NIGHTWEAVER

NIGHTWEAVER

R.M. GRAY

MERLIN'S PEN

PUBLISHING

Nightweaver
Published by Merlin's Pen Publishing

Library of Congress Control Number: 2023942536

ISBN (hardcover): 9781662942853
ISBN (paperback): 9781662942860
eISBN: 9781662942877

For Mom and Dad,
For always believing

And for my husband, Harry,
For dreaming with me

"The scariest monsters are the ones that lurk within our souls..."

— Edgar Allan Poe

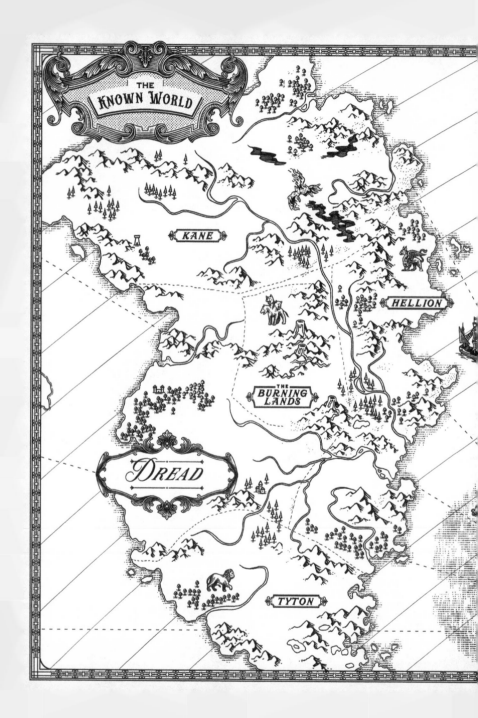

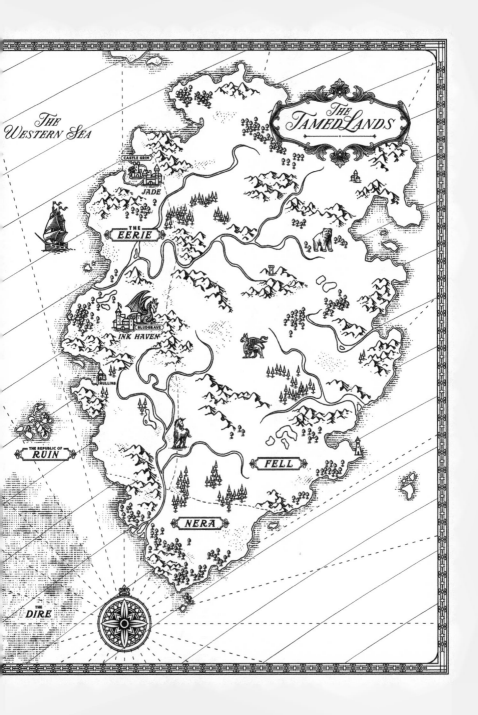

CHAPTER ONE

I'm not fast enough.

When the alarm rings out, warning of the attack, Owen is already armed and racing up the companionway.

"Don't worry, little mouse." My eldest brother casts a wry smile over his shoulder, dirty-blond hair tumbling into his tawny eyes. "I'm sure there'll still be something for you to do."

I groan, stuffing daggers and pistols into every holster and sheath strapped to my body. A knife in each boot, a dagger at either hip, four pistols at my back...Satisfied with my walking armory, I take my cutlass in hand and chase after Owen.

Before I've reached the top step, thick, black smoke chokes the morning air. I emerge onto the main deck expecting a bloodbath, but this is worse.

Much worse.

My foot slips and my back slams against the deck, knocking the breath from my lungs. The thunder of cannons trembles in my chest, a deafening crash of splintering wood. I try to gather my bearings, but something hot and sticky soaks my clothes; it drips from my tangled hair, filling my senses with the bitter, metallic bite of copper. To my left, the pool of crimson originates from a headless body.

I don't need to see the face to know whose blood saturates me from head to toe.

Mary Cross, a refugee we'd taken aboard only last week, after an enemy clan attacked her family's ship. They slaughtered the Cross clan, leaving Mary adrift in the Dire, a dark stretch of ocean plagued by sea monsters and cutthroat pirates. It seems she escaped one battle only to meet her family's same fate not a week later.

"On your feet!" Owen hoists me upright. He shouts something else, but I don't hear him over the din of clashing metal.

I grip his arm, unwilling to part with him in the blinding haze of smoke. I know of only one ship capable of creating such mayhem. In the two months I'd been held captive aboard the *Deathwail*, chained in the dank, dark hull of the cannibals' ship, I'd listened as they attacked countless vessels, stealing pirate children away from their parents in the dead of night. A year has passed since I've been rescued, but I still feel the burn of the rope those bloodthirsty savages tied around my neck. I still remember the word they'd used to justify their fear of an emaciated, unarmed sixteen-year-old.

Cursed.

"Who—"

As the word leaves my mouth, a blaze of fire illuminates the towering black sails of the ship flanking our starboard side, and I have my answer. This is not the work of the *Deathwail*. Not the work of a rival clan. A black flag, embroidered with the scarlet sun of the Eerie, billows in the wind.

Nightweavers.

I look back toward Owen, hoping to find some inkling of reassurance in his face—in his kind, tawny eyes, so much like our father's, or his cheeky, carefree grin, a mirror image of our mother's—but I'm met with an expression of fear I've never seen before. Not in him.

He grabs my shoulders, clutching me with urgency. "Whatever you do, don't let them take you." And with that, he's gone, another faceless figure in the darkness.

My fist tightens around the hilt of my cutlass. *I will not let them take me.*

But I do not fear for myself. This is not my first battle. I have tasted blood and ash. I have plunged my dagger into the heart of my enemy. I have ended a life with the weight of a bullet. Elsie—sweet, innocent Elsie—has never had to endure the sting of a knife. For eight years, Mother and Father have been careful to shield my little sister from the horrors of the life my siblings and I lead. She has never witnessed a massacre such as this.

Today will be no different.

My feet pivot, and instead of diving headfirst into the fray, I start belowdecks. But as I turn, two figures block my only path to the companionway.

"Not so fast, *pirate*," comes a rough voice as one of the men takes a step towards me, his iron blade held between us. *Humans*, I realize when I see their hard faces. But why would these humans choose to crew alongside Nightweavers?

No matter. No one stands between my sister and me.

I flourish my cutlass. "You say 'pirate' like it's an insult."

The first man lunges, and I dodge his strike with ease. I twirl, bringing my blade down in a smooth arc, slicing his chest wide open. He falls to his knees, blood spilling onto his chin. The sight of it spurs something in me—something I've felt before in the heat of battle: a sort of thrumming in my chest, like the rhythm of the waves as they lap at the hull of a ship. Before the second man can find his footing, I use the momentum I'd gained to pierce his throat. I withdraw my blade with a wet *shlink*, and he falls to the deck beside his companion.

Too easy.

I step over their bodies, my boot sticking to the first bloodied tread of the passage that leads belowdecks. That's when I hear her.

"*Violet!*" Elsie shrieks, calling for me. I spin on my heel, trying to make sense of my surroundings in the haze of smoke. Fire razes the mainmast of our family's ship, the *Lightbringer*. Our enemy's reckless attack is a declaration—the Nightweavers don't plan on looting our meager stores; *we* are the only cargo they're interested in.

I sense movement to my right and lash out, my sword clashing with that of my sister Margaret. It's like looking in a mirror. She's two years older than me, but with the same wild, untamed hair that falls to her waist in dark brown waves, crisp with blood. Tears limn her sapphire eyes as she grits her teeth, lowering her sword.

"They took Elsie," she cries over the roar of fire, her voice breaking. "Charlie tried to get her back, but—"

"Margaret!" Our most elusive brother, Lewis, appears at her side, half of his face bloodied from a gash in his head. As the ship's resident spymaster, he's always managed to keep his cool in battle. But he's still just an eighteen-year-old boy, and though it hardly ever shows, he looks every bit his age as he pants for breath, his light-brown eyes wide. "Albert's wounded. His leg—"

Another blast sends shards of wood flying past us, slicing my face and arms. Margaret appears torn between tending to Albert and addressing my fresh wounds. But Albert is only eleven. He shouldn't even be in this fight.

"Go!" I hiss through the pain.

Margaret hesitates only a second longer before she and Lewis charge into a plume of smoke. Alone again, I sip at the air, attempting to slow my heartbeat and focus on the task at hand.

"*Violet!*" Elsie shrieks—closer now as I near the starboard railing.

Before I can determine a course of action, Owen emerges from the smoke. Once again he's faster, grabbing hold of a line and leaping across the gap between our ship and the Nightweavers'. Without thinking, I follow him, careful not to glance at the dark waters below. My knees collide with the deck of the Nightweavers' ship, but I'm on my feet in seconds, my spine flush against Owen's.

"Damn it," he snarls, and I'm surprised I hear him over the roar of the cannon as it rips another hole in the *Lightbringer*.

He must have heard her, too—little Elsie, in the arms of a Nightweaver, crying out for help. But she's nowhere to be seen. And we're surrounded.

Six Nightweavers encircle us, wielding rapiers that appear darker than any metal I've ever seen, the black iron glimmering with iridescent shades of purple, green, and blue. Their black cloaks are not suited for a life at sea and their disfigured faces are hidden beneath the shadows of their hoods, but I've heard enough stories to know what I'm missing. Sallow skin, sharp teeth, eyes that shift between oily black pits and glowing red beacons. The stuff of old wives' tales, meant to scare children into behaving. Only, myths and legends won't tear your flesh from your bones in one bite. Nightweavers will.

There is a reason humans fled to the water six hundred years ago. After the Fall, Nightweavers claimed the land for themselves, hunting our kind to near extinction. The ocean was supposed to keep us safe. They weren't supposed to follow us here. But as trade has flourished between Hellion, a kingdom along the coast of Dread, in the West and the Tamed Lands to the East, more Nightweaver ships have been spotted near the borders of the Dire. They're hunting us again. And this time, we have nowhere left to run.

I swallow hard, stealing a glance across at our ship. Are Mother and Father still alive? Did they hear Elsie's cry?

My pulse hammers in my throat. Behind me, Owen's shoulders tense. How many times have we stood back-to-back, facing down our enemy, and laughed? *Why isn't he laughing?*

"I'm sorry," he breathes, his elbow brushing mine. I know what he really means. When we lose—and we will—he will not let the Nightweavers take me.

He'll kill me before they get the chance.

If we were facing an enemy clan, his promise would give me peace. A quick death at the hand of my brother is a kindness. But my stomach sours at the thought of Elsie. If the rest of us die in battle, what will become of her?

With my empty hand, I clutch the medallion hanging from my neck, my thumb grazing the embossed skull and crossed daggers on the surface of the bronze coin. I'd stolen it off the pirate who had saved me from the *Deathwail*, if only to prove I hadn't imagined him in my feverish state. Some nights, when I wake in a fit of terror, I clutch the medallion to remind myself the nightmare is over. Now as my fingers trace the symbol of death, the words he'd spoken to me as I slipped in and out of consciousness brush up against my mind. *"Now's not the time for dying, love,"* he'd said. *"Remember, you have to live."*

Dying is easy. In order to save Elsie—to save my family—I'll have to live. Because if I'm not there to protect her from whatever gruesome fate the Nightweavers have planned for her, who will?

"What about the Red Island?" I say, nudging Owen, my eyes narrowed on the Nightweavers as they tighten their ranks to close the distance between us. "You said we'd find it together."

Owen rolls his head on his neck, sighing. "I thought you'd given up on it."

I shift my weight and assume an offensive stance. "You know me better than that."

Many pirates have told tales of the mysterious Red Island, a haven for seafaring humans hidden deep within the Dire, where few ever dare to venture. For years, Owen has implored Mother and Father to search for the Red Island. Still, they refuse. "It's only a legend," they tell him. But he doesn't believe that. And neither do I.

I hear a smile in his voice when he says, "We go together, then."

Owen lurches forward, and I lose myself in the dance. I keep light on my feet, locked in battle with two Nightweavers, dodging their blows with ease. Their heavy cloaks offer me an advantage; the Nightweavers are slow, their steps unsure as the waves toss us to and fro.

I grit my teeth as the clang of metal on metal vibrates my jaw. They might not be accustomed to fighting onboard a ship, but I'm no match for a Nightweaver—much less two. They don't tire like us, and I summon every ounce of my strength to match them strike for strike.

"Violet!" Elsie wails.

I lose focus for only a second, but that's all it takes. In the instant I turn my head, searching for Elsie in the haze, the Nightweaver nearest to me lunges, his rapier aimed at my heart.

I'm not fast enough.

But Owen is.

He parries, throwing himself in front of me with enough force to knock me backwards. I stumble, landing on a heap of bodies. He's bested four Nightweavers and I couldn't handle even two. If we live, he'll never let me forget it.

I've barely found my footing when I'm yanked into the air. Two large hands wrap around my throat. Black spots edge my vision, and my cutlass clatters to the deck. A strangled yelp escapes me, though I wish it hadn't.

This time, it's Owen who turns.

His eyes—his kind eyes—find me in an instant. They widen as a deep-red stain blooms on his chest.

A Nightweaver withdraws his blade, slick with blood, and Owen's body crumples forward.

I want to scream, but the hands around my throat tighten. Owen's body blurs through my tears, but I can't look away from him. My oldest brother—my best friend—is dead. And it's all my fault.

Kill me, I plead silently, praying for death. But even as I think the words, shame claws viciously at my chest. *No.* Elsie needs me. My family needs me. I have to keep fighting. I have to live.

I struggle and kick, but the pressure builds in my head, bulging behind my eyes. Just as the world goes dark, I'm sent sprawling onto the deck. I reach for Owen's sleeve, clawing at the rough linen like I can rouse him from no more than a deep sleep.

"Get up!" I shout. "We go together! We have to go together!"

"Leave him!" barks a hoarse voice.

When I look up, I find Mother has followed us onto the Nightweavers' ship. She stands over my attacker's body, her face red with blood, her dark, untamed waves cascading down her yellow brocade coat. A crimson fountain gushes from the Nightweaver's throat, spilling onto her feet, but she doesn't seem to notice. She fixes her intense gaze on the two Nightweavers now backing away from where Owen and I lie.

"Get back to the *Lightbringer*!" she croaks, her face streaked where tears have cut through the smattering of scarlet. "Find Father—get to the jolly boat. Now!"

I know better than to disobey her, but that doesn't stop me. Elsie is still on this ship, and I will not let another sibling's blood stain my hands. Not while I have breath in my lungs and enough bullets to take down anyone who stands in my way. I press a kiss to Owen's head and lift his arm, slipping the leather bracelet from his wrist onto mine.

I draw a pistol from my back, and while Mother is distracted with the two Nightweavers, I start for the companionway. When I reach the first step, I pivot slightly, my finger resting on the trigger. He's in my line of sight—Owen's murderer—but I freeze.

The Nightweaver has his back to me, engaged in a duel with Mother—but there's something else, too.

A dark, shadowy figure seeps from the Nightweaver's body, taking on a form of its own. It looms over him, facing me, with scarlet eyes and teeth like daggers. It lets out a bloodcurdling shriek as it darts past me and disappears through the double doors of the captain's quarters.

The Nightweaver drops, convulsing at Mother's feet. His companion stumbles back in horror, and in that moment, I think he might actually seem human. *They feel fear, too.* Good to know.

Mother uses the opportunity to cut his companion down, and when he falls, she drives her blade through the other's chest, putting him out of his misery. I catch her eye and she dips her chin at me, as if she's forgotten she ordered me to retreat, or doesn't care.

"I'll find Elsie," she says, closing the space between us in a few strides. She places a hand on my shoulder, and the surrounding chaos seems to slow, if just for a moment, as her eyes linger on Owen's body. "All is well."

All is well—the customary response to death in battle. The words are meant to be both a comfort and a call to arms, but they've never felt so hollow.

Mother heads belowdecks, trusting that this time I'll obey and return to the ship, but I don't move. I stare at the double doors, my pistol heavy in my hand. Mother and Father always taught us to ration our bullets, but somehow I think this may be the last chance I'll ever get to use them. And whatever's waiting for me inside the captain's quarters won't go down without a fight.

I reach the double doors, hesitate. My family's ship, the *Lightbringer*, has gone up in flames. It will sink before dawn breaks, and my home will rest forever beneath the waves.

I have nothing left to lose.

I draw a second pistol from the strap across my back and kick the doors wide open. The neat, elegant chambers offer a reprieve from the wreckage outside. But the quiet puts me on edge. That shadow creature is somewhere, hiding, waiting to catch me unaware.

I won't let it.

Wood creaks underfoot as I take measured steps towards the door to the captain's private head. Something stirs behind it, and I think I hear breathing.

Owen's actual killer is on the other side of this door. That shadow creature had possessed the Nightweaver that ran my brother through—I can feel it. It wanted me to know; it wanted me to follow. And if I die avenging Owen, then so be it. I never thought I'd live this long, anyway.

I kick the door open, my pistols drawn, but it isn't a looming shadow I find huddled on the floor. A little girl looks up at me, her long, black hair spiraling in ringlets, her dark eyes glassy with tears. She can't be much older than Elsie. What is she doing on a Nightweaver ship?

I lower my pistols. "I'm not going to hurt you," I whisper. But before I can hold out my hand to help her to her feet, I'm struck from behind and my knees buckle. I fight for consciousness, but it's no use.

The last thing I see is the black cloak of a Nightweaver as he hovers over me, pushing back his hood. But it isn't the face of a monster hidden beneath.

It's the face of a boy.

CHAPTER TWO

I kneel beside Owen, facedown in a pool of his own blood. With great effort, I turn him over, praying to the Stars that I will see his kind eyes looking up at me. But his empty eyes are no longer kind. Shadows seep from two cavernous black pits and his mouth twists, an inhuman smirk altering his familiar features. He lurches forward and his hands clasp my throat.

I wake with a start, my threadbare tunic drenched with sweat. For a brief moment, I expect to see Mother, come to rescue me from the terror of sleep. Instead, my bleary eyes are met with soft beams of undulating moonlight. The sea rocks me gently, a comforting rhythm as familiar as my own heartbeat. Sea—not land. But this is not the *Lightbringer*.

Heavy scarlet furs blanket me, staving off the chill, and when I attempt to reach for the medallion at my neck, coarse ropes tighten around my wrists. Through the haze, I glimpse the boy in the Nightweaver cloak peering down at me from my bedside. Tangled black curls dust his severe jaw, and silver light dapples his pale hands as he gently touches my shoulder. A wave of calm ripples through my body, urging me to sleep.

My eyes close, and I see him again—Owen, shrouded by the mist. Only, this time he stands in front of me, flanked by a host of looming shadows with razor-like teeth, his dark eyes like deep wells of ink. The liquid black of his eyes drips onto his cheeks, as if he were crying.

"You should have killed me," he shrieks in a voice I don't recognize, that same inhuman smirk twisting his face.

I'm sorry, I want to cry, but my lips are pressed tight, barricading my sobs. As if incited by my despair, the shadows descend upon his flesh, teeth bared, red eyes gleaming. His arm rips, gushing blood. Then his leg. His scream is so far from human, I could pretend it isn't Owen bleeding out on the deck before me. But when he begs for mercy, he sounds like himself again—my brother, my best friend, the boy who once laughed in the face of his enemies. I want to go to him, but I can't move. I can't even look away.

When his cries can no longer be heard over the sickening snap of bone and he is fully obscured by the throng of shadows, they turn on me. Teeth pierce my left shoulder, and my eyelids fling themselves wide.

The furs are gone, my tunic dry. I'm propped against a barrel on the main deck, the rattle of chains thrumming in my chest. I blink away sleep and squint in the afternoon light. Silhouetted against the graying sky, bordered by Nightweavers in their black cloaks, the prisoners stand straight-backed despite their chains. My pulse hammers as I count the prisoners, their weary, baffled expressions mirroring my own. *Mother, Father, Charlie, Margaret, Lewis...* The knot in my chest loosens when

I spot her: *Elsie*, the stray strands of pale blond hair from her pigtail braids sticking to her cheeks. Her face is wet with tears, but her chin is held high. Beside Elsie, Albert leans on our little sister's shoulder, his right leg bent at an odd angle.

An ache creeps into my throat. Owen's absence is palpable, weighing on my shoulders, threatening to crush me flat. He should be here. He should be alive.

My stomach sinks. A single band of braided leather marks each of my siblings' arms, a unifying trait. But my wrists are bare but for the fetters, clamped tight, cutting off circulation. Owen's bracelet is gone, along with my own.

I attempt to wriggle my torpefied fingers as I glare at the assembly of Nightweavers. Which one of these monsters took my bracelets? Which one will pay for it with their life?

The Nightweaver nearest to Elsie draws her hood back, and brassy hair tumbles over her shoulders. She shouts something inaudible over the howl of the wind, and the Nightweaver at Margaret's right throws his head back, laughing. His hood falls, revealing a shock of red hair. *They're not monsters.* They're just...people.

Before I can form a coherent thought, I'm yanked to my feet. The fetters around my ankles cause me to stumble, but a second hand grabs me as I fall, and then I'm being dragged.

"Hurry now," shouts the brassy-haired Nightweaver. "The auction is scheduled to begin just after the execution. If we're lucky, we'll get to see that traitor hang *and* earn a bit of coin from this lot."

My eyes meet Mother's. She watches me, a warning flashing in her sapphire gaze. One look at her lined face and I know not to fight back. *There is a time to fight, and there is a time to survive*, she's always said. The time for fighting has come and gone. Despite my family's pride, we are unarmed and unmatched, surrounded by Nightweavers...and what we lack in coin and class, we make up for with common sense. If there has ever been a time for the Oberon clan to survive, it's now.

My gaze drifts to my feet as I'm carried over the bloodstained deck where Owen's lifeless body had fallen. His screech echoes in my mind: *You should have killed me.* Is it possible that he could have survived the blade through his heart?

No—I saw him. He was dead. Besides, it doesn't matter now. They will have thrown his body overboard with all the rest.

I'm shoved into the line, between Charlie and Father. I glance over my shoulder at Father, who bows his head slightly in greeting—ever the calm, collected sailor. Unlike Owen, Father had kept his dirty-blond hair shaven close to his head, but his short, scruffy beard had filled in since I'd seen him last. His eyes are bloodshot but just as warm and kind as they have always been—a small comfort.

"Death is the only defeat," Father whispers, so quietly I almost think I've imagined it. The Nightweavers don't see his lips move—a trick he's tried to teach me many times but one I've never mastered.

"And an Oberon is never defeated," I recite back, my voice low. The fetters bite into my skin, drawing blood. This certainly feels like defeat.

Still, I have to believe him, not for my own sake, but for my family. For little, curious Elsie and tender-hearted Albert. For clever Margaret and quiet, calculating Charlie. For Lewis with his...eccentricities. For Mother and Father, who've given us all they can, and love us more than we deserve. For Owen.

He had been defeated.

We will not.

"Where were you?" Charlie whispers, glancing over his shoulder. "Are you hurt?"

"I'm fine," I say quickly, ignoring the searing white-hot pain that envelopes my wrists. "And I don't know—a room, I think?"

"He kept you from us for two weeks, V." His low voice sounds more like a growl. Charlie, the tallest in our family—six feet, three inches of brawny muscle and a temper to match— towers over our Nightweaver captors like a mountain. His dark-brown hair, shaved close on the sides, is tied into a bun at the back of his head, exposing the tattoo of an eight-point star at the base of his neck. "Albert's been a wreck."

I squint against the dull gray light, peeking around Charlie to catch a glimpse of my little brother. Albert had tied his light-blond hair into a bun to match Charlie's a few years ago, and he only takes it down to allow Mother to brush out the tangles. I notice Albert glancing at our older brother, attempting to mimic Charlie's intimidating posture despite being nine years younger and a third his size.

"Two weeks?" I have vague memories of waking once, but...two weeks? How could I have slept for two weeks? And why keep me separated from my family? "Where were the rest of you?"

Charlie waits until the redheaded boy has passed before answering, his lip curled in a semi-permanent snarl. "They threw us in the cleanest brig I've ever laid eyes on. Gave us bread and water." He shrugs a shoulder. "I've been locked in worse cells."

The ship moans as we scrape the docks. I've seen land before—smugglers' ports all along the Savage Coast, secret trade posts where pirate clans from throughout the Western Sea come to stretch their sea legs and exchange stolen goods. But I've never left the *Lightbringer*. The water is my home, my sanctuary, my protector. Now, as we're marched down the gangplank, it's as if the ocean lashes at the Nightweavers' ship, petitioning for my freedom.

I look back, determined to remember the name of this ship so that one day I might hunt down its crew and make them answer for what they've done. My eyes narrow on the bow of the vessel, where "*Merryway*" is painted in gold lettering. In the past, we'd sunk in battle ships with names like *Stormraider* and *Soulcleaver*. Now an acrid taste burns the back of my throat at the thought of the *Lightbringer* having met her end at the behest of a brig called the *Merryway*. But the name of the ship that has taken my family prisoner is the least of my worries.

I cling to the presence of the water for as long as I can, savoring my last moments in its embrace. I might never taste this salt-laden air again—might never feel the mist on my skin, nor the gentle sway of the waves, a safe, rocking cradle. The instant my boot sinks into the marshy shore, everything within me begs to turn around. I'm forced forward another step, then another, until the towering black pines along the coast part to form a large clearing, and the wailing of the waves is no more than a whisper.

I will return. I swallow around the lump rising in my throat. *I will not let them take me.*

I think of Owen as we're paraded through the muddy streets. He used to tell me stories about the Nightweavers and the humans they sometimes keep as pets. *"They're just like us,"* he'd say of the latter, *"but the Nightweavers have them under some kind of spell."* I'd huddle between Lewis and Margaret, listening as Owen and Charlie spun tales of the time before the Nightweavers, when humans ruled the Known World. *"They were cursed because of their greed,"* Owen told me once. *"Humankind sought a power they could not control, and we've been paying for their mistakes ever since."*

As we make our way through the township of Mullins, a port just north of the Savage Coast, I don't know what to think. Aside from our escorts with their black cloaks trailing in the muck, I can't tell the humans from the Nightweavers. Even the clothes of the lowliest beggars, moth-eaten coats and herringbone caps, rival our roughspun tunics and trousers.

"Not all humans fled to the sea," Father once said. *"And of those that did, not all of them stayed."* I'd been told the humans on land were generally treated as livestock—little more than meat to the Nightweavers, with their sharp teeth and vicious appetite for human flesh. But I knew there had to be humans

living among the Nightweavers. After all, we often looted the pirate clans that frequented the human-occupied townships along the coast of the Eerie. And whenever our stores were running low, Charlie never failed to make mention of the haul waiting to be plundered aboard the Nightweavers' merchant ships—ships built by human hands, their cargo holds bursting with supplies harvested or manufactured by humans. But while most pirates that kept near the borders of the Dire would pursue the Nightweavers directly, Mother had made it clear that we were never to engage with them. That was how we survived—scavenging off those who did what we were not willing to do. All this time, we'd benefitted from the humans that lived and worked on land, but I'd never been able to fathom just how many there truly were.

Until now.

Men and women cluster in the doorways of their thatch cottages, watching our disheveled caravan as we wend our way through the streets towards the town square. On either side of the road, merchants hawk their wares to traveling Nightweavers and their human servants, who follow close behind in their plain black-and-white uniforms.

These humans might not be under a spell, but they are not free, either.

As we pass a merchant's table, his wares consisting mostly of unwanted icons and relics from times past, something catches my eye. A sword, its blade inscribed with the words *THE TRUE KING SEES*.

I glance at my Nightweaver companions, who pay the merchant and his sword no mind, my heartbeat kicking into a gallop. I would have thought the Nightweavers would have had anything regarding the True King burned and discarded. According to my people's history, after the True King created the Nightweavers, he saw their wickedness and turned his back on them, calling them abominations. But when I look over my shoulder to find that a Nightweaver man has taken up the sword, brandishing it playfully at a few of his friends, I don't know what to think.

For centuries, my people have held on to the hope that the True King would exact his justice on the Nightweavers from his heavenly realm, and we would take back the land that once belonged to humankind. But it seems the Nightweavers hold him in just as high a regard, judging by the religious trinkets engraved with the same phrase as the sword.

The True King sees. Aboard the *Lightbringer*, those words were a reminder to do good, even when no one was watching. Now I can't help but wonder…if the True King sees our suffering, why doesn't he act?

"I'm telling you, if he finds out we've taken them to auction, he'll have us gutted in the street." My ears perk as the redheaded boy whispers to the brassy-haired Nightweaver to my left. "You saw what he did to Captain Dane. All those broken bones…" He shudders. "Brutal affinity, bonewielding. I don't trust 'em."

"He was well within his rights, after what the captain did," the girl says. "Dane had to be made an example of."

The boy glares over my head at his companion. "And what do you think he'll do to us?"

"Nothing." She gives a dismissive wave. "Not if we cut him in on the profits."

"Do you really think *he* cares about splitting profits?"

"Why keep them alive if he didn't plan on making a quick coin? With the Captain dead, we're out of work for the time being. Consider this our severance pay."

In front of me, Charlie's shoulders tense. A knot rises in my throat, making it difficult to breathe. My vision swims as we pass a wooden shop, its outer wall tacked with various posters.

PROCLAMATION 63: HUMANS FOUND GUILTY OF PRACTICING SORCERY WILL BE SENTENCED TO DEATH BY HANGING.

JOIN THE LEAGUE OF SEVEN – SEE THE WORLD. FIGHT FOR YOUR KING AND COUNTRY.

WANTED: MALACHI SHADE. A BOUNTY OF TWELVE THOUSAND TENORS WILL BE AWARDED TO ANY PERSON THAT CAN DELIVER THE AFOREMENTIONED CRIMINAL TO HIS MAJESTY'S OFFICERS DEAD OR ALIVE.

The last poster, accompanied by the sketched image of a grinning, skeletal mask, causes my steps to falter, earning me a shove from the redheaded Nightweaver. Margaret must have seen the poster, too, because she lets out a small gasp, glancing over her shoulder at me with wide eyes. The infamous bounty hunter, Captain Shade, is a living legend among our people—

feeding starving clans and rescuing children from cannibal crews like that of the *Deathwail*. No one knows why he wears the mask, and no one knows what hides behind it.

Some stories claim he was cursed by a Sorcerer and wears the mask to hide his gruesome, disfigured face. Others say he'd been burned or scarred. Margaret believes he must be devastatingly handsome. Few have ever seen him face-to-mask.

But I had.

He'd rescued me from the *Deathwail* and delivered me to my family's ship just before dawn broke one year ago, then disappeared before anyone knew he'd been the one to save me. He didn't even demand the customary compensation for such a deed. He just…vanished. All I have to prove he'd ever existed is the bronze medallion hidden beneath my patchwork tunic, resting just above my heart.

"Maybe one day I can thank him for doing what I failed to," Owen had said that night as Margaret tended to my wounds.

One day.

My heart squeezes, and I look away from the poster to what lies ahead. Towards the back of the town square, an open-air pavilion plastered with signs boasting the upcoming auction sits opposite a looming wooden platform.

My mouth goes dry. *Gallows.*

Albert cries as we're herded into two rows along the side of the road, separating the men and the women. I start to lose my grip, but if I break down, the whole family might fall apart. I won't be the one to crumble into hysterics. Not yet, at least.

A muffled clomping vibrates in my chest, a steady, low thrum that shakes the ground beneath my feet. A figure in scarlet shoves me as the flow of foot traffic jostles past, knocking me into the redheaded boy. My captor hisses something, but I don't hear him. My mouth gapes as I realize what is making the townspeople quiver with fear in their doorways.

Four horses the color of midnight kick up mud as they pull a black carriage, its windows etched with the scarlet sun of the Eerie. Royal officers, their black livery decorated with an array of medals, march behind it, heading down the road from which we'd come, towards the harbor.

"Fascinating…" The brassy-haired Nightweaver cocks her head, looking at me as if I were a wild animal. "The pirate's never seen a horse."

Not true. I *had* seen a picture, once, in one of Elsie's books. But I could never have imagined their stench, or just how small and powerless the Nightweavers look beside them. A retort dies on my tongue as the carriage disappears around the bend and the crowd floods the streets. They surround the platform in the center of the town square, where the executioner, robed in black, fastens a rope around a boy's neck.

My throat burns, remembering how tight the noose had become just before Captain Shade had cut the rope. Some twisted part of me is grateful I'm not on that platform…though I'm not sure my lot is much better than his.

A trumpet sounds and a man in blue livery steps onto the wooden platform, a scroll in his hands. The crowd presses in as a hush blankets the assembly with tense anticipation. The man opens his mouth to read the prisoner's charges, but he never gets the chance. An arrow pierces the back of his throat and he falls to his knees, blood dribbling onto his chin.

Thick, red smoke fills the square. People scream, pushing and shoving, and I struggle to plant my shackled feet to keep from getting trampled.

"Sorcery!" someone cries.

"Bandits!" shouts another.

In the blind chaos, an arm wraps around my stomach like an iron band, and I'm pulled through the fog. I dig an elbow into my attacker's ribcage but he presses a pistol to my temple, halting me from any further attempts to incapacitate him.

"That's it, love," comes a muffled, lilting voice, like a deep purr. That voice—so familiar, as if I've known it my whole life. "Act nice, and there might be something in it for you."

He drags me up the wooden stairs, onto the platform, sure of his stride in the red haze. He steps over the fallen corpse of the man with the arrow in his mouth, coming face to face with the hooded executioner. My heart drops into my stomach as it becomes clear why my attacker grabbed me: I'm to be used as a shield. *Bastard!*

The executioner throws a switch and the platform gives way beneath the boy's feet, the rope pulling taut.

My attacker sighs, holstering his pistol. "Straight to the finish, then. I'll bet that doesn't go over too well with the ladies."

The executioner draws his axe, but as he lifts his arms to swing, my attacker throws out a red-gloved hand. A small iron ball attached to a metal wire shoots out of his sleeve, wrapping itself around the executioner's thick neck. The axe clatters to the platform as the executioner falls to his knees, a horrible gurgling sound coming from beneath his hood. When his body falls limp, my attacker flicks his wrist and the iron ball retracts, slicing through bone and flesh to return to its wielder.

The executioner's head rolls at my feet.

My attacker draws his sword—that same dark, iridescent metal I'd seen the Nightweavers carrying aboard their ship— and slashes the rope. The boy plummets to the ground below, coughing and wheezing for breath.

"About time!" the boy shouts, rubbing his neck. He appears to be about my age, though it's hard to tell with the way his swollen, discolored features distort his face. "I thought you wouldn't show."

"Now, now," my attacker croons, his warm breath caressing the top of my head, "is that any way to greet your captain?"

The boy shoots him an obscene gesture before vanishing into the crimson fog.

"I'll consider that as thanks." My attacker's muffled laughter has an almost musical quality as he spins me around to face him. My heart leaps into my throat as I'm met with a red, skeletal mask, its toothy smile turned upwards in a mocking grin. His scarlet tricorn, adorned with a plumage of phoenix feathers, casts shadows over his black-rimmed eyes.

Captain Shade.

I blink, too stunned to speak. The salty air of sea brine clings to the scarlet half-cloak draped over his fine red tailcoat. Through the mask, his blue eyes glitter like sunlight on the open sea.

"You little thief!" His red-gloved hand grabs hold of the chain around my neck, fishing the medallion out from under my shirt. "Weren't you pirates taught not to take what doesn't belong to you?"

"Do you even hear yourself?" I try to wrench myself free from the pirate's grasp, but he doesn't budge.

"After all this time..." He clucks his tongue as he rips the medallion from my neck and stuffs it into his breast pocket. "The Stars certainly have a sense of humor."

"Let me go!" I growl. If my hands and feet weren't bound in chains, I would have already broken his grip, but for the first time since I'd been held captive aboard the *Deathwail*, I'm totally defenseless.

"Let you go?" Captain Shade's blue eyes search mine, sparkling with mischief. "Why would I do that, when I've only just found you?"

My mouth stutters open, but no words come out. Had Captain Shade been looking for *me*? The instant I allow myself to think such a foolish thought, a sour taste coats my tongue. Of course he'd been looking for me—I stole his stupid necklace!

"You have your medallion," I say once I finally find my voice. "Now, release me!"

Shade tilts his head, eyes narrowing. "Come with me." He relinquishes his grip, taking a step back and extending a red-gloved hand. "I can hide you. You'll be safe."

The chaos taking place around us, just beyond the cloud of red smoke, fades beneath the slight ringing in my ears as my hand hovers in the air, my eyes locked on the pirate's blue gaze. He could take me back to the water. He could end this nightmare before it even begins. He'd saved me once. Now he could rescue me again. I just have to take his hand.

A breath hitches in my chest. This will have been the perfect cover for my family to make their escape. They're clever enough to sneak off, skilled enough to find a way out of their shackles. But will they have realized I'm no longer with them? If they did, do I expect them to have stayed?

My fingers hover just above his. *Safe.*

A gun fires, the bang vibrating in my chest like the rolling boom of thunder.

"Charlie!" Elsie's shriek chills my blood.

Charlie. My brother's name sharpens my mind, giving me total clarity. He needs me. My family needs me.

"My brother never got a chance to thank you," I say, withdrawing my hand.

Something flickers in the masked corsair's eyes. He reaches for me as I spin on my heels, but I evade his grasp, falling from the platform.

CHAPTER THREE

I hit the ground in a roll. The impact knocks the air from my lungs and I lie sprawled on my back, squinting into the pale gray light. The red smoke dissipates, revealing the redheaded Nightweaver standing over me, his iron blade hovering near my throat.

"Ah, there you are," I say as he yanks me up by my shirt collar. "Just the gentleman I was looking for."

I search for Captain Shade atop the platform, but he's already gone. Vanished, just like he had the night he'd rescued me from the *Deathwail*.

The Nightweaver drags me towards where my family huddles, clustered together in the mouth of an alleyway. Charlie lies in a pool of blood. A sick feeling seizes me, a cold sweat beading at the nape of my neck. *Please be okay. Please don't be dead.* I can't lose another brother. Not when I haven't even had a moment to grieve Owen.

"You idiot!" The brassy-haired Nightweaver glares at the redheaded boy. "We could have gotten thirty tenors for that one!"

"They were getting away!" The boy sneers, kicking Charlie in the side. "Have a bonewielder stitch him up. He'll be good as new."

Charlie groans, and my stomach flips with sudden relief.

"So much for a packed auction house," the girl snarls, surveying the somewhat empty town square.

"They'll come," the boy says. "If only to see *that*."

He jerks his chin at the open-air pavilion, where a skeleton hangs from the rafters, a crown of bronze atop its skull. Above, four words have been crudely scrawled on the surface of the pale stone, the fresh red paint dripping like blood.

DEATH TO THE KING.

The girl starts, "Do you think it could be—"

The boy cuts her off, his voice dropping to a whisper. "Don't even say it. We don't want a repeat of what happened in Thorn. If these humans thought for a second Captain Shade had joined forces with those rebels—"

"Duncan!" the girl hisses, smacking him on the back of the head.

"What?" the boy grumbles, giving me a shake. "They don't matter. After we've delivered them to the matrons, they won't be our problem anymore."

The brassy-haired girl rolls her eyes before barking orders at my family to get back in line. Duncan doesn't relinquish his grip on my collar as he corrals Margaret, Mother, Elsie, and me across the town square, separating us from Father and the boys.

"Charlie's survived worse." Margaret's voice trembles, but I nod. She would know—as the *Lightbringer*'s surgeon, she's always been the one to stitch him back together.

As Duncan shoves me into a makeshift stall near the pavilion, I want nothing more than to cut the smug look from his face. But I take my cue from Mother, who keeps her breath steady and her shoulders back, dignified even as the women— matrons, Duncan had called them—strip us of our clothes. If brave little Elsie refuses to shed a tear, then so will I.

The matrons work quickly, scrubbing crusted blood and a lifetime of salty grime from our skin. An ache forms at the base of my skull as an austere woman removes our chains one at a time and we're clothed in simple black linen dresses with white aprons. I watch through a mirror as the matron glares at the tattoo of a moth, inked into the center of my spine by Lewis when I turned thirteen. I'm almost inclined to scratch out her beady eyes, but my hands are limp and useless. If she weren't human like us, I'd think she could read minds, because when she refastens my bonds, they're twice as tight as they'd been before, and I have to bite my lip to stifle a wail.

Margaret spits in the face of the matron who removes her and Elsie's bracelets, but she doesn't fight back. Pain splinters my chest, knocking the air from my lungs.

I will not let them take me.

I will not let them take me.

I will not let them take me.

A matron rips through the knots in my hair and pulls it into a single, tight braid while another pries off my boots and crams my feet into a stiff pair of flats. She tosses the boots into a heap of discarded shoes, and my heart sinks. I'd been robbed of all my weapons while I'd been unconscious aboard the ship, but a part of me had clung to the hope that they'd somehow missed the knives I keep hidden at my ankles. Now, anything that had once been mine has been taken away—the *Lightbringer*, a small armory, a patchwork tunic, a pair of gold earrings, a leather bracelet, a brother. All gone.

At least Captain Shade had taken back his medallion—my most prized loot—before the matrons could confiscate that, too. And then he had disappeared—*again*—with my stolen treasure, taking with him my only chance of being rescued from whatever fate awaits me.

Come with me.

Whether they knew I was with them or not, my family *had* tried to escape. If they had succeeded, they would have left me behind. But…can I blame them? I'd been seconds away from taking Captain Shade's hand—seconds away from making the choice to leave without the rest of them. *Safe.*

But I had made a different choice. I chose to stay with my family. Now, whatever comes next, one thing is for certain: I'll never be safe. No pirate is.

I try to summon some of Mother's dignity as the austere woman leads us out of the stall and onto a platform erected in the center of the pavilion, but I'm too numb to be proud. Is this what will become of the Oberon clan? Divvied up between the hungry host of Nightweavers in their polished waistcoats, sold off to the highest bidder? I try to remember the breathing techniques Mother taught us, but the damp heat of the pavilion suffocates, and I struggle to sip air. As we're lined up along the platform, it takes everything within me to keep standing.

Duncan had been right about the crowd—the people of this township had turned out in droves. I lose myself somewhere beneath the stink of sweat and the clamor of the pressing throng as they pack in, their faces a blur. My eyes dart to and fro, searching for Father amongst the first batch of men, women, and children already lined up along the platform. I scan their faces, their heads hanging as their worth is measured in coin, but my father and brothers are not among them.

"...sold, to the gentleman in purple!" The auctioneer's ruddy face is beaded with sweat, his jowls trembling as he chants. A human woman I hadn't noticed before is dragged from the platform, inconsolable as they rip a howling infant from her arms. A stout Nightweaver man in a purple cloak steps forward to claim the mother, while a young, well-dressed Nightweaver couple take the child from the auctioneer's assistant, their faces beaming.

I wonder what purpose two Nightweavers could have for adopting a human child, but just as the thought crosses my mind, a Nightweaver in an orange waistcoat clutches my face with his clammy hand, forcing me to look away. He bends to inspect me, a silk top hat tipping low over his shiny forehead. Bloodshot eyes rove from my collarbone to my waist. He scowls, scratching his copper sideburns.

"Too old," he mutters, his breath reeking of scotch. *Too old for what?* I turned seventeen one month ago, and he can't be but a few years older than me.

Understanding churns my stomach as he kneels beside me, pressing a kiss to Elsie's shaking hand.

I don't think. I throw my body in front of her, breaking his grip on her wrist, and with all my might behind it, my skull crashes into his face. The force of it sends him stumbling backward a few steps, his eyes wide with shock as blood pours from his nose. Surprise quickly turns to outrage—but his indignation is no match for mine.

"If you touch her again, you'll die choking on your own blood," I snarl, my pulse hammering. I had worried I'd be the one to collapse into tears, but if this is how it ends, I would rather die than watch Elsie wrenched from our family by the hands of a monster and do nothing at all.

"Ungrateful *rat*," he spits, adjusting his top hat. Flanking him on either side, his friends draw their pistols, aiming them at me. "I should have you burned for that!"

"Careful, Percy," says a deep voice emanating from the center of the pavilion. Silence blankets the crowd as they part to reveal a Nightweaver in a black cloak, his hood drawn, concealing his face in shadow. "You may deal with your property however you choose. But if you lay another hand on the girls, I'll light the pyre beneath you myself."

Percy's lip curls into a snarl, but his face blanches and a weak grunt is his only protest. The Nightweaver approaches the platform, methodically making his way up the steps. The auctioneer scrambles backward, out of his path, and even Percy appears to be fighting the urge to retreat. With one gloved hand, the Nightweaver holds out a roll of parchment, and with the other, he waves Percy and his friends away, looking somewhat bored. He doesn't spare a look back at them as they scurry from the pavilion, grumbling amongst themselves.

He withdraws his hood, and my stomach drops.

The boy from the ship runs a leather-clad hand through his black curls before handing the parchment to the auctioneer. His dark-green eyes seek mine, flickering with amusement. It's as if the entire crowd cranes to hear what he's going to say next. I can't tell if they hold their breath from anticipation or fear, but I reason it's both.

He inclines his head, cutting his eyes at Elsie. "You'd die for her." Not a question, but an observation.

"I'll kill for her." I muster some of Mother's dignity, my gaze level. "Take another step, and I'll rip your throat out with my teeth."

A woman in the crowd gasps, and whispers echo through the pavilion. *Possessed. Underling. Doom us all.*

The boy's lips quirk slightly, the faintest hint of a smirk. "Tempting."

"Lord Castor, I—" the auctioneer babbles, but the boy extends his gloved hand, silencing him. The auctioneer unfolds the parchment and his brows knit. He clears his throat, bowing deeply. "Very well, my lord." He brings his gavel down on the podium. "Sold."

Panic grips me. Elsie presses closer, tiny sobs racking her body.

"Please," I beg. I hate the way that word sounds coming out of my mouth, but desperation overrides any pride I felt a moment ago. "You have to take us all."

His eyes narrow, but that flicker of amusement remains. It sets my teeth on edge.

"I don't have to do anything," he says smoothly, his voice low. Tension hangs in the air, a taut wire waiting to snap. Then he dips his head once, never breaking my stare. The auctioneer's assistant fumbles with his key ring, easing towards me as if I were a wild animal. A moment later, the fetters around my wrists are removed. Then my ankles.

The boy frowns at the raw, bloody skin circling my wrists. He seizes my arm, and that same ripple of calm overtakes me... only this time, it urges me to be still. With his teeth, he pries the black leather glove from his free hand. He towers over me, but he looks up from beneath thick lashes as if asking permission.

Words fail me, and I blink.

His fingers trail over the wounds. I wince, expecting pain. But his touch is gentle and cool, a soothing balm. I watch in disbelief as he withdraws his hand and the flesh grows anew before my eyes like a piece of fabric woven together, fiber by fiber. Murmurs of disapproval rise from the crowd as he repeats the healing motion on my other wrist, but the boy dips his head again, and in a few hasty breaths, the auctioneer dismisses the assembly.

"What of the men?" someone shouts from the street.

"Sold." The auctioneer hands the parchment back to the boy, wiping sweat from his forehead. He mutters under his breath, casting wary glances at me as he packs up his gavel and shuffles away. His assistant scrambles to remove the fetters from Mother, Margaret, and Elsie, then races after his employer.

The moment her hands and feet are free, I anticipate a signal from Mother, but she gives none. I suppose I'd been foolish to begin with to think it was only the chains that hindered us. Even if we managed to fistfight our way out of the pavilion, we'd have to find Father and the others, and Charlie will be in no shape to flee.

Charlie is okay, I tell myself. He has to be.

The boy releases me from his grip and the calm departs, leaving my heart pounding and my breath coming in ragged gasps. I jerk my arm away, a delayed reaction, and fight the rush of heat that floods my face. *He wants to eat you, stupid.*

I rub my wrists where the fetters had been. Not even a scar remains. If he plans to eat me, then why heal me? I push the thought away, flexing my fingers as sensation returns, warm and tingling.

At his signal, two Nightweavers in black cloaks approach from behind, flanking Mother and Margaret. It's as if I can feel the Nightweaver's frenzied heartbeats pulsing in the air.

"Are you the two responsible for bringing this family to auction?" the Nightweaver boy asks, his teeth clenching on the words.

"We're sorry!" Duncan drops to his knees, his hood falling back to reveal his bright-red hair. "It was Wren's idea—"

"We were going to cut you in on the profits, my lord!" The brassy-haired girl throws her hood back, her face pale. "Please—"

The boy merely raises his gloved hand, his expression neutral. "I should have made my intentions clear."

Duncan lets out a quiet sob, and Wren's shoulders sag with relief.

"Thank you!" They blubber in unison. "Thank you my—"

The boy makes a fist, and they fall silent.

"If you *ever* make the mistake of acting on my behalf again," he says with lethal quiet, "I will not show such favor. Understood?"

"Understood, my lord!"

He waves his hand and the two Nightweavers scramble away, their black cloaks billowing behind them. Alone with the four of us, the boy extends the parchment to me. "Can you read?"

I snatch it from his grasp, my hands shaking as I scan the ink. Momentary relief swells in my chest. We are not free, but we are going to be together—all eight of us. He had this certificate of purchase all along. Why let me think otherwise? Just to be cruel?

"I have no intention of separating your family." The boy holds out his hand and I extend the parchment, but I don't release it. This sheet of paper may not bind my wrists and ankles, but it is still a chain, nonetheless.

"You intend to enslave us."

"I intend to give you what a life of piracy could not."

I scowl, sizing him up. "Until you get hungry and decide we'd make a tasty snack?"

He barks out a laugh, and his reaction startles me so much that I let go.

He tucks the parchment into the folds of his cloak, lifting a brow. "You were the one who threatened to take a bite out of my neck."

"I still might."

He smiles crookedly. "Perhaps you will."

Behind me, Mother lets out a shaky breath. I follow her gaze to where Father walks beside Charlie's stretcher, which is carried by two cloaked figures. Albert limps alongside Lewis, their wrists and ankles free of chains. Just beyond their small party, a gilded train sputters pillars of thick black smoke into the dull gray sky.

The boy watches me, his smile gone, his expression unreadable.

I clench my fist, longing for the cold steel of a dagger in my palm. "If you're expecting a—"

"Thank you," Mother rasps, her hand light on my shoulder, an unspoken command to stand down. "You have shown us great kindness."

The boy bows slightly, black curls tumbling into his eyes. "Let us be on our way," he says, sweeping his arm in the direction of the train.

I wonder how many miles its hulking, golden body will take me from the shore, from the ocean, from the only home I've ever known. I wonder if, when we get there, I will regret taking Mother's advice.

Survive, her eyes say as she takes me by the arm and leads me off the platform. But this doesn't feel like survival.

It feels like surrender.

CHAPTER FOUR

"**I**'m worried."

Lewis's quiet voice startles me out of a daze. He stretches his lanky limbs, his straight, dirty-blond hair creeping into his tawny eyes, and for a moment I feel as if I'm looking at Owen. He's so at ease that if it weren't for the roar of the tracks as we barrel across the countryside, or his clean white shirt and plain gray trousers, I would think we were back on the *Lightbringer*. *He's a good liar*, I remind myself. He's hiding it well, but I am his sister, and he cannot conceal his grief from me. By the way he rubs at the bare, tattooed skin of his wrist, the host of rings that once bejeweled his every knuckle gone, he looks just as lost as I feel.

Lewis jerks his chin at Margaret in the row across from us. "I think she might eat her fingers before the Nightweavers can."

Margaret gnaws at her cuticles, glaring at the compartment door. Two Nightweavers had taken Charlie to what they'd called an ambulance car, where they could remove the bullet safely and begin healing his wound. Margaret, a gifted surgeon in her own right, hasn't been able to sit still since we boarded. And she isn't the only one.

Father fidgets in his seat, his mouth pressed in a grim line. Mother places a comforting hand over his, but her face is drawn as the landscape whirs past, a blur of rolling green hills and thick, overgrown woods. Across from them, Elsie consoles Albert, who, despite being three years her senior, has always relied on his brave little sister for comfort.

"We should have never let him go," Margaret grumbles, nibbling at her thumb.

I want to say something, anything, to calm her, but nothing comes. Before we'd boarded the train, the Nightweaver boy had taken the time to heal the raw skin at each of our wrists and ankles. He'd even straightened Albert's leg with a mere wave of his hand. But just because the boy made sure we were all in working condition doesn't mean the Nightweavers aren't hacking away at Charlie as we speak.

I grit my teeth at an image of the Nightweavers in their luxurious dining car, picking Charlie's flesh to the bone. She's right—we should have never let him go. But as they carried Charlie away, there was nothing we could do. We are not in chains, but we are still prisoners. We were shown mercy once, when we boarded this train as a family, and every pirate knows that mercy is never free. We've yet to learn the young lord's intentions behind purchasing all eight of us, and I can't help but wonder if he isn't getting more than he's given.

"Miss," says a Nightweaver in a blue uniform.

I hadn't heard him enter our car. *Focus. Keep it together. Don't let him see your fear.*

"Lord Castor has requested your presence." The officer's hand lingers on his saber, his shoulders tense, his eyes alert. There's only the seven of us here at the back of the train, seated on weathered, dusty pews, but he acts as if he were standing on a battlefield.

I fix a cold stare on him, relaxing my face so that he can't see beyond the apathy that glazes my eyes. "Request denied."

The officer clears his throat, tightening his grip on the saber. "Lord Castor won't take no for an answer."

"And yet, that's all he'll get."

His throat bobs, and he withdraws the saber halfway. Sweat rolls down his cheek, and I understand: he isn't afraid of us, he's afraid of returning empty-handed. "He's instructed me to escort you, Miss."

I stand abruptly, squaring against him. But instead of putting a saber to my neck, he cowers, his knuckles paling around the hilt. A smile tugs at my lips.

"And how did he think you were going to accomplish that without force?" I cut my eyes at his saber. "He did tell you not to use that, didn't he?" I take a step towards him and he takes another step back, nearly tripping over his own feet.

His cheeks flush. Apparently, his contempt for me is not enough to override his fear of Lord Castor. Officers on this train must not be accustomed to negotiating with pirates, and it shows in the way he sneers, his face a bright shade of pink. "Listen here, you filthy—"

Lewis is on his feet in an instant, a split piece of wood clutched in his fist. He aims the sharp, jagged end at the officer's throat. "Something you'd like to say?"

The officer blanches. "P-please," he stammers. "He'll kill me."

"Let him," Lewis growls, passing the chipped sliver of wood to me. I hadn't noticed when he'd broken off a piece of the pew. *Clever*, I think. Why hadn't I thought of that?

I keep the jagged end pointed at the officer's throat. "Why me?"

"He didn't say." He glances over my shoulder at Lewis, then down at the sliver of wood. "Please, if I don't—"

"I know," I cut him off. "There'll be one less officer on this train. What makes you so sure I won't take care of that part for him?"

He gulps. "Miss—"

"See what he wants." Mother lowers my arm. Gently, she takes the sliver of wood from my hand. "If he'd wanted to harm us, he would have."

Mother—always the voice of reason. Father has often said her penchant for diplomacy—and his lack of it—is why he surrendered the captaincy to her after she'd given birth to Elsie.

Without a word, I shoulder past the officer towards the compartment door. I've already disobeyed enough orders from my captain, and I don't feel like arguing with her. Not when we haven't spoken a word about Owen, or the *Lightbringer*, or the truth of the Nightweavers' appearance since our reunion. Besides, she has a point. I'd rather get some answers than stay here and watch Margaret chew her hand down to a stub.

Lewis grabs my hand, his brows furrowed. "I'll come with you."

The officer starts, "Lord Castor specifically asked—"

"I'll be fine, Lew." I give my brother's hand a squeeze, offering him a reassuring smile too weak to be convincing. I don't look back as the officer straightens his uniform and opens the compartment door. I grit my teeth and follow him willingly into the throng of bloodthirsty Nightweavers, with nowhere to run and no way to fight.

I will not let them take me.

I pass one scowling face after another as the officer leads me down a narrow path between plush velvet chairs and white linen tablecloths, his head held high. *Happy to be alive,* I think.

I wish I felt the same.

My eyes drift to every plate. We kept chickens aboard the *Lightbringer*; I know what their meat looks like, smells like. But the way they've prepared it is unlike Father would have ever been able. We had limited provisions at sea, but there were times when we'd make port along the Savage Coast and Father would return with a basket of herbs and spices. Rosemary, thyme, sage, garlic powder, onion powder...My mouth waters, and I can't help but imagine how well equipped their kitchen must be compared to our meager galley.

When we reach the far end of the dining car, I find the Nightweaver boy seated alone at a table, his chin resting on his bare fist, staring intently at the passing landscape as if he were seeking some answer in the branch of a tree or the slope of a hill. He no longer wears his cloak, but rather a sleek black suit and scarlet cravat. He furrows his brows at the officer as we approach.

"Did she put up much of a fight?"

The officer's lip twitches, but he maintains a neutral expression. "No, my lord."

The young lord cuts his eyes at me, smirks. "Not likely." With a subtle nod, he dismisses the officer, who takes up post at the compartment door.

The Nightweaver boy gestures for me to sit.

I don't.

"What do you want?" I demand, my arms crossed.

He clenches his jaw, but his frustration doesn't seem to be with me. "This train is much too crowded for my taste." He glares at the other passengers, but when he speaks to me, his voice is gentle. "Shall we dine alone?"

The clamor of conversation surges and every head turns away, followed by the clanging of forks and the tinkling of glasses. The young lord folds his hands, apparently satisfied. He peers up at me from beneath thick, coal-dark lashes.

"I thought you might be hungry," he says simply.

"And what of my family?" I ask, not bothering to keep my voice low. I know this isn't what Mother meant by hearing him out, but I refuse to bow to his every whim while little Albert and Elsie's stomachs ache with hunger.

"Provided for."

Not likely. My eyes flit over the spread laid out on his table—buttered biscuits, fragrant cheeses, fresh fruit. Very well. I'll hear what he has to say, and I'll leave with full pockets.

I take my seat across from him, surveying the various jams—strawberry, blueberry, blackberry—and my heart twists. Owen would have loved this. I rub my bare wrist where his bracelet would have been, longing for the feel of braided leather.

Come with me.

If I had taken Captain Shade's hand, I would have never seen any of this with my own eyes. I would have never known what the world could be like—at least, what it could be like for the Nightweavers...

The young lord watches me, his head cocked. "You're thinking of him."

My cheeks flush. Can he read minds, too? "Thinking of who?"

He dips his chin, his forehead creasing. "The one you lost."

Oh. *Owen*...My throat tightens, and I seek out the young lord's eyes—dark green, flecked with gold. Not red. Not like I'd been told. "Your men took him from me."

A frown tugs at his lips and he dips his head regretfully. "Those were not my men. I was to oversee our journey to Hellion, but the order to attack your family's ship came from the captain, not me."

My eyes dart to a butter knife and I let my hand wander, my fingers brushing the cool metal. His eyes follow my every movement, glittering with intrigue as I grip the knife, gently, weighing it in my grasp. The captain might have ordered the attack, but Owen's real killer—the shadow with the glowing red eyes—had escaped. I can feel it, as surely as I can feel my own heartbeat drumming in my chest. It's still out there, taunting me, practically begging me to give chase.

I have always found solace in the efficacy of a blade, no matter how small. But I cannot pierce shadow with blade. I cannot draw blood from that which bears no flesh.

I release the knife, but the weight of it remains. "And where is this captain now?"

The soft whisper of rain fills the silence between us. It trickles down the window, blurring the thick tangle of woods beyond the train. At sea, rain was both savior and warning. A storm was on the rise and we were to prepare for the worst, but if we were lucky and the Stars smiled down on us, we would have fresh water to drink. Now, as the engine chugs along with a lulling cadence, the rain is a comfort. Each drop brings with it the familiar kiss of the ocean—a reminder that I've not been forgotten. That the water has not abandoned me, even this far from its shore.

"Dead." He motions for a servant to fill our empty wine glasses. "I killed him."

My hands are numb as I grip the stem of my glass and bring it to my lips. Once a year, on the eve of Reckoning Day, we drink wine in celebration of our freedom, in remembrance of the blood our ancestors spilled so that we could be safe from the Nightweavers. The bitter taste causes my lips to pucker, but the warmth of it settles in my belly. I close my eyes, savoring the patter of rain as it beats against the window.

Dead. A shame. I would have liked to kill him myself.

When I open my eyes, the young lord is still watching me, as if he were trying to read my expression but finding it more of a challenge than he might have expected.

"You're not what I thought you'd be," he murmurs.

"I could say the same of you."

His mouth quirks and he looks away, searching again, as if the rain holds the answer to a question he's long been asking.

"The monsters are real," he says. "Monsters with sharp teeth." His shrewd eyes find mine, and I wonder if he's found his answer there. "Monsters with glowing red eyes."

Something within me recoils. But it creeps forward in equal measure, like a secret burrowed deep, eager to be uncovered.

"We call them Underlings," he goes on, but I can tell he senses the change in me—just as I noticed the shift in his posture, the way he leans in, as if we are connected by some shared purpose. "For those of you born at sea, it seems the legends have us confused with them."

I nod slowly, thinking back to all the stories I'd been told of Nightweavers. It seems as if Mother and Father would have known the difference between them and the Underlings—Father had spent enough time on the Savage Coast to hear things, see things—but they let us believe anyway. *Distrust breeds caution,* Mother would say. *Caution keeps you alive.*

"Some things are true, of course." He takes a biscuit from the plate and dips his knife into a jar of raspberry jam. "Both our kind come from another realm: one above, one below. Both possess power not of this world." He spreads the jam with care, his eyes flitting up to mine. "Both seek to control."

My fingers brush the serrated edge of the knife, and with my other hand, I lift the wine glass to sip. "Control what?"

He takes a bite, and the jam stains his lips like blood. "This realm, and everything in it."

I think back to the stories Owen told me. The Nightweavers were sent here to punish humans for their greed. We tried to regain power, but the Nightweavers had abilities—a new kind of magic, it would seem—that we could not possess.

"Six hundred years ago, your kind opened a door that was meant to remain sealed." He takes another small bite, chewing methodically. "You've no doubt heard of the Burning Lands?"

I picture the maps Owen used to agonize over, how he used to beg our parents to let him explore the land beyond the shore: the Burning Lands, bordered by Hellion on all sides, an uninhabited stretch of blackened earth. It's said an earthquake split the barren landscape, and at the pit of the chasm a fire rages that hasn't died out in six hundred years.

"If that's where the Underlings came from," I say, "what about your kind?"

He takes a sip of wine, wets his lips. "We were sent here to eradicate them. Holy beings from a higher realm—a glade hidden within another dimension. There we were immortal, blessed by the True King with gifts that granted us dominion over the elements, over *Manan*."

Manan—the unseen. *"That which makes all things,"* my mother once said of the glittering, golden dust. *Gurash-vedil*, she'd called it—'the dust of creation.' Father used to tell us stories about human Sorcerers that controlled *Manan* to manipulate the wind and the waves. Others used *Manan* to set enemy ships ablaze, or to keep bountiful gardens aboard their vessel. It was always thought that the Sorcerers were not merely human, but rogue Nightweavers that had taken to the sea.

"When all was said and done, we were no longer pure." Again he looks out the window, intent on whatever it is he sees beyond the glass. Beyond the hills, and the trees. Beyond time. "This world—the things we were required to do in the name of war—stripped us of our immortality; of our wings. We were cut off from our home, Elysia."

The man seated at the table across from us wrinkles his nose with distaste. *Sore subject,* I note.

"We fought alongside the humans." The young lord looks at me, now, as if he were seeing me for the first time, his head tilted, eyes keener than before. "But they turned on us. Craved our power. Eventually, they settled for the closest thing."

I nod slowly. "The Underlings."

He frowns. "Few humans that fight alongside the Underling armies remain. The rest fight for the Nightweavers that rule over them, and each kingdom in the Known World is represented in the League of Seven."

"The League of Seven?"

"A united army, tasked with keeping the Underlings at bay. Those that aren't stationed in the Burning Lands belong to internal forces, hunting the Underlings that manage to slip past the barricades."

That same, unknown part of me burrows deeper. "Why are you telling me this?"

"I know what you saw." He lowers his voice, and I lean in despite myself. He scans the dining car, a wariness about him that wasn't there before. "You're hunting an Underling—a kind we call a *Sylk*."

"How do you—"

"I had my suspicions," he interrupts. "There were signs that one of the men had been possessed in Hellion."

Possessed. I knew it. The shadow *had* possessed that Nightweaver aboard the *Merryway*, the one that had slain my brother. The Nightweaver's body had functioned as a host for the dark spirit, and when its host no longer served its purpose, the Sylk had sought another victim to control. A host that could be on this very train, right now.

The young lord glances at my hand as I reach for a block of hard cheese. *He's attentive*, I realize bitterly. All hope of stealing my family something to eat is quashed.

Out of the corner of my eye, I see the officer approaching, his hands clasped behind his back. Bounding along behind him, I recognize the girl I'd found hiding aboard the Nightweaver ship, her long, black ringlets splayed over a frilly red dress.

"Pardon me, my lord, but your sister—" the officer starts.

"*Annie*," the young lord chides, waving the officer away. He grins at the little girl, lifts an eyebrow. "You're supposed to stay in the cabin."

She pouts, hands knit together. "Can I please go play?"

He tilts his head at me, a smirk playing on his lips. "My little sister has spent the past few weeks in the company of sailors," he says. "I believe she's caught word that you have siblings about her age."

"Albert and Elsie?" I blink, not fully understanding.

"*Please?*" Annie grasps at the hem of my dress the way Elsie tugs at my arm when she wants something.

"I'm not sure if that's—"

"I think it's a wonderful idea," he cuts me off, motioning for the officer. "Escort Lady Annie to the back of the train."

The officer's shoulders slump as he follows Annie skipping down the aisle towards the compartment door from which I'd entered.

"I meant to thank you," the young lord says.

"Thank me?"

"You spared her life."

"She's a *child*."

"She's a *Nightweaver*," he counters, almost in a whisper. "You've known only fear and hatred for my kind. Yet, when you thought you'd found the Sylk, you didn't strike her down."

"It wasn't her," I murmur, staring at my reflection in the knife—dark circles under my eyes, sallow skin. A Sylk killed Owen. An Underling. "I tried to follow, but it was...gone."

Gone. But still I feel it, like a presence hovering over my shoulder, whispering in my ear, "*Come and find me...*"

He sits back rather suddenly, and I realize just how close we'd been. His shoulders lift, as if a burden has been removed.

"It's not Annie..." he breathes, half to himself. He runs a hand through his curls, visibly relieved.

"You thought she was possessed?" I whisper.

He stares at the compartment door, brows pinched. "I wasn't sure," he admits.

"You can't see them?"

He shakes his head. "And you shouldn't be able to either," he whispers. "You'd be put to death if anyone knew."

My stomach plummets. Before, I'd thought the Nightweavers only wanted to eat me—to kill without any valid reason. Now they have one.

"Why?" I barely manage the sound.

He scans the dining car. When his gaze falls on me, it softens. "Your ability is thought to be part of a curse."

Cursed. Phantom pain seizes my throat, like a noose pulled tight. Once, that word had kept me safe from the torture others endured aboard the *Deathwail*. Then, I'd thought that had been sailors' superstition. But now…

"If I'm truly cursed, why would you…" *Show mercy?* The words stick in my throat. What reason could he possibly have for taking pity on a pirate he thinks to be cursed? Someone he has been taught to hate? Someone he should have put to death?

Mercy is never free, I remind myself. But what does he stand to gain? What price will I have to pay?

"I am no stranger to curses." He looks about the dining car, speaking low. "My family is… *different.* I sent word ahead. They'd like to offer your family a home."

I drag the serrated edge of the knife along the tablecloth, eyes narrowed. "In exchange for our service."

"Precisely."

"You don't seem pleased."

He quirks a brow. "Should I be?"

"You hold all the power," I say. "We don't really have a choice."

"Ah, yes. I knew I was forgetting something." He reaches into his coat pocket and withdraws the certificate of purchase.

My heart skips a beat as he holds it over the open flame of the candle.

"If you stay," he says, "you'll be compensated. Or you can try to make your way back to the sea, only to be captured again. The choice is yours."

I sink back into the chair, watching the last few scraps shrivel into ash. I rub my wrist where the fetters had felt as if they had cut through to the bone. *He healed me.* He saved Elsie; he kept us together. And now he's given us back our freedom. What does he stand to gain?

"I do hope you'll stay." His glittering green eyes seek mine. "At least for a few days. If you still wish to leave after you see what life can be like at my family's estate, our guards will not stop you. You have my word."

I scowl, raising the wine glass with one hand, drawing his attention away, and with the other, I tuck the knife into my apron. "Why should I believe you?"

He follows the glass to my lips, his forehead creasing. "Because I'm telling you the truth."

I snort, standing and turning to leave, but he grabs hold of my wrist. At our connection, a feeling of familiarity pulses through me. My breath hitches.

"You forgot something," he says, cutting his eyes at my apron where I'd hidden the knife. He releases me to gesture at the table, but the feeling remains, full and rich, like honey flowing through my veins. "Take some food back to your family. Though I believe you'll find they've been well looked after."

I force myself to move, but I can't shake the feeling that swept over me at his touch. Eyeing him suspiciously, I stuff a block of cheese, three biscuits, and a handful of crackers into my apron. The Nightweavers fall silent again, every eye in the dining car fixed on me with blatant disgust.

The young lord stands, and the couple closest to us flinches away. But he doesn't pay them any mind. *He wants them to see*, I realize as he takes me gently by the hand, and that same, overwhelming calm washes over me, dissolving all tension, soothing all fear. I don't pull away when he presses his lips to my knuckles and the wave of calm floods through my hand, warm and pleasant.

He looks up at me, sparks of golden firelight dancing in his green eyes. "Forgive me, I haven't asked for your name."

Warmth bleeds into my cheeks. I hadn't noticed his freckles before, but now I find myself counting them, trying to remember how to breathe. "You haven't told me yours, either," I say stupidly.

He smiles, showing perfect white teeth. "Will," he says, somewhat self-consciously. "Just Will."

"Not Lord William?"

He chuckles softly, his eyes crinkling. "Only to people I don't particularly like." His thumb brushes my knuckles, where the impression of his lips lingers. "And yours?"

My stomach flips and I struggle to find my voice. "Violet." I clear my throat, jerking my hand back from his grasp. "Just Violet."

"Violet," he echoes, his mouth quirking. He sinks into a deep bow. "A name fit for a—"

I don't hear what he says next. The moment his eyes are obscured by the tangle of curls, I spin on my heels. I don't look back even once I've reached the compartment door, but I feel his eyes on me. I picture them flickering with amusement after having looked up to find me already walking away.

When the door to the gangway closes behind me, the wind whipping at my hair, I glance down at my knuckles, where his lips had left their blood-red stain. I clench my fist.

I will not let them take me.

CHAPTER FIVE

Will hadn't lied. When I make my way to the back of the train, I find trays scattered about the compartment, littered with crumbs. Annie is there, too, giggling with Elsie and Albert as if they've been friends since long before today—something I would have never believed based on the stories I'd been told about the Nightweavers. Stories that would have better described Underlings, it would seem.

I clench my fists, a hundred questions poised like arrows on the tip of my tongue. But as I start towards Mother and Father, I see Charlie seated between them, his shoulder like new. He laughs at something Lewis says, and Margaret swats them both on the back of the head, though she grins from ear to ear. It's strange to see them all like this—full bellies, smiling faces. When Charlie spots me, he beams, creating a space between himself and Father and beckoning for me to sit. I oblige him, reasoning that my questions can wait a little while longer. But the time for answers never comes, as it isn't too long before the shrieking of a whistle pierces my eardrums and the train creaks to a halt.

As we depart the train, resentment leaves a bitter taste in my mouth. We're stepping into a world without Owen—a world

I want nothing to do with. And yet…I can't help but think, as Mother and Father clasp hands, as they breathe in the humid, earthen air, *they seem happy.* If what Will says is true, we could be safe here. No more running. Already, the wear of long, hard years at sea has begun to fade from their faces. Lewis beams at a shopfront bedecked with rolls of fabric. Albert and Elsie chase Annie in circles around Charlie. Even Margaret takes in the bustling village with awe.

Again, Owen's absence bears down on me with inexplicable force.

Will's deep voice comes from behind. "I'm afraid there isn't room for everyone." I turn to find him already staring at me. He gestures at the motor carriage sputtering along the road towards us, its wheels churning up dirt.

"An *automobile!*" Elsie squeals, jumping up and down. I remember when Father had given her the book on land transports last year. She hasn't stopped talking about them since.

Will smirks, directing his attention over my shoulder, where a black horse nearly rivals the motor carriage in size. "I thought we could follow along," he says, eyes glinting with amusement as I survey the horse with distaste. "Do you mind?"

I glance at my family, already piling into the coach, and again at the horse. I swallow hard.

He laughs, patting the horse's side. "Caligo won't bite."

I wrinkle my nose. "It's not him I'm worried about."

Will climbs into the saddle and extends a hand to me. The coach pulls away, packed to the brim with my family. *They didn't even wait for me*, I realize with a pang in my chest.

I take Will's hand, expecting something to pass between us at the connection, but I feel nothing but his calloused palms in mine. *He has hands like a pirate.* The thought is swiftly abandoned as he pulls me onto the saddle behind him. I wrap my arms reluctantly around his waist, keeping as much distance between us as the saddle allows. *And he's warm.* I had been told Nightweavers were cold and lifeless—bloodless beasts; soulless, unfeeling creatures with glowing red eyes and razor-sharp teeth. I'd been told they were nothing like humans—*monsters*, I'd called them.

But Will…

My stomach turns to water as the horse lurches into a trot. But instead of following the carriage, Will tugs on the reins, steering us down another brick-paved street.

"Where are you taking me?" I demand to know, hoping he doesn't hear the panic in my voice. "You said—"

"If you're going to consider staying here," he says, a hint of playfulness in his tone, "then I thought you ought to see Ink Haven for yourself."

Ink Haven. I call to mind Owen's beloved maps. *"See here,"* he'd say, pointing at the jagged shores of the Tamed Lands, then dragging his finger along the soft slope of hills and clusters of dense forest to the deep valley at the heart of the Eerie. Here, between the towering cliffs and among the sodden green fields, lay Ink Haven: the last major township between Jade, the capitol city of the Eerie, and Fell, their neighboring nation to the east. *"Ink Haven,"* Owen would whisper reverently, *"where the streets ran black with human blood."*

I'd pictured it then as a place of nightmares—a dark, shadowy region, where Nightweavers perched on gnarled branches, human limbs dangling from their jaws. No pirate has ever made it this far inland and lived to see the ocean once more. *"No place for our kind,"* Owen would say. A valley of bones.

This can't be Ink Haven…

The setting sun bathes the hills in amber light. Narrow falls trickle down into the township, streams of water flowing throughout, whispering to my heart in the language of the sea. Colorful lanterns reflect from the canal's surface, glimmering like jewels, and the air is heavy with the aroma of freshly baked bread and damp earth. Charming storefronts line the street, and shopkeepers light candles in their windows as Nightweavers dally with their baskets, clothed in rainbows of satin, their faces bright and rosy.

"The young lord has returned!" a plump woman calls to her friends—humans, I realize. *A* plump *human!* Owen wouldn't believe it. The woman wears a servant's uniform like my own, but she and her companions are well fed, not fed *on*. They walk among the Nightweavers without fear for their own flesh. *Underlings eat humans*, I remind myself, *not Nightweavers*.

At the woman's cry, every head turns to find Will and me. Some wave, shouting greetings. The humans appear especially fond of Will. *And too familiar*, I think, recognizing the shared looks of disapproval passed between the Nightweavers among them. Will isn't blind to this. In fact, it seems he welcomes it, indulging the woman who'd first spotted him with a charming grin.

"Good evening, Mrs. Carroll," he calls to her by name. "You're looking well."

"Very kind, m'lord." The woman waves him off bashfully. "Very kind."

From this vantage point, I recognize the Nightweaver exiting a carriage to my left—*Percy*, the man from the auction. He glowers at Will, smoothing his yellow waistcoat.

"Ah, yes, the little lord returns," Percy sneers, addressing anyone within earshot. "And with a human girl for a traveling companion." He turns his attention on Will, cuts his eyes at me. "I'd heard the bulk of Bludgrave's staff had been drafted by the League. But I see you spared no time in finding more human filth to meet your...*needs*."

Will pulls on the reins to halt abruptly in the center of the street, a few feet from Percy. He climbs down, adjusts his cloak.

"My *needs* are met without having to spend a single coin," Will says calmly. "Unlike your own."

A few Nightweaver women giggle, and Percy's lip curls. He tugs on the arm of a human girl as she steps down from the carriage, her wrists bound in fetters. "This is my right," he snarls, spitting at Will's feet. "Just because you and your old man have abandoned the ancient ways, doesn't mean—"

Will opens his palm, contracts his fingers. Percy's knees buckle and he crumples to the ground. His body lists him onto his feet once more, his bones suspended at unnatural angles. Percy grits his teeth, laboring for breath, unable to form words.

"Speaking of my father." Will's deep voice commands silence from the gathering crowd. "Lord Castor has asked me to deliver a message to the Hounds of Ink Haven." He pauses deliberately and twitches a finger, pitching Percy onto his knees in front of him. He twists his wrist slightly and Percy's neck snaps back, forcing him to look up at Will. Will bends, whispers something in Percy's ear. When he straightens, I catch a glimpse of Percy—his jaw clamped shut, his face red. Will flicks his hand, apparently setting Percy's bones to rights, and Percy tumbles backward, his top hat flying.

As Will pulls himself onto the horse, Percy scrambles to his feet, dusting off his rumpled waistcoat. He grabs the girl by her arm and storms through the doors of the coaching inn, cursing loudly at the coachman as he wrestles with Percy's luggage. Will gives Caligo a gentle kick and the crowd disperses, their heads down. The Nightweavers gossip in hushed voices—I catch the word *bonewielder* more than once—but a few humans linger, watching Will with pure adoration.

Who is this Nightweaver, loved by humans and feared by his own kind?

A moment later, we round the corner. The street is relatively empty but for a few humans scurrying about in their plain black uniforms.

"What did you say?" I ask quietly, easing closer to him.

He glances over his shoulder, smirking slightly, but the expression doesn't reach his eyes. "His band of thugs have terrorized Ink Haven long enough. The next dog that nips at the heels of House Castor will die as such."

My teeth work at my bottom lip. "He thinks you're soft because of how you treat us." I struggle to keep the venom out of my voice at the thought of Percy and his clammy hands, dragging that human girl along behind him. If it weren't for Will, that might have been Elsie.

I suppress a shudder.

"Among other things." Will straightens and I pull back, suddenly aware of how tightly I'd held him. He glances over his shoulder again, but not at me. His dark-green eyes survey the crest of the mountains in the distance, the storm clouds gathering there. "I told you, Violet," he says, his voice low. "My family is different."

We arrive at the iron gate just as the motor carriage rumbles onto the long circular drive. Ahead, the stone fortress stands guard at the top of the hill, a sentinel watching over the valley below where the dim glow of Ink Haven winks, a lone candle flickering in the cloud of fog.

In the coming twilight, the estate exudes warmth. Golden light casts a halo around the head of the statue atop the fountain at the center of the drive, and towering lampposts illuminate the vast gardens ornamenting the lawn.

Father once brought Mother a bouquet of roses from our usual port along the Savage Coast, but by the time he returned, they had already wilted. I had thought the earth was harsh and unforgiving, a forgotten graveyard where life struggled to survive. I never imagined beauty like this. I only wish Owen were here to see it.

"Welcome to Bludgrave Manor," Will sighs, and I recognize the relief in his voice with a twinge of jealousy. This is his home. But I will never go home again—not to the *Lightbringer*.

The carriage pulls around, emptying my family out at the foot of the steps as double doors open to receive them. Will dismounts with ease, holding out a hand for me to take. I am considering refusing when Caligo lists forward, and in my panic I grasp for Will's fingers. He tugs me gently off the animal's side and onto my feet.

"Woah, Caligo!" A boy hurries down the steps, takes the reins from Will. He strokes Caligo's muzzle before removing his patchwork cap and extending a hand to me, a boyish grin plastered across his face. His light-brown hair sticks up in unruly tufts, but he doesn't attempt to smooth it back. "Name's Jack."

"Violet." I give his hand a firm shake, following his eyes as he watches Margaret enter the house. I stifle a smirk. "That's my sister Margaret. I can introduce you, if you'd like?" Pitching my voice, I call out, "Mar—"

"No!" Jack ducks behind Caligo just as Margaret glances back, sees Will and me studying the ground, and turns again.

Will's easy laughter catches me by surprise. He claps Jack on the shoulder. "It's good to see you, Aldrin."

"You too, Castor," Jack mutters. He shoots me a playful glare, fixing his cap atop his head. "Pleasure to meet you, Miss."

I wink. "Likewise."

Jack leaves Will and me standing at the foot of the steps and heads for the stables in the distance. Will starts for the door but I hang back, glancing over my shoulder at the iron gate as two guards clad in red livery seal it shut.

"He's human…" I murmur, half to myself.

"Of course." Will's eyes glint with amusement. "What did you expect?"

I expected him to hate you, I think. *To fear you.*

As if sensing my train of thought, he adds, "His parents were both drafted into the League when we were six. He's been with my family ever since." He flicks a glance at Jack, swallowed up by the fog. "Can't say I haven't considered making a meal of him once or twice…"

My throat tightens, but Will only chuckles.

"Joking," he says, his eyes glittering. "Come now." He extends an arm to me. "Everyone's waiting to meet you."

I take his arm and follow him to the top of the steps. As I cross over the threshold and into the house, relinquishing my tentative grip on Will's arm, it starts to rain. And I wonder…is this rain a savior, or is it a warning?

I tense as we're swallowed up by the grand foyer. I'm met with a sweet, heady aroma, reminding me of the warm spices Father once brought back from the Savage Coast. Plush scarlet carpet flows down the mahogany staircase and spills at our feet like a river of blood. The Castors' crest—the same golden dragon I'd noticed embroidered on the guards' uniforms as we'd come upon the estate—hangs mounted beneath the banister, encased in a gilded frame.

I shudder. This rain feels like a warning.

A stab of grief pierces my chest as the double doors close behind us, separating me from the downpour. Our life-before is over. Evenings spent with Father and Owen in the galley; watching the ocean lap at the horizon from the crow's nest; practicing our swordsmanship in the heat of the day, with no thought but what story Mother might tell us that night as the waves rocked us all to sleep. In the grand foyer of Bludgrave Manor, surrounded by strangers, I attend my own, private funeral.

Bludgrave—my grave, should I never leave this place again. Somewhere at the bottom of the sea, my heart rests along with the Lightbringer. With Owen.

I rub my left wrist, feeling the phantom brush of braided leather. I promised Owen I would not let them take me. But as Mother and Father are greeted by a kindly Nightweaver man and his wife, as Margaret and Charlie and Lewis exchange pleasantries with the servants in their black-and-white uniforms, as Elsie and Albert follow Annie from room to room, chasing after a fat, furry black creature about the size of an overfed tomcat, I think maybe, just maybe, they could make a home of this place. I could slip away. They might not even notice. They might not even care…

"You must be Violet," the Nightweaver woman says in a singsong voice. "Lady Isabelle." She gives a slight curtsy. "My husband, Lord Castor."

"Welcome, welcome," the tall, silver-haired man booms. He winks at Will and reaches into his breast pocket. He takes my hand in both of his, and when he withdraws, he leaves something nestled in my palm.

"Taffy?" I breathe, staring at the pink-striped wrapper. Father used to buy us a single piece each year for Reckoning Day; one piece, split between all seven children. My eyes seek Father, expecting him to appear downcast, but there's a warmth in his face that I can't quite understand. He dips his head, signaling for me to accept. "Thanks," I mumble, stuffing the taffy into my pocket.

Over Lord Castor's shoulder, I see a boy who looks about my age descending the opulent staircase. He careens onto the marble floor and flings himself at Will. They embrace, patting each other on the back.

"My little brother, Henry," Will says, gesturing at the boy, who shares the same towering, lithe frame and curly black hair.

Despite the brothers' similarities, Henry's lip wrinkles in disgust at the sight of us. As he turns his face, I notice the jagged scar that carves a line from his temple and disappears beneath the collar of his shirt, shifting in the light of the electric chandelier.

"So it's true," he mutters, his charcoal-dark eyes fixed on me. "You've brought *pirates* into our midst."

"Henry!" His mother swats at his arm.

"The Oberon family is in our care now." Lord Castor's kindly face is stern, his charcoal eyes like flint. "You will treat them with the same respect you show to all those in our employ." With that, he motions to one of the servants—an elderly man with deep-set eyes and sparse gray hair. "Mr. Hackney, I believe it's much too late for a grand tour. See them off to their rooms and ensure they have a proper supper. Tomorrow is a new day, and I shall hope to find everyone settled in. Philip, is it?" he asks Father, who nods. "We're in dire need of a chef. William sent word ahead that you seem fit for the job."

Father beams at the suggestion, his eyes wide. "Thank you, sir."

"Right, of course." Lord Castor dips his head. "Mrs. Oberon—"

"Grace, my lord," Mother offers.

At that, I fight down the title *Captain* as it threatens to burst from my mouth. How quickly she resigns herself to servitude! How humiliating this must be for her…

But as I search for any sign of contempt in my mother's dignified gaze, I find none. This is no longer survival, I realize. She has made her decision, and with it, an unspoken agreement passes through the family. "*This is a good life for us*," I hear her say in the way her eyes flit over Margaret, Charlie, Lewis, and then me. Charlie shifts uneasily on the balls of his feet, and Margaret and Lewis share a wary look. I stare at the floor swaying beneath me, my mouth dry.

"Grace, yes." Lord Castor clears his throat, motions at a frail-looking woman with a long, slender neck and a neat gray bun atop her head. "I'm afraid our beloved Mrs. Hackney has taken ill, and we'll soon be in need of a new housekeeper. You'll be well suited for the task." He turns to Lewis. "Hands of a tailor, so says my son. And you"—he nods at Charlie—"built like an ox. I believe you'll both make fine footmen."

Lord Castor takes another piece of taffy from his breast pocket, tosses it to Margaret. "A surgeon..." he muses, stroking his chin. "We've no patients for you to tend, but my daughter does need a nanny. It's not quite the caliber of work you're used to, but there's no shortage of blood in child's play."

Margaret takes Elsie by the arm as she darts past, yanking her to a standstill. "Surely, my lord."

*My lord...*They say it with such ease.

Albert continues to chase the furry black creature, which skirts my leg and leaps into Annie's outstretched arms. Now that she holds it still, I'm able to get a better look at its rotund body, its six stubby legs ending in claw-tipped paws like that of a canine. Coarse black hair sticks up in unruly tufts everywhere except on its fleshy bat-like ears, and eight insectoid eyes peek out from beneath the matted fur on its face. Its elongated snout resembles a boar's, complete with four yellowing tusks, but the grotesque little thing purrs like a cat as Annie strokes its furry head, causing Margaret to grimace.

"What *is* it?" Albert pants, his hands on his knees.

"An atroxis," Elsie answers primly, her chin held high.

"Very good." Lady Isabelle smiles sweetly at Elsie, who beams at her praise. "Atroxi are one of the few Myths protected under the king's law," she explains to the rest of us as we continue to gape at the strange creature. "Queen Anteres even keeps one for a pet, you know."

Albert wrinkles his nose. "But it's so ugly."

Annie gasps while the bell on the creature's leather collar jingles, but Lord Castor gives a hearty laugh. "You're not the only one who thinks so," he says, patting Albert on the back.

I'd almost hoped I'd been forgotten in the commotion, but now Lord Castor squints at me, his lips pursed. "William wasn't sure where to place you."

Because I don't belong here.

I clear my throat. "If I may…" I raise my voice, inject some gravitas into my words. "I'd prefer to work alongside my father. In the kitchen…*sir*," I add awkwardly.

Lord Castor chuckles and pats Will's shoulder. "You were right about this one—a formidable woman indeed." He offers his son a private smile, and a rush of heat creeps into my cheeks. "Very well. Mr. Hackney, I'll leave you to it."

Mr. Hackney motions for us to follow him through a servant's entrance hidden at the base of the stairwell. He keeps a brisk pace despite his age, and Mother leads our troop, her head held high. Behind me, a few servants bring up the rear, and through the cluster of bustling figures, I spot Will. When our eyes meet, I find no trace of amusement there—only sadness.

In that moment, his eyes tell me more about this new life—about this new world I've entered—than his words ever could. We may sleep beneath the same roof tonight, but when we wake, he will be Lord William and I, a kitchen maid. And though I dare not admit it, within the deepest confines of my heart, I share in his sadness.

I can't stay here, I think as I'm led down a dusty corridor. In the dim light, Albert takes my hand, walking alongside me.

"I miss Owen," he says quietly.

I swallow around the lump in my throat. Tears sting my eyes. *I can't stay here.* But I can't leave my family, either. The others might understand my choice to flee, but Elsie and Albert... They've just lost Owen. They need time.

"Me too," I whisper, squeezing Albert's hand. "Me too."

CHAPTER SIX

A green baize door is all that stands between my quarters and Will's—or so says the maid, Sybil. She can't be more than a few years older than Albert, but as she lights the lamp in the quarters in the upstairs hallway that Margaret and I are to share, I note the stiffness in her back when she straightens.

"Used to be more of us," she mumbles, staring wistfully down the long hall. Her forehead creases, and she sighs. "Suppose I should consider myself lucky." She brightens a bit, adding, "It'll be nice to have more people around again."

Before I can think to ask about Percy's comment concerning Bludgrave's staff—about the draft—the furtive scuffle of Sybil's footsteps fades down the hall.

Margaret flings herself on one of the two narrow cots, snuggling the pillow close to her chest. "A *pillow*, Violet!" she squeals. "And beds! Can you believe it?"

Margaret? Squealing with excitement? "I can't."

"I've always dreamed of this, you know." Her voice drops to a whisper, and in the dim flicker of candlelight, I'm shocked to find her eyes are wet with tears. "My own bed…"

She closes her eyes, and for a moment I stand perfectly still, watching the rise and fall of her chest. Margaret—warrior of the seas, terror of the tides—drifting off to sleep, with Nightweavers only a few steps away.

"Owen would want you to be happy," Margaret murmurs, almost too quietly for me to hear.

My mouth works as I search for the words I can't seem to find. "I know," I whisper finally, but Margaret's only reply is a gruff snore.

I take in the room, trying my best to glimpse what Margaret sees in this place. A narrow cot and thick blankets in lieu of a hammock and rags; an empty trunk, a rickety table with a basin for washing up. Life at sea was short on amenities. We cared little about staying clean, focusing instead on keeping sharp, being prepared for anything. But I wasn't prepared for this. There may be comforts I've never dreamed of, but I'd trade the roof over my head for a view of the stars—for my freedom.

I seek my reflection in the looking glass atop the table. Aboard the *Lightbringer,* my dark-brown hair was tangled and matted, my clothes were tattered and stank of bilge water, and my skin was coated with all matter of mud and blood. Still, I looked strong. Healthy. Happy. Now, with my hair pulled into a tight braid, my plain black uniform pressed and clean, I look frail, my skin lifeless and dull, and the circles around my eyes are darker than they have ever been. I think, with a stab in my chest, that Owen wouldn't even recognize me.

Careful not to wake Margaret, I slip out into the empty hall. We'd taken our supper downstairs, where Mr. and Mrs. Hackney gave a brief overview of our duties, but I could hardly hear them over the buzzing in my head. We had barely arrived and already I was planning my escape. While the others scarfed down stew and rolls, I memorized the layout of the servant's routes. Down the stairs, left, right, left again, and out the side door onto the west lawn. Stepping out under cover of nightfall is a small liberty, but I feel like a trapped animal breaking out of a cramped cage. I breathe in the fresh air, savoring the musk of fallen rain.

"Going somewhere?"

Jack leans against the exterior wall, his cap pulled low to cover his eyes.

In the distance, tucked between the folds of lush green hills, the lights of Ink Haven twinkle like fireflies. Where can I go? It's half a day's journey by train back to the coast, and then what? Like Will said, I risk capture—or worse. Only this time, I would be separated from my family.

Behind me, Bludgrave shelters everyone I hold dear. At sea, it was only a matter of time before we were captured by an enemy clan—before another one of us was taken by the *Deathwail*. We had only each other, and I knew that eventually, that wouldn't be enough. At least here, we can all be together. "*We have lived a life of hardship,*" Mother had whispered in my ear as she hugged me goodnight. "*It is time our family knew peace.*"

My heart sinks, and I turn my head so that Jack can't see the tears that spill onto my cheeks. Owen is at peace now. So why can't I let him go?

Before I know it, I'm running.

"Violet!" Jack calls after me, but I don't turn around.

I sprint across the lawn, the soft earth giving way beneath me. I kick off the stiff, uncomfortable flats, and my bare feet sink into the mud. Had it been only this morning that we were marched from the Nightweaver ship? Only today that Captain Shade had extended his hand to me, offering me my freedom? It already feels like a lifetime has passed. And longer still since I sat in the galley with Owen, watching him shuffle a deck of cards with ease; an eternity since I'd heard him laughing, since I'd seen his kind eyes, his cheeky grin.

"We're so close," he'd said just a few weeks before the Nightweavers' attack, jabbing a finger at the map stretched out before us. He circled an uncharted region of the Dire. *"If we can just convince Mother and Father to go deeper, into the heart of the Dire…I can feel it. The Red Island is in our reach."*

"And we'll be safe," I'd put in.

Owen had nodded slowly, his gaze lingering on the scar at my throat. *"On the Red Island, we'll never go hungry. We'll live like kings and queens. You'll see—you'll not want for anything. No clan will be our enemy. We'll stand together to protect the paradise set aside for us."*

The Red Island, a pirate sanctuary, where we wouldn't have to kill to survive—wouldn't have to murder our fellow humans for bread to eat. It all seems so far away now. Owen's dream—*our* dream—is no longer in reach. I crumple to the ground, choking down sobs.

Jack is at my side a moment later, panting for breath. "Violet, I—" He breaks off, wheezing for air. "You're pretty fast, you know that?"

I look up at him, his hands on his knees, his chest heaving. He slides the strap of a raggedy brown knapsack off his shoulder. "Will asked me to give you this," he says, offering it to me.

I wipe my face with the back of my hand and take the knapsack. Inside is a map, a canteen, a block of hard cheese, two loaves of bread, a compass, a wicked-looking pocketknife, a box of matches, and a pouch of gold coins.

"Thought you'd try to run," Jack explains, lifting his cap to scratch his head.

I slowly stand, pulling the drawstring tight. I secure the knapsack over my shoulder, fixing my gaze on the looming tree line in the distance, cradled in the mouth of the valley. I could take my chances in the wild. I could try to make my way to the coast, commandeer a small vessel and set sail. I could find the Red Island by myself.

"Stop being selfish." I can almost hear Owen's voice in my mind, chiding me. *"Our family needs you. Elsie and Albert need you."*

No, I argue. *They need* you.

I need you...

A few feet away, Jack collects my shoes, now caked with mud. "You won't make it very far with bare feet." He lets out a low, dramatic sigh. "Follow me." He takes off past me, towards the stables, where a single lantern gutters in the window. "There might be an extra pair of boots lying around."

I follow him, but I hang back at the door, wrinkling my nose. The *Lightbringer* had its own familiar stench, but it was nothing like this.

Jack laughs, waving me inside. "You'll get used to it," he says. And then, as if remembering why we'd come here, he adds, "I mean, you would, if…"

I roll my eyes, taking a few reluctant steps to appease my own curiosity. Stalls line either side of the brick path, littered with hay. I spot Caligo immediately, his black coat dappled by the moonlight streaming in through the skylight above. In the stall beside him, a white mare appears to glow silver from within, and at the crown of her head, a twisted horn tapers off to a sharp point.

"Is that…" I try to remember what Elsie had called the creature from her little book of Myths. She was obsessed with the beings and creatures that roamed the earth before the Fall: men and women with the lower halves of goats who were known to hypnotize misbehaving children with their magical flutes, or the water sprites our ancestors once commissioned to deliver messages across the Western Sea. I preferred the stories Mother and Father told us about the Stars—the brave humans who earned their place in the celestial sea above through daring feats and altruistic deeds. Now I wish I'd paid closer attention to what Elsie had to say.

Jack busies himself with cleaning my flats, dunking them in a bucket of water and scrubbing the mud with a hard-bristled brush. He jerks his chin at the white mare. "A unicorn," he says. "I thought you seafaring folk dealt with your own fair share of Myths?"

"Different kinds," I murmur, entranced by the unicorn's beauty. At sea, Myths were to be feared—great serpents that could splinter a ship into pieces, or mammoth fish capable of swallowing a vessel whole. I'd never seen one for myself, but Owen once claimed he'd spotted a hippocampus, one of the few benevolent Myths that shared our vast ocean. "*That means I'll have good luck for the rest of my days*," he'd said. I can't help but wonder if he'd actually seen a hippocampus, or if he'd simply been wrong about the luck it would bring him.

"If you change your mind," Jack says, handing me my steeped flats, "I could teach you to ride. Most of the time, Thea here only lets Annie take her out." He cuts his eyes at the unicorn and lowers his voice, adding in mock reverence, "*Unicorns can only be ridden by those pure of heart*'—and all that."

He turns, rummages through a nearby trunk. A moment later, he retrieves a scuffed pair of knee-high leather boots.

"These should fit." He extends them to me, but I stare down at the flats dripping water onto my bare feet.

"Is it difficult?" I ask, surveying the wall of various saddles and equipment. "Riding a horse."

He shrugs, patting Caligo's muzzle. "Not nearly as difficult as sailing a ship, I'd think."

I stare at Caligo, looking deep into his dark eyes. I glance at the boots. *Owen wouldn't run away*, I scold myself. He'd learn to ride. He'd work with Father in the kitchen. He'd make the best of all this. He'd find the Underling that tore our family apart and send it back to the pits of the Burning Lands where it belongs.

"If you teach me how to ride," I say, slipping my feet into the squishy flats, "I'll put in a good word for you—with Margaret, I mean."

He blushes scarlet, dropping the boots. "So you'll stay?"

I start for the door, the knapsack suddenly heavy on my shoulder. "It depends." I hear the trunk open and close behind me, and a moment later Jack bounds to my side. "What can you tell me about the Castors?"

Jack leans against the doorpost, sweeping his arms out wide. "What do you want to know?"

"Where do I start?" I settle against the opposite post, letting the bag slide to the ground. "Humans love them, Nightweavers hate them—"

"They *fear* them." Jack's boyish smile turns grim. "The Castors are nobility. Nobility control the distribution of *Manan*." His playful grin returns, and he puts the same mock reverence back into his tone. "*'They giveth, and they taketh away.'*"

I look out across the lawn, at the sprawling gardens that stretch as far as I can see. In the generous moonlight, I note several follies, ponds, bridges...even a dense orchard north of the estate.

Both seek to control—Will's words play through my mind. So the Castors control *Manan*, and Nightweavers like Percy depend on *Manan* for power. Power and control: the Castors have what every Nightweaver seeks. Yet they are not cruel. Not like I thought they'd be.

My gaze wanders to the stars, seeking comfort in the constellations I'd memorized as a child—Talia the Archer, Paul and his Ten Sparrows, Ugo the Dragon, Titus and the Twelve Keys. "What is it?" I ask quietly. "*Manan…*"

Jack follows my eyes but there's puzzlement in his gaze, as if the sky were a mystery, not a friend. "My mother once called it the stuff of souls." He shrugs. "I'm not even sure where it comes from—no one is. It's the royals' best-kept secret."

"*Gurash-vedil…*" I breathe, thinking back on all I'd heard of the mysterious substance— 'the dust of creation.' Dust that was said to be the color of pure gold. My whole life, I'd never actually thought it could be real.

Jack nods, shoving his hands in his pockets. "The Nightweavers used to consume it like sugar—in their tea, in their food. Some of them snorted it. Deadly to us, though. Didn't stop the occasional human from giving it a go." He clears his throat. "Been a shortage as of late. Even the nobles are having trouble getting their hands on it."

"Then it's true?" I ask. "It's what gives them their magic?"

"Not quite." He purses his lips and glances at me curiously. "You do know why they're called Nightweavers, don't you?"

I shake my head, a tad embarrassed, but Jack isn't the least bit condescending in his answer.

"The Common word for *night* comes from the ancient word *Manan.*"

The unseen. I take up the bag, sling it over my shoulder. "They control the unseen."

"They *manipulate* it," he corrects me. "A small supply of *Manan* exists in all things. Nightweavers pull at the strings—the *Manan*—that make up the fabric of the universe."

I start towards the house, keeping a leisurely pace, cherishing these last few minutes outside. "And the actual dust…"

"Works like a drug." He follows alongside me, hands in his pockets. "It enhances their magic—focuses it. Makes them stronger."

"More powerful."

"Exactly."

I glance at him sideways. "You're smarter than you look."

"And you're not half as unpleasant as I thought you'd be."

I thrust an elbow into his side. "Give it some time."

"Then I guess you ought to stick around." He nudges my shoulder, and before I know it, we're both laughing. It feels like I've known Jack my whole life, and we've only just met. *Maybe this won't be so bad,* I think. Maybe I can be happy here, too.

It's as if the very thought brings with it the weight of Owen's absence, even heavier than before. And then I realize—Jack's easy way, his teasing—he reminds me of him.

How can I be happy when Owen is dead?

Jack must notice the change in me because he's no longer laughing, either. "I heard about—" he breaks off, shakes his head, tries again. "I'm sorry—your brother—"

"Jack." I cut him off gently, rubbing at the bare skin of my wrist. "We're pirates. A long life isn't part of the bargain."

I think back to the battle, the memory like a fresh, bleeding wound. The vibration of the cannons still resonates in my teeth; the tang of gunpowder lingers in my nostrils.

"It was Will who called off the attack," Jack says, drawing me out of my thoughts. "He wrote that with the captain dead, it was his responsibility to have your family executed, but he insisted on taking you all prisoner. Told the officers he wanted to *reform* you," he adds with a playful lilt.

"I'd like to see him try," I mutter. If only Will had hit me a bit harder, I'd be with Owen. I would have never had to know the pain of living without him.

But I would have never known Will, either. The Underling led me to him—but why? Will protected us, kept us together. He brought us into his home. He put his family's reputation on the line to give us a fresh start.

Mercy is never free—that same nagging refrain burrows deep into my heart. And again I wonder, what does he stand to gain?

"Annie?" Jack's eyes narrow. He takes an abrupt left, headed towards the glistening, moonlit pond, where the little girl shuffles along the bank. "Annie?" he calls urgently. "Are you alright?"

Annie makes her way towards the house, having emerged from the folly on the other side of the pond. It must be a trick of the light, because at first, a network of cracks in the stone columns appear to be oozing blood. But when I look again, the domed structure is whole and bloodless, bathing in a pool of silver radiance.

Annie doesn't react to Jack's call. Her eyes are dull and glazed, her orderly gait uninterrupted. We intercept her at the edge of the lawn, among the rose bushes, but she walks right past us as if we aren't even there. Only when Jack grabs her by the arm and gives her a shake does she seem to stir from her trance.

"Annie?" Jack's voice is hoarse as he holds up her hands, wet with blood.

"I was looking for Dearest..." she mumbles, almost as if she were half asleep. Then suddenly, coming awake, she lets out a piercing cry. "Dearest! Oh, Dearest!" She collapses into Jack's arms, sobbing uncontrollably.

His throat bobs, and he glances up at me. "The atroxis," he mouths.

"Where is Dearest now?" I ask, my voice trembling.

Annie wails, burying her face in Jack's shoulder. "I don't know!" she cries. "I don't know!"

A few lights flicker in the upstairs windows. Jack hoists Annie onto his hip.

"I'll get her inside," he says, looking harried. "Maybe you should try to get some sleep."

We part ways at the west entrance, but as I make my way up the stairs, down the long hall, I can't shake the image of the columns dripping blood, nor Annie's crimson hands. Could I have been wrong? Had the Sylk possessed Annie after all?

I pause at the green baize door, my heart hammering in my chest. Annie's crying will surely wake the entire house—if it hasn't already. Is Will just on the other side of this door, wondering if Jack delivered the knapsack to me? Does he think I'm long gone? With all the commotion, he'll be so worried for Annie, I doubt he'll even stop to consider my absence.

I slink into my room, expecting Margaret to be awake, but the lamp has burned out, and she's still snoring just as loudly as she'd been when I'd left. She could sleep through anything. But I doubt I'll get much sleep—if any.

I shove the knapsack underneath my cot, where I could grab it at a moment's notice. *I can still leave this place,* I tell myself. *I can still run away.*

As I pull back the blankets and sink onto the cot, I'm certain I must be seeing things—a trick of my mind, like the bloody folly I'd imagined minutes before. But when I reach out to touch the small, dark shape resting atop my pillow, my fingers brush braided leather. Blinking back tears, I slide Owen's bracelet onto my left wrist and hold it close to my beating heart.

In the pitch blackness, I picture Owen—his kind eyes, his warm smile. Even here, in this strange, foreign place, he is with me. I'll carry his trinket as a constant reminder: I will find the Underling that took him from me, and when I do, I will show no mercy.

When my head hits the pillow, my muscles sigh with relief. Exhaustion weighs heavy on my eyelids, but I stare up at the ceiling, my mind racing. Will had taken Owen's bracelet that night aboard the ship; I'm sure of it, now. But why wait until tonight to return it to me? I ask myself again and again, but I already know the answer.

He wanted me to stay. He hoped I would. And as I listen to Margaret's snoring, Owen's bracelet secure on my wrist, I think that despite the disturbing encounter with Annie, despite the green baize door that stands between us...I'm glad I stayed.

A gust of cool air hits my face, drawing me out of my thoughts. As my eyes adjust to the dark, I struggle to make out a square grate in the ceiling, about the size of a large book. Through the slits in the brass, I think I see a pair of glowing red eyes peering down at me. Fear seizes me, and for a moment, all I can do is stare back into eyes that promise death as surely as a sinking ship. But I blink and the eyes vanish, leaving me gazing into the starless depths of darkness, wondering if I've lost more than just my home, my brother, my life before. Wondering...

Have I lost my mind, too?

CHAPTER SEVEN

ather looks as if he'd been a servant at Bludgrave long before today. He moves about the kitchen like a dancer waltzing across a ballroom floor, just like I'd seen him do with Mother on starlit nights aboard the *Lightbringer*. He whirls, chopping this, tasting that, savoring the spices with such relish that a few times, I catch myself watching him rather than tending to my duties.

I thought he had been happy aboard the *Lightbringer*, but now I'm starting to wonder if he wasn't always somewhat out of place in our tiny galley. As he rushes about in his white coat and blue-checkered pants, I have trouble picturing him lounging on the bowsprit of our ship, playing the fiddle, as if that image of him had come from a long-forgotten dream.

And still, once in a while, he forgets where he is, opening his mouth to bark an order at Owen before realizing he isn't there. In this way, I think Father might be the only one who truly understands my grief. Mother, Charlie, the others—they miss him, but not like Father and me. Owen was an extension of our work. Cooking without him feels like trying to cut through bone with a dull knife.

"Martin found the poor thing at Hildegarde's Folly," I overhear Dorothy, one of the young maids, whispering to Sybil as they wash dishes together. Dorothy has been careful to avoid me all day, as it seems even the humans that live on land have been warned of the brutality of pirates—though I've no reason to harm her, aside from her constant fearful glances in my direction. A few times I've thought about strangling her with that black velvet ribbon she uses to tie up her dark silken hair, if only to show her just how easy it would be to do what she fears I will.

"Boris thinks it was a Gore that gutted little Dearest." I don't miss the skepticism in Dorothy's tone, and it confirms my own theory as to why the staff have kept their distance since the groundskeeper discovered Annie's disemboweled atroxis this morning.

They think it was me.

Fine, I think, twirling a paring knife. Let them fear me. I don't need friends here; I have my family. Besides, this isn't permanent. I'll stay long enough to figure out how to track the Sylk that killed Owen, and then I'll be on my way.

"A Gore?" Sybil croaks, dropping the plate she'd been drying. It shatters near my feet and her eyes lock on mine. Just last night, she'd shown no signs of apprehension towards me, but as she bends to sweep up the broken pieces, her hands shake.

I set the paring knife down and kneel beside her, collecting bits of the plate and depositing them in her dustpan. "What's a

Gore?" I ask, softening my voice as best I can, though it appears my mere proximity is enough to spook her.

"An Underling," Sybil whispers, biting her lip as if the word itself might summon the creature. She stands, bows her head in thanks, and scurries to the trash bin.

I rise. "What's the difference?" I ask Dorothy, who had paused mid-wash to gawk at the exchange. "Sylks, Gores..."

Her eyes follow my hand as I reach for the paring knife. She gulps. "Sylks are shadows. They possess. Gores are"—she hesitates—"monsters. They consume..." She averts her gaze, busies herself with the dishes once more. She doesn't say the words, but I understand the implication nonetheless. I already knew the Underlings ate humans. I just hadn't realized there were so many different kinds.

I make a mental note: *Gores are Underlings. Gores eat humans.* I'll need to know all I can about the Underlings if I'm to find the Sylk, and even more if I'm to kill it.

"What is this nonsense?" Mrs. Hackney strides through the doorway with Mother close behind, both dressed in matching long black gowns and white half-aprons. "I will not tolerate talk of Gores in this household," she says sharply, casting a warning glance at Dorothy. "If there were an Underling on the property, Lord Castor would know about it. What happened to Lady Annie's atroxis was unfortunate, but it seems most likely to be the work of a lone wolf wandering too close to the house— nothing more."

I seek Mother's eyes and find she's already watching me, a reserved smile on her lips. There's something pained about her expression, as if she were looking at me but seeing someone else. I dip my head, confident that she'll catch the subtle indication of meaning. *I'm not going anywhere,* I assure her.

I lower my eyes past the half-peeled potato in my grasp, to my wrist, where Owen's bracelet forms a lump beneath my sleeve. *Not yet.*

"Who knew Father could cook like this?" Charlie lifts the lid off a silver platter, gaping at the dish of scalloped potatoes.

"Smells heavenly," Lewis agrees, inhaling deeply.

"A chef is only as good as his tools." Father whistles, garnishing the roast beef before motioning at Lewis to take the tray. "And your sister helped."

I shrug, a slight grin tugging at my lips. "Not much."

Charlie snorts. "Obviously." He elbows me playfully, almost losing his grip on the platter teetering on his palm.

"Otherwise, the Castors would be dining on pickles and eggs," Lewis chimes in, fidgeting with his uniform one last time before taking the tray from Father.

All the while Mr. Hackney corrects their posture, critiquing their form. He fusses over Charlie's rumpled collar but praises Lewis's finely pressed waistcoat. Meanwhile, he scolds Lewis for his indolent stance—"Hold your head high, boy. Shoulders back!"—but commends Charlie on his deft maneuvering as the crowded kitchen bustles with activity.

I try my best to stay out of everyone's way, observing the other servants as they scramble to collect their trays and follow commands. For a moment, noting the shrewd way Mr. and Mrs. Hackney govern the staff, doling out pride and correction with equal fervor, I'm reminded of Mother and Father aboard the *Lightbringer*. *They're like a family*, I think. *A crew*.

Most of what's left of the staff were either too young or too old to be drafted. Though over the age of fifteen, Jack, as the sole survivor of his bloodline, was exempted from service. Dorothy—sixteen and quick on her feet—provides for her sick mother back home, and Martin, the groundskeeper, is missing an arm. From what I've seen, all three would have been formidable members of the *Lightbringer*'s crew, but while the League is keen on drafting human fodder into their ranks, Lord Castor secured "special provisions" that spared the three from military service.

"You, girl," Mrs. Hackney snaps, beckoning me with a stern look. Beside her stands Margaret, looking poised and contrite—not at all like the rough, calloused sailor I share blood with.

I hadn't even noticed Margaret enter the room, since she'd changed out of her new cotton dress and into a plain black-and-white uniform like my own. Her formerly wild brown hair is neat and coiffured, and her cheeks and lips are pink with rouge. I cover my mouth to hide a laugh and her brows shoot up, threatening me to silence. But where I hadn't noticed her until now, Jack, who lingers near the side door, can't help but stare. Margaret's face flushes bright red, and this time, I outright chuckle.

This earns me a stern look from Mrs. Hackney, but even the old woman stifles a smile as she hands me a pair of white gloves. "You'll be serving dessert tonight. Follow Dorothy's lead, and remember you are to be seen, not heard. And whenever appropriate, you are not to be seen at all. Understood?"

"Yes, Mrs. Hackney," Margaret and I say in unison.

I take in Dorothy's instructions with an addled mind. It was only yesterday that I'd ridden through town with Will, and yet I feel as if it's been a week. As I follow Margaret through the servant's hall, my heart pounds in my chest. Will he even look at me? Would it be more humiliating if he did? Would I rather he ignore me altogether?

All day, through every task, my thoughts have wandered to Will. So many times I've wanted to barge through that green baize door and demand an explanation: why did he take Owen's bracelet, and why did he wait until last night to leave it on my pillow? And more than once, the thought has crossed my mind: *he was in my room*. How infuriating that he should have the right to enter my quarters, when his are forbidden to me. But rage isn't supposed to set my stomach aflutter. *Get it together, Violet*.

Before I can collect myself, we enter the dining room.

"Close your mouth," Dorothy hisses discreetly, and my jaw snaps shut.

I do as Dorothy instructs and avoid looking directly at the family. Instead, my eyes wander to the crisp, snow-white linen adorning the table, littered with a militia of silverware and delicate tableware laced in gold. Mrs. Hackney had called on us before the crack of dawn, taking pains to show us from room to room, ensuring we knew our way around the house via hidden passageways, but the dining room looks nothing like it had this morning. The candelabras cast flickering shadows on the heavy velvet curtains, and Mr. Hackney stands at attention near the sideboard, a decanter of wine in his hands. Around the table, the conversation is subdued, and out of the corner of my eye, I glimpse Lady Isabelle dressed in her finery, a tiara perched atop her elaborate up-do.

I feel Will's presence before I see him. Just two weeks ago, I had plunged headfirst into battle without a second thought, armed to the teeth with knives and pistols, but standing here now, with only a dish of pudding in my hands, I can't seem to calm the frenzied beating of my heart.

The young lord sits opposite his mother, a tuxedo clinging to his lithe figure. As I place the dish in front of him, he glances up at me, his mouth parting to fit words he doesn't say. He closes his mouth, his expression nettled. Heat floods my face and I turn away.

I seek out Annie, bracing myself for another vision of blood or of wisps of shadow seeping from her flesh, but there's nothing harrowing about her appearance. *Thank the Stars.* What was I prepared to do if I saw the Sylk hovering over her shoulder? Would I cut down a little girl—a girl of Elsie's age—because she was unlucky enough to be possessed?

No. But would I let the Sylk get away?

Could I?

"How are you settling in, dear?" Lady Isabelle's soothing voice halts me mid-step as I attempt to flee the dining room with the final shred of my dignity intact. From what Dorothy had told me, I hadn't expected an interaction with the lady of the house, and I'm sorely unprepared.

"Just fine," I answer as meekly as I can manage, knitting my hands behind my back to keep from clenching my fists.

"And you?" Lady Isabelle addresses Margaret, who responds with an all-too-natural half curtsy.

"Very well, my lady."

My lady...Was I supposed to say that?

"Ah, Philip," Lord Castor booms, taking a bundle of parchment from his coat pocket.

Father enters the dining room in his dirty apron, looking even more out of place in the velvet-swagged dining room than I feel. "You sent for me, my lord?"

"Do stay." Lady Isabelle raises a delicate finger, hindering my leavetaking once more as I begin to make my way towards the servant's passage. By the look on Mr. Hackney's face, the whole ordeal is unexpected and not at all proper, but from what I've overheard from the other servants, the Castors are notorious for breaking all manner of social norms.

Lord Castor proves thus as he stands up from the table, approaching Father with the bundle of parchment in hand. "I must say," he starts, his charcoal eyes brimming with admiration, "I haven't enjoyed a feast such as this in quite some time. Wherever did you learn to cook?"

Father glances at me, smiles graciously. "Always had a knack for it, I suppose."

Lord Castor, visibly intrigued, doesn't look satisfied with the answer, but he doesn't press. "A knack for it, indeed." He beams as he extends the papers toward Father. "I do apologize for creating a fuss, but Lady Isabelle insisted I not wait a minute longer."

Father unrolls the parchment, his brows knitted.

"I'm aware this is all very sudden," Lord Castor continues, "but there are certain items that must be addressed before you and your family can make Bludgrave your permanent residence. You are acquainted with the King's Marque, are you not?"

Father nods slowly, cutting his eyes at me as if warning me to hold my tongue. The King's Marque: the brand of the Eerie. Identification papers to be stamped and approved by a governing lord that detail a human's right to work, live, and travel within the country. For a pirate, it's more than a pardon—it's a formal declaration that states the recipient's abnegation of piracy and its irrevocable Creed. I knew that if we stayed here, we would have to sign the papers, but Will promised me time to think things over.

I glare at the back of Will's head, digging my nails into my palms. To his left, Annie peers over the back of her chair, her big green eyes pleading as if I were the one holding the King's Marque, not Father. Across from her, Henry examines his pudding with thinly veiled disgust, and beside him, Lady Isabelle watches Father, a sweet smile on her thin ruby-red lips.

Lord Castor gives Father a pen. "You don't have to sign them just yet. But I certainly hope you will consider making Bludgrave your home."

I implore Father to look at me, but without a moment to waste, Father signs the papers, folds them, and presents them to Lord Castor. Only after Lord Castor tucks them into his coat once more does Father glance at me, his kind eyes offering an unspoken apology. I want nothing more than to storm from the dining room and find Mother, but I know it would do me no good. This was a decision they made together, a decision they made without asking me what *I* wanted.

Quit acting like a child, I scold myself. *This is for the good of the whole family.* Even if it feels like I'm watching the *Lightbringer* sink all over again. Even if it means turning my back on everything I've ever known.

My eyes meet Margaret's on the other side of the table, just over Lady Isabelle's shoulder. But I don't see any of my grief mirrored in her expression. Only pity.

Am I truly the only one who sees this place for what it really is? A prison. And these people—the Castors—our jailers.

Lord Castor shakes hands with Father, and Lady Isabelle dismisses Margaret and me as Charlie and Lewis enter the dining room to collect the empty trays. As Margaret rounds the table, Henry shifts in his seat, stretching his leg to block her path. She trips, catching herself on hands and knees, and in an instant, Father, Charlie, Lewis, and I start towards the table. But before Charlie can reach her, Lord Castor is on his feet again, helping Margaret to stand.

If looks could kill, Henry would be dead.

"Apologize," Lord Castor demands.

Henry ignores him, lifting his glass of wine to drink. Just before it reaches his lips, it catches fire, but all he does is roll his eyes. He slams the glass down, sloshing wine onto the white linen tablecloth—much to the chagrin of Mr. Hackney, who seems eager to mend the stain. Lady Isabelle raises a hand, signaling for Mr. Hackney to wait. With only a look, Lord Castor extinguishes the flames before they can singe the tablecloth further, but Mr. Hackney looks as if he's just been slapped.

Henry casts a hostile glance toward Margaret. "Sorry," he grumbles.

Lord Castor bristles. "Go to your room," he barks, any trace of warmth gone from his face. "I will deal with you later."

Henry stands and shoulders past Margaret. Neither Charlie nor Lewis move, but their eyes follow Henry to the door, intent on him like two mountain cats watching a mouse. Father had signed us over into their service only a minute ago, and already my family is being forced to adapt to this new way of life. At sea, Margaret wouldn't have hesitated to slice Henry from chest to navel, and if she hadn't, Charlie or Lewis would have done it gladly.

And Owen…he would have had his own way of dealing with Henry.

"My sincerest apologies," Lord Castor says, his warmth returning, but it's too late—I can't unsee the ferocity that had taken its place. "I can assure you, my son's deed will not go unpunished."

Margaret dips her head, masterfully maintaining her composure. "My fault entirely, my lord."

As she shuffles from the dining room, our brothers and Father close behind, I feel as if I've lost more than Owen, more than the *Lightbringer*, more than my freedom. I'm losing them, too.

Margaret doesn't stop once we've reached the kitchen. I follow her outside, onto the west lawn, peeling the white gloves from my hands.

"Margaret—" I start, reaching out to touch her shoulder.

She shrugs me off, her arms crossed. "Leave me alone," she mutters, storming away from the house.

"Sister, please," I say, grabbing her by the arm. "I hate it here, too. We don't have to stay. We can still find the Red Island!"

She whirls to face me, her eyes narrow. "Don't you get it? This"—she gestures at the house—"is far better than anything we could have ever hoped for. The Red Island was just another story—something Mother and Father allowed you and Owen to work towards to keep your spirits up. *This* is real. How could you actually consider leaving your family behind?"

I'm the one who's getting left behind, I cry inwardly, but I don't dare say the words aloud. Just then, I spot Jack headed our way, his face smudged with dirt.

"How'd it go?" he asks, brushing hay from his shirt. His grin fades as he nears us. "Let me guess—Henry?"

Margaret huffs, and I nod stiffly.

"I was thinking of going for a walk." Jack tilts his head at the orchard. "Care to join me?"

"You two go." Without giving either of them a chance to argue, I slip back inside the house.

In the kitchen, Father stands near the stove, pinching the bridge of his nose, his face drawn. A part of me wants to stop and make one last appeal, but I keep going, up the stairs, down the hall.

It's too late. Just like that, Father and Mother have sealed our fate. And yet, by the looks on Charlie's and Lewis's faces when I'd passed them breaking bread with Martin and Boris downstairs, they seem to have been celebrating. As if our being captured, sold off, and inducted into service were a victory. As if our life before had been an insufferable trial and not the glorious adventure I knew it to be.

The instant I step foot in my room, a hand clutches my throat, slamming my back against the door. Just as quickly, I twist, bringing my elbow down hard, and break free, but the force of it throws me further into the room.

Henry stands between me and the door, his lip curled.

I think of the knapsack hidden under my bed—the pocketknife. But the weight of my apron jogs my memory. I plunge my hand into the apron, grabbing hold of the butter knife I'd stashed away onboard the train.

Henry chuckles mirthlessly. "When will you humans understand?" With the twitch of his fingers, a fiery sensation seizes my hand and I drop the knife. The pain spreads from my hands into my arms, then down into my legs, bringing me to my knees. I cry out, but the sensation needles its way into my brain, forcing my mouth shut.

Henry crouches in front of me, close enough to strangle if I weren't paralyzed by the fire raging within. He cocks his head and his voice is low, dripping with malice. "I could end you with a single look."

Then do it, I think. My life is over. There's nothing left for me—on land, at sea. I can't stay here, but I can't leave. This is my only way out—death my only escape. *Do it. Please. Let me be with Owen.*

"Truthfully, I wasn't expecting you." He rises, smoothing his brocade vest. The jagged scar that cuts from his temple down his neck makes his face look as though it is split in two. "No matter." He twitches a finger and a sharp pain rents my skull. "You and I will have some fun while we wait."

A spasm racks my body, setting every nerve ablaze. Black spots edge my vision. This is it. This is how I die. I'm ready for it. I give in to the pain, welcoming it.

"*I'm here, Violet.*" I know I must be dying, because I hear Owen's voice as if he were standing above me. And then, louder, as if he were whispering in my ear, "*I'm here.*"

I'll be with you soon, I promise, closing my eyes.

And then, just like that, the pain is gone. When I open my eyes again, Henry is on the floor in front of me, his body rigid.

Will towers in the doorway, a hand outstretched. "Father wishes to see you," he says, his voice gruff. He contracts his fingers and Henry's joints crack, pitching him onto his feet. "I wouldn't keep him waiting."

Will relaxes his hand and shoves it into his pocket, but a muscle in his jaw tightens. His eyes follow Henry's every movement with rapturous attention.

Henry shakes himself. "She's a *pirate*," he hisses. "She deserves worse than she got." With one last hate-filled glance at me, he shoulders past Will. A moment later, the green baize door slams.

Will starts towards me but must think better of it. There is no amusement in his eyes but rather, a deep intelligence I hadn't noticed before—intense and calculating, searching me in the way I'd seen him study a landscape. And a reluctance, as if he were looking for something he hoped he wouldn't find.

"Did he hurt you?"

My hands rove my skin, remembering the fiery sensation. "What *was* that?"

Will frowns. "Henry takes after my father. They have an affinity for heat—light, electricity. We call them firebreathers." He bends slightly, but I scramble backwards, using my bed frame to pull myself onto my feet.

Firebreathers. That explains what happened with Henry's cup at dinner—and why he said he could end me with a single look. Months ago, Elsie told me she'd been studying anatomy from one of the books Charlie had stolen off a merchant ship.

She'd said "scientists" in Jade had discovered electricity in our brains decades ago. With his deadly magic, Henry could have flipped the switch in the blink of an eye. So why didn't he?

Will chews at his bottom lip, takes a step back and surveys the room. His eyes linger on the pillow atop my bed, and then on my wrist—on Owen's bracelet. "Violet, at dinner—"

I don't give him a chance to finish. I kneel, snatch the knapsack from beneath my bed, and hurry past him, into the hall. I set a deliberate pace but he follows close behind, chasing me down the stairs, into the kitchen, and out onto the west lawn. Dorothy, Boris, and Martin watch us go, frozen in shock. *Let them see,* I think bitterly. It doesn't matter what they think of me. Come tomorrow, I'll be long gone.

I refuse to stay here, pandering to the whims of Nightweavers. I am Violet Oberon, and despite what the King's Marque states, I am a pirate, through and through. I always will be.

When I reach the stables, I whirl, facing Will head on. "You said you wouldn't stop me. You gave me your word."

Will doesn't look at me but at the iron gate in the distance, guarded by two figures in red livery. "I said my guards wouldn't stop you. *I,* on the other hand…"

That settles it. It's been too long since I've stabbed someone.

I turn and enter the stables, my sights set on the wall of rakes and sheers. Just as I reach for the sharpest tool I can find, Will tackles me, his hand covering my mouth. We land in a pile of hay inside Caligo's open stall. I struggle to break free, but Will holds a finger to his lips, the weight of his body pinning me beneath him.

"...tripped me." I hear Margaret's voice approaching and fall still. "You should have seen Violet—I thought she might filet him with a butter knife."

"I'd pay to see that." Jack laughs, halting at the door to the stables. "I've known Henry my whole life, and it seems like he was on his best behavior tonight." Then, in a softer voice, he adds, "You can't blame her for wanting to go."

"I know, I just—" Margaret breaks off. "I never wanted any of this, either. But here we are. And, as strange as it is, I'm happy. I just wish she could be happy, too."

Will's eyes flit to mine. He peels his hand back, but he doesn't move and risk alerting them to our hiding place, and neither do I.

"Do you really think she'll leave?" Jack asks.

"If I know my sister, she's probably already gone."

There's a long silence, and I avoid Will's gaze.

Margaret sighs. "I should get back to the house."

"Oh, right, of course," Jack stammers. "Goodnight, Miss Margaret."

There's a sound as if she's kissed him on the cheek. "Goodnight, Jack," Margaret calls, the squish of her footsteps fading.

A minute passes. Jack clears his throat. Over Will's shoulder, he leans against the stall door, shaking his head.

"You're early," he says, folding his arms.

Will rolls off me and we both sit in the hay, neither one of us speaking. He watches me out of the corner of his eye, but I stare at my flats, encrusted with fresh mud, as Jack disappears around the corner. He returns a moment later, a picnic basket in tow.

Will sighs softly, gets to his feet, and takes the basket from Jack. "I want to show you something," he says, fastening the picnic basket to Caligo's saddle. He pulls himself onto the horse's back and holds out his hand to me. "When we return, you can take Caligo if you still want to leave."

I glance at Jack, who gives me a hopeful look. I purse my lips, eyes narrowed at Will. "And *you* won't stop me?"

Will dips his head, looking wicked. "You have my word."

CHAPTER EIGHT

With my eyes closed, the wind casting my unbound hair behind me, I can almost pretend I'm back aboard the *Lightbringer*. I keep one arm hooked around Will's waist and one hand on the knapsack, my thoughts racing. Can I really leave here without saying goodbye to my family? What will Mother and Father think of me? I imagine Elsie and Albert hearing the news that I've gone: Albert's wailing cry, Elsie's stubborn tears. *It's better that I leave*, I tell myself for the twentieth time. They probably won't even miss me.

We pass Hildegarde's Folly and enter a tunnel of apple trees in the northern orchard. At the other end of the long tunnel, in a clearing of dense wood, a conservatory stands alone, trimmed in white lattice and hidden from prying eyes.

Will dismounts Caligo and starts towards the conservatory without offering me a hand. I remain in the saddle, feeling more unsure of myself than when Owen first taught me how to climb the rigging aboard the *Lightbringer*.

"Oh?" He turns, his eyes twinkling with mischief. "I just thought…?"

I roll my eyes, swinging my leg over the saddle as I'd seen him do, but my foot gets caught in the stirrup. My stomach plummets as I fall—right into Will's arms.

He sets me gently on my feet, his dark-green eyes locked on mine. "You can't do everything on your own, Violet," he breathes, withdrawing his hand from my back. He doesn't pull away; his nose is only inches from mine. "Would it kill you to ask for help?"

The butterflies in my stomach drop dead, and I take a step back. "I don't need your help," I say, my nostrils flaring. "I know what you're up to."

"And what is that?" He cocks his head, takes a step towards me.

I stand my ground, slipping the knapsack off my shoulder. "This"—I throw the knapsack and it lands in a pool of mud a few feet away—"the way you've treated my family." I slide Owen's bracelet from my wrist and wave it at him. "What is it you want from us?"

Will's face falls and he furrows his brows. "I can assure you, my intentions—"

"Intentions!" I huff. "I think you've made your intentions rather clear, *Lord William*. I refuse to incur any further debt to you, or your family, or any *Nightweaver* for that matter."

The use of his proper title appears to strike him. The crease in his forehead deepens. "I'd heard of the trinkets before—I know what they mean to your people." His voice is quiet, gentle. "If I hadn't taken it, someone else might have."

I clench my fist around the bracelet. "You were going to let me leave without it!"

"I knew you wouldn't leave your family," he argues, taking the picnic basket from Caligo's saddle and starting for the conservatory. He halts at the door and turns to face me. His eyes search mine, his expression nettled. "At least, I thought you wouldn't."

I bite my lip and look away, sliding the bracelet over my knuckles. I don't want to admit it, but he's right. I can't abandon my family, especially not after what happened tonight.

Will runs a hand through his black curls, his jaw clenched. "You owe me nothing, Violet," he says softly. "Now, are you coming or not?"

Without waiting for my reply, he throws the door wide and disappears inside. I glance longingly at the knapsack, half-buried in the mud, and then at Caligo, into his deep, black eyes—my freedom so close, I can almost taste the salt-laden breeze. I shuffle towards the conservatory and slip inside, where the humid, earthen air stifles any lasting notion of escape.

From the outside, the shadowy silhouette of plants clustered in the window gave the conservatory the distinct appearance of having been abandoned. But as the door closes behind me, I feel as if I've stepped foot inside another world entirely. Bright, phosphorescent globes hover in midair, and all around, tiny bioluminescent figures dart to and fro among the colorful flowers. The winged shapes flit around Will's head, their laughter like tinkling bells.

He holds out his hand, and a bright-pink form perches on his finger. I marvel at her chestnut skin, her curly black hair—like a tiny human with long, dainty ears that taper to sharp points. Gauzy wings like those of a butterfly span behind her, twitching with laughter. Pink light emanates from within, as if her very heart is glowing, casting a rosy sheen on Will's pale face.

"I'd like you to meet Liv," Will says, a rare, bashful grin on his lips. "Liv, *this* is Violet."

Liv rises delicately, flutters towards me. "*Neeshta.*" Her sweet, small voice sounds as if it is coming from the bottom of a well. Her tiny hand touches my cheek and she presses her forehead to my nose, tickling my face. At the connection, a joyful laugh bubbles up in my chest, but I swallow it down.

"What did she say?" I ask Will as Liv darts away, joining the others atop a cluster of purple blossoms.

Will smirks. "Beautiful," he murmurs, his eyes reflecting the lights like two glowing green orbs. "Although…my Pixie is lacking. She could have very well called you strange."

"*Pixies…*" I breathe. "But I thought—"

"They were extinct?" He inspects the petals of an orange blossom. The ghost of a smile touches his lips. "Not if I can help it."

"But the King—"

"The King sought to exterminate pirates, as well," he says, bending slightly to sniff the plant. It glows at his touch. He glances at me, his forehead creased. "Yet, here you are."

I clench my fist, remembering the look on Father's face as he signed the King's Marque. *An Oberon is never defeated*, I think bitterly. But we are no longer the Oberon clan, notorious pirates of the Western Sea—respected by all who knew us, feared by those that crossed us. We are what the Nightweavers tell us we are: servants, footmen—a kitchen maid. Death is no longer the only defeat. It can't be. Not when I would prefer death to this predictable, sanctioned life on land.

And still, a quiet voice whispers: *Would you?* Here, surrounded by such beauty, the sweet fragrance of the garden like an intoxicating brew, I find myself drifting farther from the sea than I ever thought possible.

No, I admit. Life on the water was an adventure. Surely, life on land could be just as exciting. But in order to stay here, in order to be happy, I have to forgive. I have to forget—the *Lightbringer*, our customs, Owen.

"Is that why the Nightweavers attacked us?" I ask. Only after I've said it do I remember that Will isn't human—at least, not like me.

His lip quirks, but he knits his brows—a conflicted expression. "The captain disobeyed a direct order from the prince of the Eerie by attacking your ship. We were not to engage with any pirates."

"The *prince*?" I squeak. Owen used to tell me stories about the prince of the Eerie. The sole heir of King Anteres, the prince is an evil, cruel monster who only comes out at night. He drinks the blood of humans, eats their hearts, impales their heads on the castle walls. Of all the Nightweavers, he is the most fearsome.

Although I know now that everything I'd been told about the Nightweavers was a lie, the mention of the prince still raises the hair on my arms.

That familiar glint of amusement flickers in Will's eyes. "Yes, the prince," he says. "He asked me to oversee the voyage, and to serve as the princess of Hellion's personal guard until his betrothed could be intercepted by the royal procession at port."

So, the princess of Hellion was aboard the *Merryway*. And the royal carriage I'd seen—it must have been sent to retrieve her. That must be why Will wasn't there when we were taken to the auction house. He hadn't yet been relieved of his duty.

I run my hand over the petals of a blue flower—blue, like my beloved ocean. "Why you?"

His expression shutters. "He trusts me."

"Why?"

"We're…friends," he says slowly, crouching to examine the soil running parallel to the bricked path. He scoops up a handful of the black dirt and lets it sift through his fingers. "We were raised together at court."

My mouth goes dry. *Friends*…with the prince of the Eerie?

"But he's—"

"Evil?" Will's lips twitch into a slight smirk. "Your people's stories would have you believe the same of me."

"Maybe you are," I say, lifting my chin. "Perhaps you're only pretending to be—" I cut myself off, my cheeks flushing.

"Pretending to be what?" His deep voice is like the distant roll of thunder. "Kind?"

I gnaw on my bottom lip. "I didn't say you were kind."

"I wouldn't expect you to," he says, his eyes darkening. "Besides, not everything you've heard of the prince is a lie. He *is* ruthless, and cunning, and deadly."

"And he's your friend."

Not a question, but he answers anyway.

"He's like a brother to me," he says, more serious than I've seen him yet. "I would do anything for him."

Anything. I swallow hard. If the prince is what Will says he is, then...

"Is that why people are so tense around you?" I ask. "That officer on the train was afraid you'd kill him if he didn't do what you asked."

Will clenches his jaw. "It is my family's job as the ruling fief of this region to keep men like Percy and his gang of miscreants in line." He wipes his forehead with the back of his hand, rising to his full height. "I'm not proud of the things I've done. But the cruelty some have come to expect from me is a necessity, one that keeps the people of Ink Haven safe from filth like Percy."

My uniform sticks to my skin in the nearly unbearable humidity. "You want them to fear you."

He dips his head. "The more people fear you, the less you need actually give them a reason to be afraid."

My lip twitches. "You sound like my mother."

He gives a low, dark chuckle, the sound full and rich. "Maybe it's not me that people are tense around," he says, his brow quirking. "You are a pirate, after all."

A few hours ago, I would have beamed at his observation. Now, my heart sinks. *"I'm not proud of the things I've done."* I know that feeling all too well. The blood I've spilled could color the tides scarlet. But in the same way Will needs to inspire dread, fear was necessary to our survival at sea. So, I became something to be feared. Someone who didn't ask for help. Someone who needed no one. Someone who shoved their grief deep below the surface, where even the sun could not penetrate.

I used to wonder who I could have been, had I lived on land—who I could be, now. But all of that grief, all of that bitterness, has become a looming wave crashing over me, pulling me under, down...down...down...

Eager to change the subject, I ask, "How did Annie end up aboard the ship?"

He runs a hand over his face. "Sneaky girl," he sighs. "Stowed away. By the time I realized it, we were halfway to Hellion. I considered ordering the captain to turn around, but..." He glances at me, looking pensive. "My loyalty to the prince is not the only reason I agreed to go on that voyage. We were given orders not to engage with pirates, but with one exception." He hesitates. "You've heard of the *Deathwail*?"

My stomach roils. Without thinking, I reach for my throat, remembering the noose that held me captive when I was sixteen. I still hear the screams that had come from the cells on either side of me—I still see the mutilated bodies when I close my eyes to sleep at night. For reasons I've never been able to understand, no one would touch me.

The other prisoners weren't so lucky.

"They took Henry when he was nine." Will's voice is raw, barely a whisper. My own hatred is mirrored in his gaze. "They tortured him for twelve days before they agreed to let us pay his ransom. It took another week to find where they'd dumped him off the coast." He scowls, his jaw clenched tight. "He was never the same after that."

Never the same. In the weeks after I'd been rescued from the *Deathwail*, I'd noticed the way my siblings looked at me—as if the girl Captain Shade had cut down from that rope was not Violet Oberon, their sister, but rather a shell of the girl they once knew. Once, Lewis startled me and I nearly cut his throat. My dagger had grazed the skin below his jaw before I realized what I'd done. Later, I'd overheard Margaret whisper to Charlie, "*She's just...not the same.*" But how could I be? Those two months had become part of me in ways I cannot amend. I left the *Deathwail*, but it has never left me.

And just like that, my ill will towards Henry gives way to pity. How can I hate him, when I understand him in a way his own brother never will?

"We're not all that way..." I murmur.

Will casts me a sidelong glance. "I could say the same."

My cheeks burn. Will and I have more in common than I would have thought. We both seek to avenge a brother—one lost, one broken.

"Did you find it?" I ask quietly. "The *Deathwail*."

A muscle in Will's temple feathers as his eyes glaze with memory. He looks up, basking in the moonlight. "No."

I watch as Liv and the other pixies swoop past Will's head, towards the back of the conservatory, where a sturdy oak tree grows amid the flowers and plants. How could I have guessed that a boy who spends his time with pixies and flowers would be driven by a dark, ravenous hunger for revenge?

"Does your family know about this place?"

He follows my eyes, a slight grin spreading across his face. "My father rescued Liv and her friends during a mission near the southern border. He asked me to take care of them."

"Why you?"

His grin widens, giving way to dimples in either cheek. "Pixies draw their magic from flowers, and I—" He holds out his hand and contracts his fingers, watching with glittering eyes as red roses sprout from the soil into full, blossoming plants. "Well, I grow the flowers."

"And what about the prince?" I cross my arms, eyes narrowed, trying—and failing—to hide my amazement. "Does he know just how *different* you and your family are?"

Will pinches his brows, his grin fading. "You must understand," he says, leading me towards the sprawling oak tree. "There are certain…*expectations* we must uphold in order to do what must be done. If we are to dismantle a system that benefits Nightweavers and seeks to eradicate all else, wouldn't you think it rather advantageous to work within that system?"

My eyes widen at his admission. How had I not considered this before? If Will and his family are not as loyal to the king as I'd previously expected them to be, what other secrets have I yet to uncover?

I plop down on a low-hanging branch and let my fingers trail along the grooves in the bark, remembering how fondly Albert used to dream of trees. Before, I had thought his dreams were foolish, indulgent. The earth did not belong to us—it belonged to *them*, the Nightweavers. But before we were driven out to sea, my ancestors tended gardens; they planted trees such as this one.

I've been so focused on everything I hate about this place that I've blinded myself to what is right in front of me. Maybe Albert's fondest dream had been my worst nightmare, but is it really so foolish to believe that we could make our home on land? After all, what better revenge, than to take back what the Nightweavers had stolen so long ago?

Will sits beside me, the picnic basket wedged between us. He takes a deep breath and I follow suit, savoring the damp, floral air. My pride would have me deny that while I still yearn for the fresh, salty breeze, there were no flowers—no smell as sweet as this—aboard the *Lightbringer*.

"Underlings hate flowers," Will murmurs, reaching into the picnic basket. He withdraws two golden-brown hand pies. "Sugar, too," he adds with a wicked grin, offering me the dessert.

I turn it over in my hands, letting it warm my palms against the chill of spring.

For all the literature that Elsie collected, there were two books Father acquired that he gave to me rather than her. One, a cookbook titled *Tastes of the Eerie* by Cornelius Drake, was filled with pictures of food I'd only ever dreamed of tasting. We could only do so much at sea, but on land, chefs like Drake did it all: teacakes, brown-bread ice cream—*hand pies*. I had wondered then why Nightweavers would care for such cuisine. I couldn't picture a Nightweaver eating anything other than human flesh, much less green-pea soup or marbled blancmange. Now, after only two nights here, I can't imagine Lord Castor favoring a human heart over a simple salad.

I bite into the flaky crust and the flavor of warm apple filling floods my taste buds. I shoot a glance at Will, chewing tentatively. "My father didn't make these."

Will smiles. "No," he says around a mouthful, eyes twinkling with amusement. "Henry did."

I fight the urge to spit apple filling at his feet. "When? Father and I have been in the kitchen all day."

His smile widens. "Mrs. Carroll owns a bakery in town. She lets Henry hang about."

I shake my head, marveling at the buttery, perfectly pricked crust. "But he's nobility..."

Will quirks his brow and takes another bite, chewing thoughtfully. "And you're a pirate," he says finally. "Strong willed, defiant, independent—to a fault, I might add." He winks, taking another bite. "But you're also selfless, and clever, and kind."

I open my mouth to argue, but he silences me with an imploring look.

"I'm a Nightweaver," he goes on. "A bonewielder, at that. But the same affinity that gives me power over someone's bones also gives me the ability to heal their flesh." He glances down at my wrists, where his touch had mended my wounds, then at me—at my eyes, ever searching.

He shifts his gaze over my shoulder, reaches out. I want to kick myself for flinching, because when he withdraws his hand, a silken pink blossom nestles in his palm.

"To grow flowers," he says softly, presenting it to me.

I inspect it, raising it to my nose. The blossom smells faintly of peppermint.

"A sorrowsnap," he murmurs. "Smells good enough to eat, but one bite and it fills you with such sadness, many have been known to take their own life. Oftentimes, one would send a bouquet of sorrowsnap to their former lover as a message: 'You, too, were sweet, but to go on loving you would be the death of me.'"

"Harsh," I mumble, setting the blossom on the trunk beside me.

He smirks, and I feel the heat of his gaze on me once more. "Perhaps," he says, his voice low. "But the truth remains: dangerous, deadly things are often the most beautiful."

My cheeks flush and I look away, stuffing another bite of apple pie into my mouth. Will gazes out at the garden once more, where Liv and the others dance and sing in their tiny chiming voices like a chorus of tinkling bells.

"Like anyone, Henry has the capability to cause pain. To be cruel, and selfish. But the same affinity that allowed him to hijack the nerves in your body also enables him to heat an oven to just the right temperature to make one delicious apple pie. His magic can bring about destruction, but it is also the only affinity known for creating light." He pauses, thoughtful for a moment. "Give him a chance. I think if you put your differences aside, the two of you might actually be friends."

Friends? With a Nightweaver? The thought crosses my mind, followed by an uncomfortable realization. I might consider Will a friend, under different circumstances; if he were not a lord, and I were not a human servant in his household. But then, who am I to care about rules? The Castors themselves show a blatant disregard for social order, treating their servants with respect and dignity. I should be able to do as I please, to befriend whomever I'd like—including Will.

Swiftly, heedlessly, I find myself forgetting. It was a Nightweaver that attacked our ship. It is a Nightweaver's fault that Owen is dead. In staying here, will I forget him completely? Will it be as if our life before never happened? As time goes by, will I no longer think of myself as a pirate, but rather, a kitchen maid?

No. If I'm to stay here, I mustn't lose sight of the task at hand. That Underling will pay for what happened to Owen. But Will's right—I can't do everything on my own.

"I need your help," I blurt out, standing to face him.

He looks up at me, his expression earnest. "You want to find the Sylk that killed your brother."

My mouth works as he stands and dusts his clothes, taking the picnic basket in one hand.

"I thought you'd never ask," he says, starting down the aisle. "I have to admit, after what happened to Dearest—"

"I know." I follow along, a burst of newfound energy nearly causing me to skip. I thought my life here would consist strictly of peeling potatoes and chopping onions. But if I can scheme, then perhaps I can maintain some semblance of my life at sea.

"It's not Annie." The words tumble out before I even realize I've made up my mind.

He halts, cuts his eyes at me. "You're sure?"

I nod. "At dinner, I thought I'd sense its presence. I don't know why, but I just…feel it. It's not her."

He relaxes his shoulders, but before he can take another step, he tenses again, dropping the picnic basket. Every light in the conservatory goes dark, and Liv and her friends flee for the oak tree, the sound of tinkling bells swallowed up by the silence. Outside, Caligo trumpets in distress.

That's when I hear it.

A gut-wrenching scream rips the air, far away and yet all around us. But it isn't the scream that chills my blood, raising the hair on my neck.

It's the laughter.

Chapter Nine

"Stay here," Will whispers, easing through the conservatory door. But I'm not one for taking orders, and I refuse to stay behind.

Blood drums in my ears. Who did that scream belong to? *Please*, I pray to the Stars, *don't let it be someone I love*. And though I try to push the thought away, if only to maintain the illusion of calm, I wonder—who did the laughter belong to?

What did it belong to?

"A Gore," Will's hushed voice answers as if he had read my mind. "I should have known."

I follow his moonlit shadow, my tread light, careful not to make any unnecessary noise. That laughter...both guttural and high-pitched, as if two voices had joined in unison. It grated against my senses like sandpaper, leaving them raw. I flinch every time Caligo shifts his stance, hold my breath every time a twig snaps underfoot.

"Why did it..." I trail off, scanning the pool of mud for the knapsack. My stomach flips, and I bite down hard on my bottom lip to keep from groaning. *It's gone*. How could it be gone? Panic rises in my chest, but I fight to keep it at bay. It must have been an animal. It had to be.

Will pulls himself onto Caligo's saddle, offering me a hand. "A Gore laughs only after it's fed."

I take his hand, pulling myself up behind him. "Does that mean..." I can't bring myself to finish my sentence. I hold onto Will unabashedly, drawing as close to him as the saddle will allow. Thankfully, he doesn't answer. He gives Caligo a swift kick, and wind whips at my face as we tear through the orchard and down the lawn, towards Bludgrave Manor.

In the few seconds before we've rounded the front of the house, I don't know whether I wish Caligo would run faster or stop entirely. Will's family has gathered at the steps. Flanked by the guards Gylda and Hugh, Lady Isabelle clutches a grave Lord Castor, sobs racking her body. Henry holds Dorothy unconscious in his arms, smoothing the hair from her face with particular care. Mother and Father are there, too; only Albert and Elsie are absent from our troop, along with Annie, Sybil, and the rest of the staff.

I smell the blood before I see it.

I hadn't paid much attention to the fountain at the center of the drive until now. The statue—a winged woman with long, wavy hair—stands with one foot atop a pile of rocks. In one hand, her sword is raised in triumph, and in the other, she carries a grail, tipped sideways as if it were poised to spill. Her anguished face is turned downward, intent on the water as it empties from the grail and filters back into the basin.

Only, the water is thick and crimson, and two human heads are impaled on her sword. Mr. and Mrs. Hackney, their faces taut with horror, their eyes missing from their skulls, and their bodies nowhere to be seen—*eaten*, I realize with a heave of nausea.

Will leaps from Caligo. I jump down without thinking, landing hard on my hands and knees. I scramble to my feet and race towards Margaret. Jack stands beside her, clutching her hand as if she were the only thing keeping him from drifting away.

"What happened?" I manage to speak, but I barely hear my own voice.

Charlie, Margaret, and Lewis share the same solemn expression. We've seen much worse than this in battle. Why, then, do they seem so shaken?

Lewis glances at me, his face full of confusion, but he doesn't say a word.

"There was a scream," Father explains. "And then..." he trails off, shaking his head. "Knocking—Mr. Hackney—it sounded like—"

"Like he was pleading for help." Mother places a gentle hand on Father's arm. "Dorothy answered." She motions at the fountain. "But this is all that was left."

"And you saw nothing?" Will asks Hugh, a man of about Charlie's age.

The guard shakes his head, his ebony skin reflecting the moonlight with a dazzling silver sheen. He glances at Gylda.

Her long blond hair is pulled into a tight braid much like my own, and her face is twisted in a bitter expression. "We heard the screams," he says in an accent I don't recognize, his voice deep. "But we failed to reach them in time. Forgive us, my lord."

The two guards drop to one knee, their heads bowed.

"There is no need for forgiveness," Will says, gesturing for them to rise. "You've done your duty. This attack was beyond your control. Whoever did this knew how to bypass our wards."

Henry snorts. He glares up at me, seething with hate. "*You!*"

Charlie pushes me behind him, his shoulders squared, but Will jumps to my defense.

"She was with me," he growls. "Father, surely you must know this was a Gore and not—"

"Of course I know that!" Lord Castor snaps, his face ruddy in the lantern light. "But in all my years, I've never seen a Gore do *this.*" He points at the heads, but as Will and I draw near the fountain, I realize why even my own family looked at me so strangely.

Carved into Mr. and Mrs. Hackney's foreheads, two words ooze fresh blood into empty, black sockets.

HELLO

VIOLET

CHAPTER TEN

Will and I glance at each other, my own puzzlement mirrored in his gaze. At the base of the fountain, a pocketknife remains, wet with blood. It's the pocketknife from the knapsack Will had given me—the knapsack I'd left to sink in the mud. It wasn't an animal that had taken it, after all.

"A Gore didn't leave this message," Will says, lifting the pocketknife to inspect it. "Gores know only two things: kill and eat. It was a Gore that killed Mr. and Mrs. Hackney, but *this*"—he cuts his eyes at the bloody message—"was the work of someone else." He turns to me. "It would seem you've a remarkable talent for making enemies."

"How do we know she isn't in on it?" Henry snarls, his eyes like daggers.

"I told you," Will shoots back, his voice dark and deep. "She was with me."

"And why is that?" Henry tilts his head. "Have you forgotten the law? Or do you think it doesn't apply to you?"

"And what of you, little brother?" Will gestures at Dorothy, faint in Henry's arms. "Do you bow to the king's law?"

Henry bites his bottom lip, his nostrils flaring. He looks as if he'd like to set both Will and me on fire.

"What law?" I whisper, burning under the heat of both my family's and the Castors' relentless stares.

The corner of Will's mouth pulls into a frown. "Nightweavers and humans are...forbidden."

I stagger away from him, my cheeks hot. "But we're not—"

"No." Will fixes a glare on Henry, his voice somewhere between a growl and a whisper. "We're not."

Lord Castor clears his throat. He takes a watch on a long, golden chain from his breast pocket and flicks it open, scrutinizing its face. His gaze slides up toward Will, and he cocks a brow. "We'll discuss this another time. Tomorrow's a busy day. I've received word that my brother-in-law, the Admiral, will be arriving in little over a month. He's to spend the summer at Bludgrave, and we're obliged to have him. There's much to do to prepare, and with Mr. and Mrs. Hackney—" he breaks off, sighs.

"No need to fret, my lord," Mother says smoothly, her countenance like that of a political advisor, not a housekeeper. "Lewis will act in Mr. Hackney's stead."

Lord Castor dips his head. "Thank you. I don't know what we would have done, had my son not brought you into our home."

Henry scoffs. "Mr. and Mrs. Hackney would still be alive, had he not brought them into our home." He glowers at me but I hold his stare, steady and unblinking. I know what he's thinking, because I'm thinking it, too: one look and I'm dead.

"Enough," Lady Isabelle barks. She turns to Margaret. Her face is drawn with exhaustion, but she speaks to Henry nonetheless. "Take Dorothy to her room. Do whatever Margaret tells you."

Henry purses his lips sourly, but he doesn't argue—not where Dorothy is concerned. Carrying her, he follows Margaret into the house. I start after them, not wanting to leave Margaret alone with him, but I've taken only a few steps before I stop short as Jack shoulders through the door behind Henry.

"The staff need not know details of what we've seen here tonight," Lord Castor says, directing a pointed look at Gylda and Hugh, whom he dismisses with the subtle dip of his head. He bids Mother and Father goodnight before following Lady Isabelle into the house, and a moment later, Lewis scurries after him.

Mother motions for me to come near, and without hesitation, I allow her to draw me close, knowing the gesture is not for comfort, but to serve as a means of passing along a message without Will's suspicion.

"Be vigilant," she whispers into my hair. "Kindness is the great deceiver."

Don't trust anyone, she means, and I hear her loud and clear: even Will. I watch him out of the corner of my eye. He's still examining the knife that had been used to carve words into the disembodied heads—two humans in the Castors' employ, impaled on a Nightweaver's blade.

A phantom pain seizes my left shoulder, and my muscles tense.

I can't forget why we're here, and I can't forgive. But there is some small part of me that, against my better judgement, wishes I could. Because despite what I've been taught, despite what I know to be true, I find myself wanting to trust Will. And though my mother's command is the only true law by which I'm bound, I feel I've already broken it.

Mother pulls away, tucks a strand of hair behind my ear, and takes Father by the arm once more. Father smiles at me, but the expression doesn't reach his tired eyes, which convey a message all their own. *We are not safe here.* Not like we hoped.

He touches my cheek, a gesture meant to offer comfort—and confidence. "This isn't your fault," he says, and at his words, the tension in my left shoulder eases. If Father is on my side, then so are the others.

I want to apologize for how I'd acted earlier this evening and tell him I don't blame him for signing the King's Marque, but by the time I've found my voice, the double doors have closed behind them. Charlie and I are left together on the steps, watching as Gylda and Hugh make the long trek down the driveway.

At sea, Charlie oversaw the disposal of bodies after a skirmish. He took special pains to scrub blood and excrement from the deck until the stain was nonexistent, and if it were one of our own adopted crew that had fallen, he made the arrangements for burial. It makes sense that he would be the one to deal with this mess. Gentle Charlie—my careful, considerate brother—

the same boy who cried for a week when he accidentally broke Mother's favorite music box—is the only one with the stomach for decapitated heads and a fountain of blood.

"Do you need me to—" I start, but Charlie shakes his head. I already knew what his answer would be; he has always preferred to work alone. But I almost hoped he'd ask me to stay. For some reason, I'd rather be with Charlie, cleaning up blood, than go back to my room, alone with my thoughts.

That same, familiar ache smarts like a bruise on my heart. If only Owen were here, I wouldn't have to be alone. He would help me get to the bottom of this—the missing knapsack, the bloody pocketknife, the message. *"Beheading is the sincerest form of flattery,"* he'd tease. *"Maybe you have a secret admirer."*

Charlie rolls up his sleeves. "Do you mind?" he asks Will, reaching for Mr. Hackney's head with his long arms. His tone implies he won't wait for permission.

"Actually," Will says, never taking his eyes off the knife, "I'd prefer you leave them be for now."

Charlie grunts. The look he gives Will betrays the assumptions I'd made about his happiness here. After all, Charlie took a bullet in the shoulder from a Nightweaver, and it doesn't seem like he's forgotten—or forgiven—just yet.

"Violet," Will calls, setting the knife down and peering into the fountain. "Come take a look."

Charlie sticks an arm out, barring me from coming any closer. "Why do you have to involve her in this?"

"It says, 'Hello *Violet*,'" Will mutters drily. "I'd consider her involved."

I lower Charlie's arm, look up at his face—softer than Mother's but just as determined. He hasn't yet mastered his temper as well as her, and it's beginning to show.

"Trust me," I say, knowing what weight that simple phrase carries among my siblings and me. In battle, those two words could be the difference between life or death, and the covenant they represent must be absolute.

Charlie nods, and though there are no cannons blasting, no banners waving, I feel as though we stand side by side on the frontlines of an inevitable war. "Always," he says, his hand on my shoulder. "I'll just be over here when you're done." He casts Will one last warning look and heads for the steps.

"Charming family," Will says once Charlie is out of earshot.

"Pirates." I shrug. "It comes with the territory."

He smirks. Then, remembering the reason he'd called for me, his face falls, and he narrows his eyes at the basin. "I have a hunch."

"I couldn't tell."

His lips quirk, the faintest hint of a smile. "There." He jerks his chin at the grail. "Do you see that?"

I squint, and in the flickering light, I catch a glint of gold. It's too far away, out of reach. I climb onto the rim of the fountain, but before I can stick my foot in the bloody water, Will seizes my wrist.

"You'll soil your clothes," he says, but something like fear flashes in his eyes, betraying his intentions.

"Fine," I say, wriggling free from his grasp. "You go."

He glances down at the basin, and I expect to see that same fear—disgust, even. But the look he gives the crimson water is one that churns my stomach. His green eyes have darkened with hunger.

He looks away, back at the house, away from me and the fountain of blood. "I can't."

"Well, I can," I say, and before he can grab hold of me again, I lower myself into the basin, first my foot, then my whole leg. I wade hip-deep in thick, warm water—*water*, I tell myself, *not blood.*

So much blood...

I reach out, taking hold of the leather band that hangs from the grail. A collar, I realize, noting the small golden bell that dangles from its clasp. I turn slowly. I've started towards the rim of the fountain once more when something seizes my leg, dragging me under. I kick, but it's no use. Whatever has me tightens its grip, claws digging into my flesh.

I can't break free, so instead, I fight to slow my frenzied heart. I am no stranger to water; it is my aid, my ally. It gives me strength. It gives me an advantage. I can hold my breath for as long as I need to, but I have to remain calm.

"He's not coming to save you," a voice says, forcing its way into my mind, gritty like sand.

I don't need to be saved. This is the closest I've been to water since I was taken from the sea. Fresh energy courses through my veins, awakening every cell. I bathe in the vitality it brings, giving me life anew. I want to stay here, beneath the surface. I *want* to drown.

Just as I begin to sink into the power that floods my body, I'm heaved free from the fountain. For a moment, I'm no longer fighting whatever pulled me under but whoever is pulling me free.

"Violet?" A voice warbles in my ears. "Violet, breathe!"

Owen? I gasp for air, choking on blood. *No,* I remember with a start. It can't be Owen. My mind clears as someone sets me on my feet, smearing blood from my eyes with the hem of his shirt. Through a red film, Charlie's blue eyes come into focus, full of panic. Behind him, Will's face is pale.

As soon as I regain my balance, Charlie whirls to face him. He grabs Will by the shirt collar, shaking him. "You were going to let her drown!" he growls. "Why didn't you do something?"

Will looks past Charlie, at me, his eyes darker than before. "The...blood..."

Charlie shoves Will to the ground. "A Nightweaver, afraid of blood? You expect me to believe that?"

Will clenches his jaw, grasping tufts of grass with his fists. He looks away from me, his brows knitted. "Not afraid," he grinds out. He shuts his eyes tight and takes a few labored breaths. The rise and fall of his chest slows, and when he opens his eyes again, they are bleak with shame. "There is some truth to the legends you've heard."

Will stands, smooths his clothes. He avoids looking at me, his gaze intent on the sprawling gardens in the distance. "When the war first began, there were some Nightweavers that sought to gain the psychic abilities of Underlings," he says quietly. "That kind of power...it changes us. The stories of Nightweavers bathing in human blood—drinking it like wine from the cup— aren't just stories. Blood is the purest source of *Manan*, but *human* blood is the most potent." He turns to me, his mouth set in a grim line. "But it drives Nightweavers to madness. We become no better than the Underlings—as savage as a Gore, and twice as deadly."

I hear what he says, but it's as if I'm listening from somewhere far away. I grasp at the hem of my dress, lifting it to inspect the wound left by the claws that had dug into my flesh. But the skin is unbroken. There are no puncture marks. Had there even been a hand?

"What did you find?" Will starts towards me, but Charlie throws his body between us, a towering shield.

I turn, searching the ground. There—the collar lies in the grass, covered in blood. I snatch it up, and without asking, I use the tail of Charlie's shirt to clear the blood away. Carved into the leather on the inside of the band are four words.

DID YOU MISS ME?

I gulp, my eyes meeting Will's.

"That's Dearest's collar," he says, his eyes narrowed.

"So, it *was* a Gore that killed Lady Annie's pet," Charlie murmurs.

"No." Will takes the collar from me, scanning the words carved into the band. "Gores can't write. Whoever left these messages is using a Gore to cover their tracks." He starts for the fountain again, past Charlie and me, focused on Mr. and Mrs. Hackney's heads.

I start to follow, but Charlie gasps, halting me mid-step.

"Violet!" he breathes, his face slack. "Your eyes!"

Will turns on his heels. In a flash, he plunges a hand into the fountain, elbow-deep in blood. Before Charlie can react, Will grabs him by the arm.

"Take care of Mr. and Mrs. Hackney," he says, his husky voice as gentle as a lullaby. "Forget what you've just seen."

Charlie's eyes glaze and he starts towards the fountain, moving as though he were in a trance. As he lifts Mr. Hackney's head from the sword, Will takes me by the arm, his grip gentle but commanding.

His eyes are no longer green, but gold. They glow with a soft, alluring light, drawing me in, soothing all fear. His hand grazes my cheek, and a familiar rush of calm sweeps through me at his touch. "Sleep," he whispers.

I try to resist, but the world around me fades. The last thing I see is Will's golden eyes as he takes me in his arms, sweeping me off my feet.

Don't trust anyone, Mother's warning echoes in my mind. Even Will. *Especially* Will.

I want to obey, to be a good daughter—a good crewman—and heed her command. But as I surrender to the gentle kiss of darkness, Will's arms feel safer to me than the *Lightbringer* ever did, and I know it's too late.

CHAPTER ELEVEN

I wake to the familiar sound of Albert's wailing cry. I leap from my bed, expecting my sheets, my uniform, my hair to all bear signs of the bloodbath I'd taken in the fountain the night before, but it's as though it never happened. My hair is clean and dry, my sheets without stain, my uniform like new. A vague memory of Will wading into a pond, washing the blood from my hair, turns my stomach to water.

Had he changed my clothes, too?

A different memory surfaces just as my cheeks grow hot. Liv and the other pixies pull the blood-soaked uniform over my head, and Will keeps his back turned away from them as they work to dress me near the old oak tree in the conservatory. And then, Will places me gently on my bed, covering me with a blanket.

Another muffled cry stirs me from my thoughts, and I race down the hall to find Mother and Father consoling Albert in his bed. Sunlight pools on the floor, where Charlie is kneeling by Albert's bedside. When Charlie dips his head in greeting, he doesn't appear to have any memory of pulling me out of the fountain, or the collar we'd discovered, or Will's golden eyes.

"But I saw him," Albert sobs, burying his head in Mother's chest. "I saw Owen!"

"Hush, now," Mother croons, smoothing his hair. "It was just a dream."

Father looks up at me, the wrinkles near his eyes more pronounced than they've ever been. "It's time," he says. "I'm going to ask Lord Castor for a break this afternoon."

I nod, my throat tightening. At sea, under normal circumstances, we would have already observed Owen's burial rites. Something within me hoped we never would. Maybe if we didn't, I wouldn't have to accept that he's really gone. But Father's right—it's time. Time to put Owen to rest.

Time to let go.

The morning passes in a fog. After lunch, when the eight of us meet on a grassy knoll overlooking a vibrant tangle of wildflowers, I feel as if I'm watching us from afar. Throughout the ceremony, my gaze remains fixed on a sprawling oak, where a raven perches on the highest branch, looking down on us with shrewd interest. Owen once told me that if he could be anything, he'd be a bird. A sad, twisted smile tugs at my lips. Perhaps he finally got his wish.

Lewis has sewn a small replica of the *Lightbringer*'s flag—canary yellow, emblazoned with nine silver stars. He presents it to Mother as she recites from memory a passage out of Captain Gregory's Psalter.

"May the waves prove monument to a life bravely endured," Mother says, concluding the ceremony, her solemn eyes wet with tears.

"And may the Stars proclaim its glory," we all murmur in response. Traditionally, we would have fired our pistols into the air—twenty-one shots to represent the years Owen spent on this earth—but since we have none, we kiss the tips of two fingers and point them at the sky, our thumbs extended. This, along with the rest of the ceremony, seems to put the others at ease. Margaret and Lewis embrace; Charlie lifts Albert onto his shoulders, and Father carries Elsie on his back as my family parades down the hill towards the house. Only Mother lingers, her eyes fixed on the horizon as tears spill onto her weathered cheeks.

"You didn't have your trinket when your sisters' and brothers' were taken," she rasps, her voice barely above a whisper. "William took them, didn't he?"

My fingers brush the band of braided leather that had belonged to Owen. Mother had made them herself when I was still a child, choosing braided leather to represent the tightly woven bond among us. According to the Creed, if a pirate is killed in battle, their trinket should be received by the clan member who witnessed their death. Even enemy clans will provide a truce to ensure that the rite of trinkets be honored after the battle has been fought.

"Yes," I say quietly.

Her eyes narrow. "He kept yours."

I'm not sure how she knows the difference between my bracelet and my brother's—I could hardly tell, aside from the slight fraying of Owen's compared to my own. I dip my head. "He did."

Since it was Will who found me that morning, just after Owen died, it seems only fitting that my bracelet remains in his possession. After all, Violet Oberon, fearsome pirate of the Western Sea, died the moment the *Lightbringer's* masts sank below the waves. He might not be a member of the Oberon clan, but Will witnessed that death. In a way, the trinket belongs to him.

I start back down the hill before she can ask any more questions I don't have the heart to answer. If I'm to stay here, I have to let go of more than just Owen, and the *Lightbringer*, and our life before. I have to let go of me, too.

Owen is gone, but his trinket will always remind me of who he was. That he was here. That he existed. That he fought bravely until the last. And as my family moves on, as they put Owen's memory to rest, my trinket belongs to someone who will always remember that I was a pirate before I was a kitchen maid. That I remain here only out of loyalty. That despite our new life on land, the sea claimed two Oberon children that day.

"Violet?" a voice murmurs from behind a cluster of rosebushes as I pass. I halt. My hand searches instinctively for the hilt of a dagger at my hip but finds nothing.

Will steps into the open, his pale face flushed pink. "I didn't mean to startle you," he says, rubbing the nape of his neck. With a rumpled white linen shirt and his knees caked with dirt, he looks less like a lord and more like one of the groundskeepers. If I didn't know better, I'd think he were merely human—enough to make me forget that just last night, he'd looked at a fountain of blood as if it were a spring of cool water and he was dying of thirst.

"You didn't," I lie, taking a step back.

Understanding registers in his eyes, and he strokes his jaw. "You have every reason to feel the way you do." He sighs, taking a single white lily from his chest pocket. "If you wish never to speak to me again—"

"I don't," I blurt out, my cheeks hot. "And I don't know what I feel."

Guilt coils around my stomach, squeezing tight. We've only just said goodbye to Owen, and rather than grieve my brother, I'm finding myself torn between my hate for Nightweavers—for what they did to Owen, for what they've done to my people— and hating myself for this odd and fervent desire to be close to Will.

He takes a step towards me, but I stand my ground. His dark-green eyes bore into mine with a deep regret I can't begin to fathom. "What I did last night, I did to protect you. If

anyone knew we were so"—he wets his lips, knits his brows—
"involved…"

"What makes you think I need protecting?"

"I don't." He glances down at the lily, his expression nettled.
"You remember what I told you about the humans that choose
to fight alongside the Underlings?"

I nod. He frowns.

"They call themselves the Guild of Shadows," he says, his jaw
tightening. "They serve the Underling's Sylk queen, Morana."
The name causes him to grimace, and he runs a hand through
his hair as if to calm himself.

"Morana?" I echo, the name sending shivers down my
spine.

He nods, his brows pinched. "Before the fall, she was
imprisoned in Havok, the realm below, but when your people
created the Burning Lands, she was set free. No one knows
where she is now—or if she's ever chosen a host to possess—
but there has been speculation for centuries that she remains
in the Burning Lands, waiting for Nightweavers and humans to
destroy each other so that she can claim this realm for her own."

He glances over his shoulder before turning back to me, his
expression softening.

"The Sylk that killed your brother knows that you can see
it," he goes on, lowering his voice. "That's the reason it followed
you here—the reason it's still toying with you. The Guild is
always looking to recruit someone with your ability, lest you use
it against them. And they do so by stripping away everything

that makes you human, including everyone you know and love." He takes another step towards me, close enough that if I had a dagger, I could plunge it into his heart before he had the chance to blink. "Mr. and Mrs. Hackney were like family to me, but if the Guild had wanted to send a more effective message, that could have just as easily been your mother and father's heads we found last night."

He slips the lily into my apron, and my stomach leaps at the proximity of his hand.

"I meant what I said," he murmurs, his eyes lingering on the flower peeking out from my apron pocket. When he looks up at me, his thick eyelashes cast shadows on his freckled face. "If you still want my help, meet me at the stables tonight, after everyone's gone to sleep."

I take a step back, wanting for breath. "Why the lily?" I ask, remembering what he had said last night about the secret language of flowers.

He looks past me, toward where Mother is beginning her descent down the hill, knee-deep in wildflowers. "They represent sympathy for that which has come to an end," he says, his eyes glittering. "And new beginnings—the hope for what's to come."

New beginnings, I think, my fingers brushing the soft petals. As I watch Mother, the vibrant earth undulating like waves, the wildflowers a sea of color at her feet, I feel as if I'm seeing her for the first time. If Mother can begin again—if she can let go of her past, of who she was before—then so can I. At least, I have to try.

Just not yet.

If I'm to have any chance of putting my past behind me, I have to put Owen to rest, once and for all. Not with psalms or flags or mock salutes. If I'm to let go—truly let go—I have to find the Sylk, and Will is going to help me do it.

CHAPTER TWELVE

I don't have to wait long before Margaret lets out her first snore. I light a candlestick and tiptoe down the hall, past Mother and Father's room, then Lewis and Charlie's. As I pass Albert and Elsie's quarters, the door creaks open slightly, beckoning me to peek inside. I squeeze through the gap, letting the warm flicker of the fire cast long shadows on their two tiny cots.

In the dim light, a figure stands over Elsie's sleeping form, his back turned to me.

My heart skips a beat. "Lewis?" I whisper.

The figure glances over his shoulder. Two red eyes find mine, glowing softly like smoldering embers. Shadows seep from his flesh, enveloping him in a haze.

Not Lewis.

The shadows lash out, extinguishing the candle, plunging us into darkness. In that instant, he leaps through the open window. The candlestick clatters to the ground as I lunge after him. I stick my head out into the damp night air, but when I look down, I find the rosebushes below are undisturbed. Above, a raven glides on moonlit wings towards the forest in the distance, where steep cliffs surround the valley and dark falls cascade over the rock face.

"Violet?" Albert murmurs, rubbing his eyes.

"Go back to sleep." My voice shakes as I close the window and kiss Albert's forehead. I take up the candlestick once more and slip into the hall. The moment I reach the staircase, I break into a sprint. I dash through the kitchen, out onto the west lawn. By the time the stable comes into view, my breathing is ragged and my heart threatens to burst from my chest.

Will is already there, propped against Caligo's stall, a black cloak slung around his shoulders. He must know by the look on my face what I've seen, because he holds a finger to his lips, his expression urgent.

"Not here," he says.

We take Caligo to the conservatory, his hooves churning up dirt as we race through the apple tree tunnel. I follow Will inside, and he closes the door behind us. Liv and the other pixies are gathered round the old oak tree, singing and dancing, undeterred by our arrival. Somewhere close by, a howl splits the air.

I start, reaching for a weapon I don't possess, but Will appears unaffected.

"Just the wolves," he murmurs.

Wolves. Mother used to read us a story about a wolf that killed a sheep and stole its skin, using it to disguise himself so that he could evade the shepherd's watchful eye. In the end, it turned out the shepherd had a taste for mutton, and by happenstance he caught the wolf. Mother said the moral of the story was those that sought to harm others often ended up in harm's way themselves. She often warned us to beware of wolves in sheep's clothing—kindly pirating clans that would come upon us under the guise of fair trade only to attack when we least expected it. But we were not helpless lambs, and their deception always cost them more than they were willing to pay.

Will sheds his cloak, draping it over my shoulders. It's lighter than I expected, and it's as if I've been robed in a blanket of relief. The tension in my muscles eases, my head clears. The terror of what I'd seen only minutes ago fades beneath the incessant fluttering in my belly as he fastens the hook loosely around my neck. Warmth seems to bleed through the fabric, caressing every inch of my skin with its soothing heat. It smells like him—like roses and damp earth.

He furrows his thick brows, his green eyes glittering. "You saw it, didn't you?"

I nod, my mouth dry. "It was right in front of me, but I didn't…I couldn't—"

"There was nothing you could do." Will's eyes darken and he glances at the ground. "I'm afraid I haven't been entirely honest with you."

I take a step back, the cloak suddenly heavy on my shoulders. "What do you mean?"

He runs a hand through his long black curls. "Last night, what you saw," he begins, his voice low.

"Your eyes," I murmur.

The muscle in his jaw twitches. "I drew power from the *Manan* in the blood. It strengthened my ability to...*influence*. It gave me power like that of an Underling." He looks down at his hands. "The humans that serve the Underling queen do so because she promises to give them such power. Those that choose to follow her are no longer human—no longer living. Not truly." He looks up, searching my face. "They become Shifters."

"Shifters?" I echo. "But how—"

"It doesn't take much." His throat bobs. "Just a bite."

"A bite?" My voice falters as I remember the dream I'd had just after Owen was killed: the teeth that pierced my shoulder.

He dips his chin, his expression grave. "When I told you that my people saw your ability as a curse..."

I stagger away from him. The cloak slides from my shoulders, lands in a pool of black velvet. "Are you saying that I'm a—that I—"

"No," he insists, taking me by the arm, drawing me towards him. I stumble over the cloak at my feet, and my head collides with his chest. He looks down at me, his eyes soft, his voice gentle. "If you'd been bitten, you'd know it. The mark it leaves would have rotted your flesh, and the Underling venom in your system would have already turned you."

In a moment of weakness, I don't pull away. "You don't sound sure."

"I'm sure about you, Violet," he murmurs, searching my eyes. "You are no Shifter."

I bury my face in his shirt, inhaling the cloying scent of flowers and damp soil. I long for Mother and Father's solace, but how can I go to them, how can I tell them what I know—what I can do—when all they want is for me to move on? Mother and Father know more about the Nightweavers than they've let on, and I believe they know more about the Underlings than they're willing to tell. If I tell them I saw a Sylk—that I'm hunting Owen's killer—will they think I'm cursed, too? Will they think I've lost my mind?

For what feels like too long, I let Will hold me, my cheek pressed against his chest, as I listen to the steady rhythm of his heartbeat. Finally, I draw back, his arms still wrapped around me like a shield.

"Your ability is rare," he says, seemingly oblivious to the way his hands press against my lower back. "On the front, soldiers have to use special equipment to detect Sylks. I've never met anyone who could see the shadows like you can. At least, not anyone who has not yet turned fully into a Shifter."

"But why?" I manage to ask, all too aware of the intimate nature of our embrace. "Why can I see them?"

He shakes his head, withdraws his hands. "I don't know," he admits, his fingers lingering near my elbow as if he's only just realized how close we'd been. "But what you saw tonight was no Sylk."

I tuck a tangle of hair behind my ear, and the movement jars him into action. He draws his hand back, rubs the nape of his neck. A bashful grin tugs at the corner of his lips, his cheeks rosy—a look all too human, too humble for someone like Will:

someone with the power to break bones with the flick of his wrist, or bring a man to his knees with the twitch of a finger.

I clear my throat, fidgeting with Owen's bracelet. "You think it was a Shifter?"

His boyish grin fades. He nods grimly. "A Sylk is just a shadow in this realm until it possesses a human, and when it jumps into a new body, it kills the former host. But Shifters can take on any form they please." He rubs his jaw. "It's just as I feared. The Guild is hoping to recruit you. If you hadn't been there tonight…"

His unspoken words hang in the air. If I hadn't been there, Elsie and Albert would be dead.

"What can I do?" I hate how small my voice sounds, how helpless I feel. At sea, I was always so sure of myself. Killing was easy when it was a matter of survival. A sharp blade or a quick draw is all I've ever needed to stay alive, to win a fight. But how can I kill something that hides in the shadows, if I do not learn how to fight in the dark? And in that darkness, will I become nothing more than a shadow, too?

"There's nothing to be done. Not tonight." Will bends, takes the bundled cloak in his arms. "The Shifter will show itself again, and when it does, it will lead us to the Sylk. Until then…" He turns away from me and heads towards the old oak. He spreads the cloak on the grass and lies down, his hands beneath his head. "Care to join me?"

I lift a brow. "That's it? There's nothing we can do, so you're going to take a nap?"

"Technically, it's not a nap if it's past my bedtime." The corner of his lip kicks up into a grin as he pats the space beside him on the cloak. "I heard you pirates have a penchant for storytelling." He points at the glass ceiling. Overhead, the night sky twinkles, the constellations like a living tapestry of the legends for which they're named.

I lie beside him, careful not to infringe on the narrow sliver of space between us, as if he hadn't held me in his arms only moments ago.

"That one," he says, pointing to Astrid and her Crown of Seven Candles. "What's its story?"

I glance at him sidelong. "I'd rather talk about what happens once we've caught the Sylk."

He sighs, mimicking one of Jack's dramatic fits. "I'm well aware of your obsession with killing," he says, letting his head fall to the side, his eyes finding mine.

I snort, fixing my gaze on the stars once more, but heat creeps into my cheeks under his probing stare. "Then surely you know what I'll do to you if you stand in my way?"

From the corner of my eye, I see him smile crookedly, revealing teeth as bright and as brilliant as the stars themselves.

"I can dream."

Chapter Thirteen

I can't shake the feeling that I'm being watched. All morning, the sensation prods at the base of my spine, raising the hair on my neck anytime a floorboard creaks or the wind rattles the shutters. Once in a while, the brass grate near the base of the wall in the kitchen catches my attention and I think I see the glowing red eyes tracking my every movement—though I'm sure it must be my imagination, because every time I look again, there is nothing but darkness.

"You're jumpy today," Father says, glancing at me out of the corner of his eye as he peels a carrot with keen precision, wasting nothing. "Everything alright?"

I swallow hard, forcing a smile. "Just a bit tired. Haven't been sleeping well."

His eyes narrow, but he nods. "Feeling okay?"

"Fine, yeah," I lie, ignoring the throbbing ache in my head that had kept me up most of the night, and the sick feeling that roils my stomach. Rays of afternoon sun stream through the skylights, all too bright, and I fight the urge to block my eyes as

I turn to fix Father with my own questioning look. "Do I look that rough?"

Father grins—reminding me of Owen—as he gestures at the tomato I was supposed to dice. "Your technique is sloppy."

I don't suppress a chuckle before I frown at the mangled red chunk of fruit. "No one likes an honest pirate."

Dorothy, drying dishes across the kitchen, shoots me a scandalized glance, and I roll my eyes.

"*Reformed* pirate," I bite out, the sweet smile on my face laced with enough venom to keep Dorothy from looking my way again.

"Get some rest," Father says warmly, clapping me on the shoulder. "I'll need you at your best for dinner tonight."

I hesitate, thinking about the red eyes I'd seen watching me from above while I was lying in bed that first night. It was the Shifter—I know that now. Even if my head hadn't felt as if it were splitting in two, I doubt I would have gotten any sleep after my encounter with the shape-shifting Underling in my siblings' room last night. I doubt I'll get much sleep now, but I agree to take a break. I head upstairs, my every muscle tense as I open the door to my chambers.

My breath hitches in my throat. There—on my bed—sits the knapsack that had disappeared the night the Hackneys were murdered. I inch towards it, my heart beating faster. All too aware of the brass grate overhead, I open the knapsack with trembling hands.

Inside, two pairs of eyeballs reek of death.

I drop the knapsack, stumbling back a few steps.

"V?" Charlie knocks on the door, waiting only a moment before barging in. He wears the crimson livery of the guards, having agreed to cover for Hugh, who had taken ill with a cold yesterday evening. It's strange to see him in uniform with the Castors' golden dragon embroidered on his chest, but I can't deny that it suits him. "Something wrong?"

I didn't realize I'd made a sound. "No," I say, grabbing the knapsack and darting past him through the open door. "No, everything's fine."

Charlie doesn't seem convinced as he flicks a glance at the knapsack clutched behind my back, but he doesn't press. "Sure." He clears his throat, starting awkwardly, "You know, if you need someone to talk to—"

"I'm fine, Charlie," I insist, already making my way down the hall. "Really, I'm alright."

He leans against my doorway, arms crossed. "Right," he says with a sigh. But when I reach the stairwell, his quiet voice reaches me, heavy with grief. "He was my brother, too."

I halt, my foot hovering over the top step.

"And Lewis, and Margaret's," he adds. "Elsie, Albert—we all miss him, Violet. You're not alone in that. You don't have to shut us out because Owen—"

"I'm fine, Charlie," I repeat, careful to keep my tone even. Without waiting for him to respond, I hurry down the staircase, my grip on the knapsack like a vise.

I know Charlie means well. After all, he and Owen were only a year apart. In a lot of ways, they were closer than most of our siblings. But Charlie couldn't possibly understand what I'm going through. The Guild of Shadows isn't after Margaret. Lewis isn't being haunted by a Shifter. Elsie and Albert are oblivious to the threat of the Underlings, living within a carefully constructed illusion of safety. I am alone in my hatred—alone in my need to avenge Owen. There is only one person in this entire house who makes me feel less…alone.

Maybe that's why I find myself wandering the west atrium of Bludgrave Manor, uninvited, in the insane hope of finding Will as alone as I feel.

Sunlight beams through the glass ceiling above, setting the scarlet staircase aflame and illuminating every shiny knickknack kept on display in this part of the house. Silver spoons, delicate pottery, hand-painted vases all reflect the light. It's somewhat blinding. I'd have to take only a few things and I could bribe my way to the Savage Coast. If I could make it there, I might have enough coin to buy myself a ship, maybe a crew. I might even be able to purchase information on the whereabouts of Captain Shade. Perhaps his offer to join him would still stand…

My grip tightens on the knapsack. If the Sylk is after only me, then if I left Bludgrave, the Guild of Shadows would have no reason to torment my family. Would they?

If only I could find Will. If I could just see him, maybe this sick feeling twisting my gut would be replaced by the incessant fluttering I feel whenever he's near.

Oh, Maker of All. How can I be so foolish? I turn around, starting towards a panel of a wall I know will open into one of the servant's passageways. Will had agreed to help me find the Sylk. That doesn't mean he'll appreciate it if I seek him out during the day, in a part of the house where I am required to make myself scarce. For the safety of both of us, neither my family nor his can find out about our secret meetings. Only Jack is to know about the time we spend together. I am not to delude myself with the notion that he should treat me any differently than he treats any other member of their staff. Even if it seemed that way last night, when his arms were wrapped around me...

"Violet?" His deep voice causes my steps to falter.

I look up toward where Will peers over the banister, his expression neutral. I don't know what I'd expected. Had I fooled myself into thinking he'd be happy to see me?

He descends the grand staircase at a leisurely pace, looking everywhere in the room but at me. A black three-piece suit clings to his lean, muscular frame, and I can't help but think he looks like a wolf in sheep's clothing—powerful, cunning. Dangerous.

Dangerous, deadly things are often the most beautiful.

When he reaches the bottom of the steps, his gaze lands on me, far too intense. "Are you lost?" he drawls, adjusting his shirt cuffs.

My heart says *yes*, but, "No."

He quirks an eyebrow. "You're a long way from the kitchen."

Still holding the knapsack behind my back, I give a quick nod. "I'll just be going, then."

Shifting the knapsack to my front as I turn, I press my hand to the panel in the wall, my chest squeezing painfully tight. *Stupid. Stupid. Stupid*—

"Wait."

I hold my breath as Will's languid footsteps draw close. His presence behind me pulses as if it has a heartbeat of its own, one that only I can hear.

"Violet," he says, his voice low.

I glance over my shoulder at the same moment he retracts his hand, as if it had been outstretched towards me. My stomach twists into knots as he looks left, then right, before reaching past me to open the panel to the servant's passage. He inclines his head, a subtle command for me to enter, and the knot in my stomach tightens as I obey, my cheeks burning. I've never felt such humiliation in all my life as when I enter the dimly lit passage. Thick, angry tears well in my eyes as I wait, listening to the door click shut, when a hand on my lower back sends a jolt through my spine.

"This way," Will murmurs, his warm breath caressing the shell of my ear.

Dumbstruck, I allow him to lead me down the passage, where we come upon another panel. The door lets out into a room I've heard Margaret extoll but have yet to see for myself.

Bookshelves line the cylindrical space, three stories high. A spiral staircase leads to the second and third landings, and in the center of Lord Castor's study, a hulking mahogany desk sits opposite a stone hearth big enough to stand inside. The crackling fire fills the space with warmth, while various lamps illuminate the piles of books strewn about the room. No skylights, no blinding white sun. Thank the Stars.

I glance about the room, wondering if Elsie or Father have seen this place. Between the two of them, the *Lightbringer* had been overflowing with books about almost everything. My favorite works in their collection were the storybooks Mother read to us at night—tales of faraway lands, of daring adventurers and runaway princesses. Mother and Father insisted we all learn to read when we were children, giving us as rigorous an education as a life of piracy would allow, but I'd never given much thought to it until we'd brought Mary Cross aboard and the poor girl admitted she'd never even *seen* a book.

"Are you well?" Will asks softly, his light touch on the small of my back like a flare of heat. The scent of roses and damp earth encapsulates me, and for a moment, I forget to answer.

"I found something." I turn, taking a step away from him.

His hand hovers where I'd been for only a moment before he adjusts his lapels, his green eyes narrowing as I extend the knapsack to him. "What is it?"

"See for yourself."

Will opens the knapsack—closes it. His expression is nettled. "My sincerest apologies," he says, taking the knapsack from me. He tucks it away inside his jacket, and as if by magic, the knapsack shrinks to accommodate the size of his interior breast pocket. "I've spent the morning attempting to locate any weakness in the wards my family has placed around Bludgrave, but there's no sign of a breach." He lowers his voice to a whisper.

"The only way an Underling could be getting in is if someone in my family *let* them in."

The roiling in my stomach intensifies. "Could it be—"

"Annie?" He rubs his chin. "I thought so, at first. But she's not skilled enough with magic to do something like that. My father created the wards before she was born. She's linked to them by blood, but it would be difficult for her to tamper with them without help from my father himself."

I chew on my bottom lip. "Would your father—"

"No," Will says sharply, his face drawn. "He's devoted his life to fighting Underlings. If he knew one had found access to the manor..." He shakes his head. "I'll keep checking the wards. I must be missing something."

Above Will's head, the fire dapples a brass grate with amber light. "Is it possible—" I hesitate. "Those...grates. I've noticed them all over the house. Could someone get in through those?"

Will tilts his head, eyeing me consideringly, before glancing over his shoulder at the brass covering. "They're called grilles," he says slowly. "Mother insisted on ventilating the manor with central heating and air a few years back. Father didn't see the point with all the fireplaces, but Mother won out in the end." He runs a hand through his hair, his brows pinched. "They're within Bludgrave's walls, so the wards would still apply." He fixes his gaze on me once more, ever searching. "Why? Did you see something?"

I lift a shoulder. "It might have been a nightmare," I admit. But after the words leave my mouth, I realize something I haven't before. Since I've come to Bludgrave, I haven't had a single night terror. Not one. Aside from the pain that kept me awake last night, I've slept soundly in my little cot. Margaret reasoned just this morning that it might have something to do with having a pillow for the first time in my life, but by the look on Will's face, I'm not sure that's the case.

"Impossible," Will says. "Years ago, after Henry returned home, he could hardly close his eyes without screaming." A muscle in his jaw twitches as he picks up a glass bottle. Inside, a miniature ship with replica black sails appears caught in a tempest—simple magic, surely, compared to what I'd seen Will do with the flick of his wrist, but wondrous nonetheless. "My Uncle Killian is rather talented with wards. His magic guards Bludgrave against nightmares for Henry's sake." He shrugs. "I can't complain. The only time I get any sleep is when I'm within these walls."

Will sets the contained ship on a stack of books. With the little bottle no longer in his grasp, the sea within the glass calms, the sails flapping as if stirred by a gentle breeze.

"What did you see?"

I pull my bottom lip between my teeth, hesitating. "My first night here, I thought…It looked like…" My right hand strays to the bracelet hidden at my wrist, and I let out a shaky breath. "Nothing. It was a long day. My eyes were playing tricks on me."

Softly, he asks, "What kind of tricks?"

My heart throbs in my chest, a dull ache. "Eyes," I whisper. "Red eyes. Watching me…"

His brows furrow. He doesn't speak for a long moment as he studies me, his eyes narrowing slightly. "Could you tell if someone in this house was possessed?"

"I think so." I scan the bookshelves, squirming under the weight of Will's calculating stare. "But, Will…"

"Yes?"

"You said the wards protect against nightmares," I say slowly, dragging my gaze back to his. When our eyes meet, I almost forget what I was going to say, but he gives a subtle nod, encouraging me to continue. "Albert had a nightmare, the morning after we found the Hackneys. He thought…" I take a deep breath, clenching my fists to keep my hands from trembling. "He thought he saw Owen."

"Owen," he echoes, his expression unreadable. "It's possible my uncle's wards have weakened since he last visited. I'll have him check them first thing when he arrives."

His confident dismissal of any other possibilities is so certain, I allow myself to sag a bit with relief. It was only a nightmare. Albert hadn't actually seen Owen. But still, as much as I want to believe that it was a fault with the wards, I can't help but wonder…is there something else going on? Something Will doesn't want me to know?

Will's gaze trails down my arm like a caress, resting on the concealed form of the bracelet. "I always thought most pirate trinkets were gold earrings and bronze medallions. Why the bracelets?"

I run my fingers over the braided leather beneath my sleeve, somewhat jarred by his change in subject. "At sea, all my siblings and I had was each other. The three strands represent our unbreakable bond." I meet Will's gaze, my brows pinched. "My brother said you kept me separated from them for two weeks. Did you decide to take my bracelets before or after you decided to keep me drugged in your chambers?"

A muscle in Will's jaw feathers as he slides his hands into his pockets. "I didn't drug you, Violet." He sidesteps around me, stopping to stand in front of the fireplace, his back turned. "When I first saw you that day aboard the ship, you were crawling towards your brother. I saw you take his bracelet, and then…I knew, when you saw the Sylk—I knew what you had seen. I'd suspected it, but I knew for certain then. And when you followed it into the captain's quarters—after having just witnessed something truly terrifying and strange, you followed it anyway, despite your fears—I knew I had to meet you."

Silhouetted against the flames, his dark outline sends a shiver through me. He appears like a shadow—like a Sylk given flesh.

I am no stranger to curses.

"But when I looked down at you, lying there…" He trails off, his deep voice barely audible over the crackle of the hearth. "I saw that you'd been marked."

My heart drops into my stomach. "Marked?"

He angles towards me, beckoning me with only a look. I shuffle across the ornate rug, towards the warm embrace of the fire. I face Will, the amber light dancing in his eyes as he extends his hand, slowly, to brush a loose strand of hair from my cheek. He tucks it behind my ear and his fingertips lightly brush the skin behind my earlobe, sending another shiver through me.

"There," he murmurs, his face grim. He traces the ink tattooed in the shape of an X—a scar I've tried my best to forget. "Henry has one just like it."

Will's fingers linger near my cheek, his calloused palm cradling my jaw. At his touch, a feeling of calm overtakes me, the tension in my neck and shoulders melting like butter on a hot skillet.

"So, you felt sorry for me?"

His eyes darken. "I felt responsible."

"Responsible? For what?"

He clenches his jaw. "I should have found them before they could do to anyone else what they'd done to Henry."

"Will," I say, my voice small, "what happened to me isn't your fault. You didn't even know me then."

His thumb strokes my cheek. "Sometimes I feel like I've known you my whole life."

My stomach somersaults, and I struggle to form words.

"When I saw you…" He trails off, his eyes prodding at my very soul. "I couldn't let them take you to the brig. Not after everything you've been through."

He sighs, withdrawing his hand. At the absence of his touch, my skin goes cold and clammy, and the ache at the base of my skull seems more intense than it had before.

"Some of my kind are gifted with unique abilities that go beyond our natural affinity," he says, pinching the bridge of his nose. "I possess a rare talent for persuasion. It's akin to the compulsion Underlings are capable of, but less...intrusive. You slept for two weeks aboard the ship because as long as you were asleep, I could keep you safe. Only the True King knows what you'd have attempted had you been awake."

I can't argue—if I had been awake, I would have done everything in my power to wreak havoc on Will and the remaining crew. "And my bracelets?" I press. "Why not give them back to me that day on the train?"

He hesitates, looking away from me, his gaze fixed on the thrashing flames. "I sensed human magic on them," he says quietly. "I wanted to inspect them further before returning something that could have had you accused of sorcery."

"Sorcery?" I rub my arms against the sudden chill. "That's outrageous."

"Is it?" He cuts a glance at me. "Why were you instructed never to take it off?"

I wince against the throbbing pain in my head, hardly able to think straight. "To remove your trinket is to renounce your clan."

Will nods. "Interesting," he murmurs, rubbing his chin. "Have you ever taken it off before?"

I make a fist, my nails biting into my palms as the pain migrates from my head into my left shoulder. "Not by choice." I grind my teeth, remembering the pile of trinkets they kept aboard the *Deathwail* as trophies. When Captain Shade had rescued me, only a small portion of the crew had been on board. He'd kept one of them alive to show him where they'd stored my trinket, and he'd made sure it was secure on my wrist before he took me to the *Lightbringer*. I still don't know why he saved me—or how he knew where to find my family—but the care he'd shown in recovering my trinket...only a pirate would have done that.

"How do you know where to look?" I ask. "The *Deathwail* never stays in the same place for very long."

"I have an informant of sorts who found them once, but most of the crew had been aboard a different vessel. He's been tracking them ever since." He blows out a tight breath. "Or rather, attempting to track them."

My heartbeat skips. "Is your informant a captain?"

He gives me an odd look, but he doesn't answer.

"Do you know him?" I whisper, my pulse kicking into a gallop. "Captain Shade?"

Will looks over his shoulder at the door to the study, his expression hard. "Well enough," he admits. "How did you—"

"I took a wild guess," I lie, my mind racing. If Will knows Captain Shade, then it might be possible for him to send a letter to the captain from me. I could still be free. I could join Shade's crew. He promised I would be safe—*safe*, where Sylks and Shifters couldn't find me.

Maker of All. What am I thinking? I can't leave Bludgrave. Not until I've brought Owen's killer to justice. Maybe not ever...

"Violet?" Will turns to face me, closer now than he'd been before, his breath the only warmth on my icy skin. "Are you sure you're feeling well?"

"I'm fine," I groan as the pain in my shoulder flares. "I'm so tired of everyone asking me that."

"You just look—"

"I look like what?" I bite out. "Like I spend my days toiling away in a stuffy kitchen? Not all of us get to parade around the manor in fancy suits all day, *my lord.*"

Will exhales sharply through his nose. "I only meant—"

"I don't care what you meant!" I've turned as if to storm out of the room when the pain in my head and shoulder intensifies in such a way that I stumble a few steps forward, then backward. I reach for something solid, grabbing at the iron tools near the hearth, but they slip from my grasp and topple onto the rug with a loud clang. Will throws his arm out, steadying me just before I tumble into the hearth.

He guides me to the armchair at Lord Castor's desk, pushing loose strands of dark, wavy hair out of my face like a fussy nursemaid. "Violet?" His voice warbles in my ears. "Are you ill?"

I'm fine, I want to say, but I'm afraid that if I open my mouth I might vomit.

"William?" Lord Castor hastens into the room, his crimson dressing gown tied somewhat askew, his hair ruffled as if he had just rolled out of bed. He takes in the sight of me sprawled in his armchair, my face wan—of Will hovering over me, the back of his hand pressed to my sweaty forehead. "What is the meaning of this?"

"I ran into Violet in the hall," Will says, his deep voice even and firm, leaving no room for doubt as he withdraws from me, sliding his hands into his pockets. "She felt cold, so I brought her here. I thought the fire might help, but she's clearly unwell. I was just about to take her to Miss Margaret."

Lord Castor's eyes narrow on Will, but he nods. "Of course. See to it that she's looked after."

Bless the Stars, the pain in my shoulder fades to a dull ache, and I manage the strength to stand on my own. "I'm alright," I insist, straightening my apron with shaky hands. "I apologize for the intrusion."

Without looking back at Will, I exit through the door from which Lord Castor had entered. The moment I've made it into the main hall, my knees threaten to buckle, but I lean on the wall for support, feeling as if I've been caught at sea in the midst of a violent storm.

"...a *human*, William!" Lord Castor's furious whisper carries through the open door as I stumble down the hall. "You put us all at risk!"

Human. In a way it never has before, that word stings like a slap to the face.

Tears burn my cheeks. I'm not sure how I make it to my bedroom without fainting, but I collapse onto my cot just before exhaustion finally overtakes me. As my eyes drift shut, I glimpse the brass grille overhead.

Two glowing red eyes peer down at me from the darkness, watching me from above, but instead of fear, pity grips my heart, and I can't help but wonder if they—whoever they are—feel alone, too.

"Why did no one wake me?" I scramble off my cot, my heart threatening to beat out of my chest.

Margaret pulls the blanket up to her chin, her eyes already closed. "Lord William insisted you get some rest," she says with a yawn. "He told Father you looked ill, and that he'd given you the rest of the day off. Said that no one should disturb you."

Pain stitches my shoulder, and I bite my bottom lip to keep from crying out as I stagger across the room. How I'd managed to sleep, I don't know. But I suspect it has something to do with Will's *talent*.

"Where are you going?" Margaret asks, her eyes still closed. "It's past midnight."

"Nowhere," I say, lingering in the doorway. "I just need some fresh air."

I wait until I've exited the house to peel back the collar of my dress and examine my left shoulder. For the pain it's caused me, I expect to find myself hideously burned, or mauled—something to explain the stinging sensation. But there is no evidence of a wound. Not even an insect bite.

Groaning, I trudge across the lawn. When I reach the pebbled bank of the pond, I strip down to my underclothes and wade into the moonlit water, letting it cool the ache in my shoulder. I float on my back for a while, staring at the moon overhead.

The True King sees. Can he see me now? Does he look down on me with pity, or with shame?

After a while, the pain in my shoulder subsides. When I draw breath, I don't wince. In fact, I breathe more clearly than I have since I'd stepped foot on dry land, as if the water revives something vital within me.

Above, a raven flaps its wings, dappled silver in the moonlight. It lands on the opposite side of the pond and perches atop the domed roof of Hildegarde's Folly, watching me with knowing eyes. Beyond the folly, the woods loom like a dark, impenetrable wave. The raven stirs, diving into the woods, and for the briefest moment, I feel compelled to follow it.

"You're up late."

Mother's calm voice beckons me from the rocky shore. I turn to face her, treading water with practiced ease.

"Couldn't sleep."

"Again?" She unfolds a towel and holds it open for me. "Father says you haven't been getting much rest."

I swim towards her, savoring the feel of the water gliding over my arms. "I'm having a hard time adjusting." A half-truth. "The house is so…still."

Mother grins, and my heart breaks. "It is, isn't it?" She sighs and looks toward the sky, where clouds conceal most of the stars. "I know this is difficult for you, Violet. But there is nothing you aren't capable of. Give it more time."

I don't say anything as I emerge from the water, and Mother wraps me in the rough linen towel. But something has been nagging at me since my conversation with Will in his father's study.

"Our bracelets," I say, fidgeting with the band of braided leather as Mother picks wet strands of hair from my face. "Will—er—Lord William mentioned that he'd sensed human magic on them." I bite my bottom lip, my voice barely a whisper. "But that can't be true…right?"

Mother's eyes flicker with some unknown emotion as she cuts a glance at the bracelet, but her expression remains innocently blithe. "Of course," she says, her tone light. "Our people's laws forbid the practice of sorcery. You know that."

Something within me deflates. "I know."

Mother cups my cheek in her calloused palm, her sapphire eyes reflecting the moonlight like two sparkling gems. "Your siblings are worried about you."

A cool breeze ruffles my hair, and I pull the towel tighter around my shoulders. "They shouldn't be."

"We have nothing else in this world if not our family. If something is troubling you—"

"Nothing troubles me, Mother," I lie, leaning away from her touch. "Like you said, I just need time."

Mother nods, her expression as soft as it had been the day Captain Shade had returned me to the *Lightbringer*. Then, she had wrapped me in a tattered blanket, her calloused palm stroking my cheek. *"The True King sees,"* she'd said as the sun peeked over the horizon. As if the True King had been responsible for sending Captain Shade to rescue me. As if he'd seen my suffering and had for once acted. But I know now that while the True King bears witness to all our misery, all our tribulation, it is not for him to act. If there is to be justice in this world, it will not come from above.

It will come from below.

CHAPTER FOURTEEN

few nights after the incident in Lord Castor's study, I lie in the shade of the old oak in the conservatory, attempting to mimic Liv's nimble movements as she weaves together a crown of hybrid purple blossoms—*mystiks*, Will had called them.

"Centuries ago," he tells me about the flowers, his brows pinched as he prunes a nearby rosebush, "a bonewielder crossbred your namesake, violets, with a rose. Only bonewielders are capable of maintaining them, and few are actually capable of doing so successfully."

Unlike Will, whose garden seems to overflow with the strange blossom.

"What about Annie?" I ask Will. "Is she a bonewielder, too?"

He chuckles softly, rolling his sleeves up to his elbows. "Children typically inherit their affinities from their parents, but not always. I took after our mother; Henry, our father. Annie, however, is what we call a windwalker. She has dominion over the air."

"I never see her use her magic."

He smiles. "She's young. She's still learning to perfect her gifts. My father wanted to send her to an academy in the capital that specializes in teaching children of nobility, but Mother wouldn't have it."

Academies—I'd heard of them before, but the concept was foreign. Aboard the *Lightbringer*, Mother and Father were our only teachers, the sea our classroom. I can't imagine attending school with hundreds of other children for hours every day. I certainly can't imagine preferring it to the invaluable education I'd received in the world beyond brick walls.

"And the fourth affinity...?"

He nods. "Bloodletters," he says, tossing aside a stem of dead flowers. "They have dominion over all the waters of the earth."

"Dominion over water?" The words leave a bitter taste in my mouth. The water has always been our sanctuary, our stronghold. But knowing that Nightweavers could have so easily taken it back from us whenever they pleased...It makes me feel weak.

"Have I met any?" I ask. "Any bloodletters."

"Not to my knowledge," Will says, his expression softening.

Yesterday, I'd heard Sybil and Martin discussing the affinities while I swept the kitchen. I'd heard that Bloodletters are considered the most powerful of all the Nightweavers—and the most deadly—but I hadn't heard them mention their ability to control water. From what I've learned through eavesdropping, the king and queen are both bloodletters.

And so is the prince.

"What is Percy?"

Will stills, tension bracketing his mouth. "Only the nobility were gifted with affinities. Nightweavers like Percy can do simple magic, but nothing more. Some like him tend to develop a dependency on *Manan* to give them some semblance of our power."

I want to ask more about this simple magic, but another thought takes precedence. "Speaking of *Manan*," I say slowly, my focus split between the subject at hand and trying not to prick my fingers as I continue to weave alongside Liv. "Jack made it seem like Father and I would be seasoning your meals with it. But I haven't even seen a speck of gold dust since we came here."

Will sits back on his heels, dusting the dirt from his palms. "There has been a shortage," he reminds me, his forehead creasing. "Regardless, my family has always given more than we take. What small supply we keep for ourselves is used to imbue our gloves and cloaks."

I start to ask him more about how one might imbue their cloak with magic dust, but something has been nagging at me since I'd first learned of the Castors' role in distributing the *Manan*. "Where does it come from?"

Something dark flickers in Will's eyes. "Once..." he draws out the word, "it could be harvested from a flower—the Bloodrose. They grew in abundance in Elysia, and when our kind were cast out of our realm, the flowers began to spring up all over the Known World. But over the years, the fields have dried up. There is only one garden left in the Eerie, and it is safeguarded in the capital, Jade, within the walls of Castle Grim."

I open my mouth to ask what other source of *Manan* they could be depending on, with so few Bloodroses left, but— "Maker of All!"

Will is at my side in less time than it took to utter the words, moving with preternatural speed. He takes my hand in his, examining the pinprick wound.

"I'm fine," I insist. "Just a stupid thorn."

But as the tiny drop of crimson wells on the tip of my finger, I'm reminded of what Will had said the night the Hackneys were murdered, what he'd done.

"You said human blood was the purest source of *Manan*," I whisper. "If there is a shortage, wouldn't that make our blood a resource?"

Will heaves a sigh, taking a handkerchief from his pocket and cleaning the blood from my finger with utmost care. "An extremely valuable one," he admits, his brows drawn. "But that's not something you should worry about. The law forbids the taking of human blood."

"But Percy does it," I say, glaring at the bloody handkerchief as Will folds it and tucks it away in his shirt pocket. I don't want to think of how many children—little girls like Elsie—that Percy had taken for that very reason.

Will takes the crown of mystiks from my lap and continues weaving, his fingers just as nimble and deft as Liv's. "I think," he says, placing the finished crown atop my head, "you would make an excellent queen."

"If I were queen," I say, rolling my eyes at how ridiculous those words sound coming out of my mouth, "my first decree would be to have Percy strung up from the castle walls."

"Surely you could think of something more creative than that," Will teases.

"Surely," I agree. "But I'm afraid it would be far too gruesome for your lordship to hear."

Will's green eyes sparkle, his smile revealing dimples in either cheek. "Now that," he says, adjusting the floral crown atop my head, "is what I like most about you."

"Oh?" A blush creeps up my neck, into my cheeks. "Are you referring to my needless concern for your gentle sensibilities or my inspired taste for violence?"

His grin turns wicked. "'Inspired' is the least of words I'd use to describe your appetite for violence," he murmurs, his hand straying to my cheek. "But the notion that you find me gentle…" His thumb brushes my lips, sending a shiver through me. "That will be my undoing."

He leans in, his breath warm on my face, his eyes drifting shut, and I find myself closing the distance between us, my lips parting on a shaky breath—

A howl splits the air and I jump back, knocking the crown of mystiks from my head. Will's husky laughter is the only thing that keeps me from getting to my feet to flee.

"Only the wolves again." He smirks, leaning back against the trunk of the old oak. "I told them not to do that while we're here, but they must have thought it would be humorous to scare you."

"I'm not scared." I grab the crown of mystiks, fiddling with the petals. "And what do you mean you *told* them?"

Will flashes a charming smile. "My affinity allows me to communicate with all living things." He pats the trunk of the tree. "The flowers, the trees, the insects—the wolves."

"That must be incredible." I think about Albert, and how he'd do anything just to have a conversation with one of the many squirrels that occupy the grounds. I can't help but feel that in a world where a boy can speak to trees and wolves have a sense of humor, anything could be possible.

"It can be," he agrees, but his face falls as he plucks a blade of grass, tosses it aside, plucks another.

"I'm sure it can also be overwhelming," I say, watching him carefully.

His mouth twists, the makings of a frown. "Would you like to know why I joined the League of Seven?" he asks, his question catching me somewhat off guard.

I nod, unsure of what to say. I'd thought the nobility were expected to serve; I hadn't realized Will might have had a choice in the matter.

Will's expression softens, but his gaze is closed off, as if he were reliving memories he'd prefer to keep to himself. "When I first joined the League four years ago," he says finally, his voice quiet, "I did so to keep Boris from being drafted."

Boris—the Castors' mild-mannered chauffer—had not spoken more than a few words to me since we'd arrived. But I don't take it personally. From what I've observed, he doesn't speak much at all.

"He'd been conscripted just one year before his eligibility would have expired, and with his eyesight already failing him at thirty-nine, I knew he wouldn't last long. Nobility aren't required to fight—it's discouraged, actually, in order to keep the bloodlines intact—but I petitioned the prince, and he accepted my offer to serve in Boris's place.

"During my first tour, we were in the trenches on the outskirts of the Burning Lands. I was cataloguing supplies when I'd heard news that an entire unit of soldiers had been possessed by Sylks. My commanding officer ordered that I be the one to deal with the executions of all sixty men and women."

"Why you?" I ask, thinking about how young Will would have been at the time—barely fifteen years old.

He grimaces, fiddling with a blade of grass. "The stronger a Nightweaver's magic, the harder it is for an Underling to possess them. Sylks shy away from possessing the nobility, as only Nightweavers who are weak in magic are susceptible to their control." He creases the blade of grass, his long, pale fingers twitching restlessly. "I knew when I joined that I would eventually be called upon to handle certain matters, but..."

His throat bobs. I've never seen him this distressed, his expression this unguarded. I remain motionless, waiting for him to continue.

"Our scientists are unable to figure out why, but wolves are one of the only creatures of your world whose bite can expel a Sylk. My commanding officer ordered me to lure a starving pack of wolves to a large pit that had been dug outside the base camp." He grinds his teeth, his jaw clenched. "Once I did, he ordered me to throw the soldiers in, one by one."

He falls silent for a long moment, his stare fixed on something far away.

"They're still *them* when they die," he says, his voice breaking. "The hosts are aware of everything that happens to them, even though they have no control over their own bodies." He pauses, his chin trembling ever so slightly, and I suppress a shudder at the thought of feeling so trapped, so helpless—a feeling I know all too well. "The Sylks—they laughed as the bodies were torn apart. Didn't even command their hosts to fight. They knew when they possessed them what would happen—they *wanted* it to happen. But the people…their screams…"

The blade of grass rips in his trembling hands. He glares at the ground, his teeth worrying his bottom lip. He takes a deep breath, his glassy eyes drifting up to meet mine.

"I never wanted to be what I am."

His words strike me like a blow to the stomach.

"I…" My voice breaks. "I didn't, either."

Will studies my face as if it were the first time he'd ever seen me. "And what do you want to be, now?"

I can't imagine why, but the memory of Captain Shade's masked face pops into my head at Will's question. What do I want to be? No one has ever asked me that. I think of Captain Shade's outstretched hand—his offer. *Safe.* Do I want to be safe? Could I be?

No. There is no safety to be had in this world. I *want* to find Owen's killer. I *want* to be left alone—free to sail the Western Sea with a purse full of coin and the wind in my hair, my compass leading me towards the sanctuary of the Red Island. But if I am to have those things, I have to be just as merciless as those who seek to control my fate.

I clench my fist around the invisible hilt of a cutlass, feeling its phantom weight in my grasp. "I want to be powerful."

Will's lips curl in a wicked smirk. "Violet Oberon, pirate of the Western Sea," he croons, "you are something much more than that." He leans forward, retrieving the crown of mystiks from where it had fallen. He places it atop my head once more, his gaze lingering on my mouth, where his thumb had brushed my lips. "You are feared."

Feared. Cursed. Hated.

That grinning, skeletal mask stains my mind's eye like a blot of scarlet ink. I look away from Will, studying the mystiks scattered around me like a ceremonial ring as I attempt to scour the bounty hunter's masked face from my subconscious. Ever the gentleman, Will leans back on his heels, his gaze fastened on my eyes as if he could see where my thoughts had drifted.

"He was there that day, when we made port." The words are out of my mouth before I realize I've said them aloud. "Your... *informant*," I add awkwardly. "He stopped an execution."

"I heard," Will says, his expression guarded. "Father read about it in the papers."

"Captain Shade didn't tell you?"

Will's lips quirk slightly. "I haven't had a chance to speak with him since I returned."

I fidget with the band of leather at my wrist. I'd never mentioned what happened that day to Margaret or the others, and they'd never asked why I'd been separated from them. Everyone had been far too worried about Charlie. Besides, if Margaret heard I'd been face-to-mask with Captain Shade for the second time in my life, she'd think I hallucinated the whole ordeal.

"He offered to take me with him." I don't know why I tell Will, but once I've started, I can't stop, as if the secret has been bursting to get out. "It's a long story. I stole his necklace. He wanted it back. We happened to cross paths that day in town. He said he could..." The words stick in my throat. "He said he could keep me safe."

Will's taciturn expression never falters, but his eyes flash with mild surprise. "He did?" He shifts to his knees, turning his attention back to the rose bush, clipping away at the diseased canes with renewed interest. "Why didn't you go with him?"

I take one of the mystiks Liv had discarded, rubbing its soft petals between my fingertips and savoring its sweet aroma.

"Charlie was hurt," I say. "And I couldn't leave Elsie—not when Owen had died trying to protect her." Protecting *me*.

Will nods slowly. "Do you know why roses are left at graves?"

His sudden change of subject sends my mind into a whirl, and I shake my head.

"Long ago, my people thought your world's roses were no different from Elysian Bloodroses," he says, his back turned to me. "They would leave them over the recently deceased in the hopes that the *Manan* within the flowers would bring their loved ones back to life."

He prunes a cane, inspecting it with utmost curiosity. A tiny rosebud had managed to survive, an isolated bloom on the dead branch, defying nature's lawful cycle with its will to live.

"In recent history, roses have been scorned by my kind," he says, tossing the branch aside. "A mockery of the Bloodrose—a reminder of the power we once held. But to your ancestors, roses represented romance, passion."

He clips a single, healthy rose from the bush before shifting to kneel in front of me. He presents it to me with a flourish, and my face goes uncomfortably hot.

"There is only one thing more powerful than fear, Violet," he says, his voice dark and deep, as rich as honey and as smooth as velvet as he tucks the rose behind my ear.

"What?" I whisper, nearly breathless.

His boyish grin reveals a single dimple in his right cheek. "Love."

CHAPTER FIFTEEN

Admiral Killian Bancroft of the King's 44th Regiment is known by Bludgrave's staff as the Lion of the Eerie. But when he arrives late on a Tuesday morning in June, Elsie thinks he takes after a tabby cat, both in looks and in manner.

"He's rather sly," she says, adjusting the wheels on the wooden model car she and Annie have labored over for the better part of a week. They sit on the kitchen floor, oblivious to the work taking place around them: Sybil panicking over the pot of boiled potatoes I'd left in her charge, Father chopping chives with rhythmic speed, Dorothy scrubbing leftover bread pudding from a copper plate.

Annie dips her brush into a can of red paint, busily applying a second coat to the coach. "Mother says he's awfully brilliant." She sighs wistfully. "He used to visit all the time, but he's been away at war since I was a little girl."

Elsie rolls her eyes, smoothing her plain gray uniform. "You're still a little girl."

Annie puts her hands on her hips, dripping red paint down the front of her frilly yellow dress. "And what are you?"

"A pirate," Elsie says primly, not bothering to look up from her work.

I smile inwardly as I knead a heap of dough with absentminded care. I glance at the sprig of blue salvia I'd discovered in my apron this morning, now sunbathing in a milk-bottle vase, along with the other secret messages Will is diligent to leave for me whenever he gets the chance. *"And this one,"* Will had told me just last night, in the colorful glow of the conservatory, *"means I'm thinking of you."*

It seems like a year has passed since we'd discovered Dearest's collar, though it's only been a month. One month, and it feels as though everyone has all but forgotten that Mr. and Mrs. Hackney had been brutally murdered, and the message that had been carved into their disembodied heads. But Will and I haven't forgotten. Every night, when the rest of the household has gone to sleep, we take Caligo up to the conservatory, where we agonize over scraps of clues and strategize about ways to entrap the Shifter. But there isn't much to go on, and with every passing day, I find myself drawing closer to Will and further away from the task at hand.

Most of the time, we lie beneath the old oak and look up at the stars. I've introduced him to the constellations; I tell him their stories, the legends of my people, of my ancestors. Some nights, as we drift to sleep under the vast blanket of the heavens, I feel as if there is no one in this world who knows me the way that Will does. But then the sun rises and we part ways, our friendship fading into memory as we become no more than strangers to each other—a young lord of a high and noble house, and a kitchen maid in his employ.

"Violet?" Margaret calls to me from the doorway. "Can I talk to you? Outside," she hurries to add. Without waiting for a reply, she scurries past Elsie, out the door to the west lawn. I don't miss the look she gives Annie over her shoulder. Margaret is rarely frightened, but the brief flash of terror in her eyes sends me darting out the door after her.

"What is it?" I whisper, scanning the landscape, ensuring we're alone. Under a cloudless sky, summer transforms the grounds into a lush haven of vibrant green trees and colorful blossoms, thriving despite the stifling heat.

"I found something," she says, taking a bundle of cloth from under the folds of her gown. She unravels it and reveals a kitchen knife, its blade crusted with dried blood and tufts of coarse black hair. *Atroxis hair*, I think grimly.

But if this is the knife that killed Dearest...

"Where did you—"

"It was under Annie's bed." Margaret's face pales, her eyes wide. "I don't know what to do. If I tell anyone, they might think I'm lying. They might think—"

"I'll take care of it." I take the knife from her, cover it with the cloth. "No one else needs to know."

"But..." Margaret tucks her shaking hands under her arms as if she were shivering, even though the summer sun beats down on us with blazing heat. "You don't think Annie could do something like this, do you? I'm with her every day. Surely, she'd show signs of…aggression…or…" She trails off, her eyes fixed on the door as if she expects Annie to appear there any moment with sharp teeth and claws, poised to strike.

For whatever reason, the Shifter wanted Margaret to find the knife in Annie's room. It's gone through great trouble to cast suspicion on the child, though I still can't figure out why. If Annie were possessed by a Sylk, I would know it. I would see it, just like I did aboard the ship.

Still, I can't explain why Annie had blood on her hands that night Jack and I saw her near Hildegarde's Folly, and why, if a Gore had been the one to kill Dearest, it would have spared a little girl. From what Will has told me, Gores don't distinguish between their victims. If a Gore killed Dearest and Annie was there, she would be dead, too.

"Don't worry," I tell Margaret, stuffing the parcel into my apron. Tonight, when Will and I meet, I'll see if he can make sense of the knife. But I can't tell Margaret about my secret rendezvous with the young lord. If anyone knew Will and I were spending this much time together—if one of the other servants found out, if they told an officer in Ink Haven—there would be consequences.

I rub my throat, swallowing hard.

"Worry about what?" Henry rounds the house and saunters towards us, a bow in his hand and a quiver of arrows slung over his shoulder.

"Nothing," Margaret mutters, keeping her back to him. She shoots me a pleading look, her brows raised.

Henry draws an arrow and arms his bow. He aims it leisurely at the sky, then at the back of Margaret's head, his eyes glinting with mischief. "'Nothing, *my l*—"

"Careful, nephew," a man in a crisp olive uniform says, slinking around the corner. His rich brown hair reminds me of his sister, Lady Isabelle, and his short beard is neatly groomed, the medals on his military jacket freshly polished. He shares Lady Isabelle's small green eyes, though his are inquisitive and playful. "I should think it would take more than an arrow to take down a nanny." He winks at me, a coy smile on his lips.

Sly indeed, I think.

Henry lowers the bow and disengages the arrow. He twirls it in his fingers. "I wouldn't waste an arrow on a pirate," he grumbles, shuffling past. Under his breath, as if only for me to hear, he adds, "I wouldn't need to."

The Admiral throws out a hand, contracts his fingers, and Henry snaps to a halt.

"Pirates, you say?" he asks Henry, but his eyes are fixed on me. Now I see where Will gets it—that searching look, that glittering amusement, that mysterious intelligence. "I'm afraid it would be a mistake to choose a pirate for target practice. I hear they're nearly impossible to catch."

Henry snorts as the Admiral lets his hand fall, releasing him. He stumbles past me, his expression smug. "Not nearly as impossible as you'd think."

If it weren't for his magic, I would have already cut that obnoxious grin from Henry's face.

"I find that hard to believe," the Admiral says. He dips his head. "Ladies, if you'll excuse us. It appears my nephew has forgotten who it was that taught him how to shoot a bow."

As they take off across the lawn, Margaret straightens her shoulders, her confident air returning. "I think this Admiral might be good for him," she says.

As if to prove her point, the unfamiliar peal of Henry's laughter rings as he and the Admiral break out into a playful tussle. I remember what Will said, about Henry's experience aboard the *Deathwail*, and I can't help but smile. It gives me hope to know, after all this time, that someone else survived that awful ship and lived to find their laughter again.

"Don't tell her I told you," Margaret adds, a tight-lipped smirk tugging at the corners of her mouth. "But Elsie thinks Henry's 'suave.'"

"*Suave?*" I burst into a fit of laughter, and the knife in my apron is forgotten as Margaret and I giggle like little children.

"What's so funny?" Jack sticks his head out the door, Albert peeking from behind him, his faithful shadow. I suppress another giggle as I realize Albert matches the stableboy in his brown trousers, wrinkled cream-colored shirt, and tattered black suspenders—hand-me-downs from Jack himself, if I had to guess.

"Oh, wouldn't you like to know!" Margaret smiles at Jack, her face rosy. And for the first time since the *Lightbringer* sank, I think, with my own, private smile, that wherever my family is—wherever Margaret and I can share a laugh—is a happy place. And even though Bludgrave Manor doesn't have sails and a stern, it could be home.

Maybe it already is.

I stroke Caligo's muzzle, humming along to Jack's melodic whistle. My hand dips into my apron pocket, feeling for the single lily Will had given me all those weeks ago. When my fingertips brush the brittle, dried petals, my heartbeat quickens with anticipation. I skim the cloth that covers the bloody knife I'd taken from Margaret, and my mind buzzes, eager to share this latest bit of news with Will.

"He should have been here by now," I murmur to Caligo, who grunts in response.

At that, Jack peeks around the corner, rake in hand. "It's not his fault," he says, wiping sweat from his forehead. "His Uncle Killian probably caught him trying to sneak away."

"You'd be correct." Will's husky voice is clipped.

I turn to find him leaning against the doorpost, silhouetted by the moonlight. He strides towards me, but his eyes, cold and distant, are fixed on Caligo. There's something about the way he carries himself—his shoulders erect, his chin tilted high—that gives him the appearance of someone twice his age. His face is hardened, his jaw set, and when he dares to glance at me, it only seems to trouble him further. Without words, he climbs onto Caligo's back and offers me a hand.

My mouth goes dry as I wrap my arms around him and we start up the hill. For a month now, I've known only warm greetings from Will after long, cruel days of maintaining the rouse of indifference towards each other. But tonight, I can't help but wonder if I've done something wrong. Was I too indifferent? I search my memory, replaying every formal exchange between Will and me throughout the week. And then a quiver of fear passes through me. *Has he changed his mind about me? Does he think I'm responsible for everything that's happened?*

He doesn't speak again until the conservatory door closes behind us and Liv and the other pixies rush to greet him, their laughter like sweet music. He waves them off and Liv darts away, her wings drooping.

"Forgive me," he says, running a hand through his mussed black curls. "I wasn't sure I could face you." He glares down at a plot of wilted roses, reaches out. At his touch, they perk up, their bright-red hue returning, but his frown only deepens. "I'm still not sure."

I take a step towards him, but he turns away from me and heads for the old oak. With his back still facing me, he lays a hand on the bark, his head bowed.

"Will…" I reach out, meaning to place a hand on his shoulder, but he spins on his heels and snatches my wrist.

"Please," he says, his voice low, his green eyes soft and tearful. He looks over my face, slowly, as if he were memorizing every detail. "Don't make this harder on me."

I swallow around the lump in my throat. *Great.* One month was all it took and he's ready to throw me out. What will Mother and Father say? Will they come to my defense? Should I even expect them to risk jeopardizing the life they're building for Elsie and Albert and the others?

"Make what harder on you?" I dare to whisper, glancing at his tight grip on my wrist, knowing full well he's capable of crushing every bone in my arm—and my spine, for that matter.

He follows my eyes, loosens his grip. Slowly, gently, he peels my sleeve back to reveal the single band of braided leather. Then he takes from his chest pocket a second bracelet—*my* bracelet.

He lifts his gaze, but he doesn't meet my eyes. "You never asked for it back."

A knot forms in my stomach, and I look away. "You know why I didn't."

He releases my hand, and it falls to my side. His fist closes around the bracelet and he furrows his brows. "I do," he whispers.

Our eyes meet, threading a tentative cord between us—a string wound tight enough to snap. And then, at the same time, we both blurt out: "I have to tell you something."

"You first," he hurries to add.

"No, please." Suddenly the bloody knife in my apron doesn't seem as important as figuring out what has Will this out of sorts. "Tell me."

This time, it's he who looks away. A dark shadow passes over his face. "My uncle brings news from the prince. As a show of good faith, the prince plans to journey to Hellion, to monitor the fight at their border. He's forming a squadron." He fidgets with the bracelet, a muscle in his cheek feathering. "He's asked me to join."

I blink, my mouth working. "And?"

"And," he says slowly, his voice quiet, "I've agreed to go."

I take a small step back, my mind reeling. "When do you leave?"

He fixes his gaze on the bracelet, refusing to take his eyes off of it, refusing to look at me. "Tomorrow."

I turn, my feet carrying me to the door, out into the cool night air.

Tomorrow.

"Violet, wait," Will pants, chasing me towards the apple tree tunnel, but I'm too far ahead. He whistles for Caligo, and just as I break out of the tunnel and onto the sloping hill, the thunder of pounding hooves vibrates in the soles of my shoes. Caligo maneuvers in front of me, blocking my path.

"I don't have a choice." Will's voice is rough, and it falters with a desperation that sounds unfamiliar from the lips of a wealthy young Nightweaver. "The prince is counting on me. He trusts me. I thought you of all people would understand that."

The weight of the bloody knife in my apron threatens to bring me to my knees. *What am I going to do?* We're no closer to finding Owen's killer than we were a month ago, and now this new discovery could be exactly what we've been looking for— proof that it wasn't a Gore that killed Dearest. That a Shifter is trying to frame Annie, all while sending me a message.

"Did you miss me?" it had written inside Dearest's collar. Why would the Guild go through all this trouble—why kill Annie's atroxis—just to have Margaret find the knife? It's almost like the Sylk *wants* me to find it, like the Shifter is leading me right to it—to the Guild. But why kill Mr. and Mrs. Hackney, and why make it seem as if it was a Gore that did it? Just to toy with me?

"Are you alright?" Will stands in front of me. I hadn't even realized he'd dismounted from Caligo, with my thoughts racing and the world around me merely a blur.

"I can't do this without you," I admit, my voice breaking. "I don't know the first thing about hunting Sylks."

His forehead creases. "My Uncle Killian's made a career of it," he says, stroking his chin. "I've asked him to assist you while I'm away."

My mouth gapes. "You told him about us?"

"*Us?*" he murmurs, blinking innocently.

I clench my fists, wishing now more than ever that I still had my dagger at my disposal. "You know what I mean."

He studies the ground, his expression pained. "When he heard what happened, about your name on Mrs. Hackney's forehead, he assumed a Sylk was involved. He asked if he could be of any assistance."

I cross my arms. "What if I don't want his help?"

"If he could find the Sylk that killed your brother, would you want his help then?"

I grit my teeth. Find the Sylk that killed Owen—that was supposed to be the only reason Will and I started working together in the first place.

Supposed to be...

"I'm worried about Annie," Will admits, his voice soft. "Would you look out for her while I'm away? Keep her out of trouble, I mean."

"You mean keep her from stowing away on another ship bound for Hellion?"

Something akin to a smirk graces his face, but his eyes are sad and dull. "If you can."

For a moment, neither of us speaks, as if the silence could last forever and we wouldn't have to part. But nothing lasts forever. I know this all too well.

"So this is goodbye, then?"

He presses his lips together, dips his head. "For now." He takes my bracelet from his pocket once more, extends it to me.

I shake my head. "Keep it," I say, hoping I sound more callous than I feel. I start past him, towards the house in the distance, wanting nothing more than to pull myself onto Caligo's saddle and ride as far away from him as possible.

"Violet?" he calls after me. "What did you have to tell me?"

My pace slows and my hand dips into my apron, feeling for the cloth that covers the knife. Instead, my fingers brush the dried petals of the white lily, and my heart sinks.

"Jack is going to teach me how to ride," I call back, using the truth to mask a lie. I glance over my shoulder at him standing in Caligo's shadow, a dark figure alone in a silver sea of rolling grass. "We start tomorrow."

I can't tell him about the knife now. It would only distract him during the hard months ahead. Besides, there's nothing he can do. Tomorrow, he'll be gone. But I'll still be here. Owen will still be dead. And with or without Will, my purpose remains the same.

I'm going to catch the Sylk, and I'm going to do it alone.

Chapter Sixteen

A heavy fog covers the estate—a thick, rolling mist that sweeps over the gardens, concealing everything it touches. I look down on the front drive from the upstairs landing in the west atrium, watching Charlie as he loads a single leather duffle bag into the idle coach parked there, wishing I could simply walk out into the fog and disappear.

"I almost didn't hear you," I say, not taking my eyes off the window. The staircase hadn't creaked, the carpet hadn't been scuffed, but I stopped relying on sound to detect someone's presence a long time ago.

"Of course you didn't." Margaret moves beside me, nudging me playfully with her elbow. "How do you think you learned to walk like a mouse?"

My sister peers down at the driveway below, where the Castors have gathered, saying their goodbyes to Will. She intently watches Jack, seated behind the wheel of the coach. "Although," she murmurs, "you're not as sneaky as you think." She casts me a knowing glance, her brows raised. "At night, when you're not in your bed…It isn't hard to guess where you've gone. I see the way he looks at you." She follows my eyes and finds Will, bedecked in a green military uniform, embracing his uncle. She smiles sadly as Will kneels to scratch his uncle's bloodhound between the ears. "The way you look at him."

My cheeks burn. "It doesn't matter, now," I say. "He might not come back."

Margaret caresses my arm, her touch as tender and comforting as Father's. "And what if he does?"

I watch as Will embraces Henry, who holds him tighter than I would have expected. When Will pulls away, he looks up at the house, searching every window, his face drawn. I turn sharply, hiding behind the curtain, and Margaret does the same. Finally, he relents, waves one last time at his family, and steps into the coach.

As Charlie moves to close the door behind him, Annie lurches from her mother's arms, and I brace myself. Beside me, Margaret tenses, but when Annie clings to Will's pant-leg, inconsolable, the two of us breathe a sigh of relief. I don't know why I had expected her to plunge a bloody knife into his ribs—not when it's safely tucked away in the trunk at the foot of my bed—but…I don't know what to think anymore. And until I can prove Annie *isn't* being influenced by the Guild of Shadows in some way, I can't let my guard down.

Lord Castor takes Annie in his arms, and Will looks up again. This time, he spots me standing in the window, pinning me to the spot. He opens his mouth, but then the door is shut, obscuring him from sight.

As the coach drives away, towards the iron gate at the far end of the drive, my hatred for the prince of the Eerie festers. It takes on a new form, becoming a vile, all-consuming desire to drive a blade through his heart, to make him bleed for taking Will from me. And as much as I hate the prince, I hate Will all the more for leaving.

"I won't hold my breath," I say, turning my back on the window, on Will.

I hurry past Margaret, into the hall, down the stairs, to the kitchen. Father is there, laboring over breakfast. He'd given me the morning; I suppose Margaret isn't the only one who knew I'd want to see Will off, even if just from afar. He dips his head in greeting, his face full of compassion. Sometimes, when I look at him, I see Owen—his kind eyes, so much like Father's—and I feel my heart breaking all over again.

I take the milk-bottle vase from the counter and hasten through the door, onto the lawn.

The buds and sprigs Will gave me have wilted. I hadn't given them enough water, I suppose. I find it funny how even Will's beloved flowers can't survive without it.

I empty the dead flowers at my feet, stomping on them for good measure. It was foolish of me to put my faith in Will; foolish of me to stray so far from what I know to be true. The earth is no place for me. Only the sea can cool my rage. Only the water can heal my wounds.

I promised Owen I would not let them take me. I've told myself I stay here out of loyalty to my family, to find the Sylk and avenge my brother's death. But now that Will is gone, I know that isn't true. I'd not only broken my promise to Owen—the Nightweavers took me from the sea, they made me their servant—but I'd forgotten who I am.

No longer.

I am Violet Oberon, pirate of the Western Sea. I need no one's help, and I bow to no king. I will have my revenge. And when I've killed the Sylk that took Owen from me, I will set my sights on the Nightweavers that seek to eradicate my people. It's the only way to ensure a future for Albert and Elsie: to create a world where they are free, a world in which they don't have to live in fear of those that consider us slaves.

Better to die fighting than to live on my knees.

A part of me always knew it would be impossible to adjust to a life of servitude. I could never let go of who I am. I can never forget, and I will never forgive. I can see clearly now that Will is gone. I have nothing left to lose.

First, I will kill an Underling. Then, I will kill the prince.

"Like this," Jack says, adjusting my grip on Caligo's reins.

"I've got it," I grumble, going over his surprisingly short list of instructions in the back of my mind. *No loud noises, stay calm, sit up straight, pull left to go left, pull right to go right.*

Jack rolls his eyes, holding his hands up in mock surrender. "If you've got it, then by all means," he says, stepping aside.

I take a deep breath, give Caligo a gentle kick, and we're off. At first, his pace is slow, steady. It's different, holding the reins rather than holding on to Will and trusting him to be in control. *Trusting him*, I think bitterly. *What a mistake.*

The wind whips at my hair, a cool breeze. I give Caligo another kick and he breaks into a trot. My plan *was* to ride past the orchard, to the old windmill near the far side of the property, and back. But—we pass the windmill. Caligo seems to be enjoying the fresh air and freedom as much as I am, and I can't help but urge him to go faster.

"*Balance,*" Jack had reminded me, "*is your main asset as a rider.*" Luckily, I spent seventeen years at sea. I was born with legs meant to weather the waves. Balance is no obstacle. I am in control. I am—

Caligo trumpets, rearing back. I grip the reins, my heart in my throat. Out of the corner of my eye, the source of Caligo's distress—a bloodhound, its ears flopping—races across the lawn, intent on the horse.

Caligo takes off, headed towards the forest that encroaches on the steep cliff-face in the distance.

"Woah, Caligo!" I shout, but it's no use.

A second set of thundering hooves rumbles in my chest.

"Easy now, easy." The Admiral appears at my side, his sister's unicorn, Thea, keeping pace with Caligo. "Easy," he says, his voice soft but commanding. At the sound of him, Caligo slows.

We come to a complete stop at the edge of the forest. The bloodhound bounds up to us, but the Admiral has already dismounted Thea and stands with his arms crossed, a stern look about him.

"Dinah." He shakes his head disapprovingly and the bloodhound slides to a halt, her ears pulled back. "What have I told you about chasing after someone your own size?" He kneels and the dog leaps into his arms, tail wagging. He glances over his shoulder at me, lowering his voice conspiratorially. "I haven't, actually. Dogs are notoriously deft at sniffing out Underlings, after all."

My mouth falls open, but no words come out. I relax my grip on Caligo's reins, my palms stinging.

"How did you do that?" I ask. "How did you make him stop?"

"Simple, really." He smooths his jacket—dark Bancroft green in place of the League's dull-olive uniform, a rampant silver wolf embroidered on his chest. "All it takes is a little magic."

I sigh. "Is that all?"

He stands, extending a hand to me. "Killian."

I give it a firm shake. "Violet."

"I know," he says with a sly wink. "My nephew tells me you're hunting a Sylk."

I have to clench my jaw to keep my mouth from flailing open. Will had said he'd told his uncle about us, but I hadn't expected Killian to be so blunt about it.

"Any luck?" he asks casually, stroking Caligo's muzzle.

"Not quite," I admit. "Even if I happen to come across the shadow, I don't have the means to kill it."

"You mean like this?" Killian hefts a flintlock from his waistband, offers it to me. "Go on, take it."

I don't hesitate, eager to feel the cool metal in my grasp. My hand molds to the form of the flintlock, my muscles breathing a sigh of relief.

"On the front, we call them Howlers," he says, a nostalgic twinkle in his eye. "That being because it's the sound a Sylk makes when you put a bullet between its eyes."

"So, you *can* kill them?"

He gives me a puzzled look, scratching his mustache. "Only after they have possessed a host, and only with bullets made of Elysian Iron. But you never actually *kill* a Sylk—you merely banish them to whence they came." He pauses, furrows his brows. "Will told me you've been hunting the Sylk together for over a month. He didn't think to tell you what would happen once you caught it?"

Shame forms a knot in my stomach. I think back to all the nights Will and I spent in the conservatory, discussing flowers and constellations. Every time I brought him another clue, he insisted he would look into it. But as many times as he detailed ways to capture a Sylk—with cords made from silver thread, or traps set with rotten meat—he was always swift to change the subject. I was so caught up in distracting myself from my grief, in wanting to be close to someone who didn't see my ability as a curse but rather as a valuable gift, that I didn't want to push too hard.

Stupid.

"I see." Killian shrugs. "It only makes sense."

I tuck the flintlock into my apron and hold my chin up high, arming myself against any more painful realizations. "What does?"

"Well," he says, climbing back into Thea's saddle. "I've only just met you, and already I've no doubt about it."

He walks Thea towards the old windmill, his head back, savoring the breeze. I give Caligo a gentle kick, and Dinah follows close at our heels.

"What do you mean?" I ask once I've caught up to him.

A familiar smirk creases his lips, deepening the premature cracks in his otherwise youthful, sunny face. "If my nephew would have told you everything you needed to know, you wouldn't have needed *him* then, would you?"

He gives Thea a firm kick and she breaks into a gallop, leaving me alone on a hillside, wondering how different my life might be if I hadn't followed that Sylk into the captain's quarters that day. If I had never found Annie hiding there. If I had taken the shot instead of sparing her life. If I had never met Will. If he had never saved Elsie; had never been so kind and generous to my family. If he had never asked me to go with him to the conservatory that night. If I hadn't stayed.

If.

Killian's right—if I hadn't thought Will could be of any use to me when Jack offered me the knapsack, I would have taken it. I would have run. I wouldn't be here, thinking about correct saddle posture, or Elysian bullets, or Will.

I don't need Will's help, I remind myself. I never have. And now that I know what it takes to banish the Sylk, I don't need anyone.

A cool, brisk wind sweeps through me. As if compelled, I twist in the saddle, looking behind. Dinah growls with the sound of low, burgeoning thunder, her teeth bared at the old windmill. But a moment later, she whimpers and chases after Killian, her tail tucked.

Mist unfurls from the nearby tree line, shrouding the hillside in a damp fog. In the blink of an eye, I see him—*Owen*—blood pooling from a wound in his chest. He reaches out to me, his eyes glowing red. Shadows seep from his body, an all-consuming cloud of darkness.

I reach for the flintlock Killian gave me, ready to take down this Shifter that dares hide behind my brother's likeness. But I blink again and Owen is gone.

Still, I hear a voice: a soft, coaxing whisper.

"*Together, we will bring kings and kingdoms to their knees,*" it says. "*You need only ask.*"

CHAPTER SEVENTEEN

The Sunday following Will's departure, Bludgrave Manor hosts a small dinner in honor of their neighbors: Baron Rencourt, a boulder of a man, making up in height what he lacks in a neck, and George Birtwistle, a frail, thin-faced ambassador from Fell who is known by the staff as the Trademaster. Accompanying them is the Trademaster's seventeen-year-old daughter, Trudy Birtwistle, whom the staff lovingly calls the Terror from Fell. According to Boris, the Castors' soft-spoken chauffer, Lord Castor and George Birtwistle have been conspiring to align themselves through a marriage between Henry and Trudy—a partnership I find rather fitting, considering her nickname.

Throughout the preparations, Mother acts as though she has always been a housekeeper, not captain of a wild, unruly pirate crew, and Lewis does his best to keep up with his duties as replacement butler and personal valet to Lord Castor, running here and there, all while maintaining the required air of superiority. Father and I work as a single unit in the kitchen, heads down, knives sharp, communicating without so much as a word. Sybil stands alone at the sink, more forlorn than usual, while Jack and Albert sit astride on the floor, shelling pecans.

Elsie had insisted on watching Margaret fix Annie's hair with what she called "the hot irons," and Charlie—missing his duties as the *Lightbringer*'s bosun—has taken to repairing a broken cabinet door in the pantry adjacent the kitchen, which nearly causes Lewis to fly into hysterics.

"There's no time!" he cries. "They'll be arriving any minute now."

Charlie grumbles a string of curses under his breath, but I don't hear their bickering over the whistle of the kettle. I'm thankful my duties lie within the realm of chopping carrots. If it weren't for the repetitive motion of the knife in my hand, a welcome distraction, I would have nothing to do but think about the voice I'd heard on the hillside, and the offer it had made.

Together, we will bring kings and kingdoms to their knees.

A Sylk killed Owen. But if the Nightweavers had never attacked our ship, Owen would still be alive. It was the prince's captain that ambushed the *Lightbringer*. It was the prince's guard that shot Charlie in the town square. It is the prince's mother and father that hunt and enslave my kind. I can only imagine the evil the prince himself must commit. The blood he's shed. He is the cause of all of this. He took everything from me—*everything*.

He will die by my hand.

But if I call on the Guild of Shadows for help, I betray Owen. My revenge lies in killing the Sylk—that hasn't changed.

However, once I've rid the world of Owen's murderer, I will set my sights on the prince, and when the time comes to skewer his heart on my blade, I won't need anyone's help. Not from a Nightweaver. Especially not from an Underling.

Dinner passes without incident, and Lewis and Charlie gush to Father every overheard compliment to the chef. I find myself enjoying the chaos, as if I were back on the *Lightbringer* in the heat of battle, and rather than wielding a cutlass, I brandish a chef's knife. When the boys return with the empty dessert dishes, scraped clean, Father waves me off.

"Take a break," he says. "You deserve it."

I don't argue. My back aches, my shoulders throb, and my hands cramp even as I wipe chocolate trifle on my apron.

By the time I've washed up, the Castors and their guests have retired for the evening. Bludgrave Manor is quiet but for Sybil and Elsie scurrying about the chambers like mice, tending the hearths. Rather than venture out into the gardens, I take the opportunity to explore the empty halls, a tenuous salve to my curiosity.

I'm shuffling through the main hall beneath the stairwell, my hand trailing along the intricately carved wood panels, when I come upon a portrait of Will. It couldn't have been painted long before I met him, but he wears his League uniform—dull olive-green, his black sash ornamented with medals. His unruly black curls have been swept out of his emerald eyes, which seem to flicker with amusement even in illustration.

He'll be halfway across the ocean by now—*my* ocean. And I'm stuck here, plucking feathers from chickens and mincing garlic for feasts I will never take part in.

The closet door beside me creaks open, slightly ajar. A quiver of movement rustles the contents within. My fingers inch towards the flintlock I've strapped to my shin when footsteps on the staircase give me pause, and I turn. But before I can see who is rounding the banister, a hand covers my mouth and I'm yanked into the coat closet.

Henry calls a flame to his fingertip as he closes the door, forcing us into the tight, dimly lit space. Despite my pity for the young lord, I resolved weeks ago to not let him catch me unawares—not again. Pressed against his thigh is the steak knife I keep in my apron at all times, ready to spill blood. He might be able to take me down with a look, but the slightest twitch of my wrist would surely take him with me.

Panic flashes in his eyes as footsteps approach the coat closet. A shadow lingers at the base of the door, and a quiet, girlish voice whispers, "Henry? Henry, darling, where have you gone?" She giggles, and a moment later, her shadow passes, her footsteps faint as she turns at the end of the hall.

With an irritated glance at the blade resting on his thigh, Henry removes his hand from my mouth. I reach for the knob, but he seizes my wrist.

"It's rude to keep a lady waiting," I say drily.

He scowls. "Trudy Birtwistle is no lady. She's a leech."

"A perfect match."

He rolls his eyes. "On second thought, just kill me and be done with it."

"So dramatic," I tut, sheathing the knife in my apron. "You sound like Jack."

"Stars forbid." He relaxes his grip on my wrist, but when I reach for the knob, he seizes my hand once more. "Promise you won't tell her where I'm hiding?"

I bring a hand to my chest in mock offense. "Now, why would I do something like that? It's not as if you tried to—what was it? End me with a single look?"

He casts off my hand with an injured air, his lip curling into a snarl. "So be it. Father intends to marry me off to that awful girl. Suppose you think I deserve it."

I withdraw my hand from the knob. "Don't you have a say in who you marry?" I ask, remembering the gentle way he'd cared for Dorothy on the night she discovered Mr. and Mrs. Hackney.

He glares at the flame on his fingertip, as if his father had been the one to set it alight. "Even if I did, who I'd *choose* to be with…" He shakes his head, and his short black curls splay over his tightly knit brows. "It isn't an option."

"Where *is* Dorothy?" I murmur, thinking back to Sybil, alone at the kitchen sink, quietly washing the dishes instead of chatting away with the young maid. Henry doesn't try to deny his feelings, but rather, he seems relieved at my observation.

His eyes flicker, face drawn with suspicion. "News came late yesterday evening." He scowls at the fur coat encroaching on his space as if it were alive and breathing down his neck. "Her mother won't be long now. Dorothy's gone to care for her until the time comes."

"Oh," is all I can think to say. Dorothy never liked me—that much was clear. She warmed up rather quickly to Lewis and little Elsie, but she kept her distance from the rest of us, maintaining her belief that we were seafaring brutes and weren't to be trusted. After that night, after what she saw, rumors swept through the staff that Percy's gang, the Hounds, had something to do with it. But I couldn't ignore the way Dorothy acted towards me—as if there was a suspicion she just couldn't put to rest. Still, I'm sorry she's gone, if only for Henry's sake.

"If you tell anyone what you think you know—"

"You'll fry my brain," I cut him off, turning the knob. "Don't worry. Your secret's safe with me. As long as you promise to be kind to Margaret."

"Your sister has nothing to fear from me," he says quietly, his expression solemn, and I wonder if he, too, is remembering the way Margaret had cared for Dorothy that terrible night.

Just then, the flame dissipates. He puts his hand over my mouth once more as two sets of footsteps approach, their shadows passing the coat closet with haste.

"Killian's already there with the others," Lord Castor whispers.

"A conservatory..." a second man muses, his voice deep and dry. "Certainly the king's men could easily discover what you're up to here?"

"Lady Isabelle has taken measures to ensure no one enters that clearing unless invited by myself or Lord William," Lord Castor replies, but he can't hide the quiver of anxiety in his voice that threatens to contradict him. "And I told you, Baron. We have—"

"Yes, yes," Baron Rencourt drawls. "This secret weapon I keep hearing about. And when do you think you might consider the Order privy to the identity of this 'secret weapon' you've got hidden away somewhere?"

"It isn't my secret to tell." Lord Castor's voice draws further away, and I don't catch what he says next.

Their footsteps fade, and Henry releases me. Before I can gather my thoughts, he creeps out of the coat closet and slinks down the hall. I tiptoe behind, close at his heels.

"Don't follow me," he whispers over his shoulder.

"Fine," I sigh, raising my voice slightly. "I'll just go and find Miss Birtwistle and—"

He groans, pausing at the front door to peer around the corner. "Bloody pirates..." he grumbles. He motions for me to be quick as he sidles through the garden. He halts again at the corner, then darts across the west lawn, taking cover in the rosebushes. When he's certain the coast is clear, we race up the hill, towards the apple tree tunnel.

I'm lighter on my feet than he is; Henry crunches leaves and snaps twigs with every other step. As we draw near the conservatory, the incoherent buzz of voices within gives us pause. I crouch low, press my ear against the glass.

"…induct pirates into the Order?" Baron Rencourt scoffs. "What's next? A Shifter?"

"They're humans, Baron," Lady Isabelle replies calmly, her voice soft but firm. "I believe the Oberon family would be a strong asset to our faction. Of all the humans dedicated to our cause, they have more reason than any to join this fight."

What does he stand to gain? The familiar question pierces my heart like a blade. Will knew about this…*Order.* Is that why he saved my family and me from the auction house? Why he spared our lives at sea?

Someone clears their throat.

"Well, George," Lord Castor booms heartily, "out with it."

"Forgive me, my lord." His meek voice is almost inaudible through the glass, muffled by the dense foliage. "But there has been talk among the Council of Merchants. By increasing trade between Hellion and the Eerie, the king has upset the balance. Those humans that were content to brave the harsh conditions of a life at sea are no longer satisfied with their lot. The time is now. I agree with Lady Isabelle. If the Order seeks to form an alliance with the pirates, it could help to have a few of them on our side."

Baron Rencourt snorts. "And how do you propose we—"

A low growl rumbles from somewhere close behind. In the moonlight, I can just make out their bristling fur, their bared teeth, their eyes glowing yellow. I recognize them from the pictures in Elsie's books.

Wolves.

Chapter Eighteen

The first wolf stalks closer, flanked by two others, snarling and snapping their jaws. I reach for the flintlock strapped to my shin, but Henry doesn't seem concerned. He only sighs, motioning for me to be still.

A sweet, soothing voice rings throughout the clearing. "That will be all." At the sound of it, the wolves turn docile and retreat into the undergrowth once more.

Lady Isabelle stands over Henry and me, her hands folded. "You've heard quite enough," she says, lifting a brow. "You might as well come in."

Henry follows her into the conservatory like a scolded puppy, but I hesitate at the door. The last time I was here, among the perfume of the flowers and the blinking, colorful orbs of the pixies, Will had told me he was leaving. Despite the small crowd gathered among the roses, Will's absence gives the garden a cold, lifeless quality. The petals have wilted, and the pixies aren't as joyful as they always were when he was near.

"Speak of the shadow," Killian says, his voice as soft and steady as his sister's. He lounges on a low-hanging branch of the old oak, one ankle resting on his knee, a cigar perched between his fingers. Liv lazes on his shoulder, kicking her feet, but as I enter, the pixie darts across the garden to greet me, touching her forehead to my nose.

"It seems you're no stranger here," Baron Rencourt says, his expression somewhat sour.

Liv stands on my shoulder, her hands on her hips. She sticks her tongue out at the old Baron, and a faint smile tugs at my lips. "It seems you are," I say smoothly.

He screws up his face, his brow cocked. "*This* is the girl?" he mutters, flicking a sidelong glance at Lord Castor.

Lady Isabelle smiles sweetly, but there's a hint of a warning in the way she flashes her brilliant teeth at him. "This is Violet," she says, placing a light touch on my elbow as she angles herself between Baron Rencourt and me, forming a motherly barricade.

Baron Rencourt's puffy lips purse with distaste.

"Miss Oberon." George Birtwistle approaches, his shoulders hunched under an invisible weight, his hands knitting neurotically, as if his thoughts were set to rights by the constant weaving of his fingers. "Surely you've heard rumors from friends about the Order of Hildegarde?"

"Don't have friends," I reply, crossing my arms.

Henry snorts.

"Wouldn't matter if she did," Killian says. "The Order is merely a whisper throughout the Eerie. Any human—or Nightweaver, for that matter—who values their life wouldn't dare speak too loudly of what took place in Thorn."

Thorn—that Nightweaver, Duncan, had mentioned it before they'd taken us to the auction house.

"What happened in Thorn?" I ask, but every head turns to watch as the door to the conservatory opens and a half-woman, half-fawn trots in on four hooves, followed by a young man with the legs and horns of a goat. Behind them, a bespectacled badger in a brocade waistcoat adjusts his bowtie in what appears to be a nervous fit. At the sight of the strange group, I feel as though I'm thumbing through the pictures of Elsie's book of Myths. But even more confusing than the two-foot-tall man with a long white beard and rosy, red cheeks who shuffles in after the well-dressed badger, is the last to enter.

"Jack?" I gasp as the stableboy closes the door behind him.

"Violet?" He looks from me, to Henry, to me, his eyes wide. "What are you doing here?" he babbles.

"Why don't you tell me?" I cut my eyes at the woman with a crown of antlers poking through shimmering waves of long green hair. *A cervitaur*, I remember with a flush of satisfaction.

Jack fidgets with the cuffs of his shirt, brushes dirt from his shoulder. "I—uh—"

"It's alright, Jack," Lady Isabelle says, turning towards me. "Violet, dear, for the past century, humans, Nightweavers, and Myths have been fighting alongside each other to bring about change in this world. This"—she gestures around the conservatory—"is only a small part of a much larger coalition."

"*The Order of Hildegarde…*" I fix my gaze on a single rose, its bright-red petals unfazed by Will's departure. "You want my family—you want *me*—to join in your rebellion?"

"Perhaps *rebellion* isn't the right word." Lord Castor steps forward, his hands clasped behind his back. His eyes flit anxiously to the Myths. "We're biding our time, you see. If we can go through the proper channels—"

"We've been through all the proper channels, Silas," Killian interrupts, an edge to his soft voice that I haven't heard before. His use of Lord Castor's first name is jarring, and it's only then that I realize I haven't heard anyone call him that before—not even his own wife.

"The Anteres bloodline has enslaved humans since the Fall," Killian continues. "Along with the rest of the Known World, they have benefited from the humans' labor, their inventions, their military service; but they have never—they *will never*—give them their freedom." He turns to me then, his expression softening. "Our kind was sent here to protect humans from the Underlings, not rule over them. Until the balance is corrected and Nightweavers and humans join forces against the Underlings, they will continue to plague this world."

He puffs on his cigar, enshrouding himself in a cloud of smoke as he addresses the assembly once more. "Now, Hellion has promised to side with the Order so long as when the time comes and King Anteres has been brought to justice, their princess will assume the throne. Until then, we must continue to ensure our prince's safety long enough for him to wed the princess of Hellion this coming winter." He turns to Baron Rencourt. "Are your men keeping a close eye on him?"

The baron scoffs. "As close as they can. He's a slippery little bastard."

"The Guild of Shadows won't rest until the prince and princess are *both* dead," Birtwistle croaks. "Whatever Hellion has promised the Order, it stands only if the princess is kept safe. For now, she's well-guarded within the walls of Castle Grim. But once the marriage is official, what's to keep the prince from murdering his own bride if he finds out what we've planned? If she dies, we'll have made an enemy out of Hellion."

I can't help but wonder what the prince might do to the princess if he were to discover the Order's plans to have Hellion seize control of the Eerie, when Killian responds to Birtwistle.

"Hellion *is* our enemy." Killian sends a pointed look at Lord Castor. "But they are a means to an end. A useful one. Once the prince and princess are wed, she'll have access to the wards that surround Castle Grim. She'll be able to lower their defenses. With Hellion's armies at our aid, we have a chance to do something more meaningful than host dinner parties and play secret society in the woods."

"You're a cynic," Lord Castor argues. "You've always been a cynic."

"Maybe if you had fought on the front, you'd be a cynic, too." Killian shifts, planting both feet on the ground. "What happened in Thorn is only the beginning. Our inaction—"

"Inaction!" Lord Castor huffs. "I have put my own family at risk to—"

The woman with the green hair clears her throat.

"When the rebels of Thorn called for assistance, it was Myths that came to the aid of the humans," she says, her voice clear. "Not Nightweavers."

The badger raises his paw, adjusts his spectacles. "Elatha speaks the truth," he squeaks in a human voice, and I bite my bottom lip to keep my mouth from falling open.

Lord Castor's face reddens, and he takes to inspecting his buttonholes. "We did not gather here tonight to place blame." He exhales deeply and addresses the man with the bottom half of a goat. "Bronmir. You bring news from the Savage Coast?"

The man does a sort of half bow, his expression austere. There is an exhaustion in his black eyes that I know all too well—the mark of a life lived on the run. When the humans fled to the sea, the Myths did not. I thought they'd been hunted to extinction, but it seems they're even better at hiding than we are. A life like that takes a physical toll, and I note every line in his young face, marred by the years added by isolation and fear.

"The number of Gore attacks has doubled since we last met." Bronmir's low, gravelly voice has a gentle quality, nearly soporific. "More humans defect to the Underlings' army every day. The Guild of Shadows is promising safety from the Underling regime and freedom from the Nightweavers—once and for all."

"Those in Thorn are not as lucky," the badger adds, fidgeting with his waistcoat.

"Tollith has been inside the facilities the king's Bloodknights built to detain the rebels there," Elatha says, and I mark the way the Myths refuse to add Lord Castor's title when addressing him.

"Bloodknights?"

This time, every head turns to me.

"The king's private guard," Jack explains, his expression sympathetic. "Deadly brutes."

The badger—Tollith—nods, adjusting his spectacles. "They show no discretion towards young nor old." His voice trembles, and the short, bearded man places a supportive hand on his shoulder. "The conditions are..." he breaks off, shaking his head. "I've never seen anything like it. Every day, they dig new pits to dump the bodies."

"And what say you of these facilities, Grendwin?" Killian asks the little old man—a dwarf, I realize.

The dwarf rubs his rounded, cherry-red nose and spits. "Death to the King," he says in a thick, lilting accent.

Baron Rencourt grins wickedly. "A worthy sentiment."

My heart quickens. So, *this* is what Will meant when he said his family was different. They speak of treason as if it were commonplace. They aren't fleeing from the king—they're facing him head on. And with the Nightweavers among the rebels, they're able to invade his ranks—dismantle their systems from the inside, just like Will told me all those weeks ago.

"Did you learn anything else?" Birtwistle asks.

"They—" The badger hesitates, casting me a sidelong glance.

Lady Castor gestures encouragingly. "Go ahead, Tollith."

Tollith nods. "I don't yet have proof," he whispers, his voice thick, "but it's suspected they're harvesting *Manan*."

"Maker of All," Jack hisses, his face pale. "But the law—"

"When has any king or queen ever lived by their own decrees?" Baron Rencourt sneers. "I knew it! They intend to keep the Bloodroses of Castle Grim all to themselves and force the rest of us to consume what has been forbidden by the True King!"

A conversation I'd once had with Will surfaces in my memory, about human blood being a possible resource for the Nightweavers. *"An extremely valuable one,"* he'd said. But he'd told me the law forbade it—nothing more. He certainly never mentioned that the king had built facilities in Thorn to detain humans who rebelled against the Crown and drain them of their blood.

I can't help but wonder if the *Manan* the Castors use to imbue their cloaks and gloves had come from one of these... *facilities.* I'd thought everything I'd heard about the Nightweavers treating humans as livestock had been false. But now...if the Nightweavers are desperate enough to break their own laws—to defy the True King, whom they claim to serve—then things are worse than I previously thought.

I refuse to let Elsie and Albert grow up in a world that sees them as no more than sheep for the slaughter. Not if I can do something about it.

"I want to join you."

Again, every head turns to find me.

Lady Isabelle raises her brows. "And your family?"

I hesitate, thinking about Margaret, probably drooling onto her beloved pillow as we speak. "They've been fighting for their lives for as long as they've had breath in their lungs. They're finally at peace. I want them to stay that way."

She dips her head. "Very well."

"You're prepared to take the oath?" Killian strides towards me, looking more like an admiral than Will's playful uncle.

"Pirates don't take oaths," I say, pulling my shoulders back, looking him square in the eye.

He smirks, and for a moment, I feel as if I'm looking at Will. "I thought you might say that."

Baron Rencourt sputters, "If she doesn't take the oath—"

"I'll vouch for her." Killian rolls up his shirtsleeve to reveal a tattoo on his inner forearm—a winged dagger and the roughly carved ancient words *nivim derai*. It fades before my eyes, then reappears as if at will. He holds out his hand expectantly.

"I said no oaths," I protest.

"This is how we distinguish friend from foe." He points to the ancient words. "*In time of need*," he translates. "It's merely an enchantment, visible only to those who possess a mark of their own—unless we choose to reveal it. If you are disloyal to the cause, your mark will reveal your intentions."

I glance at Jack and he rolls up his shirtsleeve, revealing his own winged dagger. Behind him, Lord Castor watches me carefully, his eyes narrow.

My hand curls into a fist. Everything that's happened since the moment Owen died—our capture, our new lives as servants—has been out of my control. I promised him I would not let them take me. I broke that promise. I promised myself that for the sake of my family I would try to move on. But I can't. Despite my ability to see the shadows, I've come no closer to finding the Sylk, and now, with the Guild sending Shifters to torment me, I have no option but to seek aid from those with the resources I lack.

No oaths, I remind myself. I am not bound to the Order of Hildegarde. I will use them as the Guild intended to use me. For Elsie and Albert. For Mother and Father. For Margaret, and Charlie, and Lewis. For others like us.

For Owen.

I roll up my shirtsleeve, revealing the band of braided leather, and extend my arm to Killian. "Death to the King."

CHAPTER NINETEEN

I glance around the table at my family, gathered for a late supper after the rest of the staff have eaten and gone to bed. Aboard the *Lightbringer*, we took all our meals together, but lately it's rare that even a few of us get the chance to share our supper. I wish I could tell them about the Order, about the Sylk, about the Shifter the Guild of Shadows has sent to haunt me. But I know they wouldn't understand. I'm supposed to be letting go—not holding tight.

Elsie prods at her porridge, a frown tugging at her lips. "I miss my books."

"Lord Castor has a whole library full of them." Margaret sighs wistfully. "It's wonderful."

Albert snorts. "Good for Lord Castor."

Lewis musses Albert's hair. "Someone's in a mood."

"I'm sick of all these pointless chores," Albert grumbles through a mouthful of porridge. "And why shouldn't we get to eat all the delicious food Father makes for the Castors?"

"Albert," Mother warns, her demeanor calm and collected, as if eating porridge in a drafty hallway is an elegant affair.

"What?" Albert's spoon clatters as he drops it in the empty bowl. "It's not fair. None of it. Why can't we be pirates again?"

"Albert!" Margaret gasps, her voice hushed. "You know better!"

"Does he?" I shrug, dragging my spoon through the mush in mindless circles. "Not all of us were so eager to leave our old lives behind."

"Do you think I wanted any of this?" Margaret fixes me with a glare cold enough to chill my bones. "I loved our life before. Maybe more than you ever did."

Charlie shovels porridge into his mouth, eyes flitting between Margaret and me.

"What's that supposed to mean?" I demand, my fist tightening around the handle of the spoon.

"We wouldn't have come anywhere near that Nightweaver ship if Owen hadn't insisted that we journey deeper into the Dire! If you hadn't gone along with his...his...delusions of finding the Red Island!"

"Margaret." Mother's voice is sharper than it had been towards Albert. But Albert hadn't mentioned our brother. Margaret had.

"And for what?" Margaret's face turns a bright shade of scarlet. "Because the two of you believed in a fairytale! The Red Island isn't real. It never was. It's a fantasy, Violet. It always has been." She shoves away from the table and storms up the stairs.

I glare at my porridge, my heart racing. How could she blame Owen for what happened to us? Owen *had* petitioned

Mother and Father to explore the uncharted regions of the Dire, but they'd insisted it was too dangerous. We were near the borders of the Dire when we were attacked. If anything, we would have been safer had Mother listened to Owen. He would still be alive.

Tiny bubbles form on the surface of my porridge, as if it were coming to a boil.

"I don't mind the chores," Charlie says, a thinly veiled attempt to change the subject. "Gives me something to think about other than—" he breaks off at the sharp look from Mother, his broad shoulders drooping.

"Something other than Owen?" Anger swells in my chest, and the spoon in my fist snaps in two. "It's okay to say his name, you know." I cut my eyes at Mother, who stares at my porridge, her expression nettled. "We're not pirates anymore, right? Father made sure of that when he signed our names on the King's Marque." I push away from the table. "Owen was our brother. And I don't intend on forgetting him."

I don't look back, not even when Lewis calls out to me, his voice as broken as I feel. I storm into the kitchen, where Father and Henry stand over the stove, heads down, pretending they hadn't been listening to my outburst.

As I shoulder through the door onto the moonlit lawn, the balmy heat the only remnant of summer, Henry follows at my heels. It's been three weeks since we'd joined the Order, and despite my every attempt to avoid him, he's always hanging about the kitchen with Father. I can't help but wonder if Lady Isabelle hasn't asked him to keep an eye on me, but another part of me thinks he's lonely without Will. I can't deny that he's more tolerable when his face is dusted with flour, his apron splattered with grease. And as hard as it is to see Father cooking with someone other than Owen—other than me—it seems to be good for both of them.

"I know where you're going," Henry says, catching up to me. His forehead glistens with sweat from the kitchen, and he's snacking on a handful of walnuts, each casual bite he takes only infuriating me further.

"So what?" I snap, my blood boiling.

"Uncle Killian's training you, isn't he?"

"I'm a part of the Order, aren't I?"

Henry skirts in front of me, blocking my path. "Well? Learn anything useful?"

"Sure," I say, pushing past him. *More than Will ever taught me.* In the few weeks I've been meeting Killian at the conservatory, I've learned more about Underlings than I did the entire month Will and I spent together. *Sylks smell like smoke. Shifters hate perfume. Gores can't walk backwards.*

It's clear that Will never meant for me to find the Sylk. At least, not on my own. The time I'd spent with him was time wasted. And still, I can't seem to answer the question that plays over and over in my mind when I try to sleep at night: *What does he stand to gain?*

"Is there a reason you're following me?"

Henry shrugs, pops another walnut into his mouth. "Just returning the favor." After a moment he adds awkwardly, "And I, uh—I heard what you said. I wanted to make sure you were—"

"I'm fine, Henry." I start up the hill, towards the orchard, where the trees appear to have caught fire, their leaves aflame with brilliant shades of ruby and amber, signaling the coming of autumn. "Since when do you care?"

His cheeks flush, and he shrugs. "I don't."

"Great. If that's all—"

"It's not," he blurts, taking an envelope from his chest pocket. "Will wanted me to give you this. And before you accuse me of snooping, it's spelled so that only you can read it."

I hesitate. The envelope smells of gunpowder. My fingers tremble slightly as I remove the bundle of parchment within, open the letter...

Pressed between the pages of the letter is a dried sprig of blue salvia.

And this one means I'm thinking of you.

My heartbeat quickens. He's alive—Will is alive. I've spent weeks wondering if I'll ever get the chance to see him again. But somehow, the knowledge that he isn't bleeding out on a battlefield somewhere—that he had taken the time to write me a letter—makes my stomach squirm with guilt. I've spent so much time feeling angry at Will for leaving that if I were to read what he has to say, now, while there's still a chance he might not make it home...I'm afraid I wouldn't be able to live with myself.

I scowl, shoving the letter at Henry's chest without having read a word of it, but I hold onto the flower. "I thought you hated us," I murmur, my fingertips brushing the brittle petals.

"Yeah, well, that was before I realized you were just the thing I needed to keep Trudy Birtwistle at bay." Slowly, he tucks the letter back into his pocket. "Speaking of, the Reckoning Day ball is two weeks from today. It's quite the celebration. We stay up all night to usher in the dawn. Mother spares no expense." He clears his throat. "I need someone to ward off Trudy. Keep her from asking me to dance. With a little help, you might actually pass for something more than human." He winces at the dig, apparently thinking better of it, but doesn't correct himself. "What do you say? Care to stir up some mischief?"

"No." I drop the sprig of blue salvia. It gives a satisfying crunch beneath my shoe.

"Come on," Henry whines. "You're really going to pass up the chance to be the only human at a party of Nightweavers?"

"Yes."

He huffs, coming to a halt. "Will's going to be there."

My feet falter a few paces, but I shake myself and keep going, determined not to lose focus on the night before me.

Henry jogs to my side and runs backwards, a wicked grin on his thin lips. "*And* he's bringing the prince."

My heartbeat quickens. "So?"

"*Sooo*," he coos. "The Order wants us both there to keep an eye on him."

"Why?"

He lowers his voice. "There've been rumors. That troublemaking pirate, Captain Shade, is supposed to make an appearance here, on Reckoning Day."

My heart stutters, nearly stopping altogether. "Here?"

He nods, and I get the feeling he knows nothing of his brother's informant. "My father's sources tell us he's going to make an attempt on the prince's life. You can still say no, of course, but considering it's our job to keep the prince safe…"

Right. Keep the prince safe until I can drive a blade through his heart.

"I suppose I should thank you," Henry adds, scratching his head. "Because of you, my parents finally let me join the Order."

"Why wouldn't they let you join before?"

"Apparently I have an attitude problem."

"You don't say?"

He chews lazily, looking out over the grounds like a king seated comfortably on his throne. "There's a dressmaker in Ink Haven. Jack will take you."

I groan and start past him again, through the apple tree tunnel. "Whatever," I mutter. "Just don't expect me to dance."

"It's a date," Henry calls, and though the thought of spending a night with him sets my skin crawling, I can't quell the mixture of fear and excitement rising up within me.

The prince is going to be at Bludgrave. Even if the Order won't let me drive a knife through the prince's heart, this might be my only chance to study him up close. He isn't a shadow—

he's flesh and bone. He has weaknesses just like anyone else. And I'm going to learn them all, so that when the time comes, I can be the one to put him down.

CHAPTER TWENTY

"You're distracted," Killian says. Moonlight dapples his dark hair, washing the conservatory in silver radiance and giving Liv and the other pixies the appearance of shooting stars as they flit about the old oak tree.

"I'm tired," I grouse, tracing a groove in the bark of the branch on which I sit.

Killian cocks a brow, closing the heavy, leather-bound tome in his lap. "Strange, I thought the history of the Tamed Lands was a lively subject." He scratches Dinah between her floppy ears, and the hound lets out a contented sigh. "What's on your mind?"

Finding the Sylk.

Killing the prince.

Overthrowing a kingdom.

Will.

"Nothing." I knock my head against the trunk, attempting to still the constant churning of my mind. "Are we going to talk about hunting Underlings, or not?"

"We could talk about constellations, instead?" He adjusts the buttons of his dark, striped waistcoat. It's the first time I've seen the Admiral out of uniform, and it makes him seem oddly human. "Flowers, perhaps? That seemed to be working."

I glare at the ground where Will and I used to lie as I swipe the book from Killian's lap, flipping through its pages. "Six hundred years of kings and queens. Six hundred years of war. Six hundred years, and my people have never known freedom. There've been rebellions before. What makes the Order of Hildegarde any different?"

Killian lights the cigar dangling from his lip, his face wrinkled with scrutiny. "Have you ever heard of the Red Island?"

My heart skips a beat, but I nod, trying to seem nonchalant.

Killian takes a long drag, puffing smoke. "When the war is over, a human will sit on the throne once again." He hesitates, glancing at me sidelong. "Some believe it will be a descendent of Hildegarde, the Mother of Queens, who wears the crown."

I shudder, remembering the crown of mystiks atop my head, and Will's whispered words. *I think you would make an excellent queen.*

I fidget, turning the band of braided leather round my wrist. "Why do they call her the Mother of Queens?"

Killian flicks the ash from his cigar, squinting at the smoldering embers at his feet as if he were trying to divine something from them. "Long ago, the Eerie was ruled by a queen who believed in magic, and freedom, and goodness. Hildegarde was as fierce as she was just, as wise as she was brave.

A practiced Sorceress, she healed her people in miraculous ways and protected them against deadly Myths even the most decorated warriors would not dare face. The True King, who looked down on Hildegarde with favor, sent an Elysian priestess to this realm to bless the queen with a power only he possessed."

Killian's eyes reflect the red smolder of his cigar as he pulls in a lungful of smoke. He exhales, and in the pale blue light of the moon, he gives me a curious look. "William told me the name of your ship was the *Lightbringer*." He cocks his head, searching my face. "Were you aware that was another name for Morana, the Underling queen?"

My heart drops into my stomach, heavy as a stone. Feebly, I shake my head. "That doesn't make sense. Why would Mother and Father name our ship after an Underling?"

"Morana was not always an Underling." Killian frowns, hypnotic ribbons of smoke unfurling from the cigar. "She was the True King's second-in-command."

The leaves rustle, filling the silence. Even Liv and the pixies have gone quiet, listening to Killian's every word.

"When the True King gave Hildegarde a fraction of his power, Morana lost herself to jealousy. She passed through the gates of Elysia into this realm to steal the True King's magic from the queen. Morana slayed Hildegarde, draining her of the *Manan* in her blood. But once she had the power she had craved for so long, the True King would not allow her to enter back through the gates of Elysia. As punishment, he sentenced Morana to Havok, a realm of utter darkness and despair, where she was to remain for all eternity. That was, until your people opened a gateway to Havok, releasing Morana from her prison."

The Burning Lands, I realize. The gateway through which the Underlings flooded into our world. Will had told me as much the morning after the Hackneys had been murdered.

"What does any of this have to do with the Red Island?" I ask, tugging at Owen's bracelet. The Red Island—Owen's dream. *Our* dream.

"Hildegarde had anticipated Morana's wrath. Just before she died, she gave birth to an heir, whom she hid away on an island where it is said no Underling can tread. There the descendants of Hildegarde have ruled for centuries, waiting for the time to come for them to reclaim their rightful throne."

"The Red Island," I breathe, my heartbeat racing.

A nod. "Power was not the only thing Morana stole from Hildegarde. The True King's gift to Hildegarde also came with a title."

"The Lightbringer..." That same something I'd sensed within me that day on the train, when I'd first met Will, recoils at the words. But again it creeps forward, as if craning to hear—or be heard. "Why doesn't the heir of Hildegarde just take the True King's magic back from Morana? Why hide?"

Killian snuffs out his cigar on the trunk of the old oak, his expression drawn. "Because in order to reclaim such power, one would have to drain Morana's true corporeal form of its *Manan*. But the Underling queen has not taken her corporeal form since the day she slayed Hildegarde."

The *Sylk* queen. A shadow with no blood of her own. Frustration burns the back of my throat, bitter and acrid.

Killian hefts two daggers from his belt, hidden beneath his wool coat. Their dark iron blades shimmer with iridescent shades of green, purple, and blue. "The League took me all over the Known World—Kane, Tyton, the Republic of Ruin. During a journey from the Hellion in the West to Nera in the South, we were shipwrecked. I alone survived. The family that rescued me brought me back to their home on the shores of the Red Island. They nursed me back to health. Gave me these." He extends the daggers to me. "They're made of Elysian Iron—capable of banishing a Sylk."

I grip the hilts in either fist. My stomach clenches as the muscles in my arms groan with misuse. I've let myself grow weak. But I can't think about that now. Not when I'm so close to the thing I've spent my entire life seeking. For a moment, I forget the Sylk. I forget the prince. All I can think about is the look on Owen's face that last morning; the way his kind eyes lit up at the mention of the pirate sanctuary where we could finally be free.

It's real. The Red Island is real.

"Does that mean..." I swallow hard, my heartbeat like a painful throbbing in my chest. "Do you know how to get to the Red Island?"

Something akin to grief flickers in his eyes, but it's so brief, I think I've imagined it. He shakes his head. "When I was well enough to leave, they blindfolded me. Left me on a rowboat near the Savage Coast."

I try to hide my disappointment, studying the twin blades. Citrine jewels adorn the pommel on either dagger, their cross guards shaped like wings. Fine craftsmanship—lightweight, sharp enough to cut through bone. These daggers belonged to my people—to humans. "Why give these to me?"

Killian looks up at the sky through the panels of glass, and I recognize the way he gazes at the stars. As if they were his friends. As if he knew them all by name. "I know that look in your eye. I've seen it before." He glances at the daggers, his expression hard. "If you continue down this path, you're going to need them."

When I tiptoe into our room, well past midnight, Margaret is still awake. I've hardly caught a glimpse of her tear-streaked face when she pulls me into a tight embrace, sobs hitching her breath. As much as I'd hated to part with the daggers, I'm glad I'd left Killian's gifts to be watched over by Liv and the pixies for the night. If Margaret felt them on my person, she would ask questions I couldn't begin to answer.

"I shouldn't have said what I did," she cries softly. "I'm so sorry, V."

I return the embrace, my chest squeezing painfully tight. "Don't be," I say, stroking her hair. "I provoked you."

"I'm the older sister," she half laughs, half cries. "I'm not supposed to let you provoke me." Her shoulders shake, her grip on me unrelenting. "I haven't been able to sleep. I just kept thinking you'd left and weren't coming back and I—I—"

"I'm right here, Marge," I say. "I'm not going anywhere."

She draws back, her hands on my shoulders as she eyes me suspiciously. "You aren't?" She sniffs. "It just seems like you haven't given up on it."

I open my mouth, close it. Killian had confirmed the existence of the Red Island tonight. It isn't just a fairytale or a legend or a lie Mother and Father allowed us to believe in. It's real. We could go there. We could be free. *Safe.* I want more than anything in the world to tell Margaret exactly that.

But I don't.

"You were right," I say instead. "Finding the Red Island was a fantasy. This is where we are now." But what I don't say aloud is that although I don't plan on staying here forever, I don't intend on leaving anytime soon. Not until I've found Owen's killer. Not until I've driven a blade through the prince's heart. Not until the king and queen of the Eerie have heard the name Violet Oberon and cower in fear of the girl the sea itself could not tame.

She cocks her head, her glassy, sapphire eyes piercing me in a way only Margaret's can—as if she can *feel* the childish hope that has gripped me since the first time I'd ever heard tales of the Red Island. As if it grips her, too.

She gives a heart-wrenching smile, full of the kind of disappointment known only to those who have ever dared to dream. "It was a nice fantasy."

CHAPTER TWENTY-ONE

S oft beams of apricot light illuminate the dusty dressmaker's shop as evening settles over Ink Haven. The second-story window overlooking the canal below lets in a pleasant breeze, carrying with it the scent of fresh bread from Mrs. Carroll's bakery across the street.

"I liked the first one better." Margaret tilts her head from one side to the other, her lips pursed. "It suited you."

I groan as the dressmaker unlaces yet another itchy, cumbersome gown. How Nightweaver women force themselves into these ridiculous contraptions, I'll never know. "This is exhausting."

"Tell me about it," Jack mutters, his back turned to us as he stares at the pink floral wallpaper in the tiny dressing room.

"I'll take the first one," I tell the old woman as Margaret helps me back into my plain black dress. I never thought I'd prefer my servant's uniform, but the cotton fits snug to my skin, allowing me to move freely—and take more than a shallow breath. While Margaret and Jack discuss payment and delivery with the dressmaker, I retrieve the flintlock I'd hidden in my apron and secure it to my shin once more, grateful for its comforting weight.

The dressmaker sends us on our way, glad to be rid of us, but she sends her love to Lewis, who visits the little shop more often than I'd realized. We start the long trek back to Bludgrave as the setting sun bathes Ink Haven in amber light, and boys and girls, their faces caked with soot, tend the lanterns along the bustling street.

Jack buys the three of us a single fried donut at a candlelit stall, paying with five crisp, jet-black tenors—the currency of the Eerie, branded with their scarlet sun. In the time we've worked at Bludgrave, I've seen Father pocket the stacks of tenors from Lord Castor, but I've yet to touch a sheet of the strange, ink-laden paper.

Through a mouthful of donut, Jack grumbles, "One more dress and I swear, I would have—"

He freezes as we round the corner and find ourselves at the back of a disgruntled crowd. Margaret tenses beside me. At the front, a platform has been erected in the middle of the street. Four ropes hang from the structure, pulled taut with the weight of four corpses. A man, a woman, and two children, fresh blood oozing from the crude *P* carved into their foreheads.

Percy stands at the base of the platform, his face smattered with blood, his knife wet.

Jack's throat bobs. "We need to turn back," he whispers.

But as he and Margaret turn to leave, I push forward, through the crowd. I don't know what propels me, other than the overwhelming desire to carve Percy's heart from his chest.

"*Violet!*" Margaret hisses, her fingertips grazing my wrist as I slip out of reach.

I keep my head down, trying to hear what Percy is saying over the furious drum of blood in my ears.

"Let this be a warning," he calls out. "Any human found guilty of harboring pirates will face the hangman's noose."

"What about a trial?" someone cries over the anxious whispers. "The king—"

"There is no king in Ink Haven!" Percy's lips curl into a mirthful sneer. "And there will be no trials. Only executions."

Panicked murmurs break out amongst the crowd. A few Nightweavers nod in agreement with Percy and the men, all clad in black cloaks, who stand beside him. Someone grabs me by the arm just as I near the front.

"We have to go," Jack says in a voice I don't recognize—a voice that belongs to a soldier, not a stableboy. "Now."

I take one last look at the slack faces of the children; take one last breath, remembering the itch and burn of a rope around my own neck. But as I turn to follow Jack back through the crowd, Percy fires a shot into the air.

"Ah, bilge rats." He cackles. "You pirates can't stay away from the stink of garbage, can you?"

I don't have to see his face to know he's speaking directly to me. I glance over my shoulder to find the crowd has parted, putting Jack and me directly in his sights.

My stomach plummets. One of Percy's thugs has Margaret by the arm, a knife poised at her throat. Percy grins, revealing crooked yellow teeth. He saunters towards me, but Jack steps between us.

"Lord Castor—"

Percy strikes with the back of his hand, sending a spray of Jack's blood across my face. The metallic tang invades my nostrils, sharp and sickly sweet.

"Insolent boy," Percy growls, a mad look about him, as if the mere mention of Lord Castor were enough to drive him into a murderous rage. He clutches my face, his thumb smearing the blood from my lips, across my jaw. He leans in, his hot, liquored breath causing my eyes to water. I swallow bile as his hand roams from my face to my neck. "Your little lord isn't here to protect you now."

I spit in his bloodshot eyes. "And who's going to protect you?"

Percy laughs—a cruel, grating sound. He grabs me by a fistful of my hair and yanks me forward, towards the platform.

"Foolish *and* blind." He shoves me to the ground, motions for his men to seize Jack. They bring him forward, kicking his legs out from beneath him. "You may think yourself safe behind the gates of Bludgrave Manor, but these streets belong to *me*."

A man in a black cloak heats an iron over a fire, presents it to Percy. Another man jerks Margaret forward and holds out her arm. Percy peels back her sleeve as if he were unwrapping a gift.

"You should be known for what you are," he says calmly, his eyes burning with gleeful hate. "Filthy pirate scum."

Margaret screams as Percy presses the iron to her flesh. Jack scrambles to his feet, only to be kicked back to his knees. I watch helplessly, Margaret's screams echoing in my ears long after Percy withdraws the iron. A jagged red *P* puckers the skin on Margaret's forearm. She crumples to the ground, sobbing. Jack grits his teeth, bucking against his captors.

"You can't do this!" Jack growls. "Their names are on the King's Marque! They've been absolved of their crimes."

Percy nods at one of his men. It takes only a few precise hits, and Jack's swollen face is nearly unrecognizable. Blood pours from his mouth, his nose, his ears. His purple eyelids bulge, his breath coming in ragged gasps.

Percy grabs my arm and two men grip me by the shoulders, holding me firmly in place. My heart pounds against my ribcage, but when he peels my sleeve back, the enchanted tattoo Killian had placed there leaves no trace.

I will not scream. I will not scream. I will not—

Heat sears my flesh, and I bite down hard on my bottom lip to keep from crying out, the taste of my own blood mingling with Jack's. As black spots edge my vision, I think of the flintlock strapped to my shin. I think of the daggers hidden inside my apron. I could slit his throat before he could blink. But I'm surrounded by Hounds, and as quick as I could take down Percy, I'm not fast enough to save Margaret and Jack.

"There," Percy croons, withdrawing the iron.

The stench of cooked flesh causes Jack to retch, but my senses fade beneath the pain. Beneath the anger. Beneath the urge to spill blood. And above it all, a sound: a pumping rhythm, almost as familiar as the crash of a wave or the drip of water leaking from the roof of the *Lightbringer's* galley, but something new entirely. New, and yet I recognize its voice—a voice I've heard babbling on the tides ever since I can remember.

Percy drops the iron, his eyes intent on the brand. His fingers trail from the sizzling *P* to the band of braided leather on my wrist. "What's this?"

Touch it, and you'll be the one that's blind.

I don't move. I only know that as soon as the thought crosses my mind, a steady stream of blood spills from Percy's eyes. His men release me as Percy clutches his head, shrieking in agony. *Fools.*

In that moment of distraction, Margaret wrenches free from her captors, using the knife they'd held to her throat to slit both of theirs. I draw the daggers from my apron and, before they can react, plunge the blades into the chests of the men holding Jack.

Margaret helps Jack to his feet as a whistle pierces the air, followed by the clomping of hooves. Mrs. Carroll, the baker Will had greeted our first day in Ink Haven, sits at the reins of a small wagon, her face flushed with the evening chill. When our eyes meet, she appears startled and leans forward in her seat as if to get a closer look at me. But she blinks, shaking her head slightly, and when she looks at me again, she must not see whatever she had before, for a look of confusion settles over her plump features.

"Quickly, now," she says, slowing just enough for Margaret to help Jack into the back of the wagon. I pull myself up, sheathing my daggers and drawing the flintlock instead, covering our tail as the wagon lurches forward and we barrel down the street, feeling more alive than I have since the day my feet ran aground.

Surrounded by his men, Percy shrieks, scratching at his bloody eyes. As we round the corner, the humans in the street take up pitchforks and crude weapons, descending on Percy and the Hounds. Over the chaos, I hear their cry.

"Death to the King!"

CHAPTER TWENTY-TWO

I can't dim the glow of satisfaction radiating in my chest.

Margaret and Jack huddle together in the back of the wagon, comforting each other as the guards open the gate and Mrs. Carroll starts down the long, lantern-lit drive towards Bludgrave Manor.

I know I shouldn't feel this way. I should be huddled beside them, caring for Jack, empathizing with Margaret. But every time the brand on my forearm smarts, a smile tugs at my lips.

I am a pirate—there'll be no denying it now.

My hands, soaked in the blood of those Hounds, graze the hilts of my daggers. I hear Percy's cry again and again, filling me with pride. Still, I can't explain what happened, why blood had streamed from his eyes. Could it have something to do with my curse? I don't know if my ability to see the Sylks could also give me the means to inflict such pain. I only know that I can't shake the thrum of power coursing through me at the thought of making him bleed.

The guards, Gylda and Hugh, had raised the alarm, and by the time we reach the front steps, Lord Castor and Henry are busy pulling on their leather gloves as Boris brings a motor carriage around. Warm, golden light pours out of the double doors as Lady Isabelle invites a trembling Mrs. Carroll in for a cup of tea and Albert takes the reins of her wagon. Margaret and I help Jack down, and Lewis and Charlie take him off our hands, helping him up the steps and into the house. Margaret stumbles after them, speaking softly to Jack, as if she could somehow heal him with her words alone.

Killian leans against the front columns, puffing on a cigar, his expression unreadable. He dips his chin at me and I return the gesture, thanking him silently for the daggers weighting the front of my apron. I think I see the hint of a smile before a cloud of smoke obscures his face.

"You're going back there, aren't you?" I ask Henry, turning to face him as he saunters down the steps.

He sighs, tugging the leather glove further up his wrist. "Father says Percy has had his fair share of warnings. He and his Hounds will have to be made an example of."

"I'm coming with you."

He glances at me incredulously. "Are you armed?"

I heft the flintlock from the holster strapped to my shin. "Pirate, remember?"

His mouth quirks, his coal-dark eyes flickering with wicked promises. "How could I forget?"

We follow a trail of blood. Bodies line the street haphazardly—humans and Nightweavers, their corpses left to be picked over by monstrous black vultures. The platform lies in a heap, but the family of four remains among the splintered wood, their skin blue, faces bloated with death. Henry's hands crackle with static electricity, the *Manan* in his gloves eager to be tapped.

Lord Castor steels himself as we pass, his forehead creasing. On the trek into town, I'd caught him staring at me more than once, but he hadn't objected to my joining them. In fact, he'd welcomed it.

"Percy wronged you and your sister," he'd said as I'd entered the carriage. "I think it's only right you have a chance to repay him."

My fist tightens around the hilt of a dagger at my hip. I'd removed my apron, donning a dark cloak Sybil retrieved for me at the request of Lord Castor. It isn't like the Nightweavers' magic cloaks—at least, it doesn't *feel* magical—but it serves to conceal the belt that now holds both daggers and the flintlock from Killian.

I wonder what Will would think if he could see me now. I wonder if he would care more for the grieving, desperate girl he'd purchased at the auction house, or the girl I was before the *Lightbringer* sank. Because striding towards danger with nothing more than my wits, a pair of blades at my disposal, and a few balls of lead, I feel more like myself than I have since the day Owen died.

The coaching inn leans left, wedged between a butcher and a blacksmith, its once-vibrant emerald façade faded to a pale, sickly green. Just half an hour before, the street had been packed. Now, everything is quiet. Even the moon hides her face, tucked away behind the clouds.

The motor coach stutters into park, and Henry and I follow Lord Castor to the door of the inn. Bloody handprints stain its chipped face.

Lord Castor turns the knob.

The stench of death crashes over me like a wave. In pieces strewn about the lobby and the adjacent tavern, bodies litter the wreckage of smashed chairs and shattered dishes. Again, a mixture of humans and Nightweavers, their eyes wide and vacant, mouths gaping to fit a cry that can no longer be heard. Blood covers the floor, thick enough to lap at the soles of our shoes.

Someone moans, and I lean over the counter to find the innkeeper slumped, clutching at the broken handle of a pitchfork, impaled on its rusted spikes. He looks up at me, eyes dull, blood pouring over his chin.

He's a Nightweaver, I tell myself. I should let him die.

"Please," he chokes out, one hand stretched towards me. Blood pools around the spikes that pierce his flesh, a deep ruby red. Nightweaver or human, we bleed the same. He might be someone's brother. Someone's father. If something could have been done for Owen, would a Nightweaver like Will have tried to save him?

Could Will have tried to save him?

"Henry," I whisper, turning to find him watching the man with pity. "Can't you heal him?"

He shakes his head, frowning slightly. "It's not in my skill set."

Henry follows Lord Castor towards the stairs, but I hesitate. I kneel, touch my hand to the man's cheek, his skin already cold.

"All is well," I whisper, though I don't know if I say the words to bring him peace, or myself.

At the base of the stairs, Lord Castor motions for us to wait. A few flights up, there's a cry—so broken, so faint, as if it came on a dying breath.

I glance down at my hands, looking like a pair of crimson gloves. When I'd touched the Nightweaver's face—when my fingers came away red with blood—I felt that same rush of power I'd experienced when Percy dropped to his knees. The same vitality that filled me with strength the night I'd stepped into the fountain. *Power and control*—maybe I'm not so different from the Nightweavers or the Underlings.

Maybe I'm worse.

Henry and I follow Lord Castor up the narrow staircase, past the second and third landing. With every step they take, the old, rotting wood creaks beneath their feet. *Theirs*—not mine. I shift my weight naturally, careful to remain inconspicuous. *Quiet like a mouse*, I think with a dull ache in my chest.

My fist tightens around the hilt of my dagger.

"Is the little mouse scurrying about the deck this morning?"
Owen would ask Margaret just before I'd sneak up behind him.
I can almost hear him now, whispering in my ear, *"Careful, little
mouse. If you go looking for blood, you'll certainly find it."*

Good. We didn't come here to negotiate peace. I pray to the
Stars I find blood—Percy's blood. I pray to the Stars that I have
the strength to carve his heart from his chest. And if the Stars
look down on me with favor, I pray that when we've got what we
came for, the Castors will know what the brand on my forearm
represents. They may take me from the ocean, but the water
does not forget, and neither should they. I am the killer they
fear. I am the monster in the dark. And when I find Percy, I will
be merciless.

At the top of the stairs, a Nightweaver in a black cloak
lies sprawled across the landing, skewered on the sharp end
of a crudely made spear. Metal glints in the gaslight as I bend,
inspecting the brass knuckles clutched in his rigid grasp.

Wasting no time, I break his bloated fingers and slide the
brass knuckles from his fist onto my own. Owen used to fight
with a pair just like this.

"Only when it's personal," he would have amended.

Tonight, it's personal.

We come to a halt at the end of the fourth floor, and without
delay, Lord Castor kicks the door in. Inside, Percy stands with
his back to the open window, facing us, his eyes crusted shut
with dried blood. Under his arm, I recognize the girl from my
first day in Ink Haven. Or, rather, I recognize her height and

build. The remains of her light-blond hair is in clumps; her face is so swollen and purple, I can't discern her features.

She lets out another small cry, the sound like a knife to my heart. *That could have been Elsie.* I shake my head, but I can't keep myself from imagining Percy's arm around Elsie's neck, the muzzle of a pistol pressed to her cheek.

"I know it's you, bilge rat," Percy spits. "Have you brought your masters to see the job done?"

"Let her go, Percy," Lord Castor demands. "It's over. Your men are dead."

Percy cackles, his laughter like jagged shards of glass. "The Hounds of Ink Haven!" he cries mockingly, doubling over—with pain or with glee, I can't tell. "Did you really think my allegiance lies with a washed-up street gang that can't even handle a few angry humans with gardening tools?" Shadows seep from his flesh like wisps of black smoke. Though he can't see me, he looks directly at me, his head cocked, and when he speaks, the low, gritty voice is not his own. *"The Guild of Shadows has welcomed me into their fold."*

The blood pounding in my ears fades beneath a shrill whine. I try to take a steadying breath, but the air is dry and parched. I hadn't noticed it before—the stale, ashen odor—but now I choke on the pungent stench of smoke.

He's possessed, I realize with a twinge of panic. Can Henry and Lord Castor tell? Only I can *see* the Sylk—but can they smell it? Can they see what it's doing to him?

When Percy speaks again, his voice is his own. "Is the little lord with you?"

At first, I think he means Will, but he jerks his chin at a small wooden box on the vanity near Henry. Percy licks his lips, mouth stretching wide in a wicked sneer.

"Open it."

Henry glances at Lord Castor, his brows furrowed. Tentatively, his gloved hand prods at the lid, and I crane my neck to see what's inside. I barely make out the bloody, severed finger, and the black velvet ribbon tied around it, before Henry hurls himself at Percy, barred only by Lord Castor, who throws himself between them.

"Your human pet is a lovely creature," Percy croons, his expression vile. "She was on her way back to you, I suppose, when my men took her."

"Where is Dorothy?" Henry growls. And then, frantically, "Where are you keeping her?"

Percy clicks his tongue. Sweat beads on his forehead. "Such a shame. The great Lord Castor's sons cavorting with human girls." He spits, his face crumpled with disgust. "Though, what should anyone expect when their parents are sympathizers—traitors to their own king and country." He spits again, as if the words taste like poison, but this time, he spits blood. "A disgrace to their own kind." And then, that voice that came before—that low, gritty voice—speaks in the ancient tongue. "*Palomi havella dinosh beyan.*"

I think I hear Henry sob, the sound itself inhuman and guttural, as if it had come from a beast, not a boy. "You won't get away with this, Percy. The king—"

Percy barks out a sharp laugh, and I cringe. "*Insolent child,*" says the voice of the Sylk. Percy's lips peel back, revealing bloody teeth as he slowly removes the barrel of the gun from the little girl's face. "*It has already begun. The time has come for kings and kingdoms to bow to the one true queen. All will kneel.*"

He throws a hateful glance at Lord Castor, a sinister smile pulling at the corners of his mouth. Percy's voice comes out on a trembling breath, his eyes alight with murderous joy. "Even the mighty Castors."

In the blink of an eye, Percy shoves the girl from the open window. A small cry of shock echoes in my ears, followed by a wet crunch.

A dagger is in my hand before I even realize I've lunged. The blade pierces Percy's chest, just above his heart.

I don't want him dead.

Not yet.

Percy's knees collide with the floor as I withdraw the dagger, but he doesn't attempt to stanch the flow of blood. He holds out his arms as if in invitation. I should question his surrender, but there is only one thought in my mind as I whirl, bringing the dagger down in two smooth arcs. Blood sprays my face as Percy's severed hands land with a dull *thunk*.

Those hands will never harm another child.

I shift the dagger to my left hand and draw back my right fist, the brass knuckles glinting with a heavenly golden light. *Crack.* Bone shatters beneath the weight of my hand. Again and again pain seizes my right arm, and I welcome it. I welcome the ache in my shoulder. I welcome the voice in the back of my mind that demands I spill Percy's blood. I welcome the fury as it overtakes me, white-hot and all-consuming.

"Violet—" I'm not sure who says my name, their voice drowned out by the blood beating in my ears, a savage tempo.

Percy laughs again, the sound like shards of broken glass, and I halt mid-swing. "*Violent Violet,*" the Sylk whispers, though I'm not sure how the voice could come from Percy's disfigured face. Against all rational judgement, I lean closer, as if entranced. The Sylk tsks softly. "*So much like your brother.*"

Brother. The word is like a lifeline tethering me to reality.

This is it. This is the Sylk that killed Owen.

In one fluid motion, I sheathe the dagger in my apron, unholster the flintlock strapped to my shin. I aim between Percy's swollen, bloodied eyes and—

"*Owen sends his regards.*"

I hesitate. It's as though all the air has been sucked out of the room.

"Owen?" I hear myself whimper.

I lower the flintlock just as Henry grabs me by my collar and yanks me back.

"We have to go!" he shouts, barely audible over the sound of splintering wood. A fiery beam collapses overhead, landing in the spot where I'd been only seconds ago, crushing Percy flat.

Smoke. I thought the smell had come from the Sylk, but... Thick, black smoke chokes the air, stinging my eyes. I had been so lost in my rage that I hadn't realized a fire had started.

Despite the encroaching heat, ice sluices through my veins.

Owen sends his regards.

Henry hauls me out of the room, down the steps, fire licking at our heels. "It was an accident," he huffs as we break out onto the street after Lord Castor. "Father," Henry says, releasing his grip on me. "I'm sorry." He shakes his head, tears streaming down his face. "I don't know what happened. I—I don't think I can control it."

"It's alright, my boy." Lord Castor claps Henry on the shoulder. He glances at me out of the corner of his eye, a troubled look about him.

Henry straightens and turns towards the building, gloved hands outstretched, but Lord Castor lowers his arms.

"No," he says quickly. When Henry turns to him in confusion, Lord Castor's expression is grim. "Let it burn."

Henry nods weakly. Again, Lord Castor glances at me, flames dancing in his eyes. I turn away before he realizes I've caught him staring, but I can't shake the feeling that I've seen that *look* before—the one that seeks to answer a question that shouldn't be asked. Only, not from Lord Castor. From Will.

The fire devours the coaching inn, reducing it to cinders. There, near the front steps, impaled on a stake of splintered wood, the girl Percy had thrown from the window stares up at the starless sky with vacant eyes, blood trickling from her parted lips.

"Henry," I whisper hoarsely, starting towards the child's corpse. "We can't leave her like this."

Henry is at my side a moment later, his face hard. I know he must be thinking of Dorothy as he stretches out his gloved hands once more—hesitates.

"What's that?" he murmurs.

I take another step towards the girl's mangled body, squinting to see what had given Henry pause. A playing card rests atop the child's torn blouse, as if someone had placed it there just after she'd fallen. The knave of clubs. But it isn't just any playing card.

"It's a message." I pick up the card that had once belonged to Owen—to me—and slide it into my apron. "The Sylk wants me to believe my brother is still..." The word gets stuck in my throat. "That he's..."

"Alive." Henry nods slowly, his brows pinched. "And do you?"

I don't answer.

"Look away, Violet," Henry adds gently, his palms extended.

But I don't do that, either. Not even as the child's corpse goes up in flames.

I watch. I watch as Henry turns, headed for the heap of wood in the middle of the street, where bodies had hung just hours ago. I watch as he sets the remains of the gallows ablaze, black smoke billowing into the sky. All the while, I hear the Sylk's voice in my mind—the words it had spoken in the ancient tongue. Words I know only because Owen taught me what they meant. Words that our people—the people of the sea—speak in hushed whispers once a year, on Reckoning Day. The day the sky runs red as blood.

Palomi havella dinosh beyan.

The judgement is coming.

Chapter Twenty-Three

"The judgement…" Jack runs a hand through his hair, his mouth pressed tight. In the dim light of the pantry, he examines the playing card, flecked with dried blood. "It seems Reckoning Day holds a different meaning to those of you who've spent your lives at sea."

A few days ago, in the hours after we had returned from Ink Haven, Killian had said as much.

"We were taught that it was a day of remembrance," I say. "It serves as a reminder of the blood that was shed six hundred years ago, before we were forced to flee."

Jack nods. "It's the same for the Nightweavers," he says, his voice low. "Besides the fleeing part," he adds awkwardly, rubbing the nape of his neck. "But…the judgement…"

"That part belongs to us," I say, my chest tightening. "There are some that believe that Reckoning Day is a promise. That one day, the True King will cast his judgement on the Nightweavers that purged us from the lands of the Known World, and we will return from the sea to claim what is rightfully ours."

Jack raises his brows. "Radical."

I roll my eyes. "You belong to a secret organization fighting to take down the king and queen of the Eerie. I don't think you—"

The door to the pantry swings open. I snatch the playing card from Jack and shove it into my apron before Margaret can see. She fixes a suspicious look on both of us, her hands on her hips. Behind her, the kitchen bustles with activity as Father shouts orders over the din of clanging pots.

"This was the best you could do?" Margaret arches a brow, glancing at Jack. "Surely, you could have found a clever place to hide."

Jack raises his hands in mock surrender as he sidesteps her, out of the pantry. "I've never claimed to be clever."

Margaret's lips twitch, the beginnings of a smile. "I wasn't talking to you."

I groan, holding out my arms as if I were about to be chained and led away to slaughter. "Do your worst."

Margaret snorts. "You two need to stop spending so much time together," she says, taking me by the wrist and dragging me out of the pantry. "One overly dramatic troublemaker is enough to deal with."

"I wouldn't call myself overly dramatic," Jack mumbles.

Margaret kisses him on the cheek, and Jack's face flushes. "And what would you call yourself?"

Jack touches the place where Margaret's lips had graced his skin, his eyes glittering. "Favored by the Stars."

I clear my throat. "I'm finding that what awaits me upstairs is more preferable to…whatever this is."

Margaret blushes, but Jack winks at me as Father thrusts the handle of a paring knife into his hand and begins herding him towards a mountain of potatoes. In turn, Margaret leads me upstairs, down the hall and—

The green baize door is open.

I glance at Margaret, my heart kicking into a gallop. "What are we…"

Margaret smiles, apparently pleased with my reaction. She hooks her arm through mine, leading me over the threshold that separates the servant's hall from the Castors' living quarters. "Lady Isabelle granted us use of her chambers for the afternoon."

I barely register what Margaret has said. We pass by the first door on the right, the room that shares a wall with my own, and I have to force myself to keep moving. But my gaze lingers on the burnished knob, and for a brief moment, I fight the urge to open the door to Will's chambers. Would I find him, there, on his bed? What does his bed even look like?

"Violet?" Margaret gives me a slight tug.

"Sorry," I murmur, not meeting her gaze as we continue down the hall. But I can feel her eyes on me as she gives my arm a squeeze.

"Are you ready for this?" Margaret asks.

Ready for what? To be prodded by hot irons and painted with rouge from delicate glass pots? To don a gown made of fine silk fabric that costs enough to buy a small ship? To spend the evening on Henry's arm, in a room full of Nightweavers, pretending to be something more than just…me? To meet the Prince of the Eerie? To see Will?

Will. Somehow, everything else—everything but *him*—feels manageable. But the thought of seeing him again…

"I'm ready," I lie, because the truth would mean turning back around, walking through that green baize door, and never crossing the threshold again.

"It stays." Those are the first words I've spoken since Margaret had all but chained me to the stool in front of the vanity. I hadn't argued when she dabbed a demure, rosy shade of pink on my lips and cheeks. I hadn't fought back when she curled my hair, sweeping half of it off my shoulders and arranging it in an elaborate updo. I even let her curl my eyelashes with little more than a look of protest. But I won't part with Owen's bracelet. Not for the evening. Not ever.

Margaret withdraws her hand. She nods, her eyes glimmering with a familiar fire—a look I've seen countless times fighting by her side aboard the *Lightbringer*. "It stays."

I take a shuddering breath, the tension in my shoulders easing a bit as Margaret's battle-hardened expression softens to a look of girlish mischief.

She takes the leather garment bag from the wardrobe, beaming. "Now for the fun part."

I frown. "I thought you were having fun when you combed black tar through my eyelashes?"

"Oh, that was fun," she says, brows raised as she unzips the bag and motions for me to turn around and lift my arms. "But this is going to be life-changing."

Life-changing. I've had enough of that to last an eternity.

My eyes drift closed as Margaret slips the gown over my head. The fabric glides over my skin like water, cool and soft.

Once, when I was a child, Lewis and I overheard Mother comforting Margaret as my sister cried herself hoarse. Margaret's birthday was a week away, and all she wanted—all she'd ever wanted—was to wear a gown like those she'd seen illustrated in the books Father stole. That week, Lewis worked until his fingers bled to create something from the scraps of fabric he'd looted from enemy ships. The finished result was beautiful, expertly crafted. Then, I had envied Margaret. Now, as I open my eyes and take in the canary-yellow gown, I catch a glimpse of Margaret behind me, her expression one of awe and sisterly love.

Guilt squeezes my heart like a fist. Material like this was never meant to grace a pirate's mud-slicked, blood-soaked skin. But Margaret—my loyal, devoted sister, who, despite the jealousy I'm certain she feels in this moment, wouldn't dare admit her own desires now—she deserves a wardrobe full of gowns like this.

"Wow," Margaret breathes.

I seek out my reflection in the cheval mirror. I thought once that Owen might not recognize me if he saw me in my servant's uniform. But, standing in Lady Isabelle's luxurious chambers, my ivory skin gilded in the candlelight, I hardly recognize myself.

The material clings to my frame—no longer gaunt, but well-fed in a way that I had never been onboard the *Lightbringer*—and spills over at my feet in a pool of silk the color of the setting sun. Canary yellow—the defining shade of the Oberon clan—embroidered with silver stars along the sweeping neckline. Nine stars, just like I had requested. One for every member of our family. One for Owen.

The floor-length gown leaves my arms bare and exposes the hollow of my collarbones, revealing the various scars that pucker my freckled skin. My gaze lingers on my neck, on the faint white lines left behind from the rope that marred my flesh…

Margaret clears her throat, drawing my attention to the matching elbow-length gloves in her grasp. I extend my fingers as she slides the first glove over my hand. As Margaret tugs the second glove over my forearm, where the brand marks my flesh, I catch sight of the *P* burned into Margaret's skin. Our eyes meet, and Margaret's face hardens once more.

Here, surrounded as we are by such wealth and beauty, it is almost difficult to imagine Margaret's lovely face smeared with blood, a cutlass in her either hand.

"You would forego the gloves if you could," she murmurs, a sad sort of smirk twisting her mouth.

I don't speak for a long moment. "I'm not ashamed of who I am," I say finally. But for the first time in my life, I'm not sure I mean it.

Margaret nods, tugging the glove on the rest of the way before taking my hands in hers. "Owen would be proud of you," she says, her voice soft.

I want to believe her. I'd like to think if Owen knew I was working in secret to dismantle the Nightweavers' entire system— if he knew I was hunting Underlings and scheming to murder the prince—he would be proud of me. But there is something about the way Margaret says our brother's name, the hint of fury blazing in her dark eyes, that makes me wonder if she hasn't let go of Owen, either.

"Jack told me about Dorothy." Margaret releases my hands, shaking her head. "Do you think she's…"

"Dead?" I can't be sure. "For her sake, I would hope so."

Margaret curses under her breath. "I wish I could have been there." She takes a long strip of yellow chiffon and arranges it around my neck, concealing the faded scars. "I wish I could have been the one to drive a dagger through that Nightweaver's chest."

I blink, stunned. I had thought Margaret had been more inclined than any of us to leave behind a life of violence and bloodshed. I know I shouldn't, but I begin to peel back the glove, to show Margaret the enchanted tattoo there and the promise of vengeance it represents. After all, Jack has already shared more than he is permitted to, and Margaret is my sister. She is branded, just like me. If revenge is what she seeks, the Order could give her an outlet.

"Margaret," I say, just as faint traces of black ink begin to surface on my inner forearm, "there's something I want to tell—"

"Surprise!" Annie bursts through the door. Elsie bounds along behind her, carrying a vase of flowers. The two girls giggle, no doubt caught up in the excitement of the evening before it's even truly begun—despite the fact that Annie will be attending and Elsie will be sequestered in the upstairs rooms, listening to music and laughter through the walls but unable to participate.

I tug the glove back to my elbow. I'll tell Margaret about the Order tomorrow morning, after the ball. Hopefully, I'm right about her and she'll want to join. It would be nice to not have to hide this from my sister, at least. It would be nice not to feel so…alone.

Both Elsie and Annie come to a screeching halt. They stare at me, mouths open.

Elsie gasps. "You look like—"

"—a princess!" Annie finishes.

I can't help the blush that warms my face. But as the girls continue to gush over the gown, the flowers Elsie carries snag my gaze, and my heart twists.

She presents the bouquet to me, looking mischievous. "From a secret admirer."

I swallow hard as I accept the bouquet. "For me?" I breathe in the sweet, intoxicating aroma, my stomach aflutter. The stargazer lilies, their pink-and-white petals dappled with buttery golden candlelight, send my mind into a whirl. I try to remember what Will had told me they represent but come up short.

From a secret admirer.

I was under the impression that it was no secret Will and I had...*admired* each other. But we hadn't said that—not in words. Still, I know the flowers could only have come from him. Does that mean he's back already? Is he in the house? We could be only a room away from each other.

I feel like I'm going to vomit.

"My, my." Mother's voice sends the rush of bile creeping up my throat into remission. She stands in the doorway, her hair pulled back into a neat bun. I miss the wild, untamed curls that used to crowd her cheeks, as well as her carefree grin. The woman who approaches me, carrying a small velvet box, is not the fierce pirate from my memories. But she is still my mother— strong, beautiful, wise. And the look of pride on her weathered face as she takes in the sight of me in my gown makes me forget all about Will—about the Sylk, about everything—if only for a moment.

"Do you like it?"

Mother smiles, but I don't miss the trace of sorrow in the lines of her mouth. "You were born to wear this dress."

I watch, a bit uneasily, as she counts the silver stars embroidering the neckline. She reaches out, fingertips grazing the ninth star.

"For Owen," she whispers, almost too low to hear. Tears limn her dark-blue eyes, but she clears her throat, her smile widening as she opens the velvet box. Nestled inside, two opalescent pearl earrings glow pink in the candlelight. I knew Mother and Father were making a decent salary, but I had no idea that the Castors paid enough that Mother could afford such extravagant jewelry.

I fight back tears as Mother takes the first earring from the box and finds the tiny, pinprick hole in my earlobe that I'd thought would have closed by now. "There," she says, fastening the second earring. She draws back, her hand cupping my cheek. "Tonight, you take a piece of the sea with you."

Her words threaten to unravel me, but I maintain a fragile grip on my composure. "Thank you," I murmur around the knot in my throat, my voice thick.

I see Owen in Mother's face as she grins, and something in my chest splinters.

"You've outdone yourself, Margaret dear." Lady Isabelle enters the room, looking like a vision in scarlet. Her tiara glimmers like tiny stars atop her neatly coiffured hair. She extends an arm to me. "Violet?"

I glance at Margaret, who nods encouragingly and takes the bouquet from my trembling hands. For the first time since Killian had given me the means to protect myself, I am without a weapon. I had practically begged Margaret to find a way to hide my daggers beneath my gown, but she insisted the tight fabric wouldn't allow it. I find myself wishing I had strapped something to my thigh—a butter knife, a pair of scissors—that I might use just in case I were to be found out for what I truly am. After what Percy and his Hounds did in the middle of Ink Haven, and the subsequent revolt of the humans against them, Killian claims Nightweavers are becoming even more at odds with my kind. If they decided to take their anger out on me...

"Violet," Margaret whispers, derailing my thoughts. She pats the back of her head somewhat inconspicuously. I mirror the movement, touching the back of my head, where Margaret had secured my hair with a long, sharp pin. My fingers skim the cool metal, tears pricking my eyes. Margaret had found a way to ensure I wouldn't be without the means to defend myself. I want to kiss her cheek, but I've stalled long enough.

Breathing deeply, I give Margaret a grateful smile and take Lady Isabelle's arm.

"Oh, wait!" Margaret takes an ornate amber bottle from the vanity. She spritzes me from head to toe, bathing me in vanilla perfume. I sneeze, earning an airy chuckle from Lady Isabelle.

"Shall we?" Lady Isabelle asks, smiling warmly.

I nod before I can change my mind, allowing her to lead me out of the room. Every step down the long hallway echoes the throbbing of my heart. I don't know why I expect Will to appear in each doorframe we pass, but when we make it to the end of the hall, and the muffled chatter of guests arriving below drifts up the stairwell, my heart begins to pound for an entirely different reason.

For the past week, Henry, Killian, Jack—even little Annie— have been drilling me every chance they got on the proper etiquette I'm to obey this evening. *Graciously accept invitations to dance. Do not dance with the same partner more than three times. Do not cross or enter the ballroom unattended. Do not linger at the supper table.* I go over each rule meticulously, careful to commit them all to memory, but the dos and don'ts of attending a ball are the least of my worries, as Henry will be there to guide me through.

It is not *how* I am to be that gnaws at my insides. It's *who* I am to be.

Violet Wagner, orphaned daughter of a cobbler from the Savage Coast. According to the story I am to tell concerning my false identity, Lord Castor had loaned my father, Hans Wagner, the money to start a business when I was still a child. Hans had passed away last year due to an unknown illness and I had taken over the business, which turned out to be rather lucrative. Should anyone ask, I am visiting the Castors as an old family friend.

But, Killian admitted when crafting such a tale, my so-called freedom will matter not to the Nightweavers in attendance. They see the act of liberation as a farce, one not to be taken seriously, and while I will be Henry's guest, many will see me as a plaything of sorts.

My stomach tightens, and I remind myself that it doesn't matter what anyone thinks of me. They may not know the truth, but I do. I am more than just some human doll to be paraded about.

I am something to be feared.

I am death at the other end of a blade—*er*—hairpin.

I am…way out of my element.

"Wait here," Lady Isabelle says soothingly. "Henry will be up in a moment to retrieve you."

Mouth too dry to speak, I simply nod. The moment Lady Isabelle rounds the corner, disappearing down the stairwell, a dizzying sort of feeling sweeps over me. My body tingles, my face is hot. I take a step back, turning, ready to bolt...when a low whistle gives me pause.

"Violet?" Henry's voice is quiet, tentative.

I turn to find him lingering on the top step, his eyes wide.

"Oh, don't look at me like that," I snap, flushing.

He laughs, and I'm once again reminded that Henry was held captive aboard the *Deathwail*, too. That they had dumped him off the coast somewhere and left him to die, and yet, he'd survived. His laughter comforts me in a strange way. It gives me hope. It gives me courage. Without thinking, I tug at the strip of yellow chiffon around my neck, pulling it loose as if to free myself from the memory of that rope.

Henry takes another step, towering over me in the narrow hall. His gaze catches on the scars at my throat and his jaw works, any trace of laughter now gone from his face. His eyes meet mine, his brows knitted. He opens his mouth as if to say something, but he must think better of it.

He shakes his head. "My brother is a fool."

I nearly choke, arranging the chiffon to cover the scars once more. "What makes you say that?"

His gaze shifts and he looks over my shoulder, where I know the green baize door is closed. "He'll never truly understand what he has until it's no longer his."

My chest aches, but not because of what he said about Will. "We'll find her, Henry."

He gives a tight nod, his eyes narrow. Then his face relaxes and he straightens, extending his arm to me. The corner of his mouth kicks up. "You smell like a cupcake."

I snort, taking his arm. "Is that a compliment?"

His nose wrinkles. "Not quite."

He escorts me down the first few steps, and I find myself searching for the tattoo of an *X* just behind his ear—the mark of those held captive aboard the *Deathwail*. Before we round the corner, where the landing will expose us to the gathering crowd below, Henry turns to me, and I pretend I hadn't been staring.

"You look better than any Nightweaver could ever dream of," he says, his expression sincere. Then his lip quirks into a teasing smile, and he adds, "*That* was a compliment. Though, I wouldn't be too pleased with myself if I were you. Trudy Birtwistle might try to stab you before the night is over."

"For a dance with you?" I ask with mock surprise. "If that's the case, we shall duel for your hand."

Henry laughs again, and the anxious flutter in my stomach calms as we take another step, and another. The chatter below is all but deafening. We round the corner, stepping down onto the landing, and—

Silence.

I've never seen the main hall so full of people. Every eye finds me, but rather than the hateful looks I had expected to receive, I am met with a vibrant curiosity that nearly causes my steps to falter. Some even appear envious as Henry clears his throat, signaling for me to continue down the stairwell. But the instant I manage to lift my foot to take another step, I see him, and my heart stops beating altogether.

Will.

CHAPTER TWENTY-FOUR

T he young Lord Castor stands under an archway, dressed in his finest scarlet military jacket trimmed with shimmering gold thread. Will's dark, curly hair has been cut short and he stands a bit straighter, conditioned by months spent at constant attention. His wide eyes meet mine from across the room, and I forget how to breathe.

My first instinct is to let go of Henry and race down the stairwell, into Will's embrace. To let the past three months become no more than a distant memory. But just as I've begun to withdraw from Henry, the crowd parts enough to reveal the two women in gaudy ballgowns clinging to Will's either arm. The girl to his right whispers flirtatiously in his ear, and I taste something like acid at the back of my throat as the other throws her head back in laughter.

Will never takes his eyes off me, his jaw set, face humorless even as the women break into a fit of obnoxious giggling. I tighten my grip on Henry's arm and look away, severing the connection between Will and me. My heart pounds in my throat, making it difficult to breathe. I want to keep moving, but the suffocating attention of the crowd—along with the knowledge that Will stands only a few feet away, but that he feels more like a stranger to me now than he ever has—keeps me rooted to this spot.

"Henry?" I turn to find him already staring at me, a look of sympathy in his charcoal eyes. Beneath it, however, mischief sparks.

Henry gives me a wicked grin. "If you're going to ask me to help you make my brother jealous, the answer is yes."

I'm not sure what I was going to say, but I don't suppress the smile that plays on my lips at his idea. Aboard the *Lightbringer*, Owen and I were always working a scheme. Since that fateful day at sea, I've begun to feel as if I might never find someone equally as interested in stirring up trouble. But Henry seems inclined to indulge me, and when he pulls me even closer, making a show of the way he leans in, an odd rush of excitement chases away all my fear.

"He's going to kill me for this," Henry whispers, his breath tickling my ear as we descend the steps.

I feel as though we'll never reach the bottom. The crowd continues to stare—a gathering of local merchants, aristocrats, and traveling dignitaries. All here to celebrate the dawn of an era in which the Nightweavers took control of the land and drove us out to sea. And amongst the assembly of Nightweavers, aside from the servants Lady Isabelle had employed, I am the only human—something that the Nightweavers have begun to realize, their looks of curiosity turning sour. I don't have to wonder how they would be looking at me if they knew I was a pirate. The looks they give me merely for being human are enough to tell me it wouldn't be friendly. But tonight, I don the mask of Violet Wagner, a friend of Henry's from the small coastal town of Eldritch. Tonight, I pretend I am one of the few somewhat-free humans of the Eerie. Tonight, I pretend that the months I've spent missing Will never happened.

Because how could I miss someone who so clearly doesn't feel the same way? He didn't even bother to find me before the ball this evening. Not only that, but he's arrived with a woman on each arm. That shameless, debauched rake…To think I've waited three months, just for him to act as if the time we'd spent together meant nothing to him.

As if I meant nothing to him.

Focus, Violet, I chide myself. I'm here tonight for one reason and one reason only: to learn everything I can about the prince of the Eerie. And if Captain Shade were to make an appearance… well, I'm not sure what I'll do.

"I wish they'd stop staring," I mutter through my teeth.

Henry chuckles. "They're probably trying to figure out what beautification enchantments you've cast over yourself this evening."

I pinch his arm. "Stop being nice to me."

He laughs again, and as the crowd parts, I catch a brief glimpse of Will glaring at his brother before I lose sight of him again.

"Might I remind you," Henry says, "that I am your escort for the evening? It would be impolite not to compliment you."

I snort. "I think I prefer it when you're being impolite."

The second we reach the bottom step, a reedy girl in a pale-pink gown makes her way towards us, her burgundy curls bobbing. "Henry!" She plasters on a wide smile, though when she glances at me, her eyes flash with disgust. "Happy Reckoning Day."

"Trudy," Henry replies flatly. He draws me closer, using me as a shield. "Have you met Violet?"

I tense, expecting her to recognize me. To call Henry out and expose me for what I really am.

Thankfully, she hardly spares me a second glance. "Charmed," she grits out, that wide smile giving her a crazed appearance. A haze of smoke seems to cloud the air around her head, like a halo of shadows, but I blink, and it's gone. "Henry, would you like to—"

Another hush falls over the crowd, and Trudy's words die out on a breath as she turns towards the entrance of the main hall.

He enters without introduction but not without notice, striding lazily into the main hall as if he were taking a Sunday stroll, his hands tucked loosely in his pockets. The entire household at once becomes so quiet, every step he takes seems to echo through the crowded space in an unnerving tempo.

The prince of the Eerie looks nothing like the monster from my nightmares.

He cuts a striking figure in a black military jacket trimmed with scarlet thread, the gilded epaulets on either shoulder glinting in the gaslight. I study his somewhat delicate features, his angular jaw and high, hollow cheekbones, his skin tanned from months spent on a battlefield and at sea. It appears as if he'd arrived on horseback, his chin-length, sandy blond hair effortlessly tousled, giving him a louche quality that conveys some kind of divine authority.

Dangerous. Deadly.

He surveys the crowd, his expression aloof. A few women—including Trudy Birtwistle—curtsey as if it were the only proper reaction to his sudden, imposing presence, but he doesn't appear to take notice. Even from ten feet away, his blue eyes seem to glow from within as he fixes his gaze on—oh, Stars—

Me.

His eyebrows quirk, and I think I see the hint of a smile playing on his full lips, but he looks away so quickly, I feel I've imagined the whole thing.

He adjusts his blood-red sash, bedecked with medals, his lips curving wickedly at the sight of Will. I hadn't noticed when the crowd had cleared enough to put Henry and me at the forefront, along with Will and the two women who remain kneeling on either side of him.

"You should have warned me." The prince's voice is unexpectedly light and pleasant. He speaks with an accent unbefitting a royal. Rather, he sounds like a commoner or even… "A pirate?" The prince tsks softly. "In a ballgown? And I thought I'd seen it all."

My blood runs cold. So much for pretending.

Will's expression remains unreadable as he untangles himself from the two women and strides forward to meet the prince in the center of the hall. He keeps a calm pace, his composure unruffled, but the muscles in Henry's forearm tense and he shifts slightly, as if to shield me. Will clears his throat, glancing at me out of the corner of his eye. I think I see a small measure of hurt there—and surprise. "I was unaware my brother would be escorting Ms. Oberon this evening."

Oberon. Not Wagner.

There wasn't time to inform Will of my false identity for the evening. Henry figured he would have a moment to speak to Will in private. But now… having heard that there is in fact a pirate in their midst, every guest's eye finds me again. Only this time, I can feel the heat of their hatred as if it were a tangible thing, pressing in on me, shrinking me down and—

"I should think not," the prince muses, that wicked smirk causing my stomach to roil as he turns his full attention on me. Something about his lilting voice is familiar, hovering just at the edge of my memory, but I shove the thought aside.

He stands a head taller than the Castor boys, towering over me, but he is even more lithe than Will, moving with the grace of a trained dancer as he extends his black-gloved hand to me and…*bows?*

I think I hear someone gasp—probably Trudy—but my head buzzes with static, white heat. Henry murmurs something before releasing me. I barely hear him. The next thing I know, my fingertips brush the satin of the prince's glove and my hand is in his gentle grasp.

He presses a kiss to my knuckles, and I can't help but revel in the thrill of seeing Trudy out of the corner of my eye, fanning herself as if she might faint.

"I had hoped to meet you during my visit," the prince murmurs, his lips lingering near my gloved hand, his blue eyes— as deep as the ocean itself—never leaving mine. He straightens fully, adding loudly enough for all to hear, "Your presence at this ball is a delight, Ms. Oberon. And while I graciously accept the title of guest of honor, I am most inclined to share that position with you, the only human brave enough to come here tonight and prove that a pirate can indeed be thoroughly... *reformed.*"

My cheeks heat as hushed murmurs creep throughout the room like thorny vines, tearing into my nerves with every whisper. Still, the prince's eyes remain locked on mine—a challenge.

"Ms. Oberon," the prince says, his mischievous grin sending shivers down my spine, "would you grant me the pleasure of joining me in the first dance?"

CHAPTER TWENTY-FIVE

How did I get here? I wonder as the prince offers his arm to me, my heart beating wildly in my chest. I long for the quiet solitude of the galley onboard the *Lightbringer*; the ease of going unnoticed for hours on end, lost to my duties, alone with only my own self-grievances and unabashed by the thoughts and cares of strangers—strangers with nothing better to do but gawk as I hesitate to accept the prince's offer.

Henry clears his throat and I lurch forward, latching onto the prince's arm as if it were a life raft. I cling to him, my thoughts abuzz, as he escorts me from the main hall into the ballroom in the east wing. If I had any notion that this would spare me from the prying eyes in the main hall, I hadn't considered what would await me beyond the tall oaken double doors.

"In all my years," the prince murmurs, his warm breath caressing the shell of my ear, "I've not seen even the queen herself command such attention." There's a hint of a smile in his voice, but playfulness seems foreign to me now. My stomach twists into knots.

I feel like I'm going to be sick.

I hear the voice that introduces us, but I can't make out what he says over the blood pounding in my eardrums. My gaze darts about the lavish ballroom. Lady Isabelle had taken pains to decorate the space—quaint and small, she had informed me, compared to the ballroom at Castle Grim—in a fashion befitting a royal affair, hiring girls and boys from town to assist Sybil and Lewis with the preparations. Henry told the truth when he'd said his mother had spared no expense. Crystal chandeliers bedecked in red ribbons, crimson carnations arranged in grand bouquets, black linens embroidered with the scarlet sun of the Eerie; every inch of the ballroom speaks to Lady Isabelle's elegance—and wealth.

On either side of the room, rows of double doors allow a gentle breeze to drift in, carrying with it the scent of roses and sodden grass. I fight the urge to race through the open doors, into the garden, towards the apple tree tunnel...

The prince's hand slips to my waist, his other clutching my hand in a firm but delicate manner. My body feels as though it's caught fire as his deep-blue eyes find my gaze once more. I think of the hair pin Margaret had gifted me—consider skewering his eye with it—but, unfortunately, this night is not one for bloodshed.

The musicians begin to play as the prince sweeps me onto the dance floor, gliding as if his feet need not touch the ground. I pretend I'm dancing with Jack in the stable, going over the steps in my mind as if they are vital to my survival, but in this cumbersome dress, I can hardly keep up.

"*It's like swordplay,*" Killian had said yesterday, instructing me every so often on the proper posture or movement, "*only without the threat of being stabbed.*"

I would prefer being stabbed to this.

The prince leans in as if to whisper, and I remember all the stories Owen used to tell me about the fearsome prince of the Eerie. Though I wish I could stop myself, I flinch.

He tilts his head, frowning slightly. "You're afraid of me."

Those words are like kindling to the fire that has been raging inside of me for months—years.

"Afraid?" I scoff, my blood boiling. "Of you?"

He smirks. "You flinched."

"I twitched."

"You have a habit of twitching?"

"All my life."

He laughs, and the silvery sound catches me so off guard that *dammit*, I flinch again.

"Perhaps you should see a doctor," he says smoothly.

I nearly trip over my own feet. "A physical exam would be more exciting than this," I mutter.

His thumb draws a lazy circle on my hip, and my stomach somersaults. He smiles, flashing brilliant teeth—teeth I once feared would tear into my flesh. "That can be arranged."

This time, I *accidentally* stomp on his foot. A rush of satisfaction sweeps over me as he winces. "You're exactly like I thought you would be," I say, although I hadn't expected him to be so...normal. Or handsome.

His blue eyes twinkle as he draws me closer to him, closer than Jack informed me was appropriate for ballroom dancing. "And that is?"

I open my mouth, but no sound comes out. Something about the breeze shifts, and I catch a whiff of salty sea air. It clings to his uniform like cologne, crisp and refreshing, reminding me of home.

A vibration buzzes in my chest—so soft, I hardly notice, but...my gaze settles on the pulse of his throat, on the steady thrum of blood pumping through his body, as if I could *see* the span of veins beneath his skin. It calls to me, like my beloved ocean, drawing me in, soothing me...

"Is something the matter?" The prince's breath tickles my nose, smelling of strawberry wine. I'm closer to him than I was a moment ago, but—that can't be right. Had I closed the gap between us?

His blue eyes search my face, and I can't help but wonder if that is genuine concern flickering in his gaze. "Violet?"

His casual use of my first name jars me out of my daze. I had almost forgotten where I was—who I was with. By the grace of the Stars I hadn't stopped dancing altogether, although the prince seems to be hauling me about the ballroom like a sack of flour rather than a dance partner. And strangely, even when we had been speaking, I hadn't noticed the hundred or so people watching our every movement. But I notice them now, and again bile creeps into my throat.

Baron Rencourt stands near Lord Castor, along with Lady Isabelle and George Birtwistle. All four of them watch us with a carefully casual sort of interest that hardly befits the spectacle of a servant girl from their household dancing with the heir to the throne of the Eerie. But there is something...*off* about Lord Castor's expression. He has a guilty look about him in the way he surveys the room, as if he were waiting for a hammer to drop. I realize it could have something to do with the repercussions that are sure to follow my presence here this evening. Still, a weight, heavy and uncomfortable, settles in my stomach at the sight of him.

Beside him, however, Killian smiles, toasting me with his glass, and to the Admiral's left, Henry mirrors the gesture. The weight in my stomach lifts, but the uneasy feeling remains.

Will is nowhere to be seen.

"Your name," I say, if only to focus on something other than the crowd of Nightweavers, or Lord Castor's troubling behavior, or Will's absence. "You know my name, but I don't know yours."

I curse myself for even asking. Lewis always says that it's much harder to put a knife in someone once you know their name. Still, I don't think something as insignificant as a name could overturn a lifetime of hatred.

"My name?" The prince's voice is soft. He quirks his brows, eyeing me curiously, as if I had just done some sort of magic trick that demanded explanation. "You really don't know?"

"Should I?"

"I'm the Prince."

"That's a title, not a name."

"Of course," he says, a smirk playing on his lips. "But being as I am the prince, it is unusual for one of my subjects not to know the name that follows the title."

"I'm not one of your subjects." The instant the words leave my mouth, I wish I could take them back, if only for the sake of my family. I don't fear the prince's punishment, but my disrespect could cost my family the future they've spent the past few months working to secure—and their very lives.

The prince laughs again, causing my heart to stutter. "That you are not, Violet Oberon."

My mouth parts slightly, but the breath I take never makes it to my lungs. "You...you're not angry with me?"

He quirks a brow. "Should I be?"

"I shouldn't have said that."

"I'm glad you did."

"But..." I shake my head, looking—surely—even more ignorant than I feel. "You're the prince."

"Titus," he murmurs. "My name is Titus."

Titus. The name steals whatever breath I have left.

"Like the constellation?" I manage to ask.

He dips his chin, his jaw clenched even as he smiles. "The very one."

I can't believe my ears. The prince of the Eerie, named after perhaps the most revered hero to have ever been immortalized in the stars. A human. A pirate.

The *first* pirate.

Owen used to tell me the story of Titus and the Twelve Keys. How he ruled the seas as if he had been given dominion over all the waters of the earth. He is more than a legend among our people—he *wrote* the pirate Creed. I would have thought he'd be hated among the Nightweavers—that they wouldn't deign to speak his name.

"I know what you're thinking," the prince says drily, his lip tilting up on one side. "Why would my parents name me after your people's hero?"

I study his face—his blue eyes, as tumultuous as a raging sea. I no longer hear the music. I no longer notice the crowd of Nightweavers, judging my every move, hating me with every fiber of their being. It is only the prince and me. Only this moment.

"Why?" I whisper.

His grin fades, his expression oddly serious as he leans in close—so close, I feel the ghost of his breath on my lips, warm and sweet. "Hatred is a curious thing."

He withdraws from me in one swift movement, leaving me unsteady, as if the gentle breeze might simply carry me away. I hadn't noticed when the music had stopped. I hadn't even realized we were no longer dancing.

The prince bows, his elegant posturing a betrayal to his infamous brutality, and I almost forget to curtsey—*almost*. The movement is stiff and unnatural, and I nearly fall over, but the prince—*Titus*—is there to take my hand as I rise to my feet once more. He watches me like a child might watch a butterfly, his eyes wide with wonder.

"Did you feel that?" he asks, but I can barely hear him over the music as it strikes up a new, more upbeat tempo.

"Feel what?" The orchestra drowns me out.

He stares at our clasped hands, his mouth parting on a breath. The Nightweavers converge on the dance floor, and all at once it is entirely too warm, the muggy odor of sweat and perfume settling over us like a dense fog.

It seems as if a mask slips over Titus's expression. He goes from looking curious and teasing to cool and indifferent in the span of a heartbeat. He casts a brief glance over my shoulder, his lip curling slightly, but I chalk it up to my mind playing tricks on me again, because in the blink of an eye he's grinning like a child who's just learned a new secret.

I feel a presence behind me as Titus's hand slips from mine.

"May I have this dance?" Will's deep voice sends a shiver down my spine.

Titus gives Will a terse nod, but mine and the prince's gazes remain locked together as if neither of us can bring ourselves to look away.

Did you feel that?

"I trust her to your care, Lord William," Titus says before stepping past me, swiftly exiting the dance floor, swallowed up by the throng of Nightweavers.

Something in my chest rips, and it nearly knocks the wind out of me. *Good riddance.*

I turn, facing Will and his proffered hand. He looks the same as he did all those months ago, when we first met. Only... something has changed. Rather than amusement dancing in his dark-green eyes, he looks haunted. It's as if he had discovered that the question he'd long been asking indeed had an answer— an answer he couldn't reconcile and that had left him searching still.

Has it only been three months?

I take his hand. At his touch, electricity sparks between our palms, warm and buzzing; that old, familiar feeling of comfort sweeps through me despite the barricade of our gloves. My eyes widen on a sharp intake of breath, and he glances up at me through thick eyelashes only for a moment before his gaze drifts to the nine silver stars embroidered along my neckline. The hint of a smirk crosses his face, and my heart leaps.

In that brief second, his eyes find mine, sparkling with mischief and pride, and I catch a glimpse of him—Will. *My* Will.

But he is gone just as quickly as he'd appeared, replaced by this new, callous soldier that stands before me. Gingerly, his other hand finds my waist as the music ushers us into a slower, more thoughtful sort of dance. A dance meant for lovers. Not... whatever we are.

Will's lips linger near my ear as he draws me in, and I swallow a sigh of relief at the closeness, the intimacy of the gesture. But just as I've begun to relax, to let the tension melt away, he speaks quietly in my ear, his deep voice chilling me to the bone.

"What were you thinking?"

CHAPTER TWENTY-SIX

I don't know what I had expected him to say, but that wasn't it.

I draw back, my brows raised. "I beg your pardon?"

He grinds his teeth, looking everywhere in the ballroom but at me. "Did Henry put you up to this?"

I cough out a dry laugh. "It's been three months since we've spoken and those are your first words to me?"

The shadows beneath Will's eyes seem to darken. "You shouldn't be here."

His words are like a dagger to my heart. I start to pull away, but his grip tightens on my hand, his fingers desperately clutching my waist.

"Why?" I demand, thick, angry tears forming a lump in my throat. "Because I'm not like you?"

His expression softens and he shakes his head, blinking as if to clear himself from a daze. "Violet, that's not what I—"

"For your information," I snap, "Henry invited me because we're...friends." That word sounds strange coming out of my mouth, but it feels right. True. "Unlike you and me. And furthermore, I'm not just here to make your life miserable. I'm not even sure why you'd ask me to dance when it's obvious you have your choice of more *suitable* partners. At any rate, I'd rather not speak to you at all. I'm only here because the Order asked that Henry and I keep an eye on the prince tonight."

Will snorts. "You're doing an excellent job at that."

His nonchalant response sets my teeth on edge. "You already know," I whisper, my voice shaking with barely contained fury. "You know I joined the Order."

"Of course I know," he nearly growls. "*Someone* bothered to write me back."

His fierce green eyes are full of hurt as he watches his brother dancing a few feet from us. Trudy Birtwistle clings to Henry, who appears to be attempting to put as much space between them as he possibly can. I feel a stab of guilt for not stepping in, but after having spent the past three months angry at Will for leaving, angry at myself for missing him, I can't see past the rage clouding my vision.

"Look at me," I demand, my voice breaking. "Dammit, *look at me*, Will."

His gaze snaps to mine, and at once, I forget what I was going to say.

"What?" he asks roughly.

"What?" I echo, my voice harsher than I had intended. "You lied to me. Kept secrets from me. When were you going to tell me about the Order? About everything?"

He looks away again, his throat working. "You don't understand."

"You're right," I say quietly. "I don't understand."

He tilts his head, his green eyes roving my face as if checking for some kind of injury.

"I thought..." I sigh, my rage cooling into hardened apathy. "It doesn't matter what I thought. I spent every day of the last three months wondering if you were dead. And then, tonight, I was stupid enough to think you would come to see me. That you had missed me, too."

"You missed me?" he murmurs, prompting me to meet his gaze. His eyes are wide, brimming with an emotion I can't put into words.

My cheeks blaze with uncomfortable heat. "That's not important," I say quickly. "Instead of seeking me out the moment you arrived—and I see why, now, because it appears you were preoccupied—you sent me that bouquet and—"

"A bouquet?" He frowns, his brows drawn. "I didn't send you any bouquet."

His admission is like a splash of ice-cold water to my senses. My heart twists. "Then who—"

The music stops, my voice carrying over the sudden silence. A few Nightweavers cast me hateful looks, but then Henry is there, blocking the rest of the partygoers from my view. He peels Trudy off his arm as if she were indeed a leech.

"Time to switch partners," Henry says, shooting me a pointed look.

I don't look back at Will as I take Henry's proffered hand. But as Henry sweeps me into another, more jaunty dance, I glimpse Trudy over Henry's shoulder, standing alone, with Will nowhere to be seen.

"I don't know about you," Henry says, "but I'm damn near sick of dancing." He steers us towards the edge of the ballroom. "Care for some fresh air?"

"Do you have to ask?"

"I was being polite."

I roll my eyes. "I thought we discussed that."

His lip quirks. "And what did we discuss?"

"That you shouldn't."

Henry laughs, taking my hand and nearly dragging me through a set of open double doors, onto the lawn. Once we've made it out of earshot of the guests lingering outside and are secluded by the rosebushes of the east garden, Henry releases my hand.

"So?" he asks, straightening the lapels of his tux. "What was that all about?"

"What was what all about?"

He gives me a dull look. "Did you dance with *another* prince tonight?"

"Oh," I murmur. "That."

"Yes." He smirks. "That."

I shrug. "You tell me. It's not as if I expected him to…well, notice me at all."

Henry laughs sharply. "Notice you?" He laughs again, offering his arm. "You seriously underestimate yourself."

"I do not!" I insist, taking him by the arm and allowing him to escort me through the garden at a lazy, comfortable pace.

He quirks a brow. "Whatever you say."

In the distance, the golden lights of Ink Haven shimmer as if swaddled in a blanket of *Manan*. The balmy night air is bereft of ocean brine, infused instead with the sweet aroma of flowers and pastries.

"My brother…" Henry shakes his head. "Every time he returns from battle, he seems different. But this time…" He lets out a low sigh. "I've never seen him like this."

I wrinkle my nose, ignoring the emotion clogging my throat. "He's an asshole."

"He's just come home from war."

"I've spent my whole life at war," I snap. "That's no excuse for being an asshole."

"You're kind of an asshole, though."

I dig my elbow into his ribs. "You tried to kill me!"

He chokes out a pained laugh. "I'm kind of an asshole, too."

I don't fight the smile that touches my lips. But as we pass a cluster of white lilies, my smile fades. "Henry?"

"Yes?"

I come to a halt, turning to face him. "Do you ever think of it?"

The question is as much a shock to me as it is to him.

He furrows his brows, his voice soft. "Think of what?"

"The…" I hesitate, worrying my bottom lip. "The *Deathwail.*"

Henry pulls back, putting distance between us—distance I didn't realize hadn't been there before. His mouth twists into a wrathful frown. "Why would you ask me that?"

I shed the strip of yellow chiffon intended to hide the scar around my throat, snagging Henry's gaze. Understanding flickers in his eyes, his expression softening once more.

"Right. Before he left for Hellion, Will mentioned you had…" he trails off, looking unsure of himself. "I honestly didn't believe him. I didn't realize your scar…" He looks up at me, his throat working on a swallow. "How long?"

"Two months." My voice is no more than a whisper. "I still…I still feel trapped there, sometimes. It's worse when I'm—"

"Alone," he finishes, removing the distance between us, his hand outstretched. Gently, hesitantly, his fingers trace the scar, and I don't shy away from his touch. "Not a day goes by that I do not think of it."

He withdraws his hand, his mouth pressed tight. "Stars, Violet," he says, tilting his head. "No one lasts longer than a few days in those cells."

"You did," I say lamely. Before I can stop myself, I reach out, my fingertips grazing the scar that carves a jagged line starting at his temple, down his cheek, my touch featherlight. I withdraw just as my hand brushes his shirt collar.

His swallow is audible. He gives me a *look*, and I see it— the wound. Not like a physical scar, to be worn with pride, but something...deeper. The kind of wound that never truly heals.

"Sometimes..." he breaks off, clears his throat. "Sometimes I wish I hadn't lasted twelve days."

His charcoal eyes find mine, and if it weren't for the moonlight, I might not have seen the tears glazing his scarred face. "They took everything from me." He looks away, his skin flushed with angry splotches of red. "I never thought I'd meet someone else who could understand. But two months...Violet, how did you survive?"

"Sometimes it feels like I didn't." I touch my throat, my fingers skimming the raised flesh. "They were afraid of me. Wouldn't touch me. They..." A humorless laugh escapes me. "They thought I would bring a curse on them. So they tried to hang me."

"And?"

"And it didn't work the first time."

His eyes widen. "The first time?"

I nod, my chest tightening as I remember the way Owen cared for me after Captain Shade cut me down from that rope. For the first few nights, he didn't leave my side, even after Margaret ordered him to let me be. "They thought something was wrong with their noose. So, they cut me down and tried again."

"Stars," Henry chokes out, pain—not pity—flickering in his gaze. "How are you alive?"

I lift a shoulder. I'd been dangling from the mainmast for six minutes before Shade overtook the *Deathwail*'s crew and cut the rope. "Don't know," I say. "But I…" My throat constricts, my voice coming out thick and strangled. "I *felt* cursed."

I think back to what Will had said on the train that day, about my ability to see the Sylks. *They think it to be part of a curse.* I know I'm not a Shifter, but…could it be true? Could I really be cursed?

Henry takes my hands in his. "I'm glad you lived," he murmurs, his expression bereft of any teasing.

"I never thought I'd say this, but…" I give his hands a squeeze. "I'm glad to have met you, Henry Castor."

He smiles softly. "Even though I tried to kill you?"

"Especially because you tried to kill me."

Laughter bubbles up inside me, spilling out of my mouth. Despite everything, I can't control it. I don't want to. Henry appears startled, but only for a moment. And then he's laughing, too. I'm not sure how long we remain this way, but I laugh so hard my stomach hurts. I haven't laughed like this since…since Owen.

Just like that, the laughter is snuffed out. I fall silent, grasping my wrist, where the band of braided leather forms tiny bumps beneath my glove.

Henry stills. "Violet, are you—"

A branch snaps. The sound of muffled breathing roots me to the spot. I search the gaps in the bushes, convinced I see Captain Shade's scarlet mask everywhere I look. Has he come to kill the prince, like the rumors suggested? I can't imagine he would attempt such a thing at the manor belonging to Will, his supposed confidant, but anything is possible. And if he *has* come, then Henry and I have failed to do the one thing the Order asked of us.

"Is someone there?" Henry demands, scanning the dense rosebushes.

My hand inches for the hairpin at the back of my head, ready to strike, when—

"Got you!" Albert leaps from behind a rosebush, tackling me to the ground.

It happens so fast, but the very second Albert appears, Henry throws his hand out, sparks of electricity skittering through the air. A bolt of light strikes Albert in the back and his body seizes as he rolls off me, his eyes wide with shock.

He doesn't blink.

CHAPTER TWENTY-SEVEN

66 lbert?" I shake him. "Henry..." My voice trembles with panic. "He isn't breathing. He isn't *breathing.*"

Henry shoves me out of the way, kneeling over Albert's body. He places a hand to Albert's chest, closes his eyes. The seconds drag on, spiraling into eternity.

"Come on," Henry grinds out. "*Come on!*"

Nothing. My chest squeezes tight, making it impossible to breathe. I can't lose another brother. *I can't—*

Albert's mouth parts with a strangled gasp for air. I lurch for him, cradling him close to my chest.

"I didn't mean to," Henry stammers, shaking his head. "I didn't—"

"I know," I say, stroking Albert's hair. I had been prepared to strike him myself, only Henry had been faster. "You saved him. That's all that matters."

Henry presses his lips together, his face grim. "I shouldn't have had to."

"But you did," I counter. "Thank you."

Henry snorts, shoving his trembling hands in his pockets. "I electrocute your little brother and you thank me?"

At that, Albert pulls away from me, twisting to look up at Henry. His hair stands on end, his eyes bright with wonder. "Can you teach me how to do that?"

Henry and I share a comical look, dissolving the thick cloud of panic still lingering in the air.

"I think it's time you get back to...whatever it is you're supposed to be doing," Henry says, extending his hand to Albert.

"Right!" Albert jumps to his feet as if he hadn't just suffered a fatal injury. "Jack sent me to get you. Lady Castor told him to tell me to tell you there's some people she wants you to meet."

Henry groans, rolling his eyes. "There always is." He casts me an exasperated glance, dusting off his jacket. "Coming?"

"Not yet," I say, waving them off. "I think I need a minute to myself."

Henry looks as if he might insist, but then he dips his chin. "Be careful," he says, his expression entirely too thoughtful for someone who wished me dead only a few months ago.

"You too," I say, saluting him. "I hear these waters are infested with leeches."

Henry snorts a laugh, mussing Albert's hair as they turn and make their way back through the garden. With his other hand, he makes a rude gesture behind his back, and a somewhat hysterical giggle escapes me.

I watch as they disappear around the bend. Alone among the roses, I hear the distant sounds of music and chatter fading beneath the wind rustling the bushes. Wind that carries the faint scent of briny air...

"*Violet.*"

My heart leaps into my throat.

"Owen?" My gaze darts wildly about the garden. There—a lock of dark-blond hair rounds the corner up ahead.

Owen.

I chase after him, thorns tearing at my arms as I race down a narrow pathway. I turn the corner, my pulse throbbing in my temples.

"Owen!" My voice falters as I skid to a halt.

Owen is gone.

My stomach sours. Am I losing my mind? I know it can't really be Owen. Owen is dead. I watched him die.

But the Shifter *had* taken on his likeness on the hill that day all those weeks ago...

Behind me, footsteps fill the void of silence ringing in my ears. I tense, remembering the hairpin near the nape of my neck, praying to the Stars that I'm fast enough.

In the blink of an eye, I whirl, hairpin drawn. I lash out, but a strong, calloused hand grips my wrist.

"I don't know who this Owen fellow is," the prince says, his voice light as he eyes the hairpin an inch from his jugular. "But this seems like a strange custom for greeting."

Chapter Twenty-Eight

I try to speak, but no words come. My mouth works as I stare up at the prince—at the hairpin hovering near his throat.

"This wouldn't be the first time I've rendered a woman speechless," Titus drawls, his lips tilting slightly. He cuts his gaze at the hairpin. "However, that's new."

My grip on the hairpin loosens, but he doesn't let go of my hand. His warmth bleeds through my glove, and I realize he no longer wears his own. I gape at the ink tattooing the back of his bare hand—a sparrow in flight. The mark of a seafaring pirate.

Why would he have that tattoo?

"I meant no offense," I manage to say, meeting his haughty gaze once more.

His deep-blue eyes glow like the sea set aflame. "The fault is all mine." A coy, tight-lipped smile as he releases my hand. "I clearly startled you."

"You did nothing of the sort," I argue, attempting to pin my hair back the way Margaret had styled it. The prince watches, eyes flickering with subtle amusement, as I twist the upper half of my hair and secure it in a sloppy fashion. I'm tempted to use his face as a pincushion.

"Forgive me," he purrs. "It seems I've misread the situation." His gaze rakes over me, a wry grin on his lips. "You see, usually when someone appears startled, it's because they are."

"I'm not—" I glance down at my dress, where grass stains my knees, and groan. "You didn't startle me."

"You're right." He winks. "'Startled' does seem to be the wrong word. Flustered, perhaps?"

"I'm not flustered," I grind out, starting past him.

"Of course not." He follows me, his long strides keeping a lazy, effortless pace. "You were expecting someone, obviously. Just not me."

I roll my eyes. "Obviously."

I search the ground where Henry and I had stood only a few minutes before, but the strip of yellow chiffon is missing— just like the knapsack had disappeared that night near the conservatory. My heart drops into my stomach, panic flooding my senses, when—

"Looking for this?" Titus extends the scrap of fabric, and I notice a matching sparrow tattoo on his other hand—a twin set.

I reach for the fabric, but he yanks it back. The ring on his forefinger catches my eye. The Royal signet. A fresh film of scarlet wax besmirches the sun of the Eerie, causing dread to pool low in my gut.

His brows knit. "Who is Owen?"

I make to grab the fabric again, but he's too fast, holding it over his head, out of reach. He gives me an expectant look, one that sets my teeth on edge.

"Do I know him?" he asks, a portrait of innocent curiosity.

My cheeks burn. "You wouldn't," I bite out.

"I might surprise you," he says, tilting his head conspiratorially. Moonlight casts an angelic glow on half of his face, making him appear soft and warm and tragically beautiful. The other half is concealed by shadows, giving him the sinister appearance I always thought he would have. He flashes his teeth in a smile meant to charm—like a viper poised to strike. "I know a lot of people."

"I'm sure you do." My fingers twitch, aching to lodge the hairpin in his throat. "Just as I'm also sure you don't know him."

The corner of his mouth lifts, obnoxiously playful. "And how can you be so sure?"

His boyish teasing makes a part of me almost wish I didn't have to ruin his pleasant mood—*almost*. The other part of me wants to take from him what he took from me. To make him bleed.

I pull my shoulders back, schooling my expression into one that I hope looks as cold and cruel as I feel. "Because he's dead. You have your captain to thank for that."

Titus's eyes widen slightly, his mouth forming a hard line. "I—" He takes a sharp breath, his jaw clenching. "I'm so sorry, Violet. Truly, I am. Will mentioned there'd been casualties…"

He lowers his arm, the scrap of fabric glowing gold in the lamplight. Sorrow flickers in his eyes, and his face is drawn with a look of genuine regret. He appears dutiful, like a soldier awaiting command, glancing at the strip of yellow chiffon still in his grasp. He murmurs, "May I?"

I don't know what to say. How does one accept an apology from the prince of the Eerie? Someone I've been taught to hate—to fear. The reason for all my misfortune. The reason Owen is dead.

But...he isn't responsible. Not really. Will had told me that the captain acted of his own accord. And by the look on Titus's face, what Will had said about the prince being willing to hang the man for his disobedience...Seeing the prince now, I think he would have punished the captain in ways that might have made him wish for death. And when Titus had said he was sorry...as much as I hate to believe him, I do.

Titus clears his throat. I give a stiff nod, and he makes a motion for me to turn. My shoulders tense as he brings the strip of fabric over my head, wrapping it around my throat. I brace myself for the feeling of being strangled, but as his knuckles skim my collarbone, an entirely different sensation twists my stomach into knots.

"I must apologize for being so forthright," he says, his breath tickling the back of my head. "But I feel as if I already know you."

He takes a deliberate step back, giving me room to turn and face him. I find him staring at me as if I were something worth looking at, his mouth parting slightly on a breath. There's something awed in his expression, but it's so brief, I think I've imagined it. His features smooth out, matching his indolent posture as he tucks one hand in his pocket.

"William has done nothing but speak of you." He smirks, running a hand through his tousled blond hair. "Although, he failed to mention how easily spooked you are."

I snort. For someone who has done nothing but speak of me for the past few months, Will has hardly spoken *to* me tonight. And the few words he did say...

I make a fist. "Don't you have anything else you could be doing?"

He blinks, a faintly amused smile tugging at his lips. "Don't you?"

When I don't answer, starting towards the muddy bank of the pond, he follows, his hands in his pockets. My skin itches where I feel the heat of his gaze on my face, and I think of all the nights I'd pictured this exact moment—a minute alone with the king's flesh and blood. His only heir. How I'd imagined he would beg for mercy. All the things I would say to him before I took his life. Now that he's here, trailing alongside me, all I can think about is how...*patient* he's been despite my blatant, treasonous disrespect.

It's infuriating.

"If you don't mind," I say through my teeth, "I'd prefer to be alone."

"How interesting." He brushes an invisible speck of dirt from his shoulder. "I'd prefer *not* to be alone."

"Do you prefer to be annoying as well?"

He shrugs. "On occasion."

I lift my dress as we round the pond, picking up the pace. As beautiful as the gown is, I'd give anything to wear a pair of trousers again.

"In that case, there are about two dozen women inside that I'm sure would be thrilled to be annoyed by the prince of the Eerie."

He flashes me a charming smile. "I'd much rather be here, annoying you specifically."

"Lucky me."

I glance at Bludgrave, at the warm amber glow of the ballroom, and imagine Will with one of those gaudy women on either arm. If Will knew I was alone with the prince…what would he think? Would he be jealous? Should I want him to be?

Before I know it, we've reached Hildegarde's Folly, its dark reflection looming over the moonlit water. A raven perches on its domed roof, watching me with shrewd, knowing eyes.

In the time I've lived at Bludgrave, I've explored almost every inch of these grounds. But…after I'd seen the strange vision of blood dripping from the columns, and with Martin having discovered Annie's disemboweled atroxis here, this is the one place I've steered clear of. But as we approach the stone steps, I feel a sort of tugging in my chest, drawing me forward. My skin prickles as I take a step, and another. I've almost forgotten Titus is behind me as I enter the folly, when a cool gust of wind causes me to stumble backwards, and—

"Ouch." He grunts, hands on my arms to steady me. "I probably deserved that."

I peel my foot from the top of his shoe. "That was an accident." I add, somewhat under my breath, "This time."

He gives a startled laugh, but his hands linger on my arms. "And you're not sorry about either instance in which your foot has ended up on top of mine?"

"Not in the least."

"I can't say I'm surprised."

"Oh?" My brows lift. "I don't surprise you?"

"Quite the contrary," he says, his breath on the back of my head the only trace of warmth in the open-aired structure. "For example, I'm surprised you haven't pulled away from me yet."

His words are like a splash of cold water, a reminder of where I currently stand. My vision sharpens on the statue at the center of the folly, and I find myself craning to glimpse the face of a woman, a stone crown dipped low over her brow and the carved likeness of a child nestled to her bosom.

"Hildegarde," Titus murmurs, his reverent tone like a holy prayer spoken aloud—powerful and resonant. "The Mother of Queens." He doesn't move away, his presence enveloping me as if it pulses in the air around us. It's almost as if I can hear his heartbeat pounding in my ears.

"What do you know about her?" I whisper, my own pulse kicking up.

He clears his throat as his hands fall away from my arms, and I take a few steps to the side, putting a considerable amount of distance between us, an unwanted rush of warmth flooding my cheeks.

"Only what I learned in my basic studies," Titus answers, his voice thick, hands sliding into his pockets. When I glance at him, he wears that same awed expression he'd had when he looked at me in the garden. "She was a fierce warrior and protector of the Eerie before my kind took the throne."

I shake my head. "A *human* on the throne…"

A half grin as he angles towards me, drawing my attention from the statue. "Is that so hard to believe?"

I find myself staring into his deep, blue eyes. They twinkle like the sea reflecting the stars, mesmerizing and infinite. "There are a lot of things I find hard to believe."

Another wry grin as he closes the distance between us. "Like how you've spent your whole life wishing me dead and now that you've met me you find me utterly irresistible?" He leans in, as if sharing a secret. "I know you want to kill me. You're probably thinking about it right now."

My heart skips a full beat.

"Don't tell me you haven't considered taking this opportunity to drive a blade through my heart?" His mouth twists, a cruel smirk. "I certainly would, if I were you."

Something in the air shifts—subtle, but unnerving nonetheless. As if on instinct, I glance between the stone columns at Bludgrave, its gilded lights like a beacon in the distance. I turn to take a step back, but he moves swiftly, blocking the only exit. He prowls towards me, forcing me to give up ground, his head tilted as if he were sizing up his prey. His tongue swipes over his bottom lip as my back collides with the base of the statue at the center of the dome, knocking the air from my lungs with an audible *whoosh*.

He stretches an arm out, his palm pressed against the stone an inch from my head, caging me in, barring me from any hope that I could make it across the lawn to safety. It was foolish to think I could run. He is a Nightweaver. A bloodletter. A prince.

"And you are Violet Oberon," I imagine Owen would say. *"You bow to no king."*

"Give it up, Violet," Titus purrs. "I know about the Order. I know why you're here tonight." He tsks, shaking his head, his tousled blond hair splaying over his forehead. "You've made quite the climb. Pirate to servant girl, servant girl to the object of the Castor boys' affections."

His wandering gaze takes in every inch of my face, as if ravenous for any indication of fear. Finally, I see him for who he really is—the wicked prince from my nightmares.

"When Will first spoke of you," he drawls, "I knew I had to meet this mysterious, violent creature that had managed to wrap the young Lord Castor around her finger." His thumb strokes my jaw, his touch light, almost as if he were aware of the feel of his calloused skin on my own. Shivers skitter down my spine, and my stomach twists into knots. He seems to notice this, a pained emotion I don't understand flickering in his eyes before the eager, deadly gleam takes its place once more.

"I must say, from what Will told me, I didn't expect you to be so trusting." He brushes a lock of hair behind my ear, drawing close, his whisper warm on my cheek. "You made this rather easy for me, Violet."

I clench my teeth, my hands balling into fists. *Fool.* It was foolish to allow myself to be placed in this position. Trusting that the prince could be anything more than a slimy, murderous brute should be my downfall. After all, I know better than to trust anyone—especially not the Nightweaver in line to take the throne.

But…for the first time in my life, in some way I can't explain, I didn't *feel* that Titus was a threat. Or maybe I just didn't want to believe that he was. Because if the prince of the Eerie was good, then a part of me might actually begin to hope that things can change. And that is almost more painful than believing the only way to save my people is to murder the king and his kin. Killing I can do. Hope is more difficult. And trust…

Trust *was* impossible. Until Will. Because of him, I opened myself up to his people, his kind. Trust has made me weak. It blinded me to Titus's true intentions tonight. It convinced me to see the haughty, misunderstood boy rather than the evil prince from the stories I know all too well. But I was wrong. I shouldn't have trusted Will, and I shouldn't have trusted Titus. Both are mistakes I don't plan on making again.

If I get out of this alive.

"I know the Castors are up to something," Titus murmurs, drawing back to inspect my face. "You have my word that I will give you a swift death if you just tell me what they're planning."

He snaps his fingers, but—thank the Stars—I don't flinch. I glare up into his sparkling blue eyes, my hatred like a living thing squirming beneath my skin.

Kindness is the great deceiver. I should have known.

"Better yet...Will mentioned you're rather fond of your family." He smiles, showing teeth. "You will tell me everything you know about the Order of Hildegarde, or I will tack the bodies of your brothers and sisters to the castle walls."

I spit in his face. "Bastard."

He laughs, but his eyes darken. "Sweetheart, I've been called a bastard all my life." He licks his lips, smiling fiendishly. "You'll have to do better than that."

My stomach roils. Of all the vile words, I can't think of one wicked enough to describe him.

He cocks his head and toys with a strand of my hair. "You know," he says, his voice low, "I could have you executed just for being at the ball tonight. And not just you—Henry Castor should have known better than to link arms with a human girl. He's been only one kiss away from treason all evening." He wraps the strand of hair around his finger, drawing closer to my lips with every whispered word. "And Will...do you think he would die protecting your secrets?"

His question is like a knife to my heart. *Would he?*

Suddenly, Titus's body tenses and his breathing becomes shallow. He slowly unwinds the strand of hair, his hand lingering near my neck. As his fingertips graze my pearl earring, a crease forms between his brows. He draws back, inspecting my face, his hardened expression unreadable.

Softly, he asks, "Do you fear death, Violet Oberon?"

I laugh. "There are far worse things than death."

The corner of his lip twitches, an almost imperceptible smirk. "Torture?"

I think of the band of braided leather secure at my wrist and the bond it represents. Owen was willing to die for his family—for me. He never feared what would happen to him once he faced that final defeat. He was confident he would take his place among the Stars, and that one day, we would all be together again.

Owen dreamed of a better life for us, for our people. A place where we could be safe, happy. The Order believes in a world like the one Owen always dreamed of. If I die protecting even the slightest chance that a world like that could exist, then so be it. At least when I see Owen in the afterlife, we can both have a good laugh about how the boy I was assigned to protect is the same boy who will end my life.

"Tell me what you know, and I'll let you live," Titus whispers, his gaze trained on mine with predatory focus. "Your choice."

My choice. As if any of this is my choice. As if anything has ever been *my* choice.

"Why are you protecting the Castors?" His knuckles brush my jaw. "They bought you at an auction. You're nothing to them. *Nothing.*"

Nothing. He's right; I'm nothing. No one. If I die, my family will move on. They'll refuse to even say my name, the way they refuse to say Owen's. But if I give up the Castors, it would be a significant blow to their cause. To *our* cause.

Before, if I had died in battle, it would have meant *nothing.* Now, it means I will have died to protect little Annie, and Henry, who I would have never expected to consider my friend; and Killian, who gave me a purpose when I felt like peeling potatoes was all my life had become. I will have died protecting a future for Elsie and Albert. I will have died protecting Will.

The words that leave my mouth are not easy, but they are true. "Death before disloyalty."

Titus withdraws his hand, takes a small step back. A broad smile breaks out over his face, illuminating his eyes with some kind of holy blue fire. "I think you mean…" He discards his formal coat, dropping it unceremoniously to the floor, and meets my eyes once more, a tentative curiosity tempering his inexplicable joy as he rolls up his shirt sleeve. "…Death to the King."

CHAPTER TWENTY-NINE

S wirls of black ink materialize on the surface of Titus's skin, and a winged dagger takes shape, accompanied by the phrase...

"*Nivim derai,*" I murmur, my head buzzing. *In time of need.* Which means... "*You're* a part of the Order?" And then it hits me. At first I'd thought it could be me, considering the Order's conversations concerning an alliance with my people, but if the prince of the Eerie is on *our* side..."*You're* the secret weapon!"

"Secret weapon," he echoes, brows wriggling. "I like the sound of that."

I open my mouth to curse him but—

"Forgive me," Titus whispers, allowing me only a moment more to inspect the tattoo before covering it again. "Nothing against William's judgement, but I needed to see for myself if you could be trusted." In an instant, his sheepish grin wipes away any remaining traces of the sinister, bloodthirsty prince he'd portrayed himself to be. "I'm sure you understand?"

I exhale, unclenching my fists, letting my weight rest against the statue at my back. The contours of the stone dig into my shoulder blades, but the tingling sensation of relief sweeping through my body overrides any discomfort. "Trust, but verify," I mutter, reciting another of Mother's infamous sayings with a sigh. "In that case, you should have put in a bit more effort."

"Oh?" Titus lifts a brow. "And what would you have suggested I do?"

I shrug. "Pull my teeth, pry off my fingernails…"

A wicked smile. "I knew I saw a spark in your eye when I mentioned torture."

"If you wanted to torture me, you'd need only have asked me for another dance."

"Forgive me." His mouth twists into a mock pout. "I rather enjoyed our dance, but if it didn't meet your expectations, maybe you could give me another chance to—"

"For a prince," I cut him off, "you ask for forgiveness a lot."

His lip twitches, but his playful smirk doesn't meet his eyes, which are heavy-lidded and sincere. "I have a lot to be sorry for."

He glances at my throat, his gaze narrowing, as if he could see through the strip of fabric to the scars beneath. I lift my hand to block his view, but he snatches my wrist.

"Does William know?" he asks, his voice achingly tender. Familiar. Too familiar for someone I've just met. Someone I've spent my whole life hating.

The pit of my stomach twists, but I choke out a laugh. "About my scars? It's hardly any secret."

Titus frowns, releasing my wrist. "Then why hide them?"

Something like shame coils at the base of my spine. "No one was supposed to know who I am tonight." But what I don't say is that, for once, I wanted to be someone I wasn't. I didn't fight when Killian said they would have to find a way to cover my scars because I thought that for just one night, I could be something more than human. Perfect in the way that Nightweavers are perfect. I wanted to be someone else. Someone who had never suffered aboard the *Deathwail*. Someone who didn't know the feel of a rope crushing their windpipe. Someone who had never lost their home, or their brother, or their freedom.

He cocks his head. "And who is that?"

I think of the way Will treated me tonight, after I've spent months lying awake in my bed wondering if he was safe, if he was alive. If he missed me the way I missed him.

"No one," I say, because I'm not sure how to answer that anymore.

Before I realize it, Titus reaches out, his fingers skimming my throat as he unwraps the yellow chiffon from my neck, discarding it on the stone floor. He gives me a *look*, such certainty and understanding in his deep, blue gaze that it makes me wonder if he's seen inside me, heard the words I've never said aloud. "We all bear scars, Violet," he says, his voice low. "Even Nightweavers."

He unbuttons his shirt halfway, revealing a chest marred with puckered white marks—cruel, ugly scars left from only the deepest, most intentional cuts.

My brows furrow. "Why not have Will heal them?"

The corners of his lips turn up, a sad, knowing smile. "Why not have him heal yours?"

Titus takes a step towards me, backing me against the statue once more. I let him place his hands on either side of my head, let him encapsulate me with his body, until I feel as if the sea has wrapped me in its embrace, the scent of brine clinging to his sun-kissed skin. His blue eyes seize mine, gentle yet commanding, like the tide pulling me out into the deep.

He echoes my words from earlier this evening, his breath caressing my cheek. "You're exactly like I thought you would be."

"And that is?" I manage to ask, my voice hoarse.

He inclines his head so that his lips are so close to mine, I don't dare take a breath, my eyes shuttering closed. "Brave," he murmurs, his voice as lulling and familiar as the crash of a wave. "Loyal."

At the word, he pulls away abruptly, the absence of his presence like a physical blow to my chest. When I open my eyes, he is working to button his shirt once more. He no longer looks at me, but rather, he stares out, beyond the stone columns, at Bludgrave in the distance.

"We should head back," he says, his expression hard.

My mouth works, but words fail me. *What just happened?*

Without waiting for me to follow, Titus retrieves his jacket from the ground and turns on his heels, starting down the steps. I look down, where the strip of yellow chiffon lies like a wilted petal at my feet.

We all bear scars, Violet.

The prince had called me brave. But I haven't felt very brave, lately. This place—this new life—has borne back the wild in me. It has forced me to hide scars I once wore with pride. To pretend to be less than what I am—*who* I am.

I think of Owen, laughing in the face of danger. *He* was brave. Brave until the last.

Maybe it's time I stop pretending to be someone I'm not.

Maybe it's my turn to be brave.

Titus and I walk back to the manor in silence. I follow at a slight distance, and when we've reached Bludgrave, only then does he look back at me, his expression unreadable. He opens his mouth, but I speak before he can.

"I'll see you inside," I say quickly, opening the door that leads to the kitchen and slipping through the crack before he can say a word.

Instantly, the heady savor of roasted meat fills my nostrils. I rest my back against the closed door, inhaling deeply, my lungs greedy for the aroma of baked bread, of crushed garlic and fresh-cut fruit, whipped topping and chocolate pie. I close my eyes, letting the calming babble of boiling water soothe my weary mind.

"Violet?" Father's voice rises above the din of clanging pots and pans. He stands in the warm, golden glow of the kitchen light, wiping his hands on his grease-stained apron. "You should be at the ball," he says, his head cocked.

"I…" *I'm not sure what I'm doing here.* "I thought you might need some help."

He gives me a concerned look, as if I'd hit my head. "We've got it covered," he says, gesturing at Martin and Sybil, who bustle about the kitchen in a frenzy. His eyes narrow on me. "Are you all right? You look—"

"I'm fine."

"—beautiful," he finishes, lifting his hand to cup my cheek but stopping short. His palm, coated with flour, hovers near my face. He smiles, and at once I feel like a child again.

I throw my arms around him, forgetting about his greasy apron, or his powdery hands, or my ballgown, already stained from the grass. He squeezes me tight, and the noise fades to a whisper. For a brief moment, I feel as if I'm rocked by the waves, safe in the cradle of the ocean. *Home.*

Father draws back, his face etched with concern. "What was that for?"

"Can't a girl hug her father?"

"I'm not complaining." He laughs, the sound so sweet and familiar it almost breaks me. But he stops abruptly, his finger hooking my chin. "Violet?"

Father brushes a tear from my cheek, smearing it with flour.

"I'm all right, Father, I just…" The words die in my throat.

The King's Marque lies face up on the edge of the nearby countertop. Where Father had signed his name all those months ago, a fresh, scarlet sun appears to bleed in the candlelight.

The Royal seal.

Titus...He had done it. He had all too literally sealed our fate. We are no longer the Oberon clan, notorious pirates of the Western Sea. We belong to the Crown. We belong to the Eerie.

Bludgrave—I once thought it would be my prison, my new *Deathwail*. But in this moment all I feel is...relief. The moment I've feared most has come. And yet, nothing has changed. In my heart, I am free. I am still Violet Oberon, feared and respected by all who know me. I am death at the other end of a blade. I am the undoing of queens and kingdoms. I am brave. Loyal. I am a pirate. No ring on any prince's finger can take that away from me.

Father follows my gaze, a weary sigh rattling in his chest. "Violet, please try to understand—"

"Don't," I say, shaking my head. "It's all right." I pull my shoulders back, taking a steadying breath. "I should get back to the party."

I give him a weak smile before turning my back to him, my head light from the pressure building between my ears.

"Wait," Father calls out.

I turn to find him rummaging through his apron pocket. He takes my hand in both of his, his kind eyes swimming with tears that don't fall. He smiles as I withdraw my hand to find a piece of taffy nestled in my palm.

The pressure in my head diminishes, an odd feeling of guilt building in its place. I should never have blamed Father for signing the King's Marque. He was only trying to protect his family. And after having spent these months here, at Bludgrave…I misjudged this place—these people. If the prince of the Eerie can be good, I have a chance to be a part of something worth fighting for—a world where we wouldn't have to flee to the Red Island for a better life. A world Owen would have dreamed of.

"Oh, and I almost forgot." Father turns from me, taking the milk-bottle vase from its perch near the window. "Will came here, looking for you, just before the ball." He takes the single stem of blue salvia from the bottle and tucks it behind my ear. "He left this."

And this one means I'm thinking of you.

Will *had* come looking for me, expecting to find me here. I close my fist around the piece of taffy, meeting Father's eyes— Owen's eyes—once more.

"Thank you, Father."

He looks taken aback, but he grins, and it reminds me of the mischievous look Lewis gives before he gets himself into trouble. "For?"

"For doing what you thought was best for our family." I glance about the kitchen, at the work of Father's hands: a feast fit for a prince. My gaze lands only briefly on the King's Marque, and I feel a strange sense of peace. Of certainty.

"I think Owen would have liked it here."

CHAPTER THIRTY

"Father really outdid himself tonight," Lewis whispers. I hadn't noticed when he'd appeared behind my left shoulder, carrying a tray of bacon-wrapped quail.

"Sampled the goods, have you?" I shoot him a wry look.

His lip quirks—his only answer—as he directs a pointed glance at the plate in my hand. I'd slipped into the ballroom unnoticed and made a beeline for the dessert table, tucked away in an alcove at the back of the room, where I could watch the dancing from afar. The delicate glass plate, now piled high with fruit cake, miniature silk pies, almond pudding, and the like, reflects the gilded light of the candelabras, illuminating Lewis's clean face. He had cut his hair before the ball, his long, blond locks now tapered just above his ears. I'm not sure if I'll ever get used to seeing him without dirt on his cheeks or his hair matted with grease, but there's no denying how handsome he looks, nor how happy he seems.

"Well, I've had enough of parties to last a lifetime." Margaret puffs a strand of wavy, dark hair from her face, appearing at my right, where she places her empty tray on the edge of the buffet table. I toss her the piece of taffy Father had given me, and her lips quirk into a somewhat sad smile. "Split three ways, then?"

Charlie's voice comes from behind. "Make it four." The three of us turn to find him carrying a tray bearing four glasses of blood-red wine. He grins, his cheeks rosy. "Care for a drink?"

Margaret's eyes flash as she divides the candy. "Charlie—we can't—"

"Of course you can," Killian says from across the buffet table. He flourishes his own glass. "I insist."

Margaret blushes, her jaw agape. "But—"

"The man insists, Marge." Lewis quickly sets his own tray at the edge of the table, rubbing his hands together mischievously. He plucks a meager piece of taffy from Margaret's palm and pops it into his mouth. "Bottoms up."

He reaches for a glass, but Charlie angles himself so that Lewis can't reach it.

"First," Charlie admonishes, "we toast."

Margaret gives Charlie and me our piece of taffy. It tastes of sea salt and vanilla, the flavor more vibrant than it ever had been before.

"To Owen," I say, taking a glass from the tray.

"To Owen," Margaret, Lewis, and Charlie echo before turning their glasses up and drinking them to the dregs.

"To Owen," Killian chimes in, clinking my glass.

The wine goes down smooth, settling like a comfortable warmth in the pit of my stomach. Despite everything that's happened—despite Owen's absence—this moment, drinking our customary glass of red wine on the eve of Reckoning Day, the four of us, together…it's more than I could have ever hoped for. It almost feels as if we're back aboard the *Lightbringer*—as if Owen were watching us from above, in the crow's nest, toasting to himself.

For the first time since Owen's death, I smile at the thought of him at peace among the Stars, looking down at us, smiling back.

I turn to ask Killian if he's seen Henry, but he's already gone. A hush falls over the room, and I realize the guests have turned their attention on the makeshift dais near the front of the crowd, where Lord Castor stands with Lady Isabelle at his side.

"Thank you all for joining us this evening," Lord Castor booms, his kind face full of warmth. "As I'm sure most of you are aware, my son William has just returned from Hellion." Applause breaks out, and Lord Castor graciously signals for the guests to quiet. "Yes, we're all very proud of him."

"Unfortunately," Lady Isabelle cuts in, her sweet voice carrying over the room with ease, "while our son was away, fighting alongside the League of Seven, our beloved township was attacked."

"No need to worry," Lord Castor adds, his expression serious. "Measures have been taken to ensure your safety here tonight. My wife and I thought it only right to take this time to condemn such violence, and to tell you the truth of what took place."

Lord Castor pauses as hushed murmurs trickle through the crowd.

"A criminal known by the name Malachi Shade led a brutal attack that resulted in an unacceptable loss of life—both our kind, and the humans," he says, his head bowed slightly. "Tonight, we honor their deaths with a moment of silence."

At this, murmuring turns to grumbling, and I feel the sudden urge to crawl under the buffet table. Why would Lord Castor lie? Surely there were witnesses in Ink Haven that day— those that saw what Percy and his Hounds had done, and how the humans were merely protecting themselves against his gang of murderous thugs. Why blame Captain Shade?

"I would also like to honor the bravery of my son Henry," Lord Castor booms, regaining a measure of control over the crowd, "as well as that of one of our most valued servants, Violet Oberon, who—now, where is Violet?"

I try to take a deep breath, to raise my hand, but I can't move. Beside me, Margaret looks as if she's seen a ghost. Lewis steps on my foot, and a sound escapes me. Every head in the ballroom turns to find me.

I feel faint as Henry hooks my arm in his. "Here, Father," he calls out. He adds under his breath, "Just smile."

But my face feels broken as I force a weak, pathetic excuse for a smile, and Henry pats my hand reassuringly.

"Ah, yes," Lord Castor says. I can't help but notice the sweat beading on his forehead, and the way his hand trembles slightly as he raises his glass. "Violet Oberon and her family were once pirates of the Western Sea—"

He has hardly said the words when the ballroom erupts into furious whispers. I can *feel* the heat of their glares as Henry adjusts his stance so that he's standing slightly in front of me. But the heat—the heat I feel radiates from Henry.

"—but they have since been reformed to the King's service," Lord Castor calls out, competing with the chatter of the crowd. "And tonight, our dear prince has made it official. The Oberon family is protected by the King's Marque. We welcome them into the Eerie, pirates no more. And we extend our gratitude to Violet, who served her king and country by stamping out the vile rebellion that threatened our tranquil valley."

A single, slow clap breaks up the mumbling and grumbling. All eyes turn from me at once to find Titus near the dais, leading the applause as it slowly creeps through the room. I get the feeling that if Titus stood on his head, no one in this household would be left standing on two feet.

"I'm sure you're all wondering why a human girl was invited to celebrate alongside you this evening," Titus says smoothly, brushing an invisible speck of dust from his arm. "When I heard of what transpired in Ink Haven and the courage of Ms. Oberon, I suggested that the Castors include her in tonight's festivities. I'm pleased they took me up on the suggestion. Though, I *was* surprised to see Violet in a ballgown, as some of you might recall."

Another lie, but a necessary one. If people hear that it was the prince's idea to invite a human—a reformed pirate, at that—to the Castors' Reckoning Day Ball, it could remove the blame from the Castors altogether. After all, who would deny the prince?

A few nervous chuckles throughout the room only add to the tension, but Titus carries on seemingly without care. "A toast, to the guest of honor," he says, raising his own glass. "May you always be loyal and brave. And may the sun of the Eerie shine upon your face from today until your last day. To Violet!"

"To Violet!"

I'm surprised when the crowd echoes the words, and though most look reluctant, others begin to cheer. Meanwhile, the prince climbs onto the dais as Lord Castor and Lady Isabelle make their way down the steps, giving Titus the spotlight.

As he steps into the beam of light, fear grips my chest. My memory flashes with the image of the man in blue livery that Captain Shade had struck down on the execution platform, an arrow in his mouth. If Captain Shade were to make an appearance, now would be the time to strike. But I can't help but think it wouldn't make sense for the rumors to be true, for Shade to attack the prince. Especially now that I know Titus to be working with the Order. If Shade is Will's informant, wouldn't Will know better than anybody if Shade had plans to assassinate the heir to the throne? And if so, why allow Henry and me to believe otherwise?

"William?" Titus shields his eyes, searching the room. The crowd parts to reveal Will lingering near the wall, the same two women from earlier this evening clinging to his either arm.

"Ladies, would you mind handing him over? It will only take a minute."

The crowd laughs, but as Will peels himself from the wall and leaves the two women pouting in his wake, I see no humor in his face.

"My brother-in-arms, William," Titus says, clasping Will's hand and pulling him onto the dais to stand at his side, "has indeed only just returned from our journey to Hellion, where had it not been for the young Lord Castor, we might not have succeeded in securing the eastern borders of my betrothed's homeland—the first front against the Underling forces." He pauses, letting the applause die out. "When asked to join me, Lord William answered the call of the Crown, and for that, I couldn't be more grateful. But tonight, I have another request to make."

My stomach clenches. Last time the prince had made a request of Will, he left for war a charming boy and came home a haunted man.

"Soon, I am to be wed," Titus continues. "Lord William and I have faced many battles together, and I couldn't imagine facing marriage without my most trusted friend there at my side." He turns to Will, a cheeky smile playing on his lips. "William, Lord of Ink Haven, defender of the Eerie, would you do me the honor of being my best man?"

Will grins, and at once the shadows of war flee from his face, his green eyes bright as he embraces Titus. The people seem to have forgotten all about me—the pirate-turned-servant that somehow intruded upon their celebration—as they break out into deafening applause.

Will withdraws, taking a glass of sparkling wine from Sybil's tray as she hovers nearby. "To the prince and princess!"

As Will brings the glass to his lips, his eyes find mine, that curious, questioning look I've come to know so well seeking me out from across the room. His shirtsleeve bunches to reveal a band of braided leather encircling his wrist. My bracelet.

My heart leaps. Has he been wearing it this whole time?

I lift my glass as the crowd converges once more to part us, just as the ocean between Hellion and the Eerie had separated us for the past three months. When I look around, I see that Lewis, Margaret, and Charlie had returned to their duties before I could notice they were gone, but thankfully, I am not alone.

Henry clears his throat, untangling his arm from mine. "That should smooth things over for the time being."

I take a weary breath. "How much longer until sunrise?"

"Bored of the revelry already, pirate?" he asks, turning to face me. There's something about the way he refers to me as a pirate, still, that warms my heart. His eyes widen, and he laughs, wiping flour from my cheek. "Stars, Violet, what happened to you?"

"It's nothing, I—"

A splash of liquid washes my vision red and I gasp, choking as it fills my nostrils.

Blood. I'm covered in blood. But whose blood? I can't see—I can't—

A female voice sends me spiraling into panic as a single, life-altering word pierces me like a knife, twisting deep.

"Treason!"

CHAPTER THIRTY-ONE

Henry gently clears the blood from my eyes, and I open them to find Trudy Birtwistle standing across the table, the flames from the candelabras dancing in the black of her pupils, an empty glass clutched in her dainty fist. *Wine*. It was only wine. Not blood.

Trudy sneers at the grass stains on my dress, then at Henry's handkerchief pressed to my cheek, her lips pursed with disgust. "That's what some might call it, you know. The two of you, off having a romp in the garden—"

"Trudy," Henry warns, his face twisted with hate as he dabs at the wine dripping from my chin. I remember being on the receiving end of that look and thank the Stars that those days are behind us as he narrows his eyes at her, his voice cold. "You're out of line."

"*I'm* out of line!" Trudy gasps, drawing attention to the three of us. A few Nightweavers watch as she points an accusing finger at me. "This *rat*—"

"Enough."

The authority in Titus's voice is unmistakable. He towers over Trudy, who gawks at him, mouth babbling. She dips into a curtsy so low she might as well sit on the floor.

Titus's lip wrinkles, the makings of a snarl. "Violet is a guest of the Crown, and you will treat her with respect."

"But, your highness—"

"Silence." There is no trace of the haughty, playful prince. Rather, I catch a glimpse of the fearsome ruler that I thought only an hour ago would have filleted the skin from my flesh for sport. "Say another word, and I will have Ms. Oberon cut your tongue from your mouth. Is that clear?"

Trudy nods weakly, and it looks as if she might break down in tears. Now I understand what prompted the rumors of the bloodthirsty prince of the Eerie.

Titus turns his full attention on me, and I feel as if the air has been knocked from my lungs. His blue eyes churn, two whirlpools of fury, but his voice is steady, unnervingly calm. "Are you all right, Violet?"

I open my mouth to answer, but no sound comes out.

"Off you go." Killian appears behind Titus, shooing Trudy back onto the dance floor. The moment she's gone, the sinister expression slips from Titus's face. I take a shuddering breath as he releases me—somewhat reluctantly, it seems—from his attentive gaze, turning to Killian.

"Bancroft!" He and the Admiral embrace. "I've been looking for you all evening…"

Someone taps my shoulder. Jack stands behind me, looking more out of place than I feel. He gapes at my wine-stained dress, shaking his head.

"Are you—"

"Fine," I say through gritted teeth, my nerves raw. "What is it?"

Jack nods slowly, looking unconvinced. "Will's asked to see you," he says, his voice low. "He's waiting for you at the stables."

"And what if I don't want to see him?"

Henry rolls his eyes. "Go," he says, offering me his handkerchief. "You two need to talk things out."

I take the handkerchief, surprised by its weight. "It's... heavy," I murmur, quirking a brow.

He smirks. "Enchanted," he says simply. "It possesses the protective capabilities of chainmail. Cleans itself, too," he adds, looking smug.

I glance at the handkerchief, my mouth parting with a gasp as the berry-red stains dissolve, leaving the white fabric pristine. "Fantastic."

Though reluctant to give in to Will's request, I'm eager to flee from the few Nightweavers that had witnessed Trudy's outburst, still leering and whispering from afar. Abandoning the plate of sweets I had yet to partake in—now soggy with wine—I follow Jack towards the double doors at the far side of the room. I look back only once to find Titus watching me go, before the crowd swallows him up and the crisp night air greets me with a chilled kiss.

"You should have seen her face," I tell Jack as we near the stables, wiping my cheeks with Henry's handkerchief. It comes away soiled black from the tar Margaret had applied to my eyelashes, but an instant later, the stains vanish. I tuck it away in the bosom of my dress, marveling at the enchantment. "I thought she might die of embarrassment."

The usual laughter is absent from Jack's face. "Serves her right! Trudy has always been and will always be a miserable, conniving—"

"You're not talking about me, I hope." Will peels himself from the shadows, stepping into the guttering, amber light of the stables. He pulls back the hood of his black cloak, a subtle smirk tugging at his lips.

"If I had been talking about you," Jack says, bowing dramatically, "I would have mentioned your lordship's foul mood swings and concerning inability to take a joke." Jack salutes me, turning on his heels and starting back towards the manor. Just like that, for the first time since Will's return, we are alone.

I don't waste a moment in striding past him, towards Caligo's stall, the familiar smell of leather and hay calming my nerves. "What do you want?" I demand, perhaps a bit more harshly than I'd intended.

"Let me explain." Will's deep, soft voice reaches me from the doorway. He keeps his distance, as he has been doing from the moment he'd returned. "Please, Violet."

Something in his voice breaks at the word *please*, and it threatens to unravel me. I pull myself onto Caligo's saddle, avoiding looking in his direction. "Fine," I say, walking Caligo out of his stall. "But you'll have to catch me first."

I take off at a gallop, Caligo kicking up dust in his wake, and race for the orchard. As I near the apple tree tunnel, the sound of another set of hooves pounding the earth vibrates in my chest, and I turn to find Will riding bareback on Henry's chestnut steed, Nutmeg, his midnight cloak billowing in his wake. Caligo slows when we reach the conservatory, and Will draws up at my right side, heaving for breath.

"It seems those lessons have paid off," he pants, his green eyes sparkling in the moonlight. His charming grin causes my thundering heartbeat to falter as he hops down from Nutmeg's back in one smooth motion and holds out his hand for me to take. "You're a magnificent rider."

"Jack's a good teacher," I say, ignoring his proffered hand without effort but struggling to ignore the twist in my stomach that follows his praise—praise I didn't realize I'd wanted to hear until now.

I swing my leg over Caligo's back and land with ease, indulging in the look of shock that dominates Will's expression. "Well?" I open the door to the conservatory. "I'd like to be back before sunrise."

Will rubs the nape of his neck, his boyish smile like a breath of fresh air. When he laughs, motioning for me to enter first, I feel as if I'm seeing him for the first time all evening. As if the boy who had returned from war had never left the party, and the old Will—*my* Will—had come here in his place.

"You're certainly in a better mood," I say coolly, turning to face him as he closes the door behind us.

He frowns, wetting his lips as if to say something, but he seems to forget as his emerald eyes rove my gown, up to my face—to the single sprig of blue salvia tucked behind my ear. He shakes his head, his gaze intense.

"You are entirely too lovely for this world, Violet Oberon."

I blink, dumbfounded. "Excuse me?"

Will tilts his head, short black curls splaying over his forehead. "I said—"

"I heard what you said," I snap. "I just don't know why you had to come *here* to say it."

"You know why." His boyish grin fades as he takes a step towards me, and another, backing me towards the old oak tree at the far end of the conservatory. "My indifference towards you this evening was an attempt to fix the Order's mistake."

My throat tightens. "*Mistake?*"

Will grinds his teeth. "It *was* a mistake to invite you to the ball," he says, his green eyes reflecting the colorful glow of Liv and the other pixies as they peer out from the overhanging branches. I find it odd that Liv and her friends don't surround him, swooping and giggling, but I push the thought aside.

"The king has already announced he will be sending a regime of Bloodknights to Ink Haven—to Bludgrave," he continues. "You're fortunate Titus covered for you, though I'm not sure what he'll be able to do when the king and queen find out what's transpired here tonight." He sighs, running a hand through his curls. "You've put your family in danger, Violet. It was an incredibly reckless decision, one I thought even you wouldn't have made."

Every word is like a slap in the face. "You're just angry Henry asked me, instead of you."

"Of course I am!" His voice rises above its characteristic timbre, his expression wild. "You don't think I want you with me at every party?" He doesn't give me time to answer, his nimble fingers working to unfasten his cloak. "Titus saved your life tonight, simply by dancing with you—something I could never have done—and by doing so, ensured his own punishment at the hands of the king and queen. You owe him a great deal of thanks."

"I don't owe anyone anything." I clutch my arms, shivering despite the balmy air of the conservatory. "The Order asked that Henry and I—"

"The Order *used* you," Will says sharply. His expression softens as he heaves a breath, draping his cloak over my shoulders. Instant warmth sinks into my bones. "I only learned what they had planned just before we danced."

"But Captain Shade—"

"My father fabricated the rumor concerning Shade's vendetta against the prince in order to keep Henry distracted from what the Order planned to do with you. And so that, if anything unfortunate were to happen tonight, there would be someone to blame." His jaw tightens. "No one—not even my family—knows that Shade is my informant. I intend to keep it that way."

"But why lie about what happened in Ink Haven?" I shake my head. "It wasn't a human rebellion; it was Percy and his filth. They—"

"It is the story the king would have told," Will says, pinching the bridge of his nose. "The Order was simply trying to maintain some control over the rumors that are no doubt already spreading throughout the kingdom. If the Crown suspects a rebellion in Ink Haven, it's better that we appear to have some hand in stamping it out."

I pull the cloak tighter around my shoulders as a chill runs down my spine. "Why invite me to the ball, then? Just to call me out in front of all those people?"

"Very few know of Titus's allegiance to the Order. My father used your presence to test Titus's loyalty, to see if he would risk the king's wrath to protect you—a human girl. A pirate." He furrows his brows. "And to plant a seed of doubt in the people's minds if they think you and your family have anything to do with the human resistance. It was his idea that if Titus showed favor to you publicly, few would be willing to speak out against him. If I had been here, I would have never risked—"

"But you weren't here!" I clench my fists, my blood humming in my veins. "You left."

"I had to." A deep groan rumbles in his chest. "Titus needed me—"

"*I* needed you!" The words spill out before I can stop them. Neither of us moves, neither of us breathes, staring at each other in stunned silence.

Will's face falls in defeat, and he takes another step towards me. "Violet—"

"No," I say, standing my ground. "You don't get to come back and act like you didn't get exactly what you wanted. I joined the Order. That's why you brought me here, isn't it?"

His eyes light, a subtle honey gleam shining through the green. "This isn't what I wanted," he says darkly, taking another step. "I wanted to keep you as far from this world as I possibly could."

I give ground, my back pressed against the trunk of the old oak. This world—*his* world. I should have known he'd never want me to be a part of it, after all those weeks hiding here, pretending every day as if we weren't growing closer each night.

Rather than allow him to cage me in, I maneuver around him in one swift movement, forcing him into the position he'd placed me. "Is that why you refused to teach me how to hunt the Sylk? How to banish it?"

"I told you what you needed to know." A muscle in his jaw ticks. "I took care of the rest."

"Without me."

He dips his head. "Without you."

I open my mouth, but I don't know what to say. I turn on my heel, storming back down the path between the roses, choking on their cloying scent. "You didn't have to bring me out here just to remind me why I never want to speak to you again."

"I suppose you wanted to have this conversation in front of a crowd of people who wish you dead," he says, following close behind me.

I whirl on him, the cloak twirling. "You never cared before!"

"Things were different then." He runs his hands over his face. His gaze seizes mine, seeking answers. In this moment he looks like a scared little boy—not a soldier, or a lord, or a Nightweaver. "I don't want anything to happen to you."

I can't bear to look him in the eye, so I turn my back to him, reaching for the door. "I can take care of myself."

"I know that." He grabs my wrist, halting me mid-step. "But if you were to get hurt…" he says thickly, shaking his head, his glossy black curls reflecting the soft blue and purple light emanating from the pixies overhead. "I fear I'd lose control."

I laugh, the sound broken and cruel. "No one told you?" I jerk my wrist from his grip, tearing the glove off and tossing it aside, revealing the *P* branded into my flesh.

Will stumbles back a step, his mouth parting on a sharp intake of breath. For an instant, his eyes appear illuminated, bright and burning like molten gold, as he fixes a glare on the mark. A preternatural stillness befalls him, and when he raises his head to meet my eyes, the green of his iris is a thin line, rimming the gilded honey glow. "Who did this?"

"Percy," I answer without thinking, as if he'd coaxed my voice out of me against my own will. "Don't worry," I add, attempting to regain some sense of self-control. "He's dead."

"That's unfortunate." The golden glow subsides, making Will's green eyes almost dull in comparison. His taciturn expression, his low, deep voice, send a shiver through me. "I would have liked to kill him myself."

Will removes his gloves, and though I attempt to pull away, my movements are sluggish. He takes me by the wrist, and at his touch, it's as if a shock of electricity passes between us. A feeling of warmth, comfort, and serenity floods my veins. My breathing deepens, my eyelids growing heavy.

"Don't," I manage to whisper. "Please."

His thumb strokes the brand. He looks up at me from beneath thick, dark eyelashes, his eyes glowing gold once more. "I can heal the scar," he says, his voice a deep hum.

A tear slips onto my cheek. "And what about the scars you can't see?"

His forehead creases, but before he can answer, Liv appears, hovering near my face, her tiny hand swiping at the tear. She fixes an angry look on Will. "*Sabba nesht, vira mayani bink fana shevant.*"

The golden glow retreats, leaving only Will's familiar green eyes looking into mine, and the strange hold of his compulsion releases me.

Still, I don't pull away from him. "What did she say?"

Will smirks slightly. "She told me that if I made you cry again, I'd have to deal with her."

I don't know why, but I laugh. Will watches me, a look of wonder about him. With the hand still holding my wrist he pulls me close, and with the other, he caresses my cheek.

"That laugh," he murmurs, his eyes drifting shut, lips parting slightly as if to drink in the sound. "I missed that laugh."

I glance at his wrist, where the band of braided leather seems a bit more worn than when I'd last seen it. He follows my eyes.

"When I was on the front," he says, his breath warming my face, "all I thought about was you—your laugh, your smile, your temper. All I could think about was coming home to you. It was the only thing that kept me alive." His hand cups my cheek, prompting me to meet his eyes, the emerald green more brilliant than I remembered. "You kept me alive, Violet."

And there it is—everything I've wanted to hear for the past three months. But in this moment, hidden away in the conservatory, with only the pixies and the flowers to bear witness, I realize something I hadn't before. Will can never say those words at a ball; he can never admit his feelings to his family. All this time, I thought I only wanted to hear him tell me he'd missed me, but what does any of it mean when neither of us is free to act on the way we feel?

"You're too late," I say, my voice a quiet breath. "I don't need you anymore."

As if those were the words *he* had waited three months to hear, a tentative smile breaks out over his face, though it doesn't reach his heavy-lidded eyes. "You never did."

His nose brushes my cheek, and my eyes shutter closed as his lips lightly graze my own. All thoughts of hiding, of things forbidden, flee at the feel of his mouth pressed to mine. He kisses me softly, as if I were made of glass, ever so gentle. I sink into the feeling of bliss that floods my senses, lost in the moment, in him, in the way his hand tangles in the hair at the nape of my neck as his arm wraps around my waist, holding me close.

He makes a sound, somewhere between a purr and a growl, as he deepens the kiss, and I forget that he is a Nightweaver and that I am a pirate and that the two of us should never have met. This feels right—more right than anything has ever felt before. I never want him to pull away, the scent of roses and damp soil heady in the air, as familiar to me now as the sea had once been. I want to taste the sparkling wine on his lips a thousand times, want to get drunk on it, want to—

Something warm trickles from my nose, and before I realize what's happened, Will tears himself away from me. Thrown off balance by the kiss and his sudden movement, I land on the ground, the cloak padding my fall.

"What—" I stop short. Will towers over me, his eyes fully engulfed in the blaze of golden light. Blood stains his lips crimson. *Did he bite me?* He looks down at me, his gaze devoid of emotion. Liv and the other pixies dart to hide amongst the roses, their glow diminished.

Will's gilded eyes blaze like two fiery orbs in the darkness.

"Will," I whisper hoarsely. "Will, it's me."

He blinks, dark green rimming the gold once more. "Your nose," he says, his voice rough. "It's bleeding."

I touch just above my upper lip, my fingers coming away wet with blood. "Why—"

A howl pierces the air, cutting me off. A moment later, Dinah bounds into the conservatory, ears flopping. The golden glow of Will's eyes surrenders to emerald green at the sight of his uncle's bloodhound and the blood-spattered parchment tied to her collar.

Will scans the note, his face grim. "It's from Killian."

I don't have to ask what it says. I can hear the laughter in the distance, high-pitched, guttural, and grating—a sound I'll never forget—and know.

The Underlings are here.

Chapter Thirty-Two

My heart thunders with every hoofbeat as Will and I race to Bludgrave. He pulls on Nutmeg's reins as we near the manor, and I do the same to slow Caligo to a trot. From the outside, everything appears relatively normal. Only, the music has stopped, and an eerie silence blankets the night air, heavy and stifling. No chattering voices or tinkling glasses penetrate the dreadful stillness.

I dismount Caligo and start for the kitchen door on the east wing of the house. I'm reaching for the knob, when—

"Stop," Will hisses. "You can't—"

"My family is in there!"

"And so is mine," he says calmly, placing his hand atop my own. "If we want to save them, we can't just go barging in there, guns blazing."

"Damn it," I mutter, remembering my severe lack of weaponry. "You have a gun?"

He withdraws his hand from mine, heaves a pistol from his waistband. "Follow me."

We tiptoe along the exterior wall, peering around the corner at the front of the manor. I swallow a small scream, and Will curses violently under his breath.

Impaled on a spike at the center of the drive, a woman's mauled corpse hangs limp, her face turned towards the sky, mouth open in what appears to be one last cry of agony.

"Is that—"

"Mrs. Carroll," a familiar voice answers from over my shoulder.

I whirl to find Lewis standing behind me, his face grim, a finger pressed to his lips. He turns, motioning for us to follow him back towards the kitchen, but Will seizes my arm.

"He could be possessed," he whispers.

"He isn't," I say, shirking his grip. "I would know."

"Would you?" In one swift movement, Will blocks my path. "How can you be sure?"

"I'm cursed, remember?" I step around him, towards where Lewis waits at the kitchen door. "It's kind of the only good thing about it."

But Will isn't convinced, clearly, because when we catch up to Lewis, he draws a wicked-looking knife from his jacket pocket and holds out his hand expectantly. I recognize the pocketknife with a sudden chill—the blade that slashed Mr. and Mrs. Hackney's throats.

"Your hand," Will says calmly.

Lewis lets out a long, frustrated sigh, surrendering his palm.

Will makes a quick, shallow cut. He brings the edge of the blade to his mouth, and—

I gasp as he licks the blade, collecting the blood on his tongue in a single, dutiful swipe. He closes his eyes, though it does little to hide the golden glow of his irises, and when he opens them again, they are their usual emerald green.

Until now, I never thought I would be disgusted by anything Will did. But...as shocked as I am by the shameful act, something about the blood pooling in Lewis's palm seems to call to me, its whisper as familiar to me as the lulling voice of the waves...

I shake my head. "Was that really necessary?"

Will wipes his mouth, tucking the bloody knife back in his jacket pocket. "When a Sylk is in possession of a human, the blood tastes of sulfur."

"Lovely," Lewis says, wiping his palm on his shirt. "If you're satisfied...?"

Will nods, and we follow Lewis into the kitchen. As my brother locks the door behind us, Father throws his arms around me, weeping softly.

"Where's Mother?" I whisper, looking over his shoulder. "Elsie? The others?"

Father trembles, sobbing. The room is empty but for Killian leaning against the wall, shaking his head.

I draw away from Father, and Lewis pats him gently on the back. "What's going on?" I ask my brother. "How did you slip away?"

"I came here as soon as I realized something was wrong." Lewis rubs the nape of his neck, motioning at the vast array of kitchen knives and cleavers he'd gathered. "I figured the rules didn't apply in a situation like this."

"And what exactly is the situation?" Will asks, lingering near the door, his arms crossed.

"Trudy Birtwistle is possessed by a Sylk," Killian answers, giving Will a *look*.

My stomach twists into knots. I thought I'd seen a shadow around her head this evening, but I'd been too distracted to give it any real consideration. "Is it—"

"I believe so." Killian's forehead creases. "After Percy's death, the Sylk would have needed a new body to inhabit. Trudy and her father were staying in another inn nearby; it must have thought she'd make a good host. Trudy would have access to Bludgrave—to you."

"To Violet?" Lewis demands, drawing up at my side. "Why would a Sylk need access to Violet?"

My chest tightens. "When Owen died..." I try to conjure the right words to explain everything that's happened since the day the *Lightbringer* sank. I turn towards him, but the wood creaking underfoot gives me pause. "Wait—" I look around at the doors, free of any barricades. "Are we safe here?"

Killian inclines his head. "The room is sealed by magic. No one can enter without my permission, and we can't be heard beyond these walls."

I clench my fists. "So you're hiding in here while everyone else is being slaughtered out there?"

"It's not that simple," Killian says gently. "Trudy let a troop of Underlings into the manor. They've taken hostages."

"Hostages?"

He dips his chin, his eyes dark. "They've promised to leave them unharmed. The Guild of Shadows has only one request."

"And that is?"

Killian fishes his pipe from his coat pocket, lights it. He takes a long drag, his expression grim. "You, Violet. They want you."

My heartbeat falters, my mouth suddenly dry. "Me?"

Lewis takes another step, standing between Killian and me. "How do you know that? You were already here by the time I slipped away."

"Here? What would you be doing in the kitchen?" I ask, eyeing the Admiral.

"I grew bored of the party," Killian says smoothly. "I thought I'd keep Philip company."

Philip. "I didn't know you two were friends." Truthfully, I'd never seen the two of them so much as say hello to each other in passing, much less hold a conversation. Killian had never lingered in the kitchen before, not even when Henry occupied the space.

"We share some common interests." Killian gives me a tight smile. "Don't we, Philip?" His brows draw together. "Philip?"

Father had taken a seat on a rickety wooden stool, his face a pale shade of green. "I won't..." he mumbles, his eyes bulging, the veins in his forehead like worms crawling beneath his skin. "Won't do it..."

"Get back!" The instant the words leave Will's mouth, Father lurches from the stool, a blade in his grasp. Will seizes his wrist and slams him against the wall. Father writhes, fighting to break free.

"Violet," Father sobs even as he struggles. "I'm sorry. I'm so sorry!"

Will grits his teeth, attempting to wrench the knife from Father's grasp. "He's been compelled."

"Urge him to sleep," Killian orders, starting towards them.

"I'm trying. The magic—it's fighting me—"

Father wails, the sound fracturing a piece of my heart. "I don't want to hurt her," he cries, as if arguing with someone no one else can see, his eyes glazed. "Please, don't make me hurt my daughter!"

"Philip!" Killian's voice resonates with the command. "Who did this to you?"

Father's eyes refocus, and I catch a glimpse of the kindness before something wild takes its place. "'*Look in her trunk*,' they said." Foam bubbles over his lips. "'*Wound the girl Violet Oberon, but not fatally*.' Only weaken. Weaken her. Stab her. The knife... the trunk..."

Father's body convulses as Lewis and I watch in horror. I'm helpless in a way I've never felt before.

"Who, Philip?" Killian demands. "Who told you to do this?"

At once, Father goes still, his body limp under Will's weight. His eyes loll, fixating on a spot on the floor. He doesn't struggle when Killian takes the knife from his weak grasp. Will and the Admiral share a look and Will releases Father, allowing Lewis to lead him back to the wooden stool.

"Father?" I kneel beside him despite Will's look of protest.

Father lifts his head slightly, his features stark. "Violet," he says feebly, raising his shaking hand to reach for my face. With trembling fingers, he touches one of the pearl earrings, his eyes remote. He smiles, a sad, faraway smile. "I remember the day I gave these to your mother. She looked so beautiful. So beautiful..." He drops his hand and his head falls. He stares once again at the floor, his expression blank.

"Father?" I whisper, taking his hand.

His only response is a gentle squeeze. Whatever has hold of him...Father is still in there.

I look up at Will, who is examining the knife, rusted with dried blood. "Margaret found it under Annie's bed," I tell him. "The day before you left."

His brows draw together. "Why didn't you tell me sooner?"

"I forgot." A half truth. That night, when Will told me he was leaving, I decided to keep the knife for myself. To hunt the Sylk alone. But over the past few weeks, I've thought little about the knife or Annie's connection to it, considering it only another attempt by the Sylk to get in my head.

"You forgot?" Will fixes his keen eyes on me. "Margaret found the knife that gutted the family's atroxis under my little sister's bed and you forgot to mention it?"

"Oh, so now this is *my* fault?" I stand, squaring off with Will. "If you hadn't left—"

"I didn't have a choice!" Will sets the knife on the counter's edge with a loud *clank*, and out of the corner of my eye, I see Lewis take a warning step in his direction. But Will's gaze remains locked with mine, ever-searching, as if we were the only two people in the room. "How many times do I have to tell you—"

"Enough!" Killian barks. "The two of you are acting like children."

"He started it," I grumble under my breath.

Will scoffs.

Killian fixes a stern look on his nephew. "This is not the time for a lover's quarrel." He pinches his nose with his forefinger and thumb, sighing deeply. "William, say you're sorry."

Will gapes at his uncle. "*Sorry*? I was doing my duty!"

"Not for leaving," Killian amends. "For lying. You promised Violet you would teach her to hunt Underlings, but it's obvious from the time I've spent with her that you did little of the sort."

Will frowns, turning his wounded gaze on me. "I never wanted to lie to you," he says softly, his expression tender. "But the truth—" he cuts himself off, his eyes widening as he grabs me by the shoulders, shoving me behind him.

Will stands with his back to me, hands outstretched in a placating manner. "Philip," he says, his voice deep. "You don't want to do this."

Father had stirred from his stupor and taken hold of the knife once more. Lewis, armed with two short blades, stands beside Will, facing Father head on.

"Father, please," Lewis pleads. "Drop the knife."

Father trembles, tears streaming down his cheeks. "I won't make you stop me." He nods slowly, as if he's made up his mind. "But I can't fight it." His eyes meet mine—his kind eyes, Owen's eyes—and in that moment, I know he's beaten into submission whatever compulsion had overtaken him. "My sweet Violet…I always knew they'd come for you. But I won't let them take you. I won't."

It happens so fast but time seems to slow, the seconds spiraling into eternity as Father turns the knife inward, plunging it into his chest.

CHAPTER THIRTY-THREE

I think I hear myself scream from somewhere far away. I shove between Lewis and Will, lunging for Father as his knees hit the kitchen floor with a sickening crack and he topples onto his side. Lewis is at my right a moment later, tears streaking his face. He speaks to me, but his words are muffled, drowned out by the ringing in my ears.

I won't let them take you.

"Violet." Will sounds as if he's speaking to me from the bottom of a deep well. He shakes me, his hand on my shoulder. "Violet, look at me."

"Her eyes!" Lewis sobs. "What's wrong with her eyes?"

I withdraw my hands from Father's chest. They come away wet with blood. Had I touched him?

"Violet." Killian's voice is a gentle command. "Breathe."

Have I stopped breathing? I crane my neck to look at Will kneeling beside me, his hand on my cheek.

"Breathe," Will echoes, nodding encouragingly. "Just breathe."

No. I don't want to breathe. I want to tear Trudy Birtwistle limb from limb. I want to bathe in her blood. I want to—

Before I can register his movement, Will's mouth is on mine. It's a demanding sort of kiss, meant to jar me out of this stupor. And it works. Only, the grief it leaves behind threatens to unhinge me even further.

Will draws back, scanning my face. "Violet? Can you hear me?"

I nod weakly, a sob twisting my gut. "What's wrong with me?"

"Nothing is wrong with you," Will says softly, tucking a strand of hair behind my ear. "Can you stand?"

He and Lewis help me to my feet. The moment I'm standing on my own, my brother seizes me by the shoulders, his eyes locked on mine.

"What are you?" Lewis asks, his voice cracking.

I don't answer. Numbness spreads throughout my body, sinking bone deep. I want to weep for Father. I want to take comfort in my brother's embrace as he wraps me in his arms, his own body wracked with sobs. But as I peer over his shoulder, at Killian unscrewing a vent at the far side of the room, all I truly want is to be let out of this room—to be unleashed on the Guild of Shadows. To kill every last Sylk, Gore, and Shifter I lay eyes on. I want to burn Bludgrave to the ground. I—

Killian hefts the grate aside, and out of the vent crawls a bespectacled badger in a brocade waistcoat. The Admiral meets my gaze, and I swear he looks as undone by my father's death as Lewis and me.

"I'm sure you remember Tollith," he says hollowly. "He's been keeping me informed this evening."

Tollith takes in the sight of Father lying in a pool of his own blood. The look on his face is so human, yet the sincerity in his expression goes far beyond what I've ever seen in our kind. "My condolences, Oberon children," he says, bowing deeply.

Lewis releases me, stumbling back a step. "Did that badger just—"

"Indeed," Tollith answers, pushing his spectacles up his snout. He turns to Killian, wringing his paws. "They're growing restless. They know she's here. They're threatening to..." He glances at me, rather uneasily. "They're threatening to begin with the children first."

The children.

I start forward, towards the door that leads to the servant's corridor. Lewis is close on my heels, wiping the tears from his face, now taut with determination.

"Violet, wait." Will reaches out, but I narrowly avoid his grasp.

"I'm going in there." I take two blades from the collection of knives laid out on the counter. "You can't stop me."

Will reaches out again, but I point one of the blades at his throat just as his fingers graze my arm.

"Don't even try."

He scowls. "I'm going with you."

"Fine," I say, lowering the blade. "Just stay out of my way."

The servant's corridor is dark, all but for a few dim, flickering lights. The entrance to the ballroom is hidden within a panel of the wall, so that from the outside, it appears as if there is no door at all. Will and I stand shoulder to shoulder, peering through the faux grate that marks the passageway.

I'm ill-prepared for what awaits on the other side of the ornate filigree that separates me from the rest of my family. Corpses litter the room, lying in a shallow sea of blood. One of the two girls that had clung to Will's either arm, now without arms herself, is the least horrific of the shredded, mangled bodies strewn about the floor. At the center of it all, Elsie, Annie, and Albert sit back-to-back, gagged with dinner napkins, their hands and feet bound with ropes.

Henry alone stands above the children, his hands outstretched in the direction of something just beyond my viewpoint.

"Dorothy, please—"

A shrill laugh cuts across him. "*Dorothy, please,*" comes a mocking voice. Footsteps click, and a familiar-looking girl steps into view. Her lip curls with a sneer, and my stomach plummets as I recognize her—Dorothy, the servant girl for whom Henry secretly pines. Her dark hair—always pulled back and tied neatly with a black ribbon—hangs in matted clumps; her skin is caked with dirt and excrement. Her once carefully-pressed uniform has been torn, leaving large portions of her body exposed to reveal various cuts, scratches, and bruises. Dorothy might have been taken, but it's clear she didn't go without a fight.

Dorothy prods at a severed leg with mild curiosity. "*Is that your plan?*" A different voice speaks—the voice of the Sylk possessing Dorothy's body. I don't recognize it as the voice of the Sylk that had possessed Percy; this one is deeper, more feral. "*To ask nicely?*"

"I don't want to hurt you, Dorothy," Henry says, his voice breaking.

"Dorothy, Dorothy, Dorothy," she echoes derisively. "I'm sure the poor girl would have loved to hear you say her name so sweetly, little lord. But Dorothy isn't home. I can ask her to come out and play, if you'd like?"

An instant later, Dorothy blinks, looking around, her mouth gaping in terror. "Henry?" she cries, glancing at her hands, at her missing fingers. "Henry!" She collapses to the floor in a sobbing heap. "Oh, what have I done!"

"Nothing, my darling, nothing," Henry says gently, taking a cautious step towards her. "You're going to be all right. Everything's going to be—"

Another cackle of laughter bursts from Dorothy, and she stands lazily. "'*My darling*,'" she says, faking a pout. "*How sweet.*"

Sparks of electricity jump from Henry's palms as he grits his teeth, body trembling with fury. "Let her go."

"Now, now. If I did, poor, innocent Dorothy would be dead. Surely you don't want that?"

A tear glazes Henry's pale, scarred face. "I won't let you do this." He fortifies his stance, and even though his hands shake, he doesn't drop them. "Dorothy, if you can hear me, I'm sorry. I love you. I've always loved you."

Sparks leap from his palms, and in the instant Dorothy's body falls, jerking violently, I know what he's done. He's found the switch in Dorothy's brain and turned it off. He'd tried to make it quick—painless.

Henry looks like he's on the verge of collapse, his mouth twisting as he fights back sobs.

But Dorothy doesn't stay down. The girl's body rises again. She sticks out her tongue, swiping at the blood dripping from her face, a derisive grin on her lips. "*Cute trick*," the Sylk says, cracking Dorothy's neck. "*But your power is weak.*"

She takes a step towards him, but Henry holds his ground. And though his attempt to shut off the electricity in Dorothy's brain hadn't worked, he looks somewhat relieved. Because if it hadn't worked, that means that Dorothy is still in there, somewhere.

"Take me," he says quickly. "Leave the children. Take me. I'll serve the Guild. Please, just don't hurt them."

Dorothy's lips purse in another mock pout. "I'm sorry, little lord. That wasn't part of the deal."

"New deal," I say, stepping out of the dank passageway and into the brilliant light of the ballroom, Will close at my heels. "I send you back to where you came from, and the Guild leaves me and my family alone."

A slow, echoing clap comes from my left, where Trudy Birtwistle sits on the edge of the makeshift dais. Mascara streaks her blood-spattered face, and she peels what looks to be an ear from the front of her ravaged gown as she stands, her bare feet submerged in the pool of crimson.

"*I was wondering when you'd decide to show up*," comes the voice of a Sylk. I recognize it this time, from the night Percy died. "*Violent Violet…*" Trudy tsks. "*Did you enjoy my bouquet?*"

She tosses the ear to her right, where a gruesome, hunched creature appears in a burst of purple smoke. The Gore, built like the gorilla I'd seen in one of Elsie's books, towers over Trudy by at least three feet, with skin like red leather and a face made of raw flesh. Its six reptilian eyes swivel in different directions as it catches the human ear in its wide, gaping mouth, shredding it with razor-like teeth. It laughs, the unnatural sound grating against my senses, its unhinged jaw giving it the appearance of always smiling.

Trudy grins at the expression on my face. "*Don't be afraid*," says the Sylk. "*He doesn't bite unless I tell him to.*"

I cut my eyes at Henry and see his shoulders sag in relief. He had been prepared to take them all on his own. Which makes me wonder…

"Where are the others?" I ask him, keeping Trudy in my sights.

"*Oh, of course!*" Trudy claps her hands, and in an instant, it's as if a veil lifts—revealing Margaret, Jack, Charlie, and Mother huddled near Lord and Lady Castor on the floor near the musicians' alcove, where the remaining guests have been corralled, their mouths gagged, hands and feet bound.

Despite the binds, Margaret and Jack clasp fingers, and he keeps his head pressed to hers, his eyes shut tight.

"Now, who am I forgetting..." Trudy taps her chin. "Ah! That's right..."

She claps her hands once more, and another figure blinks into sight, nailed to the wall above the dais by his hands and feet. In the instant he appears, I don't recognize him, but...his black uniform, his blond hair, streaked with blood...

Titus's face has been bludgeoned beyond recognition. His head hangs limp, but his chest rises with an unsteady breath. He's alive. For now.

"*Tell me,*" the Sylk says, kicking George Birtwistle's severed head from her path as Trudy slowly makes her way towards us. "*What good is a prince if he cannot protect his people?*" She snorts a laugh. "*He couldn't even protect himself!*" Trudy pauses, examining her nails, crusted with dried blood. "*Well, to be fair, I suppose he did put up quite the struggle. Banished twelve of my Gores before this one knocked him unconscious.*"

"I'd almost forgotten just how much you liked to talk," I say, starting towards Trudy. "Is that all you came here to do, or would you like to settle this once and for all?"

"*Settle this once and for all,*" the Sylk echoes, cackling with derisive laughter. "*My, my, you really* are *a pirate.*"

I glance to my right as I pass Henry and the children, avoiding looking too closely at Albert's red, tear-streaked face. Henry doesn't take his eyes off Dorothy, who has fallen still, as if awaiting further command.

"This ends tonight," I say, keeping one eye on Dorothy to my right and the other on Trudy. I tighten my grip on the kitchen knives in either fist, cutting my eyes at the ceiling. One more step, and I'll be below the grate...

"What are you going to do?" Trudy shrieks with laughter. "Stab me with a kitchen knife? Even if you managed to kill this host, I'd just take hold of another. Perhaps your little sister, or that darling stable boy?"

I take another step, standing directly below the grate. *Come on, Lewis. Where are you?*

"This is your last host, Underling," I say. "I intend to make you wish you'd never heard the name Violet Oberon."

More laughter as Trudy takes another step, merely ten feet from me now. "*Owen was right about you,*" the Sylk says, grinning maliciously. "*You really don't give up.*"

Owen?

I shake my head. This is just another game—another trick. But I won't fall for it this time.

"No, I don't," I say, glancing at the ceiling, where I catch a glint of silver peeking out from the grate. "And I never will."

In a flash, two daggers drop from the grate above, falling like shooting stars from the heavens. I drop the kitchen knives, catching a dagger in either hand.

Something in Trudy's placid expression falters. *"Abominations,"* the Sylk hisses, cringing at the sight of the daggers I'd used to cut off its previous host's hands. "No matter," Trudy says, attempting to recover her composure. *"You failed to finish me off last time. You will fail again."*

Will draws my flintlock from his jacket pocket, points it at Dorothy's head, and Henry turns his palms towards the Gore at Trudy's side.

"Party's over, Underling," I say, giving my daggers a twirl. "Time for you to go home."

"Oh!" Trudy giggles. *"Owen warned me that you wouldn't be so trusting, but it appears you've been misled,"* the Sylk says, its voice gritty and hollow. Trudy claps her hands together, and in a flash of purple smoke, seven Gores blink into sight. Butchered Nightweaver corpses rise from the blood-soaked floor, some headless, some with their jaws hanging from their skull, sliced wide by the banana-sized claws protruding from the Gore's fleshy stump of a hand.

Trudy smiles as the whites of her eyes turn inky black, her irises glowing red. *"The party's just begun."*

CHAPTER THIRTY-FOUR

A small army of Sylks and Gores surround us as Trudy's laughter splits the air.

"Oh, dear," Trudy says, her face drawn in mock sympathy. "It looks like you're outnumbered."

"Well, then," I say, giving my daggers another twirl. "Why don't we make this a fair fight?"

I glance over my shoulder as Margaret, Charlie, Mother, and Jack stand, shaking free of their severed binds just as more weapons drop from the grates above them. Pixies buzz around their shoulders, no longer stifling their bioluminescent glow.

Lewis drops from the grate nearest Margaret, landing in a wide stance, one hand bracing his fall, a dagger between his teeth.

"Show-off," Charlie mutters.

After Lord and Lady Castor have been freed, the pixies set to Annie, Albert, and Elsie's binds, gnawing at them with their sharp, rodent-like teeth.

"Annie," Will says the instant she's been freed, "would you mind giving us a bit of fresh air?"

She grins knowingly, stretching her hands out in either direction. The doors of both the north and south walls are thrown open on a gust of unnatural wind, and a pack of snarling wolves prowl through the open doorways on either side.

In saunters Killian, his hand resting atop the head of a massive black wolf. "I heard there was a party going on," the Admiral says smoothly. "My friends and I thought we'd drop in for a bite."

Smirking, I look, finally, at Trudy. Her expression is schooled into something akin to admiration.

"*Impressive*," says the Sylk. "*It's a shame you're the only one the Guild asked that I let live.*"

As the others fall into rank, fanning out behind me, I step forward, my sights set on Trudy and Trudy alone. "Tell the Guild of Shadows that no one *lets* me do anything."

At that, Mother raises a longsword into the air, and with a roar, launches into battle.

Chaos unfolds around me as my family fights alongside the Castors, though Trudy and I remain unmoving. For a moment, everything fades beneath the din of clashing metal and Gore laughter. To my left, Lewis uses Charlie's back to launch himself into the air, landing on a Gore's shoulders and plunging his dagger into its skull. To my right, Margaret, Jack, and Henry form a protective shield around the children as Dorothy circles them, long black claws protruding from her severed joints.

Working his way towards the makeshift dais, Killian unloads bullets from a Howler in either fist, banishing Sylks from the corpses they'd possessed, their dark, shapeless forms whisking away with bloodcurdling wails. Nearby, Lady Castor seizes control of a headless corpse just as it leaps for Mother—locked in combat with two Gores—and brings it crashing to the ground, its bones snapping as she closes her fist, crumpling its body into a ball of flesh with a gruesome crunch.

"*Violet.*" Owen's voice penetrates the ringing in my ears.

"No," I say aloud. "You're not real. You're dead."

"Am I interrupting something?" Trudy asks, blood sloshing underfoot as she takes a step towards me. She cocks her head. "You look ill, Violet. Maybe you should…*lie down.*"

Compelled by the magic in her voice, I fall face-first to the ground against my will. I gulp down blood as it fills my nostrils, drowning me with every breath I take. I try to fight against the compulsion, but it weighs on me, pushing me down with inexplicable force.

So, I stop fighting. I let go. I let myself drown. Because I know something the Sylk doesn't.

There is water in the blood.

And water has never been my enemy.

Chapter Thirty-Five

Indistinguishable whispers hiss from every direction as I surrender to my fate, the metallic taste overwhelming my senses. Just like the night at the fountain, when I'd been submerged beneath the pool of blood, a surge of vitality courses through me, like lightning electrifying my every cell. Power floods my veins, a power that feels foreign and yet more familiar to me than my own heartbeat. I latch onto it—my courage, my hope, my defiance.

The Underlings have taken everything. My brother. My father. My home.

I will not let them take me.

The pressure lifts, like a weight removed from my back, and I rise to one knee, a dagger clenched in either fist. I cough and sputter, blood dribbling down my chin, but every choking gasp fans a fire in my chest, warming my skin from the inside with radiant heat. At first, I don't look up, my gaze trained on the floor, watching as the blood undulates beneath me, rippling with my pulse…

"What an interesting creature you are," the Sylk croons. *"I look forward to picking you apart."*

I stare at the blood, at the two golden orbs of light reflected on the crimson surface. Eyes like those of a Nightweaver.

Trudy lifts her foot as if to take another step, but when I raise my head, fixing a glare on her, she stops short. A look of fear. And then—

"There you are," the Sylk whispers, *"Violent Violet. Now we can have some fun."*

"Did someone say 'fun?'"

My heart leaps at the sound of Titus's lilting voice. He appears over Trudy's right shoulder, looking no less heroic than the famed pirate for which he's named. Killian must have set to work on healing him quickly, because the swelling in his face has gone down, the holes in his hands mended.

Titus rolls his neck, adjusting his torn cuffs as if he hadn't just been pinned to the wall like a dead insect. "I'm thought to be somewhat of an expert on the subject," he says, crouching. He plunges his hands wrist-deep into the pool of blood, his eyes glowing gold at the contact. His gilded eyes slide past Trudy, to me, a sudden look of concern on his bruised face. "Maker of All…" he breathes, a roguish grin tugging at the corner of his busted lip. "You are quite the walking contradiction, Violet Oberon."

Trudy looks between the two of us, disbelieving, before throwing her head back in erratic laughter. "Isn't this quaint?

The prince and the pirate..." She tilts her head at Titus, tsks. "What would Mummy and Daddy think?"

"You know," Titus says slowly, running his thumb over his bottom lip, smearing it with blood, "I've never really given much consideration to what my parents think. But I'll be sure to ask them when Violet attends my wedding." He gives me an earnest look. "You will join William at the palace, won't you?"

My mouth stutters open. "Join Will? At the palace?"

Titus glances about the room, laughter tugging at his crimson lips. It's hard to believe that only a few minutes ago, he seemed to be clinging to life. "Is there an echo?"

Trudy rolls her eyes. "*You're lucky my master wants you breathing,*" the Sylk tells me, "*or I'd rip your heart out just to gag him with it.*"

"Now, that's not very nice," Titus coos. "If you're trying to win Miss Oberon over, you might say something like, 'Won't you please join our evil death cult?' or... 'Say goodbye to your neck.'"

Trudy's head turns like a whip as she sneers at Titus, a confused look on her face. "*Say goodbye to...?*"

The moment Trudy takes her eyes off me, I launch one of the daggers at her neck, my heart pounding as it flies through the air, seconds away from severing her spinal cord, when—

Without looking, Trudy seizes the dagger an inch from her flesh. She drops it with a hiss, as if it had burned her. Her head swivels slowly, her eyes like two smoldering bits of coal.

"*Stupid girl,*" the Sylk seethes. "*These people seek only to wield you. You are an object to them. A prize.*"

"I'm flattered," I say, flipping my one remaining dagger and catching it in midair, the metal warm in my palm. "But isn't that exactly what the Guild wants to do with me?"

A malevolent grin. "Oh, the Guild of Shadows has great plans for you. You could be free. You could be powerful. Queen Morana has taken a special interest in you. If only you weren't—"

Titus throws out his hand, and a small iron ball attached to a metal wire shoots out of his sleeve, wrapping itself around Trudy's throat. My heart drops into my stomach. What are the odds that the prince of the Eerie uses the same weaponry as Captain Shade?

Trudy claws at the garrote, her face turning purple, eyes bulging.

"How rude of me," Titus drawls. "I believe you were saying something?"

Trudy's fingers transform, long black talons slicing through the metal with little effort. She takes a triumphant inhalation, her red, glowing eyes wild with hate. When she exhales, a legion of purple, flaming bats burst from her mouth, hurtling towards me.

Everything slows. This is it. This is my moment. All of these months spent chopping onions and peeling potatoes, all of the blood that's been shed…every second since the day Owen was killed has led me to this very instant. And I know, with startling clarity, what I am to do, as if I've been riding on a gentle wave propelling me inexorably towards land, and at long last, I've reached the shore.

I don't run away. I run towards Trudy. Towards the Sylk. Towards revenge.

Death is the only defeat. And I don't intend on dying tonight.

This is for Mr. and Mrs. Hackney. For the child Percy murdered in cold blood. For Mrs. Carroll. For Dorothy. For Father.

For Owen.

"No!" Titus roars, his voice breaking, as I race towards the onslaught of fiery bats, unflinching, picking up speed and—

I drop to my knees at the very last second, sliding beneath the blazing purple swarm, headed straight for Trudy. I lash out, bracing as I strike true, slicing Trudy's stomach wide.

The Sylk howls.

I come to a halt at Titus's feet, panting for breath. I look up at him, at his bloodstained face. His chest heaves, his blue eyes wide, fear and shock and awe all warring in his expression.

"You're mad." His voice cracks as he extends his hand to me. If it weren't for the blood blurring my vision, I'd think there were tears in his eyes.

"No," I say, standing on my own. "I'm a pirate."

I turn, watching as Trudy pivots, clutching her gaping stomach. Entrails spill out over her fingers, her intestines unfurling onto the floor. But she smiles, her teeth crimson, eyes glowing red.

"*We will meet again, Violent Violet,*" the Sylk says clearly over the gargle in Trudy's throat, a voice wholly separate from the body it possesses. "*My master has great plans for you.*"

A rush of power thrums in my veins. "See, that's the difference between you and me," I say, lodging the dagger in Trudy's forehead with a squelch. "I have no master."

As the Sylk's shadowy form seeps from Trudy's flesh, dissipating like smoke, it cackles a gritty, grinding sort of laugh.

"*We are all bound to someone,*" the Sylk says, its voice fading, merely an echo on the wind. "*The question is, who binds you, child of the sea?*"

CHAPTER THIRTY-SIX

Trudy's body collapses in a mangled, bloody heap. Just like that, the Sylk that murdered my brother has been banished. I've avenged Owen. I should feel relieved. I should feel vindicated. So, then why do I feel like I just gave the Sylk exactly what it wanted?

"This isn't over," I murmur, the hair on the back of my neck prickling as I kneel to retrieve both daggers. "That was too easy."

"'Easy' is a relative term, don't you think?" Titus says, decapitating a possessed Nightweaver as it charges us, tossing a metal star from his pocket without even looking in its direction. "I'd say you make the increasingly difficult task of banishing Sylks look rather easy."

I catch sight of Gylda, the blond guard, and snag her by the arm as she hurries past. Blood spatters her face and coats her broadsword, but she smiles as if she'd just been crowned queen of the Eerie.

"Have you seen Will?" I ask.

She shakes her head. "No, but the Underlings are retreating."

I hadn't noticed before, but she's right. I spot Henry through the dwindling crowd, beyond a cluster of Killian's wolves that have descended on the last remaining Gore, where Dorothy continues to circle Elsie and Albert.

"Dorothy!" I call out, trudging ankle-deep through the blood and guts and excrement. I pick my way over bodies—*pieces* of bodies—towards the girl I'd thought to be dead before tonight. "I know you're still in there."

Her head swivels on her neck to find me, snapping bones with an audible crack. The Sylk laughs, her mouth stretching unnaturally wide as her teeth transform to sharp points. "*Dorothy is dead*." The voice that comes from Dorothy's mouth lacks any trace of the mild-mannered girl I'd spent the past few months working alongside. This voice is throaty and dark, the distorted voice of nightmares. "*We devoured her*."

Beyond Dorothy, Henry's face goes slack. Someone had supplied him with a bow while I'd been locked in combat with Trudy, and he aims it at the back of Dorothy's head, a perfect shot. But he doesn't fire.

"I can't," he mouths to me, tears streaking his scarred face. "I can't."

I move closer to Dorothy—or rather, the Sylk possessing her. "Dorothy, I know we got off on the wrong foot," I say slowly, gaining ground with every word. "But I hope you know that if I could go back, if I could change anything about my time here, I'd try to be your friend."

The Sylk cocks her head, and for the first time, I think I see some semblance of Dorothy behind those glowing red eyes.

"I would have liked to be your friend," I say, half hoping Dorothy can hear me but praying to the Stars that she feels no pain as I launch myself at the Sylk, plunging a dagger into Dorothy's heart.

The Sylk lets out a bloodcurdling shriek, its dark form dispersing into the air with a hiss, and I withdraw the dagger, black with infected blood. Henry is there to catch Dorothy's body, kneeling with her cradled in his arms. All corporeal signs of the Sylk's possession diminish, leaving behind Dorothy's fingerless hands, her dark-brown eyes, and her modest, fangless mouth.

Dorothy—the girl, not the Sylk—coughs up blood, wheezing for breath. "Violet?"

I kneel beside her. "I'm here."

Dorothy's mouth twitches, an attempt at a smile. "I would have liked that, too."

Henry half laughs, half sobs, and Dorothy looks up at him, her eyes distant and glassy, blood trickling from her lips.

Weakly, softly, she murmurs, "I love you, Henry."

A final shuddering breath rattles in her chest, and her body goes limp. Henry buries his face in her neck, his shoulders heaving as he weeps into her blood-soaked hair.

It happens all too quickly, and yet, the world seems to slow as a spark ignites and flames consume the curtain to Henry's right. Another spark ignites across the dance floor, then another, until fire consumes the ballroom, igniting like a torch. Killian shouts something inaudible over the roar of the inferno. The smoke burns my nose and throat, but I don't leave Henry. I won't.

"Henry, you have to stop this."

I tug his arm, but he doesn't budge as flames press in on every side.

"Let me burn!" His scream is guttural, his eyes glowing gold. "Let me be with her!"

"Do you really think that's what Dorothy would want?"

Tears stream down his twisted, scarred face. He throws himself back over Dorothy, his hands on her cheeks. He whispers fervently, choking on his own sobs.

Black smoke fills the ballroom, the stench of cooked flesh roiling my stomach.

I grab Henry's wrist. "Listen to me," I attempt to yell, but I can't hear my own hoarse voice over the crackle of flames as it eats away at the ballroom—destroying any evidence of the massacre here tonight. When someone finally manages to put the fire out, all that will be left behind are charred bones and rumors of a mysterious tragedy that struck Bludgrave Manor. "Call off the flames, Henry. Please."

"I can't," he bellows. "I can't!"

Can't. Won't. It doesn't really matter. Henry isn't going to leave this place of his own accord.

"You'll thank me later," I say, knocking him over the head with the blunt end of my dagger. He crumples, his body going limp. I loop my arms under his and drag him towards a gap in the flames, heading blindly in the direction of the double doors nearest to us. Henry groans, but he's too incapacitated to fight back. "Or not."

I think I've almost made it to the exit when a fiery beam collapses, landing directly in my path. If it were just me, I could easily climb over it and make my way to safety. But I won't be able to lug Henry's body over it. Not fast enough.

I cough, the smoke filling my lungs twice as fast. I attempt to pull Henry onto my back, but I'm dizzy. So dizzy…

"*Violet.*" I hear Owen's voice. "*Get up, Violet. Leave him.*"

I'm not leaving Henry behind. I'm not…

"Violet!" A different voice comes from far away. "I found them!"

Killian's voice.

"They're over here!"

I'm lifted into the air, cradled close to someone's chest. We break out of the suffocating heat into the clear air. My eyes open slightly, just enough to see Killian dragging Henry onto the east lawn, where Lady Isabelle takes her son into her arms as if he were only a small child. But my vision goes dark, my eyelids impossibly heavy.

Sleep. I just need to sleep.

"Oh, no you don't, love."

I'm plunged into cold water before I have the chance to take a breath, and my eyelids fling wide. Titus hovers over me, holding me under the surface of the fountain. I try to wrench myself free of his grip, but the moment I do, he pulls me out of the water and close to his chest. He draws back, his hands finding my face as he searches my eyes.

"It worked." His mouth parts on a shaky breath. "You're—"

"Titus!" Killian shouts from across the lawn. My head whips to the right, where I find that Mother, Jack, Annie, and all five of my siblings have made it out, along with Sybil, Boris, Gylda, and Hugh. Thick, dark smoke billows out onto the portico as the fire rages, devastating the east wing.

For a moment, it seems as if Titus doesn't plan on letting go of me, his grip tightening. But Killian shouts his name again and he relents, lifting me out of the fountain with ease and gently placing me on the grass.

"This should only take a moment," he says, a dry smirk tugging at the corner of his lip.

Titus turns towards the east wing, takes a deep breath. He lifts his hands in a fluid motion, and in response, the waters from the fountain rise like a wave. A slight flick of his wrist, and the water shoots across the lawn in a torrent, targeting the flames with keen precision.

I think of what power like that could accomplish at sea—how the very waves would bend to a bloodletter's every whim—and suppress a shudder.

But it seems his power is limited. The water crashes to the ground, just short of the manor, as Titus roars, falling to his knees. I find myself at his side as he pants for breath, looking up at me with eyes of liquid honey.

"I'm weak," Titus groans, clutching at his heart. It's as if I can hear it beating, a frenzied pulse that's almost tangible in the air around me. "You—you have to try."

"Try?" I ask, my voice trembling. "Try what?"

"The water," he coughs, blood trickling from his lip. "You feel it, don't you?"

I tear my gaze from his to look at the waters of the fountain. I gape at my reflection—at the two gilded eyes staring back at me.

"I knew it," Titus breathes.

I suppose I did, too. From the moment I learned the truth about the Nightweavers—about their magic. The way the water calls to me; the way blood streamed from Percy's eyes with only a thought. I reasoned it was part of my curse. But all this time, I've had power all my own. A power I shouldn't have.

I meet Titus's gilded eyes, as bright as the sun itself.

"But," I whisper, glad that we are far from the others, who remain clustered together amongst the rose gardens of the east lawn. "I'm human?"

"Only half," Titus says softly, his tattooed knuckles brushing a tear from my face. "You're a Nightweaver, Violet."

Chapter Thirty-Seven

My heart stutters, threatening to stop altogether.

If I have Nightweaver blood in my veins...What does that say of my parents? Have I spent my entire life hating Nightweavers, never knowing that my own mother or father had been the very thing I'd hated? Neither Mother nor Father had ever told us much about their lives before they'd met each other, or where they'd come from. Only that they'd found each other, and that was when their lives had truly begun.

My heart splinters. *Father...*

"Focus, Violet," Titus says. "You can put the fire out. Command the water to go where you want it to go."

"You make it sound easy," I half laugh, half sob.

He smiles sadly. "Easy is a relative term, love." He gets to his feet, gripping the edge of the fountain for support. "Now, take a deep breath."

I do as he says, inhaling deeply. I cough as smoke fills my lungs, gritty and unforgiving.

"That's it," Titus murmurs, his lilting voice as gentle as a lullaby. "The water obeys you. It is your servant. Make it listen. Make it yours."

The water lapping at the fountain whispers a strange plea, and I answer it, my hand hovering over the surface. My reflection ripples as the water rises to meet my palm, drawn to me, bending to my inarticulate will...

Mine. This power is mine.

I raise my left hand in a fluid motion, just as I'd seen Titus do, as if I were reaching for Bludgrave. The water climbs, hovering in the air like a gigantic wave, towering over us. Titus watches me with a look of awe as a new torrent of water crashes into the east wing of Bludgrave, stronger than what he'd wielded moments ago. My bones shake with the power thrumming in my veins, fueling me with some innate sense of belonging in this world. I am the water. The water is me. I will not relent. I will not waver.

But the power I conjure leeches from my marrow, my blood, until every last drop of *Manan* I can afford to give has been spent. My knees buckle, my muscles failing me, but Titus takes me by the hand, his fingers clasped in mine. His other hand grasps my wrist, holding my outstretched hand in the air, in the direction of the east wing. He stands facing me, his gilded eyes locked on mine, but it's as if I see through him—to the veins in his face, the blood pumping throughout his body. He speaks to me, but I don't hear him over the sound of his heart beating in tandem with my own. I latch onto the power that thrums in his chest—*mine.* I make it mine.

The force of water as I summon it from beneath the fountain cracks the stone, splitting the earth. Unbound, the water rushes past us on all sides, creating a tunnel that surges towards Bludgrave, extinguishing every last flame until I hear Titus's voice from far away, begging me to stop.

"It's alright," he says, his hand on my cheek. "It's over. You can stop now, love. You're safe. We're all safe."

Safe.

His hand squeezes mine, and his face comes into focus—his paling skin, his blue eyes, his tousled blond hair. He wraps his arms around me, solid and real and familiar in a way I can't explain.

Safe.

I collapse, and Titus lowers himself to the ground with me, heaving for breath as the smoke clears, revealing the caved-in framework of what was once the ballroom. I must have tapped into whatever power Titus had left—whatever small store of *Manan* he'd reserved—and spent it, too. I don't understand how this magic works, but by the looks of it, he's been drained of any energy he might have had a minute ago. His body goes limp, but I can still hear his heartbeat, and the rise and fall of his chest lets me know he's unconscious but alive.

Alive. *Thank the Stars.* Earlier this evening, I would have reveled in knowing I had been the one to end the prince of the Eerie. But now...In only a few hours, everything has changed.

Everything.

I lay Titus gently on the ground and make a move to find Killian.

"Annie?" Elsie cries, her small voice breaking through the chaos. I spot my little sister across the lawn, her face covered in soot. "Where's Annie?"

I start towards her, but the ache in my head splits open, causing my vision to blur.

"*Violet.*" I hear Owen's voice again, this time even louder than before. It bores into my skull, drilling into my subconscious until I cannot tell if the voice comes from within or without.

"No," I say through gritted teeth. "You're dead. You're—"

A gunshot rattles my chest. No—not a gunshot. In the distance, fireworks erupt over Ink Haven, thundering like cannon fire in my skull. Each blast brings me back to the *Lightbringer*—back to the day Owen died. At sea, I couldn't flee. There was nowhere to go. But now…

I think someone shouts my name as my feet carry me west, bile creeping up my throat as I bolt, a mad attempt to outrun the pain that follows me despite the distance I put between myself and Bludgrave. Bludgrave—where my father lies dead on the kitchen floor. Bludgrave, our gilded cage, exposed for what it truly is. A battlefield. A prison. A tomb.

I couldn't save Father. I couldn't save Owen. What if Elsie is next? Or Albert? Lewis? Margaret? Charlie? Mother? I'm doomed to lose the ones I love. *Cursed.* Tonight is only the beginning. The Guild isn't going to stop until they've torn everyone I've ever loved from my grasp and left me with nothing. Nothing but this hollow grief, this violent rage. Nothing. Nothing. *Nothing.*

Agony cuts me like a blade and I fall to my knees, clutching my skull as a keening wail bursts from my lips. But just as I've begun to feel the burgeoning heat of anger rising up within me, something cold douses my senses. The air shifts, and my voice is lost to the wind.

Nothing. Nothing. Nothing.

Almost too low to hear, a growl raises the hair on the back of my neck. Through bleary eyes, I make out the shape of a dark, cloaked figure kneeling over a limp corpse about ten feet from where I'd collapsed. Blood coats his pale mouth and chin, his eyes glowing gold as he pierces me with a ravenous look like that of a wild animal.

Will?

He cocks his head, a preternatural stillness about him as his lips curl back, revealing bloody teeth.

"Will?" I squint through the darkness, my pulse racing. He crouches over the lifeless body like a wolf protecting its kill. And the body... "Oh, Stars...Martin?"

Will winces as if I'd struck him. Another low growl makes my blood run cold as he shifts towards me. I realize with a chill that in this moment, he appears exactly like I'd always expected Nightweavers to look. Like something out of my worst nightmares.

Like a monster.

"Will, it's me," I say on a shaky breath. "It's me, Violet."

He grunts, his posture feral as he creeps on all fours over Martin's corpse. His tongue swipes out, licking his lips.

I look past him, to Martin's face, his empty eyes; his expression, so calm, as if he had felt no pain in death. The gaping wound in his neck stains his pressed white shirt, sodden with blood.

"Human blood is the purest source of Manan," I remember Will had told me the night we found Mr. and Mrs. Hackney. *"But it drives Nightweavers to madness. We become no better than the Underlings—as savage as a Gore, and twice as deadly."*

"What did you do?" I whisper, unable to look away from the mangled wreck of exposed arteries and tissue. "What did you *do?*"

Will continues towards me, his golden eyes pinning me to the spot. My breath hitches at the sight of him, framed by the white lilies, all spattered with crimson. *"Sympathy for that which has come to an end,"* I hear Will's voice from all those months ago. *"And new beginnings."*

I taste salt before I feel the tears streaming down my cheeks.

Will is so close now, I am almost certain he can hear my frenzied heart as it leaps in my throat. He leans in, his breath—tinged with the sickening stench of metal—warming my face. *Warm,* not cold. Will—*my* Will—is warm. He is thoughtful, and loyal, and kind. He is a boy—not this beast that looms over me, drenched in innocent blood.

"Will?" his name escapes me in a panicked whisper. "Will, please. I'm here. I'm right here."

He sniffs, his face hovering near the crook of my neck. His nose brushes the exposed skin of my throat, and something in his posture shifts, more human now as he lifts his hand, his thumb tracing my scar...

When he speaks, his voice is raw, deeper than his usual tenor, and so low I can barely make out the word.

"*Run.*"

CHAPTER THIRTY-EIGHT

I blink, stammering, "Will, I—"

"Run!"

I scramble out from underneath him and race past, leaping over where Martin lies, headed for the stables. I can't lead Will back to the house, where he might hurt Elsie, or Albert, or anyone else. But if I can lead him away, into the woods...

A bone-chilling howl erupts from the garden. I stumble, tripping over my own feet, but I don't stop. Not even when the grass behind me crunches and I know, without turning, that Will has given chase. I realize, with a pang in my chest, that I can't outrun him. I'm not fast enough. I'm never fast enough.

But I don't have to be faster than a Nightweaver. I just have to be smarter than one.

I race through the open doors of the stable, my feet catching on something that sends me sprawling forward onto my hands and knees. I spit dirt, scrabbling onto my back. Cold horror washes over me, flooding my veins with ice, when I realize what caused my fall.

A torso, half-clothed in a shredded teal gown. The other Nightweaver girl from the ball, one of the two that had clung to Will's arm. I'd seen her giggling not but a few hours ago.

Will stands over the dismembered corpse, staring down at it, his head cocked.

"Will," I start, my mouth painfully dry.

His jaw twitches, lips peeling back in a snarl. He doesn't look away from the girl's torso, his gilded eyes narrowing—that familiar, questioning look somewhere beneath the bloodlust that glazes his stare.

"Come back to me, Will," I say softly, rising to my feet. "Your family needs you. *Annie* needs you."

His gaze pierces me like a knife. It's as if all the air has been knocked from my lungs.

"Annie is missing," I say, taking a tentative step towards him, attempting to ignore the body between us.

He snarls, but his face softens, his features smoothing out— if only in my imagination.

"She needs you." I reach out, my hand trembling as I press my palm to his cheek, wet with blood—blood that thrums at my touch, vibrating through my fingers…

I swallow hard, choking on the knot in my throat, and whisper, "*I* need you."

A tear drips onto my knuckles. Will catches my hand in his as he squeezes his eyes shut, nuzzling into my palm.

"The blood..." he chokes out, his voice like gravel. "There was...so much blood..."

He opens his eyes, revealing a thin rim of gold bordering the emerald green. Tears spill onto his cheeks. "I ran, but there were...others." His throat bobs. "I couldn't stop. I tried. I tried to stop."

He folds in on himself, his shoulders shaking, as I wrap him in my arms. "I know," is all I can think to say. "I know you tried."

He draws away swiftly, gripping my shoulders with heavy hands. "Annie?"

I shake my head. "She made it out of the fire, but then she disappeared."

He gives a tight nod, half leading, half dragging me to Caligo's stall. He lifts me onto the saddle with otherworldly strength before starting out on foot.

"I'll search the conservatory," Will calls over his shoulder. "Go to Hildegarde's Folly. She might have wandered off again."

"Wait!" I gallop after him. "Why not take Thea?" I ask, jerking my chin at the unicorn.

Will doesn't look back, doesn't answer as he disappears into the darkness, moving at a dizzying speed I hardly comprehend.

Wind whips my face as I ride for Hildegarde's Folly. The sun begins its ascent, a seam of crimson light on the horizon. Where earlier in the night the grounds had been raucous with laughter and music, now there is only Caligo's pounding hooves and my own beating heart as I race across the lawn.

"*Violet.*"

I dismount Caligo, clutching my aching head as I stumble up the steps of the folly. "Annie?" I call out. "Annie?"

"*Violet!*"

"Stop!" I shriek. "Get out of my head! Get out! Get out! *Get out!*"

A blinding pain sears my mind and I stagger, catching hold of the statue in the center of the folly. I blink away the black dots spotting my vision, certain I must be hallucinating as I look out through the stone columns, at the looming border of the wood. There, a figure stands, cloaked in shadows. They turn, melding into the darkness, and before I know it, I'm chasing after them.

I fling myself down the steps of the folly, ignoring Caligo's whine as I scrape through the thickets, his neighing swallowed up by the thick undergrowth of the wood. Ahead, the figure moves swiftly, leaping over fallen logs with ease. I scramble, keeping pace, and all the while my mind screeches for me to stop. Turn back. Find Will. But I can't stop. Something inexplicable propels me forward. I have to keep going. I have to be fast enough. I have to—

Just when the muscles in my legs threaten to give out, the figure breaks through the brambles up ahead. I hiss through my teeth, a stitch splitting my side, and clamber after them.

I stumble into a small clearing, heaving for breath, my vision adjusting to the pitch blackness. In the center of the clearing,

Annie rocks back and forth, mumbling something inaudible, her wide eyes fixed on an empty patch of dirt.

Pressure floods my head and I fall to my knees in front of her, pushing the black ringlets from her face. Other than her odd state, she appears unharmed.

"Come," I pant, taking her by the arm. "We have to get you back. Your brother—"

Annie jerks her arm from my grip, her mumbling growing louder, more urgent. I lean in, straining to hear. If only I could make out the words...

"She can't leave with you." Lord Castor's weak voice comes from somewhere to my left. I squint, barely able to make out his broad figure bound to a tree, his face bloody and bruised. After Titus pulled me from the fire, I hadn't even noticed Will's father wasn't among the survivors. I'd just assumed he'd made it out. But now that I think about it... I hadn't seen Lord Castor since the pixies freed him in the ballroom.

"Why not?" I demand, starting towards him. I reach out, my hands nearing the ropes that bind him, when a presence at the edge of the clearing gives me pause.

"I wouldn't do that if I were you." A familiar voice sends a chill down my spine.

I turn slowly, no longer breathing, towards the voice—the voice that haunts my every waking moment. I'd almost forgotten what it sounded like, constantly wondering if I had remembered it falsely, somehow, but no. It was him. It was always him.

At the edge of the clearing, propped carelessly against a tree, a ghost dressed in a fine purple suit winks at me, as if this were all some kind of cruel joke.

"Took you long enough, little mouse."

CHAPTER THIRTY-NINE

"Owen?" My breath hitches. I stumble a few steps, starting towards him. "Is that...Is it really you?"

Owen flourishes a bow, lips curved in a taut smile. "In the flesh."

A sob chokes my voice, and for an instant, I feel like a child. Small. Helpless. Weak. I'm dreaming—I must be dreaming. I want to run to him. Want to throw my arms around him and never let go. My brother—my best friend—stands not but ten feet away from me, looking more alive than he ever had before.

Alive. My chest squeezes, painfully tight. "How?"

Owen pushes off from the trunk with fluid grace, his dirty-blond hair creeping into his eyes—eyes that I find are no longer kind. His eyes...they're all wrong. Shrewd. Empty. Mocking. Not like Owen's.

"You're not really him," I say, staggering back. "You're... you're just a Shifter pretending to be Owen. Owen is dead. I saw him die."

"You're only half-wrong," he says, using the same patient voice he'd used when he taught me how to cut an onion without crying and the proper technique for giving someone a quick, dignified death with a knife.

He takes a slow step towards me. "You saw me die." He opens the purple coat, unbuttoning the black shirt beneath to reveal a gruesome scar where the blade had pierced his heart. "I died, Violet. But I was…reborn. The Guild of Shadows made me a Shifter; they gave me a new purpose. A new life."

I can't believe what I'm hearing. And yet, it all makes sense. "It was you," I say. "You were in Albert and Elsie's room that night." I stagger back another step, blood beating in my ears. "The card I found on that poor girl…it was yours."

He dips his head, encouraging. "Very good," he says, the way he might have if I landed a blow during a sparring match, his eyes lit with pride. "What else?"

Cold horror floods my veins. "You carved the message into Mr. and Mrs. Hackney's foreheads." My throat tightens. "You left their eyes for me to find."

Another nod. "I never thought it would take so much effort to lure you here, beyond the boundaries of their estate," Owen admits. "But that *Nightweaver*…" A muscle in his jaw tenses, his lips curling into a sneer. "Every time I left a clue for you to find, he steered you away."

Will. He *was* misleading me, just not for the reasons I'd thought.

"You killed Dearest." My voice is barely a whisper. "You hid the knife under Annie's bed."

Oh, Stars. No. *No.*

"You compelled Father," I croak, my legs swaying beneath me. I search Owen's eyes for any trace of kindness, for any trace of our father, but find none. "He tried to kill me."

"I specifically instructed him *not* to kill you." Owen heaves a terse sigh, examining his tar-black nails. "But really, Violet, after the lengths I've gone to get your attention, I thought it might be easier to have someone drag you here. And considering you'd put up a fight, I figured wounding you would give whoever brought you a fair chance."

A scream builds in my throat, strangling me. "He's dead, Owen! Father is dead!"

There—something flickers in his eyes. Something human.

He arches a brow, glancing away from his nails to examine me with a cold, dull look. "How unfortunate."

The childlike feeling I'd had at seeing Owen alive, standing before me, is replaced with unbridled, all-consuming rage, like fire in my bones. "*How unfortunate?*"

He shrugs his shoulders, rolls his eyes. "For you, of course." He takes another step, closing the distance between us, merely five feet from me now. "I know it hurts, but it doesn't have to. It won't." He draws a black dagger from a sheath strapped to his back, its dark blade inscribed with glowing purple script— ancient words I can't make out. "Not for much longer."

The pit in my stomach deepens. "You intend to kill me, then?"

"There is no death for people like us, Violet," he says, taking another step.

"People like us?" I step back. I wonder if Owen would know—if he knows that I'm half Nightweaver. Wouldn't that make him half Nightweaver, too? "I'm not—not like you."

"Not entirely. But we're more alike than you think."

"There is a ballroom piled high with corpses because of you," I snarl. "We are *nothing* alike."

"Oh?" His brows perk. He grins cheekily, but the expression no longer reminds me of Mother. "Don't pretend you're innocent, little sister. I've seen you kill. The ocean is full of bodies you disposed of. Men, women." He glances at Annie, still rocking back and forth, muttering wildly. "Children."

Something in my chest splinters. "I didn't have a choice."

Owen laughs, but it sounds foreign. "You're still telling yourself that lie, then?" He takes another step, nearly backing me against a tree, but I pivot, standing between him and Annie.

He gives me a conspiratorial grin as he shakes his head. "You had a choice. You've always had a choice. You chose *them*— Mother and Father, Margaret, Lewis, Elsie." The grin fades, a sneer taking its place. "You killed to protect them. That was a *choice*."

He takes another step. "You could have left here so many times, but you chose them over your own happiness." Another step. "Over your own freedom." Another. "Tonight, you chose to give your life rather than expose the Castors. Yes," he adds when my eyes widen. "I've been watching you rather closely."

I remember the raven, perched on the roof of Hildegarde's Folly. All this time, Owen has been here. Watching me. Tormenting me.

"Why?" I ask, blinking back tears. "Why are you doing this?"

Owen runs a finger over the edge of his blade. "Do you remember Mary Cross?"

I blink, startled. An image flashes into my mind: Mary Cross, the refugee we'd picked up along the Dire...her decapitated body.

Owen exhales, twirling the blade, his hardened gaze fixed on something over my shoulder, beyond the clearing. "It's all my fault, you know," he says quietly. "The *Lightbringer*..." His throat bobs, and he pierces me with a stare that makes me feel as if I'm watching him die all over again. "You still wear it? My trinket."

Instinctually, I reach for the bracelet, running my fingers over the band of braided leather. I swallow around the knot in my throat. "Why wouldn't I?"

He watches me, his eyes lingering on the bracelet. "She regrets not being more specific with that Nightweaver of yours."

"Who?" My brows furrow. "Mary?"

He heaves an exasperated sigh, and I see, for the first time since he appeared, just how tired he looks. "Haven't you wondered why, after we'd spent our whole lives at sea, the Nightweavers finally managed to catch up with us?" He takes slow steps, circling the perimeter of the clearing. "I did—when I woke to this second life."

He flicks a glance at the bracelet. "Old magic," he says. "That which came before the Nightweavers fell from Elysia; before they stole our lands, our thrones—*our* magic." He touches his own wrist, where the band of braided leather once resided. "Mother and Father lied to us about a great many things." His fists clench. "I'll admit, it was clever to use the trinkets. Easy to ensure we wouldn't take them off—wouldn't question their…usefulness."

I cover the bracelet with my other hand as if to shield it. As if to shield myself. All the while, he circles.

"They were enchanted."

"Enchanted?" I balk. "But—"

"Yes, enchanted." Again, that patient voice. "Mother and Father paid quite a bit of coin to have a protective charm placed on each of our trinkets. A spell that would ensure that no one could ever find us." He stills, his expression hard as he surveys the edge of the clearing. He looks back at me, his eyes brimming with guilt. "So that no one ever found *you*."

"Me?" My voice is small. "Why me?"

A knowing look. "You're cursed, remember?"

A knot forms in my stomach as Annie's senseless mumbling fades. Owen's slow, methodical footsteps are the only sound in the silent wood.

"We were children when it happened," he says conversationally. "Mother and Father had been forced to go ashore to find food somewhere just off the coast of Hellion." He doesn't look at me, his gaze trained on the brambles and thickets encircling the clearing. "You were bitten."

The knot in my stomach tightens. "Bitten?"

A slow nod, his expression unreadable. "Nearly took your left arm."

I reach for my shoulder, the feeling of teeth piercing my flesh like a remnant, lingering on my skin, in my bones.

When I look up, Owen has stilled again, watching me.

He scowls. "Mother took you to a Sorceress—a human, well practiced in the magic of our ancestors. The woman managed to heal the wound and shield your heart, keeping the venom from turning you fully into a Shifter. But there had been a Sylk present when we were attacked—it had picked up on your scent. No matter where we went, we could be traced. Even on water."

Above the treetops, the sun reaches its midway point in the dark, crimson sky. The leaves appear to glisten, wet with blood.

"Our trinkets were supposed to keep us safe," Owen says, his voice quiet as he takes a step towards me, his gaze trained on the bracelet. "We were never supposed to take them off."

"We didn't—"

He cuts me off with a dismissive wave. "No, none of you did." His jaw tightens, and he looks out at the edge of the clearing once more, glaring at something I can't see. "For years, I searched for the Red Island. Devoted my life to it. But Mother and Father wouldn't even consider looking. 'A myth,' they told me." He sneers, a look so unfamiliar on his features that I wince. "*Liars.*"

My hands stray to the daggers at either hip—daggers Killian claims had come from the Red Island, from our people. Owen's gaze follows my movement, and he smirks slightly.

"We were right," he whispers, tawny eyes glittering. In them, I catch a glimpse of the boy my brother was before the Underlings made him into...*this*. The adventurer. The navigator.

The dreamer.

"The week before we came upon the Cross ship, I prepared a rowboat," Owen says as the stars in his eyes twinkle out. His lip twitches, the makings of a frown. "I knew Mother and Father were never going to listen to me. I decided to find the Red Island on my own. I took my bracelet off—left it for someone to find."

A long, tense silence stretches out between us.

"I couldn't do it, though." He smiles sadly. "I couldn't leave you behind."

His eyes meet mine, holding my gaze as he takes another step.

"I determined to wait another year—to let Elsie have a bit more time with you—before I tried convincing you to leave. 'We go together,' right?" His expression twists, full of a raw, mangled hurt I can't begin to make sense of. "But I knew, even then, that you never would. You would never have chosen me over the rest of them."

The splinter in my chest shatters. "Owen, I—"

"A week later," he says, swiftly cutting me off, "we brought Mary aboard the *Lightbringer*." He looks away again, at the border of the clearing, his brows furrowed. "You see, when I removed my bracelet, I broke the enchantment. The Sylk had begun hunting us again. Hunting you."

Realization dawns on me, a searing pain just behind my eyes. "Mary Cross was possessed." The Sylk that had killed Owen; the Sylk that jumped from one unknown Nightweaver into another, then to Percy, and finally to Trudy. I thought, all this time, that I had been hunting the Sylk. But it had been hunting me my whole life. It had been aboard our ship for an entire week, parading as Mary Cross, a mild-mannered girl whom no one would have ever suspected brought such evil into our lives.

Owen flourishes his dagger, looking pleased that I'd figured it out. "Mary was merely a harbinger," he says, taking another slow step towards me, attempting to close the distance between us once more. "Queen Morana has searched for you for quite some time. 'The child that should have been a Shifter.' A human girl that possesses your unique talents, with enough Underling venom in your body to transform a host of Shifters, and yet continues to live." He fixes me with an odd look of curiosity, somewhat pitying. "Your Nightweaver never mentioned you should be dead, did he?"

My heart pounds against my sternum, a throbbing ache in my chest.

Owen shakes his head, laughing sharply. "No, I didn't think he would." He takes another step, merely three feet away from me now—the closest we've been since the day he died. His tawny eyes bear a trace of kindness, as if the Owen I know is still in there, somewhere. "The ocean aided the enchantment around

your heart, keeping the venom subdued while hindering your…
abilities. But from the moment you stepped foot on land, the
enchantment began to weaken."

He takes another step, forcing me backward. I almost
stumble over Annie, but I plant my feet, trembling hands
lingering near the hilts of my daggers. He closes the gap between
us, and for the first time, the metallic stench of blood and decay
that clings to him causes me to gag.

"You *will* get sick. The venom will poison you from the
inside out." He looks as if he is about to take another step, but he
wrinkles his nose, and I remember the perfume Margaret had
spritzed me with just before the ball tonight. It appears to stave
him off; he keeps at least a foot of distance between us, his eyes
narrowed.

"It will kill you slowly, Violet." Owen searches my face, his
cold stare lingering just above my lip, where blood had crusted
my skin. "It already is."

CHAPTER FORTY

Tears burn my cheeks. "You're lying."

Owen's eyes darken. "I wish I was," he says softly, his knuckles paling around the hilt of his dagger, which he holds between us like a promise. "Your Nightweaver knew this. He's known since the moment he laid eyes on you exactly who and *what* you are."

My mind whirls. I am Violet Oberon, daughter of Captain Grace and Philip Oberon. I'm a pirate. A kitchen maid. I am the reason my father is dead. The reason so many people have died. The reason Owen is an Underling. I am nothing. I am no one.

Except, that's not entirely true. Not anymore. "What are we?" I ask quietly, feeling as if, for a moment, we aren't so different after all.

"We're abominations," Owen answers, his smirk almost teasing.

"And our brothers and sisters? Are they part Nightweaver, too?"

Owen rolls his eyes. "They do not possess an affinity, if that's what you're asking. Not like you and me. And no," he adds as I open my mouth, "I don't know which of our parents befouled our blood. I don't care. Neither should you."

In a flash, I draw my own dagger, causing Owen to lose his footing. He surrenders a few feet and I claim that ground, pushing him backwards. "How did Will know about my affinity?" I demand. "Tell me what you know, Owen. I can help you. We can—"

A broken, hysterical laugh escapes him. "Help me?" Owen shakes his head. "I don't need help, sister. I've defeated death. And you could too."

He and I stand five feet apart, daggers drawn. For a moment, it feels as if we could be back on the *Lightbringer*, preparing to spar with wooden knives. But we are no longer children. And these blades are meant for killing, not play.

Owen straightens a bit, dusting his breast pocket. The rich, deep plum of his ensemble shows just how pallid he's become, having spent the past months living in shadows. "If it will make you understand," he says, a slight smirk curling his lip as he flourishes a conceding bow, "let's play a game, shall we?"

I don't answer, my grip on the dagger tightening.

"Annie," he says softly, "come here."

I turn, attempting to put myself between the two of them, but Annie skirts me to stand at Owen's side. Her body trembles, her lips pressed tight. But her eyes are vacant, devoid of any emotion as Owen crouches, using his dagger to brush her black ringlets over her shoulder.

"I'll give you three guesses," he says, taking a knife from a sheath strapped to his ankle. He presents it to Annie. "Guess correctly, and I'll share my secrets—secrets your Nightweaver has kept from you. Guess wrong, and I've instructed Annie to inflict pain upon her poor, defenseless father. I, for one, am interested to see how she interprets such a command."

My eyes widen. "You can't—"

"I already have," Owen shoots back, his face lit with carefully subdued madness. "Now, let's begin. Your Nightweaver took our bracelets when he first captured you, didn't he?"

I open my mouth, but Owen waves his hand dismissively.

"No, no. That's far too easy." Owen grins, but it doesn't reach his eyes. "Besides, you need not tell me; I already know." He inspects his dagger, tracing the glowing purple script with a pale finger. "Ah, here's a better question." He flips the dagger, pointing it at me. "By what creatures were our ancestors able to communicate across great distances?"

I stare at him, wondering if his question is meant to trick me somehow. I glance at Lord Castor, who sobs quietly, as if he'd been compelled to silence.

"Water sprites," I answer slowly.

"Correct!" Owen flourishes a bow. "Would you like to know a secret, Violet?"

I set my jaw, glaring at him.

"Of course you do." He smiles sadistically as he lowers his voice, glancing about the clearing with mock vigilance. "A Sylk stowed away aboard the *Merryway* in Hellion."

"That isn't a secret," I bite out. Will had already reasoned that a Sylk had gained passage aboard the *Merryway*. However, I had believed that the Sylk that followed me to Bludgrave and the Sylk that boarded the *Merryway* in Hellion were one and the same. But if Mary had already been possessed before she joined us aboard the *Lightbringer*, that means there was another Sylk—a Sylk that had possessed an unknowing crewmember of the *Merryway*, just as Will had suspected. A Sylk that could be watching us at this very moment.

My stomach sinks. The Sylk that had possessed Mary, then Percy, and finally, Trudy, had been a distraction. A ruse. And Will and I had fallen for it.

"Perhaps," Owen concedes, his eyes alight with mischief. "But do you know *why*?"

I grit my teeth. "Why?"

Owen tsks. "You know the game. I ask the questions." He clears his throat, flourishing his dagger. "How do you think the *Merryway* was able to find you?"

"Owen—"

"Think." His eyes darken. "I'm sure you can figure it out."

I groan, clenching a fist. "A Sylk compelled the captain of the *Merryway* to seek the *Lightbringer* out," I say, putting it together. "Mary must have provided the coordinates by way of water sprite."

Owen claps, looking genuinely impressed. "Very good."
He shrugs. "Before we were attacked, the Sylk compelled Will
to take you prisoner and bring you back to the Eerie. She had
him remove the bracelets, rendering the protective charm the
Sorceress had placed on them useless and allowing the Sylks to
track your movements with ease."

She. So, the Sylk that stowed away aboard the *Merryway* is
female.

"Next question," Owen says, tapping the flat end of his
blade against his chin. "How—"

"No," I say, my voice shaking. "I'm not playing your game."

He sighs, pinching the bridge of his nose. "I suppose I
should have explained the rules in detail."

Annie takes the knife he'd given her and plunges it into Lord
Castor's thigh. He lets out a muffled wail through his tightly
pressed lips, but Annie remains expressionless as she removes
the blade. Blood drips from the knife, coating her hand.

My heart stutters, threatening to stop altogether.

"If you guess wrong *or* you refuse to play, Annie has been
instructed to inflict pain." Owen rolls his neck. "No matter, I've
grown bored of the game myself." He kneels, taking the knife
from Annie and sheathing it at his ankle once more. "We've
little time before your Nightweaver comes looking for you. She
underestimated him," Owen goes on, claiming ground as he
takes another slow step towards me. "I will not."

"*She?*" I ask, my heartbeat quickening. "Who is she?"

"*She* is the reason you're here," he says, his voice pitched, as if his patience has finally begun to wear. "The Sylk that compelled your precious Nightweaver never dreamed the Castors would take you in. She certainly didn't think William Castor, of all brutes, would keep your bracelets, much less return them to you." He casts a lingering glance at my bracelet. "Accidental or not, it seems he found a loophole."

What was it that Will said to me, just after I'd arrived here? *"If I hadn't taken it, someone else might have."* Is it possible that Owen is telling the truth, and Will did so because he'd been compelled?

"He would have told me," I say, though even as the words leave my mouth, I can't help but wonder... *Would he?*

"He couldn't. For all he's done to get in the way, that part of her compulsion stuck." Owen shrugs. "She believes it has something to do with your Nightweaver's talent for persuasion. Perhaps he wouldn't have been strong enough to impose his own will, had he not spent years strengthening his gift through the consumption of human blood." A slow, wicked smile touches his lips at the stricken look on my face. "You've seen him feed, haven't you?"

Bile creeps into my throat. What I'd seen tonight...could it be that this isn't the first time Will has lost control? It's hard to imagine the calm, composed Will I spoke with on the train that day had already made a habit of feeding on humans.

"I've been told that just before he'd arrived in Hellion, the great William Castor had sufficiently gorged himself on *Manan*." He takes another step, his dark eyes glittering with mischief—a look I once found exciting. Now, as a sly smile curls his lips, my stomach roils.

My loyalty to the prince is not the only reason I agreed to go on that voyage.

Owen tsks. "I'd considered finding them myself after I turned," he says, twirling the dagger. "But that was before I was informed about your Nightweaver's little detour."

His grin is wickedly gleeful as the rising sun washes his skin the color of fresh blood.

"He found it?" I ask, my voice barely a whisper. "The *Deathwail*."

"Oh, he certainly thought so." Shadows wreath Owen's eager eyes as he takes another step. "Rowed out to meet them by himself in the middle of the night. Turns out it was just a poor, starving clan of pirates." Owen shakes his head, his expression somewhat mad. "From what I've heard, even once he realized he'd attacked the wrong ship, he slaughtered them anyway. Missed one, though. Left poor Mary Cross adrift in the Dire."

I'd heard of pirate clans flying the *Deathwail*'s flag to warn off attackers. But if Mary Cross was already possessed, that would mean it was no coincidence that Will had mistaken them for the *Deathwail*. The Sylk that had coordinated the attack on the *Lightbringer* and our subsequent capture must have known Will was searching for the *Deathwail*—she had to have planned for him to attack that ship. For Mary to get away. For us to find Mary...

The sun creeps higher, bathing the sky, the clearing, and everything it touches in bloody red light.

The judgement is coming.

Owen sucks his teeth. "When William realized you possessed gifts like that of a Shifter but were still alive..." He sighs, rolling his neck. "He just couldn't let you go. Thought you might be the key to finding the Sylk that he suspects had compelled him aboard the *Merryway*." A wicked smirk curls his lip. "He has quite the appetite for revenge, your Nightweaver."

I look down at the bracelet on my wrist—Owen's, not mine. The Sylk had tampered with Will's memories. She had made him forget why he'd taken my bracelets in the first place. But by giving me Owen's trinket, Will had protected me, all this time, without even knowing.

Something nags at me—something I can't make sense of. "Why kill the atroxis?"

Owen tilts his head, his expression sinister. "I had to improvise." He motions at Lord Castor, tied to the tree to my right, blood surging from the wound in his thigh. "With the right motivation, he was more than willing to ensure tonight's success."

I glance at Lord Castor—at the tears streaming down his ruddy face. He never takes his charcoal eyes off Annie, who stands motionless, her hand dripping blood.

"What do you mean?" I ask, my palm slick as I adjust my grip on the dagger.

Owen smiles like a child with a secret. When he speaks, his voice is calm, but his tone is threatening. "Tell her."

Will's father grimaces, straining against the ropes. "They had Annie," he says with a furious sniff. "Lured her into the woods. Percy and...and his thugs. *He*"—Lord Castor glances at Owen—"claimed they worked for the Guild of Shadows. That Annie had been compelled to...to..." he breaks off, sobbing.

"There, there," Owen drawls, rolling his eyes. "Really, I don't know what has him all worked up. I merely told him that if he didn't cooperate, little Annie here would do to herself what I had her do to that pitiful atroxis."

My heart catches in my throat. All the odd looks from Lord Castor; his strange behavior tonight. He knew Owen and the Sylk were here, that they were behind everything that had happened—Dearest, the Hackneys, Dorothy being taken, Trudy's possession.

Lord Castor meets my eyes, pleading. "What would you have done?"

I think about Elsie—picture Percy's knife pressed to her throat. I can't blame Lord Castor for what he's done. I would have left a trail of bodies in my wake to save my sister.

I look at Owen. My brother. My best friend.

"Anything," I say. "I would do anything to protect my family."

"I'm glad you said that." Owen throws out a hand, and an invisible force knocks the dagger from my grasp. I'd expected him to be a bloodletter, too, but...only a windwalker could have done that.

He takes advantage of my surprise, seizing ground. The tip of his blade rests lightly on my throat. "I won't let you suffer any longer, sister."

The dark magic radiating from the dagger causes me to grind my teeth. He means to give me a quick death—just like he'd promised that day aboard the *Lightbringer*. To make me like him. A Shifter. An Underling.

Cursed.

I think about Mother, back at Bludgrave, holding Father's limp body in her arms—of Elsie and Albert. Margaret and Charlie. Lewis. How I might never see them again. How if I do, I won't be myself anymore—not really.

"No need to worry," he says, as if sensing where my thoughts have gone. His free hand dances in the air below my collarbone, counting the nine silver stars embroidered there. "You won't miss them. Besides, they'll forget about you just as easily." His lip curls. "You've seen that firsthand."

"That isn't fair," I snap back. "You've been alive this whole time! You could have come to us. We could have been a family again. You could have—"

"Could have what?" He grits his teeth, his eyes glowing red. "I'm not *human*, Violet. I'm an Underling now. Don't you know what that means?" He gives a half-insane laugh, the glow in his eyes subsiding. "I need blood. We can't live among them. Not without consequence."

We. As if I were already a Shifter.

I glance at the dagger hovering near my throat, at Owen's pale hand gripping the hilt. A quick death by my brother's hand is a kindness, I remind myself. All this time, Owen and the Sylks had access to me. They could have killed me whenever they pleased; turned me into a Shifter. Owen could kill me now. So then...why does he hesitate?

Again, in the way only Owen can, he senses my thoughts. "The bracelet protects you in more ways than one," he says, cutting his eyes at the trinket. "It not only keeps you from being tracked, but it makes it almost impossible for you to be compelled by Underlings." His jaw clenches, his knuckles bone white. "And as long as you're wearing it, no harm can come to you by an Underling's hand."

My chest squeezes. "You can't kill me," I say, my head flooding with relief.

He dips his chin. "Not until you take that off."

"What makes you think I will?"

Owen's slow, corrupted smile sends a chill through me. "The bracelet protects you," he says, cutting his eyes at Annie, "but what about her?"

"You wouldn't."

"Wouldn't I?" He removes the dagger from my throat. "Have you not seen what I'm willing to do to get your attention?"

I glance at Lord Castor, at his face full of defeat. I understand now. It was him. He lowered the wards and gave the Guild of Shadows access to the manor. Owen used him to orchestrate all of this; Lord Castor has known for months what Owen planned to do—how he planned to use Annie as bait. He knew that I would have to make a choice: my life, or Annie's.

"I'd hoped your hatred for the Nightweavers would have made this rather simple," Owen says. "That perhaps you would seek the Guild out of your own accord. I even revealed myself to you that day, near the edge of the wood. But the more I watched you, the more it became apparent that you'd begun to *care* for your captors." He wrinkles his nose again. "So, I waited."

I search his eyes for a glimmer of remorse, of anything other than empty darkness. "Why now?"

Owen closes his eyes, tilting his head back to bask in the tainted light of the blood-red sky. "Once a year, on Reckoning Day, the Nightweavers' dominion over *Manan* is weakened." A cold, mischievous smile as he opens his eyes. "Meanwhile, our Underling magic grows stronger. And yes," he adds impatiently, as if answering a question I hadn't yet thought to ask, "because of your human blood, your power remains at full strength. I suppose you can thank our ancestors for that little discrepancy."

A part of me wants to ask what he means about our ancestors, but I can't pull my thoughts away from what he'd said about the Nightweavers' dominion over *Manan*. I'd wondered how Titus had been so easily overcome; how Henry's attempt to shut off the electricity in Dorothy's brain had failed. And again, how Titus hadn't had the strength to put the fire out.

Owen seizes my wrist, his hand encapsulating the bracelet. "In a few minutes, it won't matter that I can't remove this by force," he says. "After I've drained little Annie of her blood, I'll be strong enough to channel my magic through this cursed blade and break the enchantment around your heart myself."

The ground sways beneath me. I can't breathe.

"But," he adds, "I'm offering you the choice. Because you are my sister and I care for you deeply, I'm willing to let dear Annie go free. All you have to do"—he runs his thumb over the braided leather—"is take this off."

Mercy is never free. How many times have I heard Mother say those words? And yet, they've never felt truer. Letting Annie go would be a small mercy, but the price is my life.

A hysterical laugh escapes me. "That isn't a choice."

"Isn't it?" His brows perk. "You'd be more than willing if it were Elsie here instead, wouldn't you?"

Blood pounds in my hands, my throat, my ears. If I do this— if I allow Owen to turn me—I'll never feel my heartbeat again. I try to memorize the sensation, savoring the wild, frenzied tempo.

I cover his icy hand with my own, meeting his cold, tawny eyes with a look I hope conveys all the hatred I feel in this moment. I remember what Titus said hours ago, when he'd told me his name: *Hatred is a curious thing.* And he was right. Because for all the hatred I feel…

"I love you, Owen," I say, giving his hand a squeeze.

His mask falls, if only for an instant, and he withdraws his hand as if he'd been stung.

Rain spatters my face, cool and invigorating, giving me newfound strength. I hold his gaze, slipping the bracelet over my knuckles halfway. "I'm sorry." The bracelet lands in the blood-soaked leaves. "I'm sorry I couldn't save you."

Owen takes a ginger step towards me, raising the dagger with what appears to be great effort. "Oh, sister," he whispers, his hollow expression void of any cruel mischief or wicked glee as he points the tip of the blade at my chest, poised directly over my heart. "I was never worth saving."

Cold metal pierces my flesh. An agonized roar splits the night, like a wild animal caught in a trap—but it doesn't come from my lips. Owen's eyes widen, and I think I feel him withdraw the blade through the haze of pain. Black spots edge my vision as I collapse, staring up at the blood-red sky, my breath coming in short, ragged gasps. Ice creeps through my veins, swift and paralyzing. I try to fight for consciousness, but the darkness drags me under.

The last thing I see is a raven taking flight, dissolving into the light of the scarlet sun, and a Nightweaver hovering over me, pushing back the hood of his black cloak. My vision swims but I can just make out his dark hair, his green eyes, his unique constellation of freckles. It isn't the face of a monster that looks down at me, murmuring fervent words I'll never hear, a tear glazing his porcelain cheek.

It's the face of a boy.

CHAPTER FORTY-ONE

"I wish I were a star," I pant, hoisting myself into the crow's nest. From here, I can see everything. Below, the warm glow of the lanterns makes the *Lightbringer* feel like the safest ship in all the world. Beyond, the black waters of the Dire seem to go on and on forever, a dark boundary that separates us from the monsters on land. And above…a sea of twinkling lights that leave me breathless in a way climbing dozens of feet of rope cannot.

I shiver, plopping down on the weathered wood beside Owen. "Elsie says that stars are like little fires in the sky."

He smiles slightly, offering me a tattered blanket Lewis had sewn together from woven sacks and scraps of cloth. "Who comes up with all that rubbish she reads?"

I wrap the blanket around my shoulders, grateful for the small reprieve from the chill. "The Nightweavers think themselves all-knowing. Call themselves 'scientists.'"

Owen gives a short laugh, his gaze trained on the sky. I can't help but envy how at ease he is, as if this crow's nest were the throne from which he ruled his own private kingdom in the sky.

Despite the frigidity of the night air, he props himself carelessly against the railing, one leg swung over his knee, unbothered by the raging wind that billows his shirt and rustles his dirty-blond hair. "I'd rather be a bird," he says, lacing his hands behind his head. "Free to go wherever I please, whenever I please."

"We *are* free," I say, searching the constellations for my favorite cluster of stars. It takes me only a moment to locate the shape of a helm—Titus's Keys, with which he ruled the ten ancient kingdoms of the ocean. I smile a little. "We're pirates."

His carefree grin falters. "Freedom doesn't come with restrictions, Violet. Pirates or not, there are places we cannot go. Things we'll never see. Sometimes I just—" He breaks off, sighs. Moonlight limns his eyes with silver. "Don't you ever want more than these endless waves?"

I shrug. "The ocean keeps our family safe. That's all I can ask for."

"What about that chef you're always reading about, Cornelius Drake?" Owen argues, a slight edge to his conversational tone. "Don't you want a chance to cook with fresh ingredients? To taste the kind of food he talks about in that book of yours?"

"Of course I would. I can't tell you how many times I've imagined a world without Nightweavers. But…Mother and Father are right. The land is theirs. The water belongs to us." I hesitate. "You can't still be angry—"

"They won't even try." Owen's jaw clenches. "I've found it, Violet. I know it. The Red Island—it's so close." He gets to his feet suddenly, pointing east, where Astrid and her Crown of Seven Candles mark the sky. "Just there. We could go. We can—"

"Owen," I say gently. I stand, placing a comforting hand on his arm the way Father often does. "They're just trying to do what's best for our family."

He tilts his head back, lips pressed tight. I know what he wants to say: The Red Island *is* what's best for our family. But he doesn't say anything. Not tonight. Something tells me he's tired of talking. So, I stay with him in this darkness, far above the waves. After a little while, Margaret's laughter drifts from belowdecks, accompanied by Charlie's shouting and Lewis's cheers.

"Come on," I say, nudging Owen. "Albert wants to play Clubs and I need a partner."

A cheeky grin touches his lips, but it doesn't reach his eyes. He takes a pack of cards from his pocket, plucking the knave of clubs from the deck and tucking it up his sleeve with a wink.

As I begin my descent, I look up to find him searching the sky, his tawny eyes reflecting the glittering night.

"One day, we'll all be Stars," Owen says quietly, fiddling with the band of braided leather at his wrist. "Then, we'll truly be free."

"The poison is spreading." A lilting voice reaches me from far away. It sounds devastated, though I can't imagine why. It's peaceful here, in the silent dark, surrounded by an infinity of twinkling lights. "The enchantment around her heart is failing."

Warmth wraps itself around me like a cloak. *I'm a Star.* The thought greets me like a gentle embrace. All around me, the other Stars come into focus, welcoming me in a language that goes beyond words.

"I can't—" The boy's voice breaks. "I can't contain it much longer."

"You have to!" another voice snaps, deep and rich. It comes from somewhere distant, where the howling whistle of a train and the rattle of a train car remind me of a time not too long ago, when I was taken from my beloved ocean. "If the venom reaches her heart—"

"I won't let it!" That first voice, his lilting accent familiar in a way that stirs something within me, calls every fiber of my being to attention. He whispers, closer now than before, "Wake up, love. Now's not the time for dying."

Drawn to that voice, I kick, as if swimming towards the surface of the night sky. But my body is heavy. Too heavy. I struggle with all my might, clawing at the inky darkness in search of that lilting voice.

"*Live, Violet*," he whispers. I feel his warm hand on my cheek, the only sensation in this unending void. "Remember you have to live."

Those words—the same words Captain Shade spoke to me the night he rescued me from the *Deathwail*—awaken something within me. Something that goes beyond my natural understanding, and yet feels more real and familiar than anything ever has.

"We're losing her," Will moans, his voice shaking. "Come back to me, Violet. Please, come back to me."

Please. My heart breaks at the sound of that word—so broken, so desperate.

"Can't you do something?" Will demands.

"I've done all that I can," says the first voice. "It's up to her, now—fight the change or accept it. It's her choice."

My choice. When has anything ever been my choice? It wasn't my choice to abandon the land for water six hundred years ago. It wasn't my choice to return to the land. Wasn't my choice to come to Bludgrave Manor.

But…I *chose* to stay with my family when Captain Shade offered to take me with him. I *chose* to stay at Bludgrave Manor. When Will gave me the opportunity to leave…I stayed. I chose to work alongside him to find the Sylk. I chose to join the Order of Hildegarde, to fight in secret against the king and queen of the Eerie and all of the injustice they've committed against my people.

Owen—he didn't give me a choice. Letting Annie die in my place was never an option. I didn't choose to let him turn me into a Shifter. He took that choice away from me.

Now, I'm taking it back.

I will not let them take me. Not the Nightweavers, not the Underlings. Not even the Stars.

Live, Violet.

I choose to live.

CHAPTER FORTY-TWO

reath floods my lungs. I cough, sitting up abruptly, my skin slick with sweat. I clutch the medallion around my neck, my calloused fingers brushing the familiar grooves of the skull and crossed daggers. A nightmare. It was only a nightmare.

"Mother—" My voice scratches my throat, too weak to be heard over the creak of wood as the familiar, loving cradle of the ocean rocks our ship. I squint against the gentle, golden light, expecting to find Lewis still sleeping in his hammock in the bunkhouse aboard my family's ship. But this is not the *Lightbringer*.

Gauzy curtains frame the finely carved four-post bed where I lay, surrounded by a fortress of fluffy feather pillows. At the center of the opulent chambers, a masked man in red sits behind a heavy desk littered with maps and spyglasses, the open windows at his back letting the scent of briny sea air in on a gust of wind.

"There she is." His muffled, lilting voice greets me like a swiftly fading dream. "A week is a very long time to take a nap."

A week? My heart skips a beat as my hands are met with the soft linen of a white gown instead of cool metal, in the same instant that I spot my daggers lying atop the desk. The feeling of ice piercing my chest lingers, a dull ache, and I glance down at my wrist, at the band of braided leather. *My* bracelet—not Owen's.

It hadn't been a dream.

"Will?" I manage to rasp. "Where is he? Where am I?"

"No need to fret. William should be…around." The man in red stands from behind the desk and offers an elegant bow, his blood-red half cape billowing in the breeze. "Welcome aboard the *Starchaser.*"

I gape at the plumage of phoenix feathers atop his scarlet tricorn, set aflame by the morning light.

"You!"

Captain Shade flourishes another obnoxious bow. When he raises his head, he winks. "Miss me, love?"

I attempt to stand, but my legs give way beneath me. In an instant, Captain Shade holds me in his arms. His blue eyes search mine, his scarlet mask only a few inches from my face. Something electric charges the air between us, making it difficult to breathe, difficult to think. For a moment, I feel like the sixteen-year-old girl he'd saved aboard the *Deathwail*. Safe. Alive.

Someone clears their throat. Shade pulls away, steadying me with a firm touch on my elbow. I look to my right, where a cloaked figure stands in the open doorway, silhouetted by the brilliant light.

"Why didn't you tell me she was awake?" Will demands, his voice deep and dark.

He takes purposeful strides, his black boots pounding with each beat of my heart as he pulls me from Shade's arms and into a crushing embrace. One hand grasps the nape of my neck, his fingers tangling in my hair as he nuzzles his head into the crook of my shoulder. It's hard to tell if he holds me up, or I him. I only know that I can't find it in me to let go.

I inhale the scent of roses and damp earth that clings to his hair, his skin. *Home,* my heart cries. But we're far from Bludgrave now.

Will draws back, searching my gaze. He looks at me as if he'd finally found the answer to the question always lurking in his eyes. He presses his forehead to mine, his face wet with tears that continue to fall. "I thought I'd lost you."

My heart wrenches at the thought of Will finding me there on the forest floor, covered in blood. "It was him," I croak, my voice weak. "It was Owen. He did this—he…"

"I know," Will murmurs, his voice soothing. "I know."

Pain splinters my chest. "Am I…did I turn?"

"No," he murmurs, his thumb stroking my cheek. "We found Henry's handkerchief in the bosom of your dress. It kept the blade from penetrating your heart."

Henry's handkerchief! He'd told me it was enchanted—that it possessed the protective capabilities of chainmail. I'd forgotten all about it, but…when I'd tucked the handkerchief in the bosom of my dress, I hadn't considered that my brother would return from the dead to stab me in the heart. Henry had saved my life, and he hadn't even meant to.

Will watches me, his expression tender. "You're still human."

My pulse leaps into my throat—a thrilling sensation that causes my lips to tingle. *Still human.* I never thought I'd be so relieved to hear those words.

"Annie?"

"She's safe," Will says, drawing back to inspect me once more. "She's safe because of you, Violet."

"And your father?"

The muscle in Will's jaw ripples as a shadow passes over his face. "I took care of him."

I open my mouth to ask what he means, but a memory seizes me, blurred by my own tears as the poison from Owen's blade tore through my veins, jarring me in and out of consciousness. Someone held me in their arms as I'd watched Will kneel before his father in Hildegarde's Folly where, under the violent skies of Reckoning Day, the water surrounding us looked like blood.

"You know what I have to do," Will says, pulling black leather gloves over his pale hands. "You won't remember anything."

"Your mother and I can help you," Lord Castor whispers, clutching Annie, unconscious in his arms. "We've helped you before."

Will adjusts his shirtsleeves, his eyes dark. "This isn't about me," he says, his voice clipped. "No one can know about Violet."

Lord Castor stammers indignantly, "I am a senior member of the Order—"

"Who allowed himself to be used by the Guild of Shadows." Will glares at the statue of Hildegarde, refusing to look at his father. With half of his face concealed by the shadows of the folly, and the other half painted scarlet with the light, he looks like a beautiful nightmare. "Violet is not safe if you know."

Lord Castor shakes his head, his gaze resting on my writhing form. "She's doomed, boy," he says, looking back at Will, genuine remorse flickering in his charcoal eyes. "You can't save her."

Doomed. Cursed. If Owen was telling the truth, and the Underling venom will change me into a Shifter sooner or later... I've only prolonged the inevitable. The Guild isn't going to stop coming for me. Owen isn't capable of giving up. No one is safe as long as I'm alive.

I take a step back, wresting myself from Will's grip. "When did you know?"

All the care, the devotion in his gaze, is replaced with something cunning and measured as Will's face hardens—the face of a soldier. "About what?"

"About me," I say, my voice steadier than I feel. "About my... affinity."

Will grinds his jaw. "I had my suspicions." He sighs, running a hand through his disheveled hair. "Most halflings die in their mother's womb. Some Nightweavers view them as a threat. They believe humans with an affinity to be more powerful than themselves. But you..." He shakes his head, huffing a bitter laugh. "You have Underling venom in your veins and a potent supply of *Manan* in your blood. You shouldn't be alive, and yet, you've just survived a fatal amount of poisonous dark magic."

My stomach coils into knots. And there it is—that familiar thought, like a relentless refrain. *What does he stand to gain?*

My heart twists. We're only two feet away from each other, but it still feels like we're an ocean apart. "You lied to me—"

"I didn't know enough to tell you!" His eyes widen, somewhat pleading. "What would I have said? All I knew was that you possessed abilities like that of a Shifter, and yet you appeared to be fully human. It wasn't until the night the Hackneys were murdered that I first realized you were part Nightweaver."

Your eyes—Charlie had said something about my eyes that night after he'd pulled me out of the fountain. Will must have seen them change.

"When I came to you, that night I thought I saw the Shifter in Albert and Elsie's room…" Tears choke my voice. "You could have told me then!"

Will looks away sharply, his jaw twitching. "I was afraid. You were determined to put yourself in as much danger as you possibly could." His throat bobs. "When a Nightweaver is bitten by a Shifter, we don't turn right away—not like a human would. It is a slow, painful death. It corrupts you from the inside out. I thought…" He surveys the maps atop Shade's desk, his eyes dark. "I thought that if I told you, you might seek out the Guild on your own."

I can't help but glance at Captain Shade, who gives nothing away in his posture. But behind the mask, his eyes are a storm, swirling with a turmoil I can't even begin to understand, never once wavering from me.

"Did you know about Owen?" I manage to whisper. "Did you know my brother was alive?"

Will's mouth forms a grim line. "I took a wild guess."

"And you thought I'd want to be like him?" My voice shakes. "That I would let him stab me in the heart? Turn me into a Shifter?"

His teeth grit. "I didn't know what you'd do. I couldn't risk—"

"Couldn't risk what?" I shout, my voice raw. "Your precious halfling?"

"I couldn't risk *you*, Violet!" Will shouts back, his entire body trembling as he reaches for me, only to stop himself halfway, clenching his fist. His gaze seizes mine, and in an instant, his eyes convey all of the words we've never said—words we still might never say. "You deserve to decide for yourself what you're willing to die for."

Tears spill onto my cheeks as the weight of my grief threatens to crush me flat.

"I should have told you," he says, his face flushed, the color of the roses he once cared for. "But I was afraid that if I gave you the choice…"

"That I wouldn't choose you?" My eyes narrow. "What changed?"

Will glares at his boots, his face drawn. "Henry told me you'd joined the Order. You made the choice before I could extend the invitation." He clenches his jaw. "If anyone else would have discovered your abilities—even within the Order—it would have put you in danger." He looks at me now, his gaze intent, studying my face the way he always has. "I wrote to you—told you everything I knew. Keyed the ink to your blood so that only you could read it."

The letter. Henry had tried to give it to me, but I was so frustrated with Will for leaving that I'd refused to read it. *Stupid.*

My eyes narrow. "How would you have *keyed* anything to my blood? We were an ocean apart when you wrote that letter."

"The night you pricked your finger in the conservatory," he answers, his expression almost sympathetic. "Your blood was on my handkerchief."

I think back to that night, how he'd used his handkerchief to clean the tiny wound. While the thought of him using my blood to perform any sort of spell makes my stomach churn, I can't help but admit it was rather clever to ensure prying eyes couldn't see what he'd revealed in his letter.

He watches me carefully before sighing, the tension melting from his face. "I realized when I saw you that night at the ball—I knew you hadn't read it." It's as if I watch him replace his brooding mask with that of the charming lord from my early days at Bludgrave. "If you had, you would have known that your access to all three forms of magic—Nightweaver, human, and Underling—could turn the tides in favor of the human resistance. And you would have understood that you are far too important to the Order to allow yourself to be turned by the Guild of Shadows."

I look from Will to Captain Shade as I'm struck by the full weight of his words.

I swallow hard around the lump rising in my throat. "What are you saying?"

Will's green eyes glitter with amusement as a slow smirk curls his lip—a look that makes me realize what I should have known since the first time I laid eyes on him at the auction house. The way the crowd reacted to Will's presence. The way that officer on the train feared the young lord's wrath. The way Percy cowered under the force of his power.

Kindness is the great deceiver. And in a world ruled by monsters, Will is far too kind. He never intended to keep me from this world. He intended to throw me to the wolves.

No—he knew when he met me that I was more than even I have been led to believe. More than a pirate. More than the venom inside of me. More than a bloodletter.

I am the wolf. He intended to throw this world to me.

"You're more powerful than you could have ever hoped to be, Violet Oberon."

I feel as if I've been kicked in the gut. "You used me," I say, inching closer to the desk, the citrine jewels of my daggers sparkling in the dusty beams of light. "You knew a Sylk had stowed away in Hellion, and you were going to use me to find her."

Will's mouth tightens, his eyes flashing. "That was my intention, yes," he rasps, his voice momentarily taking on a rough, smoky quality I've never heard from him before. He clears his throat, and when he speaks again, his voice is smooth. "But when I took your bracelets—with no clear reason as to why—I knew I'd been compelled. I knew, right then, that the Guild had taken an interest in you."

I think back to what the Sylk that had possessed Trudy told me, about how Queen Morana had taken a special interest in me. Later, Owen had echoed that sentiment, claiming that Morana had searched for me for quite some time. Owen spoke of a "*she*" that had possessed someone aboard the *Merryway*—that "*she*" had been in communication with the Sylk that possessed Mary Cross. I can't help but wonder…would Morana herself have been so bold as to possess a Nightweaver aboard the prince's vessel?

"Bludgrave was the safest place I could think to bring you," Will goes on, drawing me out of my thoughts. "The Guild was never supposed to be able to get to you there." His gaze dips to the bracelet at my wrist, lingering on the band of braided leather. "But I was a fool."

"A fool?" I bite out, grabbing one of the daggers. "It's your fault!" I point the dagger at Will. "Those people you killed, when you were searching for the *Deathwail*—they had a daughter who'd been possessed by a Sylk. My family found her. Brought her onto our ship. She's the reason the Guild knew how to find me in the first place. She's the reason we were attacked."

"Those people I killed were eating their own children!" Will bares his teeth, his cool demeanor slipping further, revealing a somewhat manic gleam in his eye. "When I came upon their ship, there were only four adults left. I set Mary free from a cage—a *cage*, Violet—before I took vengeance on those monsters."

Monsters. Mary Cross had been birthed to monsters. And before she died, she'd become a monster herself. I can't help but wonder…before this is all over, will I become a monster, too?

Will's chest heaves as he searches my eyes, his emerald gaze desperate in its pursuit. "I can't change the past, but I don't regret what I did. I'm only sorry for the pain I've caused you." His face falls, his mouth twisting into a boyish frown as he glances from my dagger to me, looking more human in his exhaustion than I've ever seen him. "I agreed to go to Hellion with the prince because I had sensed there was an enchantment on your bracelet. I wanted to know if it had something to do with your ability to see the Sylks."

Will exhales, rubbing his chin. "Titus knew of a Sorcerer in Hellion. The old man recognized the craftsmanship of your bracelets—sent me to an old friend of his, a Sorceress who lived along the coast. She admitted she'd made the trinkets. Told me what she'd done for you—the enchantment she'd placed around your heart, as well. How, because you were a bloodletter, the ocean's magic would keep the enchantment strong."

I remember what Owen had said, about the enchantment weakening. He had told me the truth, then. What else had he been telling the truth about?

"I told Shade to meet me at dawn on Reckoning Day," Will goes on, his expression hard. "I asked him to take you with him, back to the sea." His eyes slide past me to the open windows, where sunlight dazzles the surface of the water. He grimaces. "But then you were attacked, and so many others were dead. On my suggestion, the Order seized the opportunity to blame the massacre on Captain Shade and his crew. Titus testified that he'd seen Captain Shade kidnap you from the grounds—you, Violet Oberon, a human girl that had been willing to sacrifice her own life to save Lady Annie from Captain Shade's men.

"Word spread of your heroism like a wildfire through the Order's channels. With the king struggling to contain the rebellion amongst the enslaved humans of the Eerie, he declared you an honorary member of the king's army. I've been sent to rescue you and bring you back to the Eerie to be knighted."

A small sound escapes me. "Knighted?"

Will dips his head, his brows pinched. "The king believes giving you a place at court will satiate the humans long enough for him to regain his foothold. He's hoping to make an example of you—a reformed pirate fighting alongside the Nightweavers of the Eerie."

I watch him carefully. "But?"

"*But*," Will says slowly, the hardened mask of a soldier concealing his expression once more. "I'll be coming home empty-handed."

Captain Shade takes a step towards Will, his arms crossed. "That's not what we discussed."

Will doesn't tear his gaze from me, his green eyes locked on mine. "I won't argue this. I want Violet safe."

Shade snorts a laugh. "She'll never be bloody *safe*, mate! Not when Morana is—"

"I said," Will cuts him off through gritted teeth, turning to face him squarely, "I won't argue this. I don't want Violet involved."

Captain Shade's eyes narrow on Will before he turns abruptly to me, blurting, "Morana possessed the princess of Hellion."

I gape. I'd begun to suspect Morana had been the Sylk that boarded the *Merryway* in Hellion, but… "The princess?"

Will casts his eyes skyward, as if praying to the Stars for patience. He drags his hands over his face. "You cannot prove this."

"No, but she can." Shade flicks his gaze over me before turning to face Will once more. "If I'm right, there might still be a chance at finding a cure."

I look between Shade and Will. "A cure?"

Will's eyes are murderous as he glares at Captain Shade. "Don't."

Shade props himself precariously on the edge of his desk, fiddling with a spyglass. "The Sylk queen is the only Underling capable of breaking the curse inflicted by a Shifter. If we could trap her, somehow—force her to remove the venom—"

"If you're right, it would kill the princess," Will says, cutting him off. "You would ignite a war between Hellion and the Eerie."

"And it would save *both* of your lives," Shade argues, his muffled, lilting voice familiar in a way that quickens my heart.

It's clear that he and Will are closer than I'd previously thought, but…why would he care if *I* live or die? *I'm no one to him*, I tell myself. Other than my value to the Order, I'm just a girl he'd saved from the *Deathwail*. And, for some reason, that realization causes my chest to ache.

"Violet can see the Sylks," Shade says. "If your curse allowed you to confirm the princess of Hellion is in fact possessed by the Sylk queen, we wouldn't be having this conversation."

My eyes meet Will's. "Your…curse?"

Will looks away, his throat bobbing. "I told you, I'm no stranger to curses."

Shade inspects the spyglass with great care, his black-rimmed eyes narrow. "He's dying."

Dying. Will can't be dying. He looks perfectly fine. He…he can't be dying.

Shade takes from his breast pocket the bronze medallion, dangling it from his red-gloved fingers. He must have stolen it off me when he'd caught me in his arms. Bastard!

Captain Shade extends the medallion to me—the same medallion I used to clutch when I'd wake from the terror of sleep, reminding myself that the nightmare was over. That I was safe. But this nightmare has just begun, and it is one from which I fear I'll never wake.

"This trinket is worth an entire fleet of ships," he says. "If you agree to help me discover the truth about the princess, it's yours. And if I'm right, and we manage to trap Morana and force her to take her true, corporeal form, you'll be cured. You can go on your merry way, free to roam wherever your little heart desires. Or," he croons, his muffled voice stirring something within me. "You can refuse to join Will at Castle Grim, where the princess currently resides, and lose your only chance at ever finding the Red Island." His blue eyes search mine. "It's your choice."

My heart twists. "The Red Island?" Our dream—mine and Owen's. But now that I know the Red Island is real—that I could go there—it means nothing if I'd be going alone.

Shade inclines his head, his blue eyes devious. "This medallion once belonged to the heir of Hildegarde. If the current leadership found out that it was in your possession... why, I believe they'd offer you a royal escort."

The chain slips from his fingers—only a fraction—the medallion swinging back and forth like a pendulum. The last time Captain Shade's hand had been extended to me, he offered me safety. Now, he offers so much more. And none of it is safe. It's dangerous and thrilling and everything I've ever wanted. If I agree to do what Shade asks of me, I could have it all. Revenge. Justice. Freedom.

Coin.

I glance at Will, but he refuses to meet my eyes. He'd lied to me. He'd kissed me. He'd wept for me. He's dying. And so am I.

A cure. I could help Titus find the cure for Will. For me. And if we can trap the Sylk queen, I might be able to force her to release Owen from her service. Maybe he can still be cured, too.

"I'll do it," I say, reaching for the medallion.

Shade withdraws his hand, stuffing the medallion in his pocket once more. I imagine his face to mirror the grinning mask he wears, but despite my agreeing to do what he's asked, his blue eyes seem almost sad, as if he, too, remembers a time when he'd asked me to come with him. To leave everything behind. Then, I'd thrown myself from an executioner's platform. Somehow, this doesn't feel all that different.

"We'll make port along the Savage Coast by noon," Shade says, skirting his desk to stand at the open windows, his back turned to us. The breeze ruffles the rare plumage of phoenix feathers atop his hat. "Arrangements have been made to take us to Castle Grim, where the king eagerly awaits your arrival."

"Us?" I glance at Will, who glares at the back of Shade's head as if he could set fire to it with a single thought. "Why would *you* be traveling to Castle Grim?"

"Because the princess of Hellion—the one possessed by the Underling queen who'd like nothing more than to see the three of us rotting in Havok…" Captain Shade removes the scarlet mask, his back still turned to me. I hold my breath as he pivots on his heels, his cerulean eyes meeting mine. Eyes as blue as the ocean. Eyes that belong to someone I'd danced with only a week ago. Someone I've spent my whole life hating.

Titus—the prince of the Eerie—smirks, flourishing a final bow. "She's my fiancée."

CHAPTER FORTY-THREE

y mouth works as I glare at him, my mind struggling to reconcile what my eyes now see—Titus, clothed in the striking red garments of Captain Shade. A hero. *My* hero.

It was him. *He* had been the one to save me from the *Deathwail. He* had delivered me to my family. The pirate who had so thoughtfully searched for my trinket after he'd slashed the rope meant to end my life—all this time, it was the prince I've so despised. The boy I've wished death upon more times than I can count.

I feel as if I already know you, he'd said to me that night in the garden. How could I have been so blind? The tattoos on his hands. The weapon he keeps hidden up his sleeve. His name. I should have known that the most successful pirate of my time would turn out to be a bloodletter.

Oh, Stars. He was Will's informant. When I told Will about Captain Shade—how he'd offered to take me with him…Will knew this entire time that it was Titus behind the mask.

Without a word, I spin on my heels, shoving past Will.

"Violet," Will calls after me, his voice soft, but I don't turn around.

I burst through the double doors that lead onto the quarterdeck as a familiar ache in my shoulder ignites, sending a bolt of pain directly to my heart. I stumble a few steps, squinting in the bright light. The *Starchaser* bustles with activity—people shouting, people laughing. But their voices fade beneath the low hum of silence as I see it—*really* see it—for the first time in so many months. Spanning in all directions, the Western Sea borders the horizon, straight and true. My ocean. My home.

I breathe in the fresh, salty air, feeling as if I'm fully awake for the first time. I follow that feeling down the steps, towards the taffrail. My hands grip the rough wood as a splash of cool water kisses my face. For a moment, I could convince myself this is the *Lightbringer*; that I might turn around and find my family smiling back at me. Together. Happy. But the moment passes, leaving behind a hollow, unending grief as vast as the ocean itself.

"Hey!" someone shouts. "Get down from there!"

I hadn't made the decision to climb onto the taffrail, as if it had been long decided—a delayed reaction set in motion the instant I'd been ripped from my beloved ocean. As I loosely hold myself to the rigging, the breeze billows through my hair, reminding me of the way the wind would glide over my skin as Caligo soared across the open fields. If I close my eyes, I could pretend I'm back there—back at Bludgrave, where Father waits for me in the kitchen. Where Dorothy and Henry steal secret glances at each other from across the dining room. Where Elsie and Annie paint little wooden cars and Albert follows Jack to the stables every morning and evening, happy and safe and full of hope for the future.

My heart wrenches. *Home.*

My dagger slips from my fingers, plummeting to the water below.

"Hold my hat," I hear Titus say as I let go of the rigging, allowing the wind to sweep me off my feet, and dive headfirst into the water.

I don't *hit* the surface—the water softens for me, greeting me with a gentle embrace. I look up, where through the haze of bubbles, Titus climbs onto the taffrail and without a breath of hesitation dives in after me.

I don't swim away. I let the current continue to drag me under, my lungs burning. Only the ocean can take away this awful grief. Only the water can heal these wounds that gape and bleed deep inside, where the names of my father and brother have been carved into my heart, a ruthless reminder of all I lack. A reminder that I'm not fast enough. Not merciless enough. Not brave enough.

How could I have saved Father? Or Owen? When the crew of the *Deathwail* tied that rope around my neck, I couldn't even save myself.

A sharp gasp of anger sends precious air bubbling past my face. I hate that I'd been lied to. But what I hate—what I truly, deeply hate—is that I believed every single lie.

Pressure builds between my ears, and my vision blurs. I consider letting go. Letting the water fill my lungs. Letting the ocean take me to its depths. But then he appears before me, his scarlet half-cloak undulating like blood in the water.

He'd removed his gloves, his tattooed hand floating between us. His blue eyes never leave mine, apparently cataloguing the way my muscles tense as he reaches out. He frowns as his fingertips brush my skin, cradling my cheek in his calloused palm. His gaze drifts to my lips, his brow furrowed.

My lips part, releasing whatever breath I'd had left, in the same instant that Titus presses his mouth to mine, filling my lungs with air.

At the feel of his lips on mine, the ocean pulses. He draws away sharply. *No*—he's pushed away, as if the water had sent him barreling backwards.

At once, the ocean becomes so dark, not even the sun can penetrate its surface. All around us, gold dust shimmers like the innumerable stars in the heavens. The water begins to swirl, spinning faster and faster, forming a whirlpool of sorts. It encases me in a pocket of air at the center of the vortex, and I fall to my knees on the sandy rock-bottom of the ocean, gasping for breath. Alone.

"Titus!" I scream, my voice hoarse as I attempt to stick my hand through the cyclone of night-dark water surrounding me. I withdraw the instant my fingers skim the rushing current, afraid that if the water were to catch hold of me, it might never let me go again.

The gold dust glows in the air like thousands of pixies, and I stand, reaching out to take hold of it when—

"*Daughter of the sea.*"

At the sound of the woman's disembodied voice, the roar of rushing water quiets, the gold dust glows even brighter than it had before. It casts its light upon the ocean floor, where my dagger blazes as if the hilt had been fashioned from a beam of sunlight.

I pick it up, the metal warming my palm.

All around me, the brilliant gold dust shimmers in the air, encapsulating me in its dazzling glow. A figure takes form, gilded dust in the shape of a woman, nearly too bright to look at. I shield my eyes, cowering slightly.

"*The queen of this world has risen. She who lurks in shadows, devouring the light. Only blood can heal the land. Only truth can mend the past.*"

She presses her hand to my cheek, her touch like fire. "*The True King sees,*" she whispers, her voice gentle and firm—a reminder, a solemn vow—before the dust dissipates, leaving me alone once more. The roar of the water intensifies again, almost deafening. I'm lifted into the air as the gold dust spirals around me like a cyclone of light. I tighten my grip on the dagger, unwilling to surrender it to the raging current.

"*Palomi havella dinosh beyan.*"

The woman's voice booms over the sound of the water as it grows louder, swirling faster, propelling me up, up, up—

I gasp for air as my head breaks the surface. Instantly, two pairs of hands haul me into a rowboat. I cough up water, rolling onto my back, the dagger still secure within my grasp.

Will and Titus stare down at me, chests heaving, and beyond them, the sky mirrors the dark of the ocean depths far below. It had been morning when I'd gone into the water, but now the stars glitter overhead, almost dull in comparison to the gold dust that had encapsulated me only moments ago.

"What happened?" I ask weakly.

Titus and Will share a serious look.

"You were under the water for twelve hours," Will answers, his deep voice breaking as he smooths the hair from my face, his gaze ever searching.

"I tried to get to you so many times, but…" Titus trails off, shaking his head. In the dim light of the lantern, his blue eyes appear glazed—haunted. Whatever had happened in the past twelve hours, he was soaked to the bone, his slick blond hair stuck to his face. His gaze roves from my head to my toes, looking everywhere but my eyes. "I couldn't reach you."

Twelve hours. But it feels as if only a minute had passed. And the woman…could I have imagined her?

Palomi havella dinosh beyan. The judgement is coming. Words I've heard on the lips of humans, Underlings, Myths, and Nightweavers alike.

I glance at the dagger in my fist, still glowing, though no longer as brilliant as it had looked below the water. My eyes meet Will's. It hides beneath the immediate concern, but I see it—the glimmer of amusement in his green eyes. As if he knew what had happened beneath the surface. As if he knew what it all meant.

For the first time, I think I understand the question he's long been asking. And I finally know the answer.

Will must know that I will not leave Castle Grim until I've spilled blood. The king and queen will pay for what they've done to my people. To my family. To me. And when I strike, the king and queen and all those that follow in their wicked acts will know me for who and what I truly am.

I am the one they fear. I am the monster in the dark.

I am the judgement.

ACKNOWLEDGEMENTS

Writing a book is hard.

It's also exciting, and rewarding, and lots of fun. It requires copious amounts of caffeine, a profound lack of sleep, and most importantly, other people.

But writing the acknowledgements for this book? Hands down, that's been the hardest part.

It isn't that I'm not incredibly grateful to everyone who played a part in putting this book in your hands. No—it's because I am SO incredibly grateful that I have no idea how I could possibly do this the justice it deserves. I mean, where do I find the words—how do I form a sentence—that could properly convey how thankful I truly am to everyone who has shown *Nightweaver* their support?

I'm at a loss. But, I'm going to give it my best shot!

First and foremost, to God be the glory. Throughout this journey of writing and publishing *Nightweaver*, I have done a lot of praying. And a lot of waiting. And a lot of wondering, "Should I quit? Can I really do this?" Without my faith, and without the Lord's grace and mercy on my life, I wouldn't be here.

Mom and Dad, thank you for teaching me to dream, to believe in myself, and always reminding me that I can do anything if I put my mind to it. The lessons you've taught me and the examples you've set in your own lives are more valuable to me than all the buried treasure in the world. Thank you for giving me the time and the space to write, for buying me all the books, and of course, for not only reading *Nightweaver* but letting me ask you a million questions about what you thought. Most importantly, thank you for never letting me give up and for never giving up on me. You are the best parents a girl could ever hope to have.

Harrison, my beloved husband and best friend, when the storms of life threaten to throw me off course, your unwavering support is the anchor that holds me fast. Thank you for believing in me at a time when this felt impossible. It would have been so easy for you to think I was crazy (well, crazier) but instead, you've championed my dreams in ways I could have never expected. And more than that, you have always been there, dreaming right alongside me. For that, I could never thank you enough. You are my fairytale love and my greatest adventure.

To my editor, Susan, you truly are my literary fairy godmother. Thank you for believing in this story. Your guidance and encouragement kept me from pressing "delete file" more than once.

To Srdjan, for bringing this book to life with your mind-blowing talent—for taking my scribbles and turning the vision in my head for the Known World into one of the most beautiful maps I've ever laid eyes on, for designing a cover more perfect than I could have ever dreamed of, and letting me email you a dozen times a day (maybe not a dozen, but enough times to drive anyone bananas).

To my dearest childhood friend, Ashlee, who read *Nightweaver* when it was just a messy, incomplete draft—thank you for being excited about this story, for every kind word, and for making me feel like a somebody when I felt like a nobody.

To my siblings, who have always believed in me—thank you for keeping me humble.

To everyone else who contributed to bringing this book to life, from the bottom of my heart, thank you.

And finally, to you, dear reader, for going on this journey with me. Thank you for your love and support for these characters and this world, and for being so kind to me. It means more than you'll ever know.

Last but not least, to the dreamer who has made it this far: don't ever give up. You are capable of more than you could even imagine. I believe in you.

Esther 4:14